KU-274-196

CHRISTINE
FEEHAN
SAVAGE
ROAD

PIATKUS

PIATKUS

First published in the US in 2022 by Jove, Berkley,
An imprint of Penguin Random House LLC
First published in Great Britain in 2022 by Piatkus

1 3 5 7 9 10 8 6 4 2

Copyright © 2022 by Christine Feehan
Excerpt from *Phantom Game* copyright © 2022 by Christine Feehan

The moral right of the author has been asserted.

*All characters and events in this publication, other than those
clearly in the public domain, are fictitious and any resemblance
to real persons, living or dead, is purely coincidental.*

All rights reserved.
No part of this publication may be reproduced, stored in a
retrieval system, or transmitted in any form or by any means, without
the prior permission in writing of the publisher, nor be otherwise circulated
in any form of binding or cover other than that in which it is published
and without a similar condition including this condition being
imposed on the subsequent purchaser.

A CIP catalogue record for this book
is available from the British Library.

ISBN: 978-0-349-43244-1

Printed and bound in Great Britain by Clays Ltd, Elcograf S.p.A.

Papers used by Piatkus are from well-managed forests
and other responsible sources.

MIX
Paper from
responsible sources
FSC
www.fsc.org   FSC® C104740

Piatkus
An imprint of
Little, Brown Book Group
Carmelite House
50 Victoria Embankment
London EC4Y 0DZ

An Hachette UK Company
www.hachette.co.uk

www.littlebrown.co.uk

For Maureen Gianinio,
I appreciate your friendship and the way
you always champion my books. It means so much
and never goes unnoticed.

Dear Reader,

When I first began to form the idea of Torpedo Ink, I knew it was going to be a very gritty, edgy and raw series, certainly not for everyone. In fact, at first, although I *had* to write the stories because I felt it was necessary, I doubted if I would ever publish them.

I had learned over the years that males, when molested, were often not given the same treatment as female victims. Often families were too ashamed to have the child go into counseling. They didn't want friends and family to know what happened. Sometimes the family members would even applaud the boy if the offender was a female and tell him how lucky he was. Other times, the males in the family would shun the boy or even want him sent away if he was molested or raped by a male. To me, it was a tragic situation. I hope that over time, these responses have changed a little, but I don't think they have by that much.

Why a motorcycle club? First, most motorcycle clubs are not running around the nation committing crimes. Often, they are men and women getting together because they like the freedom of riding. Many clubs fundraise for all kinds of causes. There is a real club that stands for victims like the children I portray in my novels. Usually the perception of those riding motorcycles is that they are tough. I wanted men and women my readers saw as tough. These are men and women who started out as victims. They survived abuse and understandably have PTSD and issues with sex due to their backgrounds. I needed readers to understand and be sympathetic toward my heroes and heroines.

Nevertheless, even by portraying them as close to reality in these conditions as possible, these are still works of fiction. I have tried to handle these situations with understanding and compassion and without judgment. I read as much as possible on each issue and then consult with primary sources before I feel able to write on the subject without prejudice or judgment. I don't ever want to depict one moment where a character is in an abusive situation and has no choice. The books are intense and some of the situations can be abusive, especially in Savage's books, as he is a sexual sadist. I want any reader to be clear on that fact before choosing to read this book. Savage's first book, *Annihilation Road*, stopped prior to Seychelle's training. That was a deliberate choice I made so that readers demanding his book, knowing what he was but also knowing they would have difficulties, would still have a satisfactory, happy ending to his story.

Savage Road is much more difficult to read and much truer to life, after the beginning of the love story between two people who truly love each other and have made a commitment but come from very different worlds. Savage's world could easily be one of abuse. There is a very important moment where Savage makes certain the heroine knows she can speak with her friends and receive support about their relationship if she needs to.

Again, it is important to me when writing a book to research the subject matter heavily so I can write without prejudice. There are many different lifestyles and needs, and not all people are alike or have similar pasts. People are shaped in many different ways by their experiences. Seychelle entered consensually into Savage's world because she needed the same things he did, which made them a perfect couple. She entered the relationship knowing what he was and wanting to share this lifestyle with the man she loves and trusts wholeheartedly with her body, mind and heart.

For the readers who have decided to continue the ride with Seychelle and Savage, I hope you feel that I've done their story justice.

Christine Feehan

FOR MY READERS

Be sure to go to christinefeehan.com/members to sign up for my private book announcement list and download the free ebook of *Dark Desserts*. It's a collection of yummy desserts that we all certainly could use right now. Join my community and get firsthand news, enter the book discussions, ask your questions and chat with me. Please feel free to email me at Christine@christinefeehan.com. I would love to hear from you.

ACKNOWLEDGMENTS

As in any book, there are so many people to thank. Domini, for hanging in there with me on this one. It was tough, but we did it—even in the worst of times, when neither of us could see. Thank you for always editing, no matter how many times I ask you to go over the same book before we send it for additional editing. Denise, you took over so many jobs for all of us, handled so much business when everything was so difficult. I admire you so much. Thank you. Brian, you got me through all those hours of writing, keeping me on track and insisting I could do it! You are the best!

TORPEDO INK MEMBERS

Viktor Prakenskii aka *Czar*—President

Lyov Russak aka *Steele*—Vice President

Savva Pajari aka *Reaper*—Sergeant at Arms

Savin Pajari aka *Savage*—Sergeant at Arms

Isaak Koval aka *Ice*—Secretary

Dmitry Koval aka *Storm*

Alena Koval aka *Torch*

Luca Litvin aka *Code*—Hacker

Maksimos Korsak aka *Ink*

Kasimir Popov aka *Preacher*

Lana Popov aka *Widow*

Nikolaos Bolotan aka *Mechanic*

Pytor Bolotan aka *Transporter*

Andrii Federoff aka *Maestro*

Gedeon Lazaroff aka *Player*

Kir Vasiliev aka *Master*—Treasurer

Lazar Alexeev aka *Keys*

Aleksei Solokov aka *Absinthe*

Rurik Volkov aka *Razrushitel/Destroyer*

NEWER PATCHED MEMBERS

Gavriil Prakenskii

Casimir Prakenskii

Fatei Molchalin

PROSPECTS

Glitch

Hyde

SIBLINGS WITHIN THE GROUP

Viktor (Czar), Gavriil and Casimir

Reaper and Savage

Mechanic and Transporter

Ice, Storm and Alena (Torch)

Preacher and Lana (Widow)

TEAMS

Czar heads Team One

> *Reaper, Savage, Ice, Storm, Transporter, Alena, Absinthe, Mechanic, Destroyer*

Steele heads Team Two

> *Keys, Master, Player, Maestro, Lana, Preacher, Ink, Code*

OLD LADIES

Blythe, Lissa, Lexi, Anya, Breezy, Soleil, Scarlet, Zyah

SAVAGE
ROAD

ONE

Seychelle Dubois sat on the bathroom floor staring at the toilet for the second morning in a row. She felt like an idiot. "No, Savage, I'm not pregnant. And I'm not a secret drinker either."

"What the hell is wrong? Should I call Steele? I want you to go see him."

She pushed herself up, glaring at him. "I do not need to see a doctor. Do you remember the talk we had on privacy?" Stumbling over to the sink, Seychelle washed her face with cold water, rinsed out her mouth and then started the process of brushing her teeth.

Savin "Savage" Pajari continued to watch her in the mirror. He leaned one hip against the doorjamb, arms crossed over his chest. His eyes were arctic blue, so cold they made her shiver. It didn't help that he wore a thin pair of drawstring pants, indicating he was going out to practice with his whip. She had been avoiding watching him the last couple of days because for some unexplained reason, just the sight and sound of it turned her on like nothing else in the world possibly could. That was the last thing she needed to know right now on top of everything else—that she was truly messed up in the head, or body, however one wanted to look at it.

"Seychelle, we did have a talk about privacy, and I told you how I felt about it when it came to my woman. Now fuckin' tell me what's going on."

She took her time finishing with her teeth, rinsed her mouth multiple times and then turned to face him, leaning her butt against the sink, arms crossed to match his. "I'm having hideous nightmares. Really vivid nightmares. They make me sick." She did her best not to make it an accusation, but she knew it came out like one. What was she accusing him of? He wasn't in her nightmares.

Savage studied her face for a long time without speaking, those blue eyes burning like ice over her. He was gorgeous. That was half her problem. She could stare at him endlessly—forever. He had a body on him, all man, more muscles than was good for him, tattoos over scars and burns. He had the words *Whip Master* burned into his skin on his chest and *Master of Pain* burned into his back. The tats didn't cover either burns, although she knew Ink, a brother in his club, had done his best with the beautiful artwork on him.

"You gonna stop there and make me ask or you gonna tell me what these nightmares are about, angel? If they're making you sick, they're fucked the hell up."

There was a warning in his voice, but no expression on his face, just those blue, blue eyes, cold as a glacier, telling her he wasn't going to let it go.

They had agreed to have truth between them, but that really meant *she* told him the truth and he withheld things he didn't want to talk about. They'd been together for months, and she loved him far too much. It wasn't a good thing by any means.

"Last chance, Seychelle, start talking."

"It was a nightmare, Savage. People have them."

"Two fuckin' nights in a row. The same nightmare. Bad

enough that you puke in the toilet and you don't want to tell me about it."

That was a straight-up accusation. Worse, he was right. She didn't want to tell him. That stance. Arms across his chest. Those eyes that wouldn't let her look away no matter how much she wanted to. He'd given her space the day before because she'd asked him to. She'd been upset. Joseph Arnold, a stalker, had been sitting in her cottage waiting for her with a gun, and Savage thought she was upset about that. She had been, of course, but that wasn't the only reason. There was a multitude of reasons she was questioning her sanity. Mostly, it had to do with herself, the things she was discovering she needed in her own sexual relationship, and that truly frightened her. She needed to come to terms with it.

There were just so many things coming at her so fast. She wasn't a person who took things in fast. She just wanted everything to slow down so she could take a breath and assimilate everything at a much different pace than they were going.

"It isn't me that is going to have the sore ass. I'm not asking again."

She detested the little flare of dark excitement that sent heat to her sex. It didn't matter how annoying she found it that he just stood there so casually. He was unmoving, those eyes of his holding her in place, probably seeing that flicker of reaction she couldn't control, knowing blood pounded in her clit and her sex fluttered just at the thought of what he intended in spite of her absolute abhorrence of his intentions.

"I shouldn't be punished because I choose not to talk to you about a nightmare I have, Savage. If I ask you about nightmares, you wouldn't tell me if you didn't want to."

"I have them all the time, angel, or I used to until you came into my life. You want to know about them, you ask me. I'll lay that shit out for you."

Of course he'd say that now. Her fingers formed two tight fists in frustrations. Why couldn't she just lie to him? Make something up? People did that all the time. She wasn't a liar. She'd never been, but maybe this one time it would be okay.

She shrugged. Tried to look away. She couldn't lie looking at him, for heaven's sake.

"Damn good thing you're just wearing that little robe, angel, and nothing else. Take it off, hang it on the hook inside the bathroom right by the shower and come on out here. I'll be waiting for you, and the longer you make me wait, the more punishment I'm going to add on."

He turned and walked away. Out of sight. He didn't go sit on the end of their bed, where she might see him. He walked out of sight, which meant he might have gone over to the chair close to the spanking bench. She nearly groaned aloud. She could close and lock the bathroom door—except there were no locks on the bathroom door. Why? Because her man had a thing about privacy.

She didn't have to go out there. She didn't have to do what he said. She was a grown woman. She made her own choices. That was the bottom line, and Savage always made that very, very clear. Everything they did together was ultimately her choice. She walked over to the mirror and stared at herself. Her eyes were dilated. Her face flushed. Already she was breathing too fast.

Why was she like this? Why did she respond sexually to something painful? Her body craved whatever Savage did to her, even when her brain refused to want it. She knew he would never stop until she told him what he wanted to know. She didn't want to tell him because what if she was right? What if the man in her nightmares was really Savage, and it was one more thing she was going to have to sort out? She was already at a breaking point.

Seychelle rinsed her face again with cold water, hoping to clear her mind. Savage was her choice. She had to sort through her problems fast. She was committed to him—to their life together. She wasn't so committed to his club. To that life. She didn't really understand it, and that was part of who he was. She needed that piece of him. He pulled her into it, then pushed her back out, and she resented it.

She took a deep breath, her lashes lifting so she found herself staring at herself in the mirror, realizing she'd just had a revelation. She didn't resent the fact that Savage had a psychic gift that allowed him to take on the anger, the very real rage his brothers and sisters of Torpedo Ink felt that made him the way he was. She was actually proud of him for that. She resented that all of them shared deep secrets and he shut her out. At the same time, he expected her to use her gifts to aid them and him when the club needed those gifts. Where was the fairness in that?

Ordinarily, Seychelle would gladly help anyone in need. Especially Savage. Any one of Savage's friends. But not like this, not when she was shut out and she was supposed to be his partner. He demanded 100 percent from her. He told her he was giving her 100 percent of him, but he wasn't.

She pushed at the hair tumbling around her face. When she did, she noticed the ring on her left hand. How could she not? It was gorgeous. A rare fancy teal-blue diamond, surrounded by diamonds that appeared to be petals hugging her finger. The entire thing glittered every time she moved. It should have been ostentatious, but it wasn't. It was simply beautiful. Savage had a way of knowing exactly what she would love.

He was trained to read body language. Every facial expression. Every single subtle hint, from elevated breathing to the parting of her lips. He knew her. And she was an open book anyway, even when she tried not to be. He had been trained from childhood in the arts of sex: giving, receiving, training one to do what he commanded, and he was very, very good at what he did. He had too many weapons to use against her, and she had fallen too fast to get her armor in place.

It wasn't that she didn't want to be where she was—she did. She had come on board with her eyes open—sort of.

Living in reality was always a far cry from being dreamily in love. "Let that be a lesson to you, Seychelle," she whispered.

She couldn't blame all of it on Savage or all the frightening things he brought to their relationship. She hadn't realized the extent of the lure of mixing pain and pleasure. She'd been so attracted to him, to that darkness in him. The first time he'd spun her around in an alley, lifted the hem of her dress and smacked her bottom, she'd gotten so damp, reacting to him when no one had ever made her body come alive before. That had been a revelation—a bit confusing, actually.

She went home and immediately delved deeper into spankings and even floggers, but she didn't really understand it. She had no idea why her body would respond to such a thing when no matter what she'd tried, she'd thought she was absolutely frigid. The deeper into his world Savage took her—and granted, it wasn't very far, but she saw where they were going—the more alarmed she got. She was intrigued. Terrified, but intrigued. That wasn't a good thing in her opinion.

In her mind, when she'd gotten together with Savage, she believed she would give herself to him and there would be that moment when she would have to "suffer" for him. He suffered for those he loved, and she would do it for him. She was very confused with the way she felt about pain and the effects on her body. She didn't want to crave pain. Did she? Or did she crave Savage? She didn't even know anymore what was right or wrong. She only knew that she loved him, and she had to find a way to come to terms with all the rest of it.

⌒

Savage stood looking at the array of tools he had lined up in his cabinet over the wooden drawers built along the wall next to the tall wooden cabinet where the jewelry he had for Seychelle was kept. She hadn't even seen the majority of it. He had orders in to have so much more made for her. Now that he had her in his life, he was more than comfortable with his needs. He just had to get her to a place where she was accepting of their lifestyle.

He was a sadist in the bedroom, and he owned what he was. He had exhausted all the avenues open to him to change and knew there was no way for him to be anything but what he was. He needed to see his woman in pain in order to be aroused. He got off on that shit. Putting his handprints or his marks on her gorgeous ass aroused him. But the thought of using his floggers or whips, that was the ultimate for him—that would put steel in his cock like nothing else could. Her tears were his. Her ultimate pleasure was his, and he could give her pleasure like no one else ever could.

She had gone into their relationship fully aware. He had been careful to tell her what he was so there would be no surprises on that score. He'd laid it out as plainly as possible, but talking about it wasn't the same as experiencing it. He had been bringing her into his lifestyle faster than he wanted to. He knew that was frightening for her. She responded so beautifully though.

Her body was aroused with clamps. She loved nipple play. He loved it. They hadn't gotten to the more exciting stuff for him, but they were getting there fast. She would both love that and hate it. She was coming to enjoy her spankings a little too much. She wasn't altogether certain she liked the crop that much, but he doubted if she would care for very many of the straps, slappers and tawse he was looking at in his cupboard at the moment.

These were specialized tools, and he chose three tawse, one that would warm her little backside up properly. He would ask her questions and hope she would answer him without lying. She'd never lied to him, but she'd been considering it. The second tawse, also crafted in the rough-hewn center-split leather like the first, was slightly larger and delivered a more punishing strike. She would definitely feel it. The split leather wouldn't feel anywhere near the same as the thicker crop he'd used on her. He'd ask again, and if she still didn't answer him, there was the larger tawse, which she definitely wouldn't enjoy. It was for a severe punishment. A lie. A holdout when there was no reason. He hoped—and doubted—it wouldn't come to that.

Savage would lay it out for her like he always did. She would choose her own consequences. During a punishment she knew there was no calling out "red" for stop. Any other time during sex, she had that right. This was a different circumstance and one she'd agreed to when they first laid down the rules to their relationship.

He'd been somewhat lax about keeping the rules. He'd let them go, didn't keep a guard on her like he should have all the time. It was his fucking fault that his woman was nearly gunned down by a madman. If Seychelle hadn't kept her head and been so resourceful, he wouldn't have gotten there in time. She had essentially gotten herself out of the cottage and was running when the club showed up to deal with Arnold, but it so easily could have gone the other way. All because he'd tried to be someone he wasn't.

He loved her so damn much he would have roped the moon and given it to her if he could have. What he did was let that fucker live the first time he'd turned up stalking Seychelle. Savage knew he should have killed him right then and thrown his body into the ocean or buried him in the forest somewhere deep where he never would have been found. Seychelle's entire ordeal rested squarely on his shoulders because he hadn't done what he was supposed to do—protect her. He was too busy worrying about her leaving him because he was asking her to accept too damn much in their relationship already.

He was who he really was. She had to know him, not some fucking choirboy he pretended to be. And he damn well wasn't letting her go. She could learn to love all of him, even the not-so-nice parts. She might be afraid of what they did in the bedroom, but she fucking loved it. It was this part, having to answer to him, that upset her. She didn't like that his world had to be so controlled. She didn't understand yet just how dangerous he could be if he didn't have everything in place. That meant her—his everything. The center of his universe.

He wasn't taking her bullshit anymore, and she might not realize it, but he was counting every fucking minute she was making him wait. He collected the three leather tawse and closed the cabinet and then crossed to the chair beside the spanking bench. He laid the three tawse out on the table, where she could see them when she came in. They were beautiful examples of Scottish craftsmanship. The leather was perfectly split just right, and each handle fit his palm exactly as he'd instructed.

He knew he had a well of rage in him, and this time it was dark and deep and ugly. He would have to be damn careful, because he wasn't going to punish her for his sins. He was pissed at himself. Not at her. She deserved punishment, and he liked when he was stripping her bare and giving it to her. He'd told her how much he enjoyed it. It aroused him, and he made no secret of it. It aroused her as well, but this time there would be no satisfaction for her at the end of it. He'd asked her several times to tell him what was making her sick, given her every opportunity. His woman had a stubborn streak. Sweet as candy. A fucking angel, but did what she wanted when she lifted that little chin of hers at him.

He would have smiled at that thought, but the way she had looked at him a few times worried him, especially when she'd said she'd had a nightmare. He'd been the one to interrogate that sick fuck Arnold, and he hadn't been polite about it, but then, Savage was known for getting answers when he questioned his prey. He'd never failed the club. He hadn't failed when he was first learning the techniques. He'd studied every poison. Every kind of weapon and where to insert knives to cause the most pain without killing. He'd studied anatomy, ways to lop off body parts without killing and ways to prolong life. At the club, he had cabinets with all kinds of tools and interesting oils and poisons he'd been taught to use from the time he was a young teen to extract the truth.

He was careful around Seychelle. He was too good at disassociating, far too good at it, and it made him a monster, lost him the humanity Czar, the president of Torpedo Ink, had fought so hard to keep in all of the club members. He had brought them to Sea Haven to give them a chance at life, but they were all so fucked up none of them really fit into society. They didn't understand the rules. They had their own code, the one Czar had given them, and they stuck with that. But Savage . . . He shook his head. He still had a difficult time even with that.

His emotions seemed to come and go. Either he felt nothing, or he was as cold as ice or absolutely enraged. All three of those things were dangerous and would get people killed. Then there was his circle, the people he protected, those he rode with and cared for. His emotions for them were strong, and anyone threatening them should have been killed and buried the moment that threat was found to be real. Like fucking Joseph Arnold. Yeah, he needed to go back to his strict rules, where he knew the people he let into his life were always safe. That meant getting his stubborn, sassy, cute-as-hell, gorgeous, sexy woman under control.

She had that psychic gift of reading his mind when things were too vivid and close. He couldn't go from an intense interrogation that might not raise the blood pressure of a sick fuck like him, but would stick in the corners of his dark soul, and come home to where an angel like Seychelle could see. Who knew? But it happened. And it might have happened again.

He'd showered multiple times and changed his clothes and burned his interrogation clothes before he'd gone home to Seychelle. He'd had breakfast with another brother, Ice, and his old lady, Soleil, allowing more time to pass and putting other things in his mind. He'd showered again at home before going to bed. He'd taken every precaution, but that didn't mean she hadn't slipped inside his soul.

He sat in the cool leather of the chair, looking at the various views he had from that one spot. The two armchairs were set close, facing the long fireplace built into the wall itself. It was a good twelve feet long and when turned on could flicker low, providing small tongues of orange or red flames or leaping, rolling red-hot scorching blazes. The curve below the fireplace provided the long bank of hand-crafted wooden drawers made by his brothers specifically for his whips and floggers. Fortunately, they were able to fit them into the room with few modifications. The tall jewelry cabinet they'd made for him fit nicely in the corner.

The woodworkers, Master, Player, Maestro and Keys, four of his brothers from Torpedo Ink, also made the rectangular, thinner cabinet housing his straps, slappers and tawse. In all honesty, they made cabinets in all shapes and sizes as they talked music and just messed around together in the shop. One would come up with a design and they'd put it together. If someone wanted it, they could just go get it. Savage had scored several beautiful cabinets that way. He'd needed them and found them at the shop.

Movement caught his eye, and his woman emerged from the master bath. Her hair always seemed a little bit wild, as if no matter what she did to try to tame it, there was no way it would fall in line. It was gold and platinum mixed together, streaks of light honey, thick, flowing down her back like a waterfall in waves.

Her eyes were a spectacular blue, like teal, deep and intense, stealing his breath if he looked too long, so that he had the feeling of falling, of drowning, and who the hell gave a fuck if he did, because just look at her. She had a woman's figure. She had tits. Nice round woman's flesh. Nipples he could see, could touch and play with. She had the kind of hips that cradled a man and an ass that invited a man to play. He fucking loved her body. He loved her skin. Smooth and soft, and it marked beautifully for him.

She walked, shoulders straight, back straight, chin up, hips and ass swaying, straight to the spanking bench. She stood, back to him, awaiting his orders. She could make his scarred cock stretch like no one could, just at the thought of what he was about to do to that sweet little ass and pussy.

He kept his relaxed position and dropped his hand to the first of the tawse, which was a bit smaller. "This is a tawse, Seychelle. It will warm your ass and get you ready for your punishment. I'll warn you, this is a cut above what you've felt before. It may not look like much, but it delivers. You will feel it."

Her gaze slid to him, and he caught the lift of her eyebrow. His cock jerked hard. She didn't intend to tell him. She was definitely challenging him. He flashed her a grin. He indicated for her to lay over the bench. She did, presenting her ass to him without hesitation. He got up and, using a lazy, silent prowl, came up behind her, put one hand on the small of her back and kicked her left foot out wide.

"You know how to present your ass to me." He bent down and fit a cuff around her right ankle to hold her in place.

She frowned and looked over her shoulder. He'd never used any tie she couldn't get out of. He'd always asked her first. They'd talked over everything. He'd told her up front punishments were different. Safe words were off the table. He was solely in charge, and she'd agreed. She might cry foul eventually, but he knew her well enough to know she was stubborn as hell and he would have to do something a lot worse than this to get her to run from him.

He cuffed her left ankle and then did the same with each wrist. He pulled a scrunchie from his pocket, gathered her hair and secured it into a messy knot. Some would escape, but she couldn't hide from him the way he knew she wanted to use her hair to do.

"Now I think we're ready. You look beautiful as always, Seychelle." He curved his palm around the back of her neck gently to give her courage, something he couldn't help doing with her, then ran his finger down her spine as he walked around her again and picked up the tawse.

Already his body was anticipating this. He could feel

himself sinking into that place of a sexual rush, a sexual high, and he hadn't even gotten started. It was in his mind, his blood already hot. He rubbed her bottom. Cupped her pussy. Teased her pussy lips. Flicked her clit with the tawse, letting her feel the leather.

"You like that, baby?" He patted her pussy with it gently. "We'll see how well you like it, when we're done."

He struck her without warning, using a little muscle, because honestly, this little thing hardly gave much of a sting in his opinion, but she jumped and then settled. He peppered her bottom with the tawse, lighting her up on both cheeks and then the backs of her thighs. He was right about his woman. Her pussy glistened; her clit was inflamed. Her ass was marked, but she didn't make a sound. After several minutes, he stopped and picked up the second tawse.

"Okay, baby, we're at the main event. What are you being punished for, Seychelle?"

"Because my man loves this shit and wants an excuse to use his fun little toys on me."

He rubbed the marks, his cock swelling to alarming proportions. *Bog*, she was killing him, challenging him like this. He fucking loved it. His hand slipped over the curve of her red bottom, fingers dipping into the heat of her pussy. She was so hot and greedy, her silken sheath tried to suck his fingers deep.

"So needy, baby. You want more, don't you? That is exactly the answer that will buy you more. I'll ask again, why are you being punished?"

"Because my man is being a total asshole right now?"

He patted her ass, smiled and let loose with the medium tawse. Her breath hissed out, and two thin lines that looked like they could welt appeared on her left cheek. Savage rained down more strokes, letting himself enjoy the way her skin bounced, taking the thinner split leather, that terrible bite, and smacked her over and over.

She jerked and moved her bottom, as if trying to get away, but there was nowhere for her to run. He stopped with the vertical stripes and rubbed them with the heel of his hand and then his fingernails. He had spent time on those stripes, taking them from the tops of her buttocks to the sweet curve and then down the backs of her thighs. This tawse was a more moderate punishment, especially if you used it the way he had, careful of his woman but still making sure she felt every stroke he laid on her.

"You want to tell me why you're lying over that bench with your gorgeous ass in the air and your pussy on display for me to punish, Seychelle?"

A quiet little sob escaped, and then she sniffed. "You asked me a question and I refused to answer you."

"That's right. Would you like to answer it now?" Deliberately, Savage continued to rub her sore bottom to keep it inflamed, but he gently circled her clit and then strummed it and flicked. When her body shuddered, he bent and used his tongue, stroking caresses and then devouring the liquid spilling from her. He wanted to keep her on edge, mix pleasure and pain until her body didn't know one from the other, until she needed them together to get that explosive rush.

He'd promised to train her, and he used every opportunity, even their punishments. He straightened and tapped her back with the tawse to remind her to answer him immediately. He had to get control back, not necessarily of her. He had to get his control back before he got her, or a member of his club, killed.

"I had a damn nightmare, Savage. I barely remember it. It was all jumbled up. Monsters chasing me in the forest or something silly like that." Seychelle's voice was a barely heard whisper, her tone not matching the defiance of her statement.

Adrenaline mixed with a dark sexual need rushed through his veins like a freight train. Like a drug he was addicted to. "You are fucking lying to me, Seychelle." He kept his tone velvet soft. Low. In total command of her. "You just fucked up big-time, and I told you what would happen."

He peppered her ass with the tawse, this time putting

more muscle into it until she was sobbing, really crying this time. He stalked over to the table, dropped the medium instrument and lifted the large one. He would have to be a little more careful—no—a lot more careful. This one could make a grown man cry. In the right hands it could deliver a blow that would go right through skin and muscle and jar the entire body with a streak of pain so severe it could incapacitate a man and leave him babbling and begging. Savage knew, because when he'd been training, he'd done that very thing multiple times. Of course, he'd been supposed to back then. He'd been thirteen years old and learning how to use all sorts of tools of the trade.

"I cannot believe you fucking lied to me." He bent his head down to snarl the accusation in her ear as he stalked around her, tracking the end of the much longer leather down her spine, causing goose bumps to rise all over her body. Yeah, she was getting it now.

He moved behind her, taking in the sight of her, trembling, barely able to control herself but not asking him, or demanding him, to let her loose. She didn't scream. Or curse. She tried to muffle her sobs as best she could, and he was damn proud of her for it. He ran his nails over the mottled skin of her cheeks, and his fucking cock swelled more, pushing hard at the scars.

He smacked her with the larger tawse, laying a double line of agony right across those perfect lines he'd already put there. She nearly came off the bench despite the cuffs, her cry choked off, and she forced herself back down. Immediately, he used his fingers to slide into her, stroking, letting her ride them, letting her settle, concentrate on that, lulling her. He smacked her again. Then again. Using some force, putting horizontal stripes over the vertical.

He was going to explode. Fucking explode like a teenager. She'd better give up her secrets soon. And he didn't want to hurt her.

"Seychelle." He stalked around to her face, caught her hair and yanked up her head so her eyes were staring into his. Tears poured down her cheeks, but he'd taught her well. Those were his tears. No screaming. She'd been silent. Held it in—for him—giving him this. He crouched down to look into her eyes. "Baby. Fucking tell me."

She swallowed a sob. "I keep having a nightmare about a man being tortured. It was horrible. He was in a chair bolted to a floor. There were men in the room, but I couldn't see them, only part of him, his legs, his lap. He was naked. There was blood everywhere. Someone smashed his legs over and over with a huge hammer-like thing. They did other worse things—with a drill. With bolts and then knives. I'm serious, Savage." She hiccupped. "It was so bad, the things I could see. I was afraid it was you doing them. I was certain the man was Arnold. Look at me, Savage. Did you kill Joseph? I have to know."

He hadn't realized he had been holding himself rigid, but his gaze never once left hers. Relief swept through him. He leaned in and licked at her tears, taking them from her face. He kissed her eyes and then found her mouth with his. "No, baby. I wanted to do it for you, and I'm sorry it wasn't me. I wish it were. He is dead, but I didn't kill him. I feel like I let you down because I didn't kill him." He kissed her again before she could protest. Before she could ask any other questions, because he would have to tell her the truth.

He moved around her once again, taking his cock out, stroking, feeling the heavy weight, moving behind her to look at her dark purple ass and thighs. She was going to have trouble sitting, and he had so many plans for her. He dipped his finger in her liquid heat and painted between her cheeks, finding her forbidden little star.

"One of our dirty, sinful things we have yet to explore, Seychelle. You love our lessons." He pushed the head of his cock into her hot entrance, throwing his head back and hissing at the tightness of her silky, wet sheath. "Maybe while I've got you helpless and you've been so bad, I should give you a lesson here." But he would never do that. Never. Not as a punishment.

He smacked her ass when she tightened up and turned her head to look at him over her shoulder, fear in her eyes. "You should know better. We haven't discussed that, and it isn't for punishment."

Before she could reply, he surged forward, driving deep into her sheath, burying himself to the hilt, watching himself disappear into her, watching the way her body swallowed his. The sight was sinful and dirty. Beautiful and miraculous. Fucking poetry. He was a big man and her body felt as if it was strangling him, a fist of scorching-hot, wet silk, twisting as he slammed into her with brutal force.

He wasn't making love to her the way he did most times, even when he was going at her hard. This was fucking her, using her body for his own personal satisfaction. He'd never once done that with her. Never. Never thought of it. He tightened his hold on her hips and pumped into her fast and hard, over and over, refusing to let her move. Never once giving her inflamed clit the necessary friction to get her off. This wasn't about her satisfaction. This was punishment, no longer for not answering him but for lying to him. That was a hard line to cross.

He let his sadistic streak roar with pleasure, let it revel in the sight of her suffering for him. Her purple, mottled ass, the glorious welts that were rising beautifully, the rakes of his fingernails, her sobs and the perfect tight, hot pussy that nearly strangled his cock drove him past all point of control, and he let it. He gave himself up to the pure ecstasy of driving in and out of her, watching her body take his. Feeling his girth swell even larger, the rigid scars scraping against the silken walls adding to the glorious friction.

Savage wanted to stay right where he was forever, giving his cock absolute freedom, giving himself permission to be who he was, but it was too good. Already, he was on fire, his entire being, blood so hot he was already a volcano, magma roiling in his balls, rocketing in brutal, jerking explosions to coat the walls of her sheath. Hot ropes of his seed that seemed a never-ending eruption, flinging him into some other place, where nothing could touch him. His fucking past was wiped out for those precious few minutes, or hours—he didn't know how long, he only knew she took it away.

He had no idea how long he stood behind her with his cock buried deep, his fingers digging into her hips so hard he was certain he had left bruises. His cock was still pulsing when he became really aware. His body buzzed, blood still roaring hotly through his veins, the rush still on him, but Seychelle was shaking and needed care.

He pulled out of her gently and reached down to unlatch the cuffs circling her ankles. He had to be a little careful. Surprisingly, his legs were rubbery. "Just a minute, baby. Let me take care of you and I'll get you free."

He had set everything he needed out beside his chair. As he passed the table, he swept up the three tawse he'd used on her and pushed them into the drawer out of sight to clean the leather later. Lotion containing a topical numbing agent as well as arnica to help against bruising was right beside the chair. He used a wet, warm cloth between her legs and thighs to clean her first and then applied the lotion.

Her breath hissed out of her, and he could hear her muffled sobs, but she didn't protest. When he had made certain he'd covered every welt and potential bruise, he removed the cuffs on her wrists and helped her into a standing position. Her knees gave out, and he caught her up.

Seychelle pushed him away and reached for the support of the spanking bench. "I'm okay." She rubbed at her face with her hand, effectively hiding from him. "I need some tissues." Her chest heaved, and her body gave another shudder.

He reached for her again. "Let me take care of you."

She went stiff. "You took care of yourself, Savage. Taking care of me is more taking care of yourself. You're doing it for you to make yourself feel better."

Savage ignored her clear resentment and lifted her into his arms, cradling her against his chest, taking her over to the chair. She struggled a little, but there was no way she was going to win when he had her trapped, and she gave up fairly quickly. He sank down onto the cool leather, keeping Seychelle on his lap, his arms firmly around her.

"Look at me."

She shook her head.

"I'm not playing around anymore, Seychelle, look at me." He poured steel under the velvet of his voice.

Her chin snapped up, and she glared at him. Her eyes were bluer than ever, that amazing teal that a man like him could drown in.

"That's where you're wrong, baby. I feel just fine. I was straight with you about what I am from the very beginning. I get off on punishing you. You give me a good reason, you're going to get your sweet little ass turned red."

"Do you really think it's necessary for me to tell you about my dreams, Savage?"

Seychelle laid her head against his chest as if she was so exhausted, she couldn't keep the weight of it up another moment. She probably was. He'd been very hard on her for more than one reason. Training her body should have gone much slower, taking much longer, but he knew they just didn't have the time. He'd used heavier instruments on her and kept her body on edge in order to continue training her body to need his. He was very worried that an upcoming club run was going to tip him over the edge, which meant regardless of whether she was ready or not, Seychelle was going to bear the brunt of his sadism.

"Yeah, Seychelle, when you have nightmares bad enough that you're puking in a toilet two mornings in a row, I'm going to find out what's wrong. As far as I'm concerned, that's my fuckin' business. I take care of you. If you're sick, I call the doctor. If you're upset, I figure out why and fix it. You're puking in the toilet, I'm going to ask why and you're going to tell me."

He massaged her scalp with strong fingers and then the nape of her neck, easing the tension out of her body. "I love you, baby. I'm not a good man, but you promised to love me the way I am. I'm doing my best to try to take care of you. I can't have stalkers pointing guns at you and you being so upset you're throwing up and afraid to tell me why." His fingers went back up to her scalp. "We set some ground rules, and we're going to abide by them. I told you I needed certain things in order to keep my life sane. You're the center of my world. I'm not taking chances on losing you."

She sighed. "I'm struggling with all of this, Savage. I feel overwhelmed."

"I know you are." He brushed kisses on her temple. "I'm a lot to ask you to accept, but you already made the commitment. We both did."

"I didn't mind the punishment, although it hurt like hell," she admitted. "I did mind the fact that you got off and I didn't."

She raised her eyes to his and he could see the misery there. He brushed another kiss over her lips. "It was a punishment, baby. You weren't supposed to feel good. I fucked you as part of the punishment because you lied to me, and you didn't deserve to get off and you know it." He kissed her gently. "That's part of the lesson."

"I hated that lesson."

"But you'll remember it, won't you?"

"Yes." She laid her head against his chest again, cuddling into him. "If you didn't kill Arnold, how do you know he's dead, Savage?" Her voice trembled just the slightest.

It took discipline to stay relaxed. He didn't want to answer questions about Joseph Arnold, but he'd just told her they didn't lie to each other. On the other hand, he could skirt around subjects that she couldn't handle—and right now he could see she was at her limit.

"Code found out that Arnold had stalked a couple of other women. Those women had disappeared. One of them was the sister of the member of another club." That was very true. "We turned him over to the club. When it was determined that Arnold had murdered her, they indicated that they killed him."

Savage chose his words very carefully. He had interrogated Joseph Arnold when Code had found that two other women had been stalked and he was suspected in their disappearance. One of them was the sister of a member of the Genesis club, a major player they could always use goodwill with. Favors came in handy when running through territories hot. Czar had put in a call asking if they wanted Arnold and saying he would be taken as far as Sacramento if they wanted him. They did.

He felt Seychelle sag with relief and knew he'd made the right decision not to tell her everything. Coming clean might be right, but he would lose her. She was overloaded, struggling to come to terms with his need for control, the punishments and her body's arousal when she experienced pain. She wasn't completely sold on the club either. The last thing she needed to deal with was knowing her man took human beings apart and didn't break a sweat or feel remorse.

"Let's get you in a bath. I've got a couple of things I've got to do today, babe, but one of the prospects will be outside, and any time you want to head out to do your thing, just message me and let me know where you're going, and then tell him. Do you already know your plans?"

He lifted her and took her on through to the grotto, where he sat on the edge of the tub, Seychelle still cradled on his lap. The water poured in, and he threw healing salts in. "When you've soaked for twenty minutes, I'll come back and apply more lotion."

"Eden Ravard has a card game today and needs a fourth person. I told her I'd join her. As usual, her sister, Nina, can't make it. Another emergency. She seems to have them a lot."

"You don't think they're real?"

Seychelle shrugged. "Nina annoys me. She's older than Eden by quite a few years but acts like Eden should do everything for her, and Eden does. In any case, Eden asked me to go shopping for her and come early to help her prepare the snacks for everyone. After that, I promised to go visit Dirk and Harriet Meadows. Then I thought I'd go for a walk on the headlands if it wasn't late before I came back here. Unless you want to stay at the cottage tonight."

He couldn't miss the hopeful note in her voice. "We could do that. Master and Player sent a text asking if you might want to join them tonight at the bar. Nothing big, just for fun. If you'd rather not, or you're tired, we'll just meet at the cottage."

She slid off his lap into the hot, steamy water, wincing as her bottom came in contact with the salt water. He'd placed the cushioned ring so she could lower herself onto it, but she was going to be sore. He wanted her to remember this lesson and any lesson afterward. He wasn't like the others in the club, and he knew that—other than perhaps Maestro, who believed the same way he did.

"We'll see how I feel," she murmured, closing her eyes.

TWO

Savage lay with his head on Seychelle's belly, his arms wrapped around her hips, listening to the sound of the waves and her steady breathing as she slept. Most nights, he couldn't sleep. He'd been that way most of his life. He'd spent too many nights in that damn hellhole, freezing, expecting to be dragged out any moment to be used by the "instructors" at the school. Sleeping lightly was a habit. Self-preservation. He had to know what was coming at him at all times.

Sometimes he slipped out of bed, and if they were at the other house, he practiced with the various whips. No way was he ever going to leave permanent marks on her skin—unless she wanted his name there, declaring she belonged to him. That was far down the line. That would hurt like hell where he wanted to put it. Just the idea of it could put his cock into a frenzy that made him so full and hard the scars threatened to tear apart. Sometimes the pain was excruciating, and he needed the relief of her scorching-hot, tight sheath, just to milk him dry.

He fucking loved her. She was doubting herself, thinking something was wrong with her and he wouldn't love her the way she was. He could see her rejection of her sexual needs. The more he developed them, the more ashamed, guilty and embarrassed she became. She put that shit on herself, not realizing he had taken what little tiny kernel of interest she had and developed it quickly. That was his expertise. He'd tried to explain that to her, but the more she got off on it, the more she took on herself.

Savage rubbed his bristled jaw gently over her belly. He'd made the decision to back off training her for a few days to see if that helped to give her peace of mind. He'd pushed her pretty hard with the tawse. Part of that had been selfish when he'd seen how she'd reacted. She was incredible. Everything he could ever want in a woman. He meant what he said to her. If they couldn't go any further, he would find a way to live with what they had. He wouldn't lie to her or himself—it would be difficult at times, but he would do it because he loved her more than he needed to have whip marks on his woman. He'd live with handprints and flogging welts. He'd have to be careful when he was at his worst, because some of his floggers were as bad as, or worse than, his whips.

The other reason he had pushed her was knowing what was coming up so fast. He would not be using any other woman to take the edge off when the monster came out. It was Seychelle or no one, so it had to be Seychelle. He was doing his best to come up with a plan to take it easy on her, knowing if he didn't train her body, she wouldn't be ready, and she needed to be. The monster was coming, and he couldn't stop it. That wouldn't be quite the same thing as handling him when he was in the mood to play.

Once Torpedo Ink went on the run with the other clubs and he had to take care of club business the way it looked like it was going to play out, he would need her almost immediately when they returned home—if he could last that long. Oftentimes, because they resided in Diamondback territory, they were required to ride with them on one of their events. They'd all but been ordered to go. It was a fucking mess.

"*Bog*, baby," he whispered. "What the fuck am I going to do? I brought you into this, and I can't give you up."

Just the thought of losing her was worse than anything he could think of. He hadn't believed anyone could love a man like him, and yet she lay there in his bed, her bottom sore, but she hadn't hesitated or held back when he'd made love to her as gently as possible, grateful that just the sight of her bottom was enough to arouse him. He didn't need to add any additional stripes to her already sore ass.

Seychelle had whispered the words to him, kissing his throat, his neck, then pouring that love into him. He felt it every time she touched him—when she looked at him. He wasn't giving that up because she was afraid. He just had to figure out a way to help her through this adjustment period and still give her the real man and not some choirboy version.

"I'll never be that man, angel. I'm a fucking devil, not a choirboy, no matter how much I want to be that for you." Sometimes he just watched her sleep because she was so beautiful, he had to make certain she was real.

Her laughter was muffled by the pillow, a low musical raining of golden notes that teased at his skin, feathering over his nerve endings until little electrical pulses beat in time to the music she created.

"Are you having delusions, honey, or did some misguided soul, one of your many admirers, actually tell you that you were a choirboy? I can rid you of that misconception right now." Her little giggle came again, along with those notes spilling over his body. He actually saw her laughter in golden notes. He saw her music that way as well. When he was a child, he'd been able to see people's voices in colorful notes drifting around them, but that had been wiped out abruptly when all joy had been stomped out of him.

Seychelle turned her head toward him, her thick braid moving across the pillow as she looked over her shoulder at him. Light came through the open window. She refused to close the damn thing, no matter what he said about security.

She liked it open, and he liked the way the moonlight managed to shine perfectly on her.

Laughter was in her eyes, that totally relaxed look she got on her face whenever they were here in her home—her little cottage by the sea she loved so much. He had tried to recreate a space on the bed in his master bedroom just like hers, but he'd failed. She still wasn't as relaxed, all tension gone, ready to tease him and play like they had for months before they made their relationship official, not in his master bedroom.

In retaliation, he nipped her hip and then soothed the sting with his tongue. "I've been a fucking choirboy for an entire day." That laughter was killing him. He loved the sound of it.

"You can't say *choirboy* and *fuck* in the same sentence and be a choirboy."

She sounded all prim and schoolmarmy, which made him smile. His first reaction was to roll her over so she was sprawled over the top of him and he had access to her bottom. That was his usual response when she teased him like this, but he didn't want any bruising, not when he'd made up his mind to ease up and give her a few days to adjust. He would always be a controlling bastard, wanting everything his way, and maybe taking one thing at a time was the best way to go.

"Babe, I told you I was going to hell. Might as well do anything I want. And that's mild in comparison to all the things I *think* about saying and doing."

Her laughter was contagious. "You should have seen your face last night when the Red Hat ladies showed up at the bar to hear me sing. All those darling ladies, Zyah's grandmother leading the way. She's so cute, by the way. I adore her, and she adores you. Obviously the two of you have a past, and she made it clear last night that you, Destroyer, Maestro and Player are her little darlings."

"You're going to get yourself in trouble if you bring that

up," he growled against her pristine skin, settling his teeth against her in warning.

She didn't pay him heed in the least. "Who knew you were so popular, Savage? All those sparkly hats and all of them wanting to dance with you. I had more requests for songs. The other bikers in the bar last night were quite enthusiastic about making certain the right music was requested. Everyone had ideas. I even saw Jackson and Jonas slip in. They were grinning from ear to ear, and at first it looked as if they might have been there on official business."

That did it. At the mention of the cops, there was no way he was going to be a saint. Savage rolled and took her with him, so that she sprawled over the top of him, her sore, bare ass in the air, legs on either side of his hips. Her amazing blue eyes laughed right down into his, causing his heart to perform some silly, weird melting sensation. He rubbed her bottom, hoping she would consider that a threat.

"You didn't tell me I had so many rivals for your affection. I went into that blind. All those ladies giggling. They brought cookies, Savage. There were plates of cookies with your name on them."

If a man like him had the ability to blush, he might actually have done it when the Red Hat ladies marched in with their crazy purple-and-red hats and their wild clothing, as if each had tried to outdo the others in outlandish skirts and layered dusters. Secretly, he applauded them for their carefree apparel and their insistence on living out their lives the way they chose. If they wanted to go to a biker bar dressed as a cross between fairy godmothers and something out of *A Midsummer Night's Dream*, more power to them.

Ten of the Red Hat women had shown up, all bearing plates of cookies. And then Zyah, Player's wife. She had come along to keep an eye on her grandmother. Anat Gamal, her grandmother, had unofficially adopted all of Torpedo Ink as her grandchildren. Savage wasn't going to admit to his woman that he might really be one of the favorites, because she would give him no end of grief over it. She was already far too amused over how the evening had played out.

"I shared the cookies with you, you little monster," he pointed out. He kissed the hollow of her neck. She always smelled so good—a wild strawberry fragrance that was just so subtle.

"You weren't very generous with the bar."

"They were snickering."

"Because you wouldn't dance. Those ladies wanted to dance."

"I don't dance."

"You dance with me."

"You've got something I want, baby."

"What would that be?" She traced one of his scars with her tongue, and then the tattoo that ran over the top of it.

"That mouth of yours. Love your mouth, Seychelle. I'm going to love seeing your lips stretched around my cock. You've got the most amazing tits. Firm and round, more than a handful. Impressive nipples, and you let me play. I've decided to see if I can make you come for me just by playing with your nipples, baby. Your sweet little pussy. It's hot as hell and so tight you strangle my cock when I'm inside you. Then there's your perfect ass. I love the shape of your ass cheeks, the way they show my marks. The way they bounce when I strike them. I think about fucking your ass while you scream and come over and over even though you don't want to, and it makes me so hard, I think I'll explode. So, yeah, I've got reasons to make the effort to dance with you and make a fucking fool out of myself."

All the while he spoke in a low, velvet tone, he rubbed her sore cheeks gently. He could feel her heat growing as he continued. He slid his fingers lower, between her legs, to find her slick, just like he knew she would be. She was always responsive to him. He loved a hell of a lot more about her than he told her. It wasn't all physical; in fact, there was a lot that wasn't physical, but making more of a fool of himself than he already looked with those women wasn't happening.

"Is that why you dance with me, honey?"

She rubbed her chin on his chest and then looked up at him, those long lashes feathering over her eyes and then lifting, nearly stopping his heart.

"Maybe. Or maybe I just like to hold you." He was rewarded with her smile. It was slow, curving those full lips so that her straight little teeth gleamed at him and her eyes picked up a shine.

"Maybe you are a fucking choirboy after all, Savin Pajari." She lifted her head and framed his face with both hands, looking innocent and sweet as only Seychelle could do. "It never lasts more than five seconds, but in those five seconds, that choirboy deserves all those Red Hat ladies and their adoration and cookies. I'm absolutely certain of it."

She leaned down and kissed him. Just a brush of her lips, but she gave him a taste of wild strawberries. Just a small elusive hint that lingered in his mouth. He had to resist fisting her hair and holding her head in place while he devoured her. She was still in teasing mode. He caught her lower lip between his teeth and bit down gently, trapping that soft curve and pulling it in warning, narrowing his eyes at her.

She giggled like a little kid, forcing him to release her. Immediately, she rolled off of him and scooted to the headboard, her favorite place. He pulled her legs down so he could lay across her hips, pillowing his head on her belly, his favorite place.

"You really didn't mind all those women there last night, did you?" she asked.

"That's your question? You're going to waste one of your questions on a silly one like that?" She knew the answer.

Hell no, he didn't mind. It ruined his badass image, but then one look at him restored it immediately. He liked the old ladies, particularly Anat Gamal. There was just something about those older women that got to him. They needed someone to defend them, he was there. He wasn't the only one that thought that way. All of Torpedo Ink did.

"No, baby, I didn't mind them coming out to hear you sing. They had a good time, and the bar wasn't too crowded. It would have been different if we'd had a couple of clubs standing off against each other, but last night no one was there challenging each other, and the ladies had their night of fun."

He rubbed her hip. This was what they did together. Lay on her bed and asked questions. The rule was, they had to answer honestly. They'd started their relationship that way, and he always enjoyed hearing her answers and her questions. "What bothers you most about our club?"

He looked up at her, watched her face. She bit her lip, not wanting to answer. He'd hoped he'd been wrong and she wasn't bothered about the club, but it was clear she was. He'd known she wouldn't like the question, but she wasn't a coward, his woman. She might take her time, but she wouldn't call a halt to their game.

"It's a closed club. I'm not in it, but I'm expected to live with it, with the rules, and to help all of you whenever you need it."

He turned her answer over and over in his mind. There was some truth to that. Torpedo Ink was closed off in some ways. All right, if he was honest, in all ways. They let their women in by loving and protecting them, but it wasn't the same. No one had gone through the things they had together. They'd been torn apart. Shredded. They weren't whole, not unless they were together. One didn't survive without the others. It was difficult to explain to anyone else. So, yeah, he got it. She wasn't exactly wrong. Still, she was his woman, and the club accepted her as such, which meant she was theirs to protect.

"That's not exactly right, Seychelle. Every member of Torpedo Ink would lay down their life for you."

"Maybe. I don't want them laying down their life for me. I want, for once in my life, to be someone's first."

He frowned. "What the fuck does that mean?"

Her lashes fluttered. "It isn't your turn. It's my turn."

"Then get on with it." He ran his palm over her hip and down her thigh possessively, because really? What the fuck did she mean by that?

"Did you always want to belong to a motorcycle club?"

"I didn't know what a club was until I saw the worst of them. We rode with the Swords, one of the nastiest clubs on the planet. They ran a huge human trafficking ring and treated women and children like shit. I loved the brotherhood I shared with my people, and riding on my Harley, but didn't want anything to do with the Swords. I didn't want to be like them. We came into contact with other clubs, and over the five years we rode with the Swords, we learned not all clubs were like the Swords. Czar set the rules for us, and we knew it was our best way to function in society."

Her hand moved to his scalp, fingers beginning that slow massage he had come to love. From the first time she'd ever done that, she'd made him feel cared for.

"So, what the fuck did you mean when you said for once in your life you wanted to be someone's first?"

Seychelle shifted her weight from her bottom to her hip. He turned his head slightly so he could look up at her face. There was no pain there, none in her eyes, but there was some other emotion that had his gut knotting. She looked almost haunted. Those teal-blue eyes looked sad. Deep sorrow. The kind that didn't just go away easily.

"Baby." He gentled his voice. "What did you mean by that? Tell me. This is our honesty time. We always talk to each other right here in the safety of this room."

Deliberately, he wanted to point out they were in her safe place. Her sacred spot—*their* sacred place. He had to acknowledge that even for him, this cottage and this bed had become that. Maybe he didn't want to give up the cottage either. He rubbed his palm up and down her thigh and then found the scars on her leg that she'd gotten saving his life, tracing them gently with the pads of his fingers.

She turned her face away from him, staring out the window to look at her beloved sea. He gave her that, not forcing her to face him. It mattered more that she gather the courage and tell him what she meant. Whatever it was, it was too damned important for him to insist on controlling how she told him.

"For you, your brothers and sisters in Torpedo Ink are a part of who you are, Savage. You kind of said that to me, right? That somehow, to survive, you're all woven together, and you wouldn't make it apart."

He nodded, afraid to speak aloud. Instead, he rubbed his chin along her belly and then kissed the faint abrasive red marks he'd put there. All the while he continued to trace those scars to soothe her. She was used to his touch. He willed her to continue.

"Everything you do, you do for the club. You have secrets with the club, things you share with them you don't share with me. They dictate your life to you. They come first for you, and they always will."

He saw where she was going with her statement, and his first reaction was to protest, but what exactly was she saying that was incorrect? The club was his life. He did share things with the club he couldn't share with her. His life did revolve around the club. He wouldn't say he put them first before her, but it would seem that way to her. He could understand that.

"My parents really loved one another, and when my father realized my mother was going to die, he couldn't see me, only her. At first, I had Mom, but then when Dad developed the heart condition, she began to focus more and more on his illness, and I was the odd man out. I didn't blame them. I really didn't. I had so much to do all the time, and they couldn't do much at all, so they spent their time with each other. Don't get me wrong, we spent time together as a family, just as I know I'll spend time with you and your family. But I always thought I'd be first in someone's life. That's the dream, right? At least my dream."

"You're my world, Seychelle. I don't want you to doubt that."

"What's your dream?"

She hadn't replied to his statement. When she asked her question, there was the slightest tremble to her voice, but when he looked up at her, there were no tears. Her lower lip trembled for just a moment, just as her voice had, but she bit down and stilled it.

"Keeping you happy for the rest of your life," he answered sincerely, without hesitation. "Finding a way that allows you to see and love the real me so that you want to stay with me. That's the dream for me, Seychelle. The real man. The monster and the man."

A wall of water thundered toward the shore, the waves crashing against the bluffs and sea stacks in a wild display of nature in turmoil. His heart beat faster, while his blood seemed to match the rhythm of the tumultuous sea.

Her fingers massaged his scalp, the one thing that kept him believing she was hanging in there with him. Why did she feel as if she was so damn elusive? They had a problem. A real problem. This was much bigger than getting her body to accept pain with pleasure.

"I laid out everything for you—how I was, what I was—Seychelle, before you agreed to our relationship. That I had to have things a certain way. That I'd be in control. That I'd want to punish you when you broke the rules. That I'd train your body to enjoy pain with pleasure so you would better be able to enjoy sex with me. You agreed to all those terms. Have you changed your mind?"

"No."

She hadn't hesitated.

"Do you really believe men can be faithful to one woman?" she asked.

"The right man can, yes." He didn't wait to hear what she had to say about that. "Do you believe you can love the real me?"

"Only if you actually share the real you with me."

There was a challenge in her voice. That deep sorrow was back. That haunting note that broke his heart. Damn it, this was about his club. About the fact that she felt she wasn't first in his life. She was—and she wasn't. She *was*. She was his fucking world. The center of it. The heart of it.

"Do you think I'm not in love with you?"

She hesitated. His entire body froze. He didn't know the first thing about relationships. He didn't. He only knew that he believed she was his. Every cell in his body knew she was right for him. There was no one else, and there never would be. He had to be right for her. He might be rough and too controlling, but he would move the world for her, if she needed it moved. He just needed her to give him a little direction.

It wasn't going to be the sex that was going to destroy their relationship, it was this distance. The way she felt about not being first in his life. How the hell did he combat that? What about the other members of Torpedo Ink who had women? Blythe felt first with Czar, their president. Breezy did with Steele, their vice president. Ice, another member, with his wife, Soleil. Even Anya did with Reaper and Scarlet with Absinthe. There was Player with Zyah. What was the difference?

Savage buried his face in the hollow along her hip bone. It was him and not only what he did for the club but the way he sometimes needed to do it. He took apart men for information. She might live with that. He took apart pedophiles because they fucking deserved to feel what they'd done to him and every boy and girl they'd ever touched. He hunted them, and he brought them to justice. He made certain they knew exactly what they had done to the little children they'd taken. The lives they'd destroyed.

Yeah, that was part of what he did for the club and part of what he did for himself. He was the club assassin. When the club was paid to make a hit, he was the one to do it most of the time. Sometimes Maestro, another member, carried out the order, but most of the time, it was on him. That wasn't something he was going to share with his woman.

"Seychelle? Do you think I'm not in love with you?" He repeated the question, turning up his gaze to her face.

Her tongue touched her lower lip. "I think you love me, Savage," she said slowly.

"That isn't the question." He gripped her thigh. This was far worse than he thought. She really had mixed feelings about the club and their relationship, and he had no idea how to fix that shit. None. He could tell her a million times he loved her because it was the truth, but it was also the truth that when the president of his club called, he would go and he wouldn't tell her why.

Her breath left her lungs in a little rush. "*In* love with me? What does that even mean to you? I don't know anymore. I thought I knew. When we started down this road together, I thought I did, but things are different."

"It means I love you with every fuckin' breath I take. That's what it means to me. How are things different, Seychelle? Tell me how you think they're different."

Her fingers continued to move on his scalp. That was the one thing that kept him from leaping up and pacing across the small room, his stomach churning. He was *not* going to lose her.

"There's this distance between us, and no matter what we do, we can't make that go away. It's like this very large space. I know you feel it too, Savage. We've always been in sync, and suddenly we're not. There's this huge chasm." Her voice was sad.

He couldn't deny it. He did feel it. How could he not? Had he done that? Or had she? Was she right? Was it his club? The club had always been there. What had changed? What was different?

"When did it start?" He wasn't going to deny it and pretend he didn't know what she meant. If she was brave enough to admit it, they had a chance to fix it.

"When the Diamondbacks came to the bar for a meeting. You brought me there that night to sing with the band. You didn't tell me until the last minute that there was some important meeting and you needed my voice to keep everyone calm."

"I apologized for that. I know you have to process, and I should have warned you ahead of time that there could be trouble." He rubbed his palm along her thigh and then down over her scars. She was too damn perceptive.

"You did apologize, Savage, and I accepted your apology. Had that been all that was happening, it would have been all right, but it wasn't. There were all kinds of undercurrents that night. The thing was, the other wives weren't there."

"Some were there. Scarlet. Lissa. They were there."

"Scarlet and Lissa can shoot the wings off a fly. They weren't there as wives that night, and you know it. They were there in the same capacity as Alena and Lana and every other member of Torpedo Ink. If something went wrong, they were there to fight for the club. I'm not stupid, Savage. It wasn't just an important meeting. Torpedo Ink was expecting trouble, the kind of trouble where all of you could have been killed."

He sat up, swearing under his breath, his bare feet hitting the floor. She was absolutely right. They had been expecting trouble, or at least ready for it.

"I was the only one not informed, yet you were using me. They all were."

"Seychelle." He turned to look at her. "Baby, it wasn't like that, and you know it."

"It was *exactly* like that. You needed my voice and you didn't want to include me in knowing whatever it was that was happening, so you just didn't bother to give me the information. Isn't that right? Club business. I don't need to know. I can serve you. Serve the club. But I don't need to know."

"Damn it, Seychelle. I'm your man. Why the fuck do I have to explain myself and what I'm doing to you? Why would I have to spell anything out? I say it, you should trust me enough to just fuckin' do what I say because I say it." Adrenaline poured through his veins, and he caught up his jeans and yanked them up.

"I did exactly that, didn't I, Savage?" she said. "I did what you said. If I go on the stupid run with you, I'll most likely do what you say, even though I'll be the only one that doesn't know what's going on."

He spun around to face her as he dragged his T-shirt over his head. "You're going on the run with me, Seychelle." It was a command, nothing less. He was so done with the argument because, damn it to hell, she was right about that too. She wouldn't know what was going on because he wasn't about to tell her he was going to kill a couple of people after he got information out of them first. And yeah, the club knew all about that shit. He stomped into his boots and pulled on his jacket and was gone, slamming the door like a fucking child.

What was wrong with him? If she'd walked out on him, he'd be after her, throw her over his shoulder and smack her ass so hard she wouldn't be able to sit down for a month. She was right, and he didn't have a leg to stand on. He didn't have a way to combat what she was saying, so he walked out instead of having the courage to just admit it.

He wanted to hit something. Anything. Head down to San Francisco to the fight club and get a few matches. He sucked at relationships. Five minutes in, and he blew it already because she spoke the truth and he had no answer for it.

He settled his ass on the familiar leather seat of his matte-black Night Rod Special with its dull gunmetal-gray trim, blacked out chrome and the image of a dripping skull. He found he couldn't move. He didn't want to go anywhere, not without her. Not leaving her like this. She had all the courage in the world to answer him honestly, and he'd run like a coward because he knew he couldn't give her the truth. He'd promised her to be all in, and yet he was the one holding back. He expected everything from her, and she knew it. She'd called him on his shit, and instead of taking it like a man he'd thrown a tantrum.

"Fuck." He was off the bike and stomping back to the cottage.

Seychelle sat in the same place, but she had a T-shirt on and her knees pulled up, arms wrapped tight around them. Her head was down, and she didn't look up at him when he walked in and sat on the edge of the bed next to her.

"Shouldn't have stormed out like a fuckin' kid, baby. I didn't know how to make this right and took the coward's way out. I don't know how couples do this. You have one of those books you're always reading?" He ran his hand over the back of her head. Down that long fall of silky hair.

"I wish I did, honey." Her voice was muffled. She didn't look up.

His stomach dropped. Flipped. His heart clenched. "Oh hell, Seychelle. You're not crying, are you? Baby, don't do that. I mean it. You can't cry."

"You like me to cry."

Oh *Bog*. She was crying. The real deal. He felt a little panicky. "No, it isn't the same. Stop it. We'll figure this out. Maybe not right away, but it will get done. We're new at this shit."

When she continued to cry, he picked her up and carried her to the chair so he could hold her on his lap. Cradling her to his chest, he just held her, cupping the back of her head, trying to soothe her with his body. Clearly, he wasn't good with words.

After a few minutes she seemed to quiet, but he continued to hold her, rocking her gently, liking her in his arms. "This is my fault, baby. I don't know what I'm doing yet. I'll figure it out, Seychelle. You just have to hang in there with me. I know it isn't easy, but I swear, if you do, in the end, I'll be worth it."

He didn't have a clue how he was going to make himself

or their relationship worth it to her. She was the one doing all the giving, and he was the one doing all the taking.

"We're supposed to be partners. *Partners*. You don't leave me out, Savage. You don't try to control my every move. I love my life, the people I visit, the places I go. They might not be anything to you or to anyone else, but they're very important to me. They're elderly people everyone overlooks, but I love them. I don't want you to tell me I can't go see them like I'm some child. Sea Haven is very small. Everyone knows everyone's business. It's not like if someone is mean to me you aren't going to know about it in three seconds. And I'd text you. I did text you."

He knew she was referring to her stalker. She had come home to her little cottage and he'd been inside.

"I was almost too late, Seychelle." Just thinking about those minutes after he heard her voice asking Arnold why he had a gun in her home had his stomach in knots.

"What happened with Joseph Arnold wasn't your fault or mine. He was sick."

"Yes, he was. There are a lot of sick people out there, Seychelle," he pointed out.

"I know, but it was a fluke that he attached himself to me."

He sighed and kissed her neck. "You know that isn't true. I want to agree with you, but you know it isn't the truth, baby." He kept his tone gentle. Pure velvet. This had to hurt worse than the punishment. She loved to sing. She had the voice of an angel, but that voice of hers was also her downfall.

She pushed her forehead against his chest. "I can switch how I sing. I tap into emotions and sing for particular people to help them, but I can find a way to stop that."

"No, you can't. You know you can't any more than you can stop yourself from trying to heal someone who is really sick. You draw men to you, babe. You just do. And if you weren't singing, you'd say hello on the street and one day you'd say hello to the wrong man and it would be someone like Arnold. He'd hear your voice and it would work its way inside him."

"Is that why you're with me? My voice? My body?"

His first reaction was to tease her and give her a sexual answer, but he caught the underlying note of despair in her voice. She didn't want him to be with her for either reason.

"I love all of you, Seychelle Dubois. I fell so hard for everything you. You bring me sunlight. You taught me how to laugh. I didn't have hope, and you gave that to me. I had no future and you gave me one. There's a brightness in you, and you were generous enough to share that with me, knowing what I am and what I'll always be."

"Don't, Savage," she whispered, pushing her face into his throat.

"No, baby, I don't have a lot to give you yet. I'm learning. But I can give you this: truth. I was all but dead inside. Just dark and gone, soulless. Then you came into my life and somehow you managed to bring me back to life. So, to answer your question, do I love your body? Hell yeah, I fuckin' do. Does your voice get to me? You sing like a fuckin' angel. I tell you that because it's true. But more than those two things, it's how you look at me and see the man inside that I can't even see. You're capable of loving that man when I didn't believe there was anyone on the face of this earth that could love that monster."

"Savage."

He felt the wet of her tears again. *Bog*, he detested making her cry, but these were sweet tears for him. Loving tears, and he felt the difference. He was learning. He might be slow, but he was finding he was capable of learning because she mattered to him.

"I want that partnership with you, it's just that keeping you safe has to be a priority. You have to understand and accept that. You can't resent it any more than you can resent it when I pull you off the stage or out of a room if someone is too sick for you to be in the room with them. I'm protecting you. Shielding you. That was the promise I made to you, and you agreed to it, didn't you, Seychelle?" He kept his tone low. Tried to state facts, not be a dictator.

"Yes. I just didn't think in terms of having to answer to you every minute of the day for my time. It feels wrong, like I'm a child instead of a woman. Should I be doing the same for you? Shielding you from Torpedo Ink because you take on their anger? Their rage and pain?"

It took discipline to stay relaxed. He kept rocking her. Running his hand down the back of her scalp to soothe her while he considered what to say. He didn't want her to ever blame the other members for what she would have to suffer on their behalf. Already she resented the club. He hadn't expected that.

She had never indicated that she would blame them, even knowing that one of his psychic gifts was to take on the rage of his brothers and sisters so they could better function. He'd been doing it since he was a little kid, and it was automatic now. He doubted he could stop even if he wanted to.

He sighed and brushed his lips gently over her ear. "I know it has to be difficult to know that you're the one who will ultimately be suffering for them . . ."

"No, Savage. You suffer for them. I take on pain for you. I do that for you, and I choose to do it. It's my choice, just as it's your choice what you do for them. I'm just asking you if I should be stepping in front of you."

"Now you're just throwing shit out there to make an argument that doesn't even make sense, Seychelle, and you know it. Don't do that. We have so much real shit to work through, we don't need made-up issues. I'll do my best to make it easy on you when you want to go places. One of the prospects will go if I can't. Either Glitch or Hyde. If things are dicey, and I ask you to stay home, I'll expect that you will. You have to trust me. I don't want to have to explain myself. My woman should trust me."

"But that should go both ways, Savage. I shouldn't have to explain myself."

He hated when she fucking had a good point. "Take your

bath and remember to use those salt crystals. After, you need the lotion. We'll go easy for the next couple of days to let you heal."

She needed time they didn't have to come to terms with their relationship. He needed time they didn't have to figure out how to give her the things she needed and deserved when he didn't have a clue what he was doing.

THREE

Seychelle dressed in her favorite vintage blue jeans, grateful she could wear them. Two days had already gone by, and her bottom wasn't sore at all. Okay, maybe a twinge now and then, but the lotion and salt baths did a world of good. That, and although at the time of the punishment it had felt as if she would have marks forever, Savage had made certain she wasn't really wearing more than a few handprints and a couple of raised stripes that went away almost immediately.

At night Savage hadn't really touched her other than to kiss her and wind his body around hers. Truthfully, she hadn't liked that very much. In fact, she was over it, but she knew he was deliberately trying to give her space. She'd been the one to ask for it. Now she didn't know what to do to get him to resume their very active sex life. She needed it as much as he did.

Savage had brought her back to his gorgeous home. She knew he wanted her to start to become comfortable in it, and she was determined that she would. She did love the master bathroom. She'd never seen anything more beautiful. She loved taking baths, and the grotto called to her. The tub filled fast and the water was hot and steamy. She had to be careful not to spend half the day there.

The house wasn't that much farther for her to drive into Sea Haven if she wanted to make her visits to her older friends. The list of the elderly she checked on was growing. Word had gotten out that she would look over their medication and ensure they had their groceries. She also thought, because Savage often did repairs, she was welcome in more homes. She didn't mind. It was important that someone look after the seniors in town.

Seychelle pulled on a T-shirt and soft sweater, found a pair of boots and went into the kitchen for coffee. The house seemed huge at first, but once she managed the layout, she realized it was the high ceilings and open floor plan that gave the illusion of space. The coffee was freshly made and very hot, just the way she liked it. Savage had put out a teapot and tea, but she put the coffee in a to-go mug. She had things to do, and she'd slept in and then spent too much time in the bathtub. She loved that tub.

She knew Savage would be outside in the courtyard off the master bedroom, practicing with his whips. He had told her it was imperative he practice every day. She hadn't wanted to come back to the house because she hadn't wanted to face the fact that just seeing him handle the whips was such a turn-on for her. That part of her had been difficult for her to confront. It still was. Maybe she never would come to terms with it.

As she made her way back through the master bedroom, she found her heart beginning to accelerate. It didn't take much for blood to start rushing through her veins. Sliding the door open, she stepped out onto the covered deck. There were two chairs there, but she ignored them and set her coffee on the railing and kept walking out toward the stairs leading to the grounds where the rows of mannequins were set up.

There was a breeze carrying salty mist toward her, and with it, Seychelle could hear the sound of Savage's voice.

"Why are you particularly concerned this time, Czar? It isn't the first time someone's taken a hit out on me, and it won't be the last."

She stopped immediately. A hit? As in someone wanted to kill him?

"Yeah, I get that. It's not like we didn't know it was going to be dangerous. I don't like taking her on this one, but I don't have a choice. Especially now. You're certain Code has the information right and it's me they're after, not you? They expect to make their try on the run? Yeah, I'll be careful in the meantime."

Savage had been stalking back and forth like a caged panther, coiled whip in one hand, his cell in the other. He looked up, his eyes meeting Seychelle's. "Gotta go, Czar," he said immediately. He sent her a smile. "Good almost-afternoon. I expected you to sleep the day away."

He came right to her and bent his head to kiss her, pulling her to him, one hand spanning her throat, the other fisted in her hair and holding her head absolutely still for him. His kisses were never fast little pecks. He took his time. All heat. All fire. Taking her over.

The minute his mouth was on hers, the world dropped away and there was only Savage. She slid her palms up his chest, her body feeling as though it went boneless, melting into his. Electrical sparks leapt over her skin, and hot blood rushed through her veins to pound low and sinful in her body.

When he lifted his head, his blue eyes searched hers. "You good, Seychelle?" His hand slid down her back, over the curve of her bottom.

"I feel fine, Savage." She tipped her face up so she could press her mouth to his neck. Already she could feel anxiety setting in. She knew he was going to act as if nothing had happened—as if she hadn't overheard that small snippet of conversation between him and the president of his club. He was going to force her to bring it up.

He stepped away from her and half turned, indicating the

mannequins. "I've been practicing. Do you want to see what I've been doing? Very intricate work."

He was definitely deflecting. He caught her hand, taking her with him, taking her right down to the waiting rows of male and female bodies posing for him in all kinds of directions. The one facing the verandah was female and fully developed. The thin paper covering the material over her body was only broken in thin lines along the bottom, right over her mound.

Seychelle felt her own instant reaction to that sight and what it meant. Heat rushed. Blood pounded. Her panties were damp. She knew Savage would see and hear the difference in her breathing. He was trained for that. Looked for it. His name was there. He had patiently, one line at a time, carved *Savage's* into the paper. Little marks with the whip formed the *S*.

She swallowed hard and went closer to examine the mannequin. Beneath the paper, the letters had sliced into the material beneath it. Deliberately. They would cut into the skin, not raising welts, but leaving lacerations that would leave permanent marks. Her heart pounded. So did her clit. She was so far gone that even the thought of this permanence appealed to her when it should have repelled her.

She wrapped her arms around her middle as if that could protect her from herself—and from him. She stepped back. "That takes incredible control."

His eyes were so compelling, so intense, she actually felt a fluttering in her sex, as if he could make her orgasm by simply staring at her.

"It does, but the end results are worth the hundreds of hours of practice."

"It looks like it would really hurt."

"Intense pain. Each tiny part of the letters is separate. You would have to hold very still and you would have to be very committed before we ever did this. Fortunately, it is long down the line, and I have plenty of time to be ready if you ever decide you want to go that far."

She couldn't help but step close again and examine the

mannequin one more time. The work seemed an impossibility, yet Savage had done it, clearly over and over. She ran the pads of her fingers over the lettering, feeling the way her body tuned itself to every stroke.

"Why is someone trying to kill you, Savage?"

She kept her gaze on the whip marks, not looking over her shoulder to see his face. It wouldn't tell her anything anyway. His silence was much more telling. That and the way he stepped back when he'd been crowding her before. She'd felt his heat against her back. His breath on her neck. Now there was the cool ocean air . . . and emptiness in the pit of her stomach.

"Don't worry about that, Seychelle. No one is going to kill me."

His voice was matter-of-fact. Dismissive. Definitely a warning to drop the subject. She did turn then and look at him, trying to keep the hurt from her face and voice. What was the use? She knew he was trying, doing the best he knew how. She was as well. It was just that neither knew what they were doing.

"I am worried about it, Savage. If I hadn't overheard the phone call, you wouldn't have told me, would you?"

"No."

His lack of remorse made her feel as if all hope was really gone, but she still tried. She loved Savage with every breath she took, and he was worth fighting for. "We agreed to talk about everything. Communication, you said."

"Not about club business."

There it was again. His club. It all came back to his club. No matter how much she tried to be okay with Torpedo Ink, she wasn't. The idea that he would share what she considered their personal business with the club and not with her was heartbreaking. How were they supposed to build a relationship together? It was impossible. They would have sex and little else.

"What you're saying is, if someone wants to kill me, I don't have to tell you."

Savage sighed. "Don't be a smart-ass, Seychelle. You tell me. I take care of it."

She turned and walked back up to the verandah, where her coffee was. She needed coffee. She needed something. She wasn't going to cry with disappointment when she'd already known Savage would choose his club every time. She had held out hope, certainly over something this big, that he would share with her. The idea that he could act so dismissive was probably the worst of it, as if she were a small child and he needed to be patient with her.

She reached down and picked up the mug of coffee, wrapping her fingers around the ceramic. "Having someone threaten the man who is *supposed* to be my partner isn't club business, Savage. It's *my* business. *Our* business."

They stared at each other for what seemed to Seychelle an eternity. Savage's expression was closed off to her. Completely. She forced air through her lungs. They were new, she reminded herself. They were finding their way. He'd only had her a few months. He'd been with the others since he'd been a toddler. It was only natural that he turned to them first. It would take time for him to let her in. She had to be patient.

"Babe."

She waited. That was it. His one-word answer, as if invoking that pet name for her said it all. "Savage, you said you were going to try. How is that trying? I just heard that someone put out a hit on you. I think that's something any couple would discuss."

"You think wrong. We're not discussing it. I told you from the beginning, when it's club business, you stay out of it, Seychelle." His voice had turned hard. Implacable.

She took a sip of coffee in order to stay calm. It wouldn't do any good to get angry or to show him how hurt she was. "Savage, you don't get to claim club business just because you don't want to discuss something with me. Someone wanting to murder you is something you share with me, not Czar."

His eyes went flat and ice-cold, his expression hard and unyielding. "You don't get to say what's club business, Seychelle. You know that."

What was the use? If he couldn't see that something this important needed to be discussed between the two of them, they weren't ever going to have anything more than a superficial relationship, and she needed to come to terms with what that would mean for her future with him.

"Fine, Savage. You don't get to say what relationship business is. We're just going to have to disagree on this very important subject. That will bring us to a standstill, won't it?"

"What the fuck does that mean?"

She waved her hand at him. "I suggest you call your all-knowing head of the club and ask him, since he seems to know everything." She really was beginning to dislike the president of his club, even knowing that wasn't fair to the man. "I'm running late. I'm supposed to meet Doris Fendris and some others she wants to introduce me to at high tea, but why I'm sharing that information with you, I have no idea."

"You're not running off in a snit." He made it a decree. "If you're going somewhere, you can wait for Hyde or Glitch to get here."

"I'm not your child. And I'm not in your club either, Savage. Since all of those members will be privileged to know why and who wants you dead, but I won't, I don't particularly want to be around them right now. I feel out of place."

"This is fucking bullshit, Seychelle." He sounded as frustrated as she was.

"*Exactly*, Savage. I'm glad you see it my way." She turned, taking three steps toward the sliding glass door.

The sharp crack was her only warning, and fire wrapped around her waist, effectively stopping her. The heat spread through her body, up toward her breasts and down toward her sex, rushing through her as if a volcano had erupted. Her heart pounded as she felt Savage at her back, pressed tight against her. His breath was hot against her ear as his palm curled around her throat, his thumb tipping her head back so it fell against his shoulder.

"You're not walking out the door pissed at me, Seychelle. And you don't leave without someone with you."

"I'm not angry, Savage. There's no point in being angry. We're going over and over the same thing, and it isn't ever going to be resolved. I get that. It just makes me sad, not angry."

Savage was silent for a moment, and then he skimmed his lips over her ear and down the side of her jaw. "It isn't a big deal, baby. You're making too big a thing over nothing."

She turned her head to look at him, head on his shoulder. "I'm supposed to be your partner. If someone threatens to kill you, I think it's pretty important for me to know about it, but you don't seem to think the same way. I don't care about your stupid club business, Savage. Have your secrets. I'll stay here or at my house every stinking time you want to go to your little boys' club. But this is something else altogether."

His expression shut down. Eyes those twin points of ice. He might not realize he went that way, put his mask on, but he wore it. He was impossible. He wasn't going to listen, no matter what she said. Someone was trying to kill him, and he wasn't even going to talk to her about it, only with his club members. Yeah, that made a lot of sense.

"Don't you fuckin' cry."

She hadn't realized she was, because she knew tears were useless. "I'm not crying. Let go of me."

"You are crying. You think I don't know when you're crying?"

His lips moved from her ear to her cheek, soft, sipping at her tears in that way that stole her heart, even as she wanted to shove him away from her. He had her body tipped back so she was nearly off balance and couldn't move.

"All right, baby, stop. Don't cry anymore."

"You don't understand, Savage. You said we'd find ways

to compromise, but you don't think in terms of compromising. It's going to be your way."

"I told you that. From the very beginning, I was honest with you that some things had to be my way."

"Not this. This is an emotional need, Savage. *My* emotional need. There's a big difference. You promised to see to my emotional needs, remember? Isn't that part of our relationship? Our agreement. We talked right from the beginning, and you said you would make me happy. There is no way for me to be happy if you insist on ignoring my emotional needs."

His thumb rubbed back and forth along her cheek in a soothing caress. She wasn't certain who he was trying to soothe, her . . . or him. There was nothing to say. There wasn't going to be a marriage though. She might live with him, but she wouldn't let him put a ring on her finger.

"We'll figure it out." His hands went to her waist, and he helped her straighten slowly even as he slid the whip from around her. "We'll work it out."

She took a step away from him. "That's what you said a few days ago, when this kind of thing came up. We didn't work it out though, did we? We had sex, and the sex was great, but we didn't talk about what was wrong. We didn't resolve it."

"Seychelle. I can't talk about club business, no matter how much I might want to."

"But then, you don't really want to, do you, Savage?" she challenged.

"Damn it, Seychelle, why are you making this so fucking difficult?"

"You're right, Savage. I am being difficult. I shouldn't want you to care how I feel, and I sure shouldn't care that someone wants you dead."

"That's a bullshit thing to say."

"It seems that everything I say is bullshit. I'm not certain what you want me to say. I don't want to fight. Keep your secrets, Savage. Tell them to your brothers and sisters and leave me out. I'm getting used to it. I really am. I don't know if that's a good thing or a bad thing."

"Damn it, baby. We'll find our way. Just give us some time."

She didn't look at him, just shrugged her shoulders and took another step toward the house and escape, because they weren't going to really work it out. They'd have sex, and it would be great sex. It always was. It wouldn't solve their problems though. She would feel alone more and more. She would want to discuss her business with him less and less, and there would be more resentment toward his club and the members, even though the problems she had with Savage weren't their fault.

She glanced down at her beautiful engagement ring. The last thing they needed to do was get married. Living together was one thing, but she refused to take a vow that wouldn't mean anything in the long run.

"Seychelle. I can read you like a fuckin' book."

"You're always so sure of yourself, Savage."

"Because you don't know how to guard your expression. You just looked down at your engagement ring and I never saw anyone look so fucking sad. We are going to get married."

"I'm rethinking, just like you had to rethink things. Nothing is going to change for you, other than you'll have everything you want. I need a full partner, Savage. I thought we'd have that. I have to rethink whether or not I can manage to be in a relationship or how far I can honestly go into this without getting all my emotional needs met. Eventually, how that will affect us, I don't know, because I know it will affect me."

"Damn it, Seychelle, it isn't going to affect us, because we're working it out. This is the first bump. We don't run from it. That's what we don't do. We figure it out."

"Because that's so easy when you just have to decree it's club business and that's the end of the discussion. I say it's not. I call complete bullshit." She forced herself to shrug. "It doesn't really matter what I say or think. In the end, you'll do whatever you want to do. I need to go before I'm late. Just like your club business is important to you, my time with the older people in Sea Haven is important to me. If one of your prospects is supposed to be following me around, they'd better get here fast, because I've got to go now."

"You're still fuckin' crying, Seychelle. I told you to stop." Savage pulled her into his arms and held her tight against him. "We'll get this figured out. I can tell you I've got enemies. Lots of them. I told you that going into this, baby. You knew that. Now stop crying."

"Why do you have so many enemies?"

"I told you, I'm not a nice man. Now go wash your face. I'll text Lana and have her take you in. She was heading into Sea Haven anyway."

"I need my own car. I have some other errands today."

"If she can't take you to do your errands, I'll get there. Just text me and let me know when you're ready to go."

She had no idea what he did, and she didn't ask him. She already knew he worked for the club and he wouldn't tell her a thing. She was tired of him not telling her anything.

Seychelle decided not to argue the point about needing her own car. Once she was in Sea Haven, she could walk wherever she wanted to go. She had never minded before, not even if she had done heavy shopping.

He was so certain she'd just fall into line with whatever he decreed. She turned away from him and hurried inside, avoiding the fact that he clearly had wanted to kiss her. She would have kissed him back—fallen into the trap he always set, just the way she always did. She had to get used to this. This was going to be her way of life if she stayed with him. And what was the alternative? Living without him? This was the same exact dilemma she found herself in over and over.

Seychelle went straight to the master bathroom and stared at her swollen, red eyes. Savage was right. She'd been crying, and she wasn't the pretty kind of crier so many movie stars portrayed. After splashing cold water on her face and trying cover-up, she did her best to master her wayward hair.

The entire time she was aware of the crack of the whip. The way it whistled through the air right before that sound as it struck the intended target. She stood at the long bank of windows in their master bedroom to watch him. He wielded the whip like an artist. It wasn't long before she realized he wasn't creating art with those vicious cuts. At first, it frightened her to see the precise way he could cut into bodies, thinking they might be a substitute for her. After a few minutes, she became aware it was just the opposite. He didn't know how to resolve the situation, and he was working it out in his mind. Savage was genuinely worried he was going to lose her. The sad thing was—it was a real possibility. The lashes weren't for her—they were for him. Tears burned behind her eyes all over again because, like him, she was really worried for the two of them.

"What's he upset about?" Lana asked, her gaze fixed on Savage as he struck with the whip, turned in a circle and struck a second time, hardly having time to coil the whip in between.

Seychelle whirled around. She hadn't even heard her come in. "We had a fight. Though you couldn't actually call it a fight because it takes two people to do that, and Savage dictates. This is one of many that doesn't look like it's going to get resolved. He said things. I said things. Not good things." She pressed her lips together and turned to look back at Savage.

"Seychelle," Lana said softly. "This isn't good. I can see, just looking at him, this is serious. Can you talk about it? Maybe I can help."

Seychelle shrugged. "Apparently, it's club business, not between us, so I'm certain you're going to hear, as are all of the other club members, just not me. I overheard him talking to Czar and someone wants to kill him. He won't discuss that with his partner. Me. Although if it was the other way around, he would expect me to immediately confess any threats to him. I don't agree. Some things aren't just the club's business, Lana. They are between partners as well. I shouldn't be locked out of the important things in his life. Someone wanting to kill him is important. If he can't see that, I don't see how we're ever going to last. It won't matter how much I love him; in the end, I'll feel so far apart from him there will be no going back." She shrugged. "He can't see that I have certain emotional needs and if he refuses to meet them, no matter how much I love him, I won't be able to stay."

"Savage isn't going to be able to handle life without you very well. Give him time. This is the first time he's ever fallen in love. We all know it's very real and it's going to be the only time for him. Let him think it over. He'll figure it out." But she sounded worried. "Come on, honey, you don't want to keep the ladies waiting."

Seychelle knew Savage wasn't going to change his mind. She felt utterly sad and defeated as she followed Lana outside to a very sporty Porsche.

"How is Tessa doing?" she asked. Lana had taken in an eighteen-year-old girl they'd rescued from a man named Brandon Campbell.

"She's coming along nicely. We're taking it slow, working on her self-esteem. I take her to Blythe's so she can hang with Darby and Blythe when I'm gone and I can't be with her. Sometimes I have her go to Crow 287 to help Alena out. She's really interested in fashion design, so she works with me at the shop when I'm there. She's good too, Seychelle. I think, eventually, we can put her through school. In the meantime, she can intern with me. The most important thing is to keep working on her self-worth. She has to believe in herself. She went from a mother who abandoned her, to a drunken father who molested her, to Campbell, who all but mesmerized her with his voice into thinking she was worthless." Lana had gotten more and more indignant on Tessa's behalf.

"I'm so glad she has you. And your house is safe? Brandon can't get to her there?"

"No. You'll have to come by sometime. It's really quite lovely and very secure. Most nights Alena stays as well. Tessa is very safe."

"Good. Thanks for taking her in, Lana." Seychelle unbuckled her seat belt as Lana pulled the Porsche into a parking slot just in front of the Floating Hat. The tea shop was one of Seychelle's favorite places in Sea Haven. "I appreciate the ride."

"Anytime. I'll see you later." Lana waved as she drove away.

Seychelle stood on the sidewalk staring after the Porsche, debating whether or not she wanted to go right into the Floating Hat and face the ladies inside. Sometimes just walking helped, but she knew they were waiting for her, and she hated letting Doris down.

Doris Fendris was bringing a woman by the name of Phillis Gimble with her to introduce her into their circle of friends. Phillis and Benjamin Gimble had been attacked when a band of robbers had come to Sea Haven targeting the elderly. Phillis still had trouble leaving her home. Anat Gamal, Player's mother-in-law and the adopted grandmother of Torpedo Ink, had also been attacked. She had insisted Phillis come to tea with Doris to meet Seychelle. Both women were doing their best to help Phillis overcome her fears.

The other woman being introduced into their circle was the "snobby" one who had recently moved there from Los Angeles, who the group had discussed at an earlier time. Rebecca Jetspun had run into the woman, Ava Chutney, and she seemed lonely and sad. Rebecca felt sorry for her and, before she knew it, had invited her to high tea. She had texted everyone that she was very apprehensive afterward but was determined to try with Ava.

With a little sigh, Seychelle pushed the door open. At once the string of little hats began to create a merry song, lifting her spirits almost before she even stepped into the store. The fragrance hit her next, enveloping her in the sub-

tle scent of lavender with just the faintest essence of berga-
mot and perhaps a delicate hint of lemongrass. Seychelle
couldn't be certain what the combination was because it
was so faint. She just knew that the moment she entered the
store, her spirits lifted and her anxiety lessened.

Her ladies had taken the largest table. Phillis Gimble sat
between Anat and Doris looking a little strained but still
happy to be there. Eden and Rebecca had Ava seated between
them. As usual, Nina, Eden's sister, was nowhere in sight.
Doris waved wildly to her, and she hurried to their table.

"Everyone got here before me. Am I that late?" She didn't
look at her watch. She took the remaining chair, at the head
of the table, out in the aisle a bit.

"Only by a couple of minutes," Doris said. "We know
what you like, so we just ordered for you."

"Technically, Sabelia knew exactly what Seychelle orders," Eden corrected. "Which means you come in here way
too much."

"You can never come here too much," Seychelle corrected. "Wait, Nina's not here yet. I'm not the last one."

"Nina couldn't make it," Eden said. "She said to tell
everyone she was sorry, but she'd make it up next time.
Something to do with one of her customers."

"I feel bad that she always misses out on the fun," Seychelle said. She turned to the newcomers. "I'm Seychelle
Dubois, by the way."

"I'm sorry," Rebecca apologized instantly. "This is a new
friend of mine, Ava Chutney. We met recently, and I thought
she might like the Floating Hat and to meet all of you. Ava,
this is our dear friend Seychelle. None of us can live without
her. She comes to our homes, sees to just about everything
and makes certain we're all right when we're not. I can't say
enough about her."

"Don't listen to her, Mrs. Chutney," Seychelle said. "The
next thing she'll tell you is I walk on water." She never made
the mistake of addressing one of the older men or women in
a familiar way until invited to.

"Please call me Ava," Rebecca's guest said. "I've heard amazing things about you, but not that—yet."

Seychelle laughed. She couldn't help it. These women had a way of lifting her spirits just the way the shop itself did.

"This is my guest, Phillis Gimble," Anat announced. "A dear friend. Phillis, this is Seychelle, the young woman I've told you so much about."

"Again, Mrs. Gimble, if you know Anat, she's always too kind in her assessments of people. Look how she is with Savage and Destroyer. She adores them both. Have you met them?"

Phillis shook her head. "Please call me Phillis. I've certainly heard Anat sing their praises. She's such a flirt though. They must be handsome."

Anat trilled in the way she had that let them all know she was reprimanding Phillis yet still made them laugh.

"It's true, you are a flirt," Seychelle pointed out. "She's crazy about both of them. And yes, I'd say they are incredibly handsome in a rough sort of way."

"Someone is named Savage? And Destroyer?" Ava asked.

"Seychelle is engaged to Savage," Doris was quick to point out.

"You're engaged to someone named Savage?" Ava asked again.

Doris grabbed Seychelle's wrist and held up her hand to show off her ring. Ava gasped. "Oh my God, that's an Ice original. I can spot one a mile away. And that stone is exquisite. A fancy teal-blue diamond. There aren't very many . . ." She trailed off, staring at Seychelle. "I know diamonds, and that's real." She almost whispered it. "You're really engaged to a Savage?"

"On and off. When I'm not wanting to hit him over the head. But I keep the ring on."

"How would he ever get his hands on an Ice original? It's almost impossible. I've never heard of anyone able to have a wedding ring designed by him."

Instinctively, she protected Ice. "You'd have to ask Savage. He surprised me with the ring. Before that I just called him my fake fiancé."

"I can tell you, you're one lucky woman," Ava said.

Seychelle held up the ring. It was beyond beautiful, but she would have traded it for a real relationship, one where her man wanted a partnership. She swallowed back the sudden lump in her throat threatening to choke her and forced a smile. "I am."

Anat watched her with knowing eyes, and Seychelle was very happy Sabelia arrived with the two towers of pastries and sandwiches. She left and returned with the various teapots, each containing a different variety of tea.

"How did you get to be such an expert on diamonds?" Rebecca asked.

Ava poured tea from a pink teapot into her delicate floral teacup. "I took a class on a cruise because I was bored out of mind. My husband gambled quite a bit when we were a young couple, and I was on my own. I thought the class might be interesting. I didn't really know anything about gems or stones—why one would be worth so much more than another. I found the subject fascinating. Not just diamonds, but various gems and their origins. How they came to be, how they are mined, some, by the way, quite horribly, and we shouldn't have anything to do with those diamonds."

Seychelle was gratified to hear Ava say some diamonds were mined in a bad way and shouldn't be bought. She didn't know why it surprised her that Ava would know and care about the origins of those diamonds, but it did. She was a little ashamed that she'd judged the woman just by that first conversation the ladies had had over her man desperately trying to purchase a scarf from Rebecca because Ava wanted it and he thought he'd be in trouble if he came back without it. That conversation had also taken place at a tea in the Floating Hat.

"I never considered that the study of gems would be a fascinating subject, but you make it sound as though it might actually be," Phillis said.

The others nodded as they took little sandwiches off the multilayered trays and selected their teas from the choices they had.

"I polished stones for a while," Eden volunteered. "I thought they were beautiful. I liked to learn about them and how they were formed. In doing so, I learned quite a bit about crystals, but not actual gems. I always told myself I would, but I never got that far. I went back to work after I lost Reggie, my husband, to take care of the children. I heard you worked in the film industry, Ava."

"I did work in television for a while. On the publicity end. I really enjoyed the work, and I was good at it," Ava said. "But then Logan was already making a name for himself, and he thought it would be better for me to be working in film with him. It wasn't quite as much fun, but I did okay there as well. I never really liked it the way I did my first job. After a while, I quit. We didn't need the money, and I wanted to have a baby. I thought I couldn't conceive because I was working too many hours."

She fell silent while she drank her tea and ate a small macaroon. "Turns out, without consulting me, Logan had decided to have a vasectomy. That way he could have as many affairs as he wanted without worrying about unwanted pregnancies."

There was silence again at the table while the women looked at one another. Rebecca reached over and patted her hand. "I'm so glad you decided to come with me today and meet all my friends. We have such a good time together. Last week we were discussing taking classes right here at the Floating Hat on casting this strange little spell that involved toads filling up a car or truck."

Ava laughed. "That's impossible."

Rebecca nodded. "I thought so too, but when Hannah, the owner, was young and her boyfriend ditched her for another girl, his bedroom was suddenly full of toads. Now, whether she actually had anything to do with it or not, no one really knows, but—and he's her husband now—he came in the other day and his truck was full of toads. They'd had a disagreement. I'm not condoning such things, or saying that she had anything to do with it, just that they might be fun to learn."

Anat did her little trilling sound, this time in approval. She looked around. "Just making certain my daughter isn't in here. When is this class being held? Phillis, dear, we must take this class. If Hannah and Sabelia are teaching it, no doubt it will be fun, and there can't be anything wrong with it. Hannah isn't into the dark arts."

"I'm in for certain," Phillis said, "if the rest of you are."

Seychelle laughed. "I'd better start talking to Sabelia and get her to agree. We were just joking around when we first came up with the idea."

The little chain of hats over the door sang out merrily. A frisson of pure heat raced down Seychelle's spine, and every nerve ending came to life. Seychelle turned her head. Even before she looked, she knew Savage had entered. He looked larger than life, striding purposefully toward her. Savage looked the consummate biker—jeans that fit like a glove, tight tee, motorcycle boots, his jacket with his colors, tattoos and his shaved head. He looked dangerous. Menacing. He wore no expression, and his blue eyes were ice-cold.

He walked right up to the table and reached for her hand. Her left hand. He tugged until she stood, pulling her tight against him. His thumb slid over her ring. "Ladies, I'm sorry I have to cut my woman's visit with you short, but we have an important appointment I forgot to tell her about. To make up for stealing her from you, I called ahead and told Sabelia your tea was on me. I'll be more careful next time of our scheduling."

He leaned over, brushed Anat's cheek with a kiss and then Doris's before he turned and walked out, taking Seychelle with him. She went without protest until they were outside, and he took her straight to his Harley and handed her a helmet.

"What are you doing, Savage?"

"I told you I was going to figure out a way to fix this, baby. We're going to get help. I don't know what the hell I'm doing, and I'm not losing you. We're going to the nearest thing we have to a counselor."

Shocked, Seychelle put on the helmet. That was the very last thing she'd expected Savage to say.

FOUR

Czar and Blythe lived in a two-story house that sprawled out huge. Very thick walls, Mediterranean tile, banks of inviting windows facing the forest both upstairs and down. Lots of gables and balconies. There was *space*. Lots of it, inside and out. The house looked inviting and gave the impression that it was a home. The house was built in the shape of a U with a courtyard inside because, according to Czar, Blythe had always wanted one. She'd had the house built that way before he'd ever come home.

Seychelle stood by the Harley, her helmet in her hand, staring up at the house without moving. "What are we doing here, Savage? Don't they have like a million kids?"

He took the helmet out of her hand and hooked it on his bike. "I texted Czar and asked for a quiet meeting. That's code for no children. Told him I'd be bringing you and would like Blythe here if possible. In their world, it's difficult, but he got back to me right away and said to come. They have Darby, already eighteen, and Kenny, about to turn eighteen, Zoe, Emily and Jimmy."

"I see." She still stood reluctantly looking up at him, clearly nervous.

"Haven't had a chance to talk about Brandon Campbell, Seychelle. We still need to get that done, because in my opinion, he's a dangerous man. Arnold and the rest of it got in the way, but that's an important conversation and part of the reason I want someone watching out for you," he said.

Nearly a week earlier, Seychelle had been at the Floating Hat with Lana and some of the older women, and Brandon Campbell had come in with an eighteen-year-old girl who was completely under his influence. Seychelle had managed to get the girl away from him by using her voice but also tricking Brandon in front of the older women he wanted to maintain goodwill with. Savage knew Lana had brought Tessa home with her instead of to Blythe to add to her adopted crew. That had been a bit of a surprise, but he was grateful it was one less problem he was going to run into trying to get Blythe and Czar alone.

She sighed. He had the feeling she would have rolled her eyes if she thought she could get away with it.

He threaded his fingers through Seychelle's as they stood beside his Harley. Just looking down at her face, those blue eyes surrounded by that sweep of long lashes and her faint smile as she looked up at him, sent heat rushing through his veins. He ran his thumb over her lips, brushed down and over her chin a little possessively. "Proud of you for taking on that vindictive little shit Campbell again, Seychelle. I am. But you gotta know he's going to come after you. You've set yourself up as a target."

"Is that why I'm in trouble?" She was stalling. Looking at the house. Not wanting to go in. Willing to pick a fight instead of facing his club president.

He caught her stubborn little chin as it began to tilt. He was in love with that chin. He bent down to kiss it, thought better of it because then she'd know he was totally gone on her. He bit her instead, catching all that stubbornness between his teeth and taking a bite out of it. She yelped, tried to pull back, couldn't and glared at him.

"You're so oral."

"You say that as if it's a bad thing when we both know you love it."

Her long lashes fluttered, but she didn't admit it. "You didn't answer the question. Are you upset over the Brandon thing? Because he's a wimp. And I had to take the opportunity when it presented itself. Who knew when it would come around again? I've dealt with him before. Remember? He asked me out before I ever met you, and I knew he was a creeper. He likes to use his voice to influence women. You even helped me get Sahara away from him."

She referred to another young woman Campbell had under his control before Seychelle discovered her and managed, with the help of the club and her incredible, persuasive voice, to get her back to the safety of the woman's parents. He clenched his teeth. That should have told her something about Campbell right there.

She didn't get it, because as much as she could read people, she relied too heavily on that gift of her voice and her own innate goodness. She couldn't conceive of people like Campbell—or him. She saw the evil in Brandon, but she thought in terms of him using his voice on women to take away their self-esteem. She didn't think he might do anything else to get back at her. She saw Joseph Arnold as a nuisance, a man to avoid, but she didn't think his disgusting behavior would escalate. And Savage, her lover, the man she looked at with close to adoration in her eyes at times, she saw danger in him, but she steadfastly refused to see the killer he hid from her, but if she looked closer, she would discover him.

"Didn't say you were in trouble, babe, but it was too dangerous, and you know it was. You knew it before you ever started a war with Campbell. You're a good judge of character, so right from the moment you met him, you knew he was the kind of man who gets his kicks from tearing women down." His thumb brushed back and forth over her soft skin in a deliberate, mesmerizing caress.

Twice she started to refute his statement and then stopped

herself. Finally, she sighed, but she didn't pull away from him. "That's the point, Savage: he uses his voice. His voice can't compete with mine."

"Baby, look at me. You keep looking anywhere but at me." He gave her the command very gently, but it was a command, nothing less.

Seychelle was her own person. She proved that to him every moment she was with him. Everything she did was her choice. That was what made her so special to him, that was why her gift, her sacrifices for him, were so special. He knew everything she gave to him was her choice. She could resist him any time she wanted to. She was susceptible to his voice, but she still made her own choices.

Seychelle's blue eyes met his, and his heart did that funny lurch in his chest it nearly always did when she looked at him. At least she kept the damn ring on her finger. He knew if he put it there in front of those women, she wouldn't take it off. She would never embarrass him. Now, he just didn't want to call attention to it until he was safe.

"I'm going to say this one more time, and I want you to hear me and trust me on this. I know men. I know that kind of man. Brandon Campbell is a weasel. When I say that, it comes from a place of knowing his kind. You took two women from him before he was through with them. I think his endgame was to get them to commit suicide. I think he's that big of a sick fuck."

He framed her face with both hands and bent his head down to hers, maintaining eye contact. He needed her to really hear him. "He wants that ultimate power. He knows you stripped him of it, and he's going to come after you. He knows his voice won't work on you, so he'll come at you some other way, and it won't be out in the open because he's the kind of man who doesn't have the guts to confront you like that. I swear, I'm not trying to control you. I know it looks like that, but I wanted you to have fun with your friends. I know you like going to the Floating Hat. I'd rather have my fingernails pulled out one by one than go there.

Lana was concerned when she saw him with that young girl and knew what you were doing that day. She saw into Campbell's character the same as me."

He brushed kisses across her soft lips when she frowned. He didn't want her blaming Lana for telling him. Already, she could be blaming the club members for the monster building like a dangerous predator in him. She knew, ultimately, it would be her who would pay the price. He didn't want her to hate them for it. They were his family. He wanted her to think of them as her family as well.

"Lana was looking out for you. She wanted you to get Tessa from him. She was so proud of you. I am too, Seychelle. Don't ever think I'm not, but I'm afraid for you. You take too many fuckin' chances with your life."

She stood looking up at him, those eyes of hers so loving but so sad, it shook him. The very reason she was the right partner for him, her strength and indomitable will, her courage, was the reason he could lose her. She wasn't going to roll over for him because she loved him. He'd made promises to her. If he couldn't keep them, she wasn't going to keep her side of the bargain either. He would lose her.

"I know we said we'd keep everything we did sexually between us, and I tried to change those rules on us for this upcoming run. That was wrong of me. We'll stick to what we agreed. As far as the other, if you're not happy, Seychelle, you're right, this isn't going to work, because I won't be happy unless you are. I told you I was all in with you, and I am. We're going to figure this out, and that's why we're here. Czar's the president of Torpedo Ink. I've got to tell him straight, that when you ask me something, and you're upset about it, I've got to be able to talk it over with you. If he gives me an ultimatum, I'm not certain where we're going from there, but wherever it is, we're going together."

Seychelle's eyes widened in shock. She shook her head. "Don't even think that way, Savage. You are Torpedo Ink. That's who you are."

"It won't come to that." He hoped he was right. He believed in Czar. He had to. Czar had said to come to him if there was a problem, and this was a pretty big fucking problem.

He took her hand and began walking to the house, his steps slow and measured. "I'm not willing to lose you, Seychelle. You mean too damn much to me."

"I'm beginning to see that." Her voice was low, but she took her other palm and rubbed his rib cage. He could feel her hand tremble. "We'll talk about the other at home. The public thing, on the upcoming run. Nothing is ever set in stone, Savage, other than our promise to make one another happy and put each other first. I think we're both trying to do that. And I do hear you about Brandon. I'll stay away from him."

Savage brought her hand to his mouth and kissed her ring finger as they went up the stairs to the heavy front door. He'd been in the house hundreds of times. The club often had breakfasts, barbecues or shared dinners with Czar's entire family. The club members were always welcome, no matter what time of day it was. They had movie nights with the family. The children on the farm were homeschooled, and all the adults pitched in to teach various classes. Torpedo Ink taught survival skills, often to Blythe's and the other women's dismay.

Savage had never been nervous going to see his club president, but there was some trepidation walking up to that door this time. He could receive orders to take out enemies, and he would do so without flinching. It didn't matter how dicey the assignment was. This was the first time, for him, the stakes were so personally high. He knew only one thing for certain: when he walked back out that door, he would be taking his woman with him.

Czar opened the door, his piercing eyes moving over Savage first, then Seychelle and then their joined hands. Czar had always been able to see too much in a man. When they were children, he could look at their enemies and know instantly the worst of them. Which ones they had to protect themselves against before the others. He knew which of the children were weak and would break. He didn't like knowing those things, but he did. He looked into people and he saw inside them.

Savage had never hidden what he was from Czar. Hell, Czar had had a hand in shaping him into being a cold-blooded killer. They had needed someone to crawl through the vents and kill the worst of their torturers before they themselves were killed. The others were lookouts or distractions. Sometimes they were the ones being tortured or raped as a distraction. But it was Reaper or Savage who had been assigned to do most of the actual killing.

It wasn't like the others hadn't done their share of ridding the world of murderers when necessary. They had. It was that Reaper and Savage never hesitated to kill, and Czar was well aware of that. He saw that in them, whereas the trait wasn't always in the others when they were young. They developed it over time, but when they were children, they were still soft inside. Both Reaper and Savage had lost any softness when their sisters were murdered and Sorbacov gave them to his friends for their "special" play.

"Seychelle. Please come in. Blythe is happy that you've come to visit us." Czar stepped back to allow them to enter.

Savage wrapped his arm around his woman and guided her inside into the very spacious living room. Blythe was sitting in one of the many comfortable armchairs. She rose immediately, a welcoming smile on her face. She came to them, both hands extended toward Seychelle, but leaning toward Savage. He obliged by kissing her cheek. Seychelle took her hands.

"I'm so glad you both came. Savage, I have your favorite coffee made fresh. And Seychelle, I hoped you were a tea drinker. I made a fresh pot, but if you prefer coffee, I can get you a cup of that."

"Tea would be lovely," Seychelle said. "I take mine with milk but no sugar."

They followed Blythe over to the chairs. A small table was set with a tray holding coffee, tea and fresh-baked pastries. There was also a vegetable tray with dip. Savage was happy to see that. He immediately took one of the small bowls and scooped up plenty of the vegetables and added some dip before handing it to Seychelle.

She laughed. "You're always trying to get me to eat."

"Because you never eat."

Seychelle laughed again, her golden notes floating to the ceiling, the sound real this time, relaxing the tight knots in his gut so that the burning in his lungs eased.

"Before we get to the reason you're here," Czar said, "I just want you to know ahead of time, I'm in full-blown crisis mode."

Blythe rolled her eyes. "You're not. You're just being silly. Take a breath and eat a pretzel. They're warm. Fresh out of the oven. They're your favorites."

"They're *Savage's* favorites," Czar corrected, taking one of the fresh pretzels anyway and glaring at his wife. "Don't discount this, Blythe. It's a big deal."

Savage looked to Blythe for an explanation for Czar's out-of-character behavior. Either he was striving to put Seychelle at ease, or he really was upset. With Czar, it was impossible to tell.

"Darby was asked out on a date."

"She gets asked out all the time," Savage said.

"She said yes this time," Czar declared. "She's going out with a perfect stranger. And he already has a *child*. He's a fireman, for fuck's sake. He's too old for her, Blythe. He's looking for one thing."

"If he were her age, you'd say that," Blythe said, calmly drinking her tea. "And you'd be right. I suspect this man is looking more for a mother for his child."

"She doesn't need to be a mother at eighteen," Czar declared. "She's hardly started her life. And she's so protective of the girls and Jimmy. Even Kenny, whether he likes it or not. She needs to have some time for herself so she knows who she is."

"I'm well aware of that, honey," Blythe agreed quietly.

"I'll pay him a visit," Savage volunteered immediately. "Have Code get an address for me." Damned if some man was going to take Darby from her home to play mother to his child. That was some bullshit right there.

"You won't be paying him any visit, Savage," Blythe decreed. "Czar, this man is off-limits. Do both of you understand? He's off-limits."

Czar sighed. "I see no reason why I can't just have a talk with him, Blythe. He's way older than she is. I won't embarrass her."

Blythe rolled her eyes. "Don't be obtuse. You know darn well you've already embarrassed her just by riding with six of the boys past Crow 287 when he was coming out of it. You did it on purpose. Twice. It was no coincidence, like you told her. I'm not that naïve. And he isn't all that much older than she is."

"You did a rollout and I wasn't called?" Savage objected.

"We thought you might be a little busy," Czar said, then grinned sheepishly at his wife. "It wasn't really a rollout. We were just riding together."

"See the kind of thing you're going to have to deal with when you have children, Seychelle? Especially girls." Blythe sipped her tea and chose a pretzel.

Savage was happy to see that Seychelle was relaxed enough to eat a few of the vegetables with the dip. He realized that was another of Czar's gifts. He knew she was extremely nervous—that even Savage wasn't his usual calm self—and he'd deliberately introduced a topic that would make everyone have a lively conversation involving someone else. It also gave him the opportunity to see how Czar and Blythe interacted when they disagreed.

"Darby is a very headstrong, stubborn young woman, Czar. If you push her, or threaten this man in any way, she will turn that protective nature of hers straight to defending him, and she'll rush right into his arms."

Czar flashed her another grin. "I notice you never give me his name."

Savage realized that Czar didn't disagree with Blythe. Czar read people too easily. He would know his daughter's nature inside and out. He knew if he pushed too hard against her dating the fireman, she would rebel. He also knew she expected his resistance. And there was no way Czar would ever allow Darby to date a man without knowing his name.

Blythe burst out laughing. "You know very well his name is Asher Larkin and his two-year-old son is Caleb. He has full custody of the little boy and takes excellent care of him. You even know his shoe size."

Seychelle's laughter joined Blythe's, and Savage saw those golden notes drifting toward the ceiling. He was dazzled by her musical notes and the fact that, after so many years of not being able to see people's musical colors, he could see hers—and once in a while, others'.

"Tell me this Asher at least rides a motorcycle. A Harley. He does ride." Savage made it a statement as he watched the notes mingling with Blythe's notes of reds and pinks.

There was silence. Czar sighed and snagged another pretzel. "Code hasn't done a DMV search yet, and I've seen no sign of one, but he always has the boy with him. He's being safe with his son." That was said grudgingly.

"I thought Lana was going to bring Tessa here today," Blythe said, clearly to change the subject. "She called to ask permission and then suddenly changed her mind. Tessa's come a few times, but I haven't had time to actually visit with her. She disappears into Darby's room."

"Lana had to get some work done in her shop," Czar said. "Tessa was going to help her."

"A while back, Darby had actually talked to us about Tessa. It was months ago. Before Jimmy." Blythe looked down at her hands. "I should have insisted on Darby bringing her here then. At least to meet us. At the time, Tessa was still going to school and living at home with her father."

Czar reached over and put his hand over Blythe's. "I remember the conversation. Darby was extremely worried about her. We told her she could bring Tessa here on a weekend to meet us. Darby said Tessa's father was an alcoholic and there was no mother around. Said her home life was awful and she suspected her father not only beat her but molested her. Tessa never admitted that, and Darby had no proof—it was just a suspicion on her part."

Blythe nodded. "I couldn't sleep a couple of nights and reminded Darby to invite her, but then Code came to us about the little boy being put up for auction online." She looked at Seychelle with tears in her eyes. "His parents were murdered by a man known only as the Collector who sold him to a pedophile who had 'ordered' him from a brochure. He had no other relatives, so eventually everyone stopped looking for him. When Jimmy got 'too old' for the pedophile's taste, he was auctioning him off, bragging that no one would ever come looking because they had forgotten his existence. He was in a cage."

"Oh my God." Seychelle turned to Savage as if to ask him if that could possibly be the truth. He slid his arm around her.

"He's safe now, baby. Czar and Blythe have him. They're adopting him."

Blythe dashed at her tears. "I forgot all about poor Tessa. It took us forever to actually track down Jimmy and get him away from those vile people. But that's no excuse. I just left that poor girl in a terrible situation."

"Blythe. Don't," Czar said. "Tessa isn't your failing or mine. We can't save every child. It's impossible." He put his hand over Blythe's again and waited for her to look up. "We would have taken her in, you know that. We would have welcomed her, but it wasn't in the cards. Sometimes things happen for a reason. Lana might need her as much as she needs Lana right now."

Seychelle nodded. "The only time Tessa appeared to show any interest at all was when she told us that she liked fashion design. Apparently, at one time she thought she was good at it and wanted to get into it. Lana has launched a very successful company and has been looking for an assistant. I think she plans on offering Tessa the job. At least, I think she's working on giving Tessa the self-esteem she would need to attend a school that would help her along in that career if she chooses after working with Lana."

Czar frowned. "Lana does have a big house. So does Alena. The two of them have always house-hopped. Now they're staying at Lana's with Tessa."

"Do you really think they're equipped to help her?" Blythe asked.

Savage could tell she was being very careful. Even so, Czar's penetrating gaze moved over his wife's face.

"I would say, if anyone knows anything about poor self-esteem and having to rebuild their lives, it would be Lana and Alena." There was no reprimand in his tone; in fact, Czar sounded gentle, even loving. He reached over and took Blythe's hand again. "I imagine we will be seeing a lot of that young lady."

"I imagine so," Blythe said. Her smile was intimate. For Czar alone.

Savage realized that it had been the relationship between Czar and Blythe that had started the change in him. Czar had brought the members of Torpedo Ink here, to this place, hoping to give them a chance at a different life. He'd given them Blythe and then the children to show them they could be something other than what Sorbacov had turned them into. Czar had them come to his home and be with his wife and children nearly every day until his family were their family.

Blythe became their symbol of hope. She accepted them unconditionally. She took in the children no one else wanted. She showed them, through her actions, how it was possible to love the unlovable. All along, Czar was slowly showing the members of Torpedo Ink, just by sharing Blythe and his children with them, what it was like to have a family and someone to love them. More, to be part of something bigger—a community.

Just watching Czar and Blythe together, Savage knew

that he'd been so closed off that it was impossible to allow anyone into his life until he'd come to this place that seemed to hold some kind of magic, until he'd seen the real possibilities.

Czar looked at him then, those eyes seeing right into him. "I know you came here for a reason, Savage, and it must be serious, or you wouldn't have asked that the children not be present. That isn't your style. You wanted both of us here. Is that right?"

Savage knew what he meant. Czar knew about his sexual needs. He was there through the entire growth of the monster. Blythe knew nothing about that side of Savage, and he would prefer it that way, just as he would prefer that Seychelle never know what his responsibilities included for the club.

"We had a talk when I first went to you about how I felt about Seychelle. Told you she was special, and I wanted to marry her." Savage lifted her hand and showed both of them the ring. "I intend to make her my wife as soon as possible. She's a little reluctant at the moment to fully commit to me, with good reason." He had to admit it because it was the truth, whether he liked it or not. He was determined to be as honest as possible. "You said if we ran into a problem, we could come to you. We're here. How do you separate club business from partner business?"

There was a small silence. Seychelle sat very still in her chair, completely taken off guard, her eyes on Savage's face. He felt the intensity of her gaze and couldn't help looking at her. She had that look again. The one that always threatened to do him in. The one that made him feel stripped bare. Raw. Naked. Vulnerable.

Seychelle looked at him with such stark, utter love. She didn't try to hide it. It was right out there, plain on her face, in her eyes. Complete adoration. She just gave that to him for no fucking reason. He had the urge to frame her face with his hands, take her mouth and devour her right there in Czar's living room.

"I don't want to know club business," Blythe said. "Unless I can see that it really upsets Czar in some terrible way. I don't ask unless I know I can handle the answer. I love Czar and I trust him completely. Whatever the club feels they have to do, that's their business. They don't run drugs; they don't traffic. I do know they do their best to stop trafficking. That's how we got the girls, Kenny and Jimmy. They put themselves in dangerous situations at times, but again, I trust Czar to get them in and out of those situations, so I don't ask unless I can see he needs to talk something out. Then I refuse to make a judgment. I asked and he answered, so it would be wrong to put a judgment on it, in my opinion. That's how I handle it."

Czar sighed and shook his head. "Seychelle, I presume Savage hasn't explained to you that sometimes what we do can be extremely dangerous to the club members. If you decide that you really want to marry Savage—and seeing the way you look at him, there's no doubt in my mind that you're in love with him, so I believe you do—you have to know what you're getting into."

The knots in Savage's belly tightened. It wasn't like he'd already given Seychelle enough to decide against staying with him. What sane woman would want to be with him? "Czar," he cautioned.

Czar shook his head. "It's only fair to her, especially if you want the kind of relationship that Blythe and I have. I think it's incredibly risky and even foolish, but under the circumstances, I can understand why you're asking."

"I want to hear what he has to say," Seychelle said.

She reached over the arm of the chair and put her palm on Savage's thigh. He didn't know if she was looking for comfort, but he covered her hand with his, because even if she didn't need the comfort, he did.

"Belonging to Savage is belonging to Torpedo Ink, Seychelle. They aren't separate. It isn't just his club, it's his family. It's who he is. It's who we are. All of us. Blythe. The children. What happens to one of us, happens to all of us.

We take care of each other first. It's always family first. What happens in our family stays in it. It's never taken outside of it. Never. You have a problem, you come to me with it. You go to Steele. Or Reaper. You put your trust in us. No matter how bad it is, or how scared you are, you never go outside the family. We watch each other's backs at all times. You need anything, you say so."

Seychelle hadn't taken her gaze from Czar's face, but her palm pressed hard into the muscle of Savage's thigh. "What you're saying to me is that Torpedo Ink sometimes does things that are illegal, and I might not agree with them. I might inadvertently find out about them, and you don't want me to go to the police."

"We take back children from pedophiles, Seychelle. We find them using illegal means, and we track them and then we take them back. We do things law enforcement can't do. These people are trafficking in children, and they have a pyramid, a hierarchy. There is someone or a group of people at the top, running the operation. We're trying to find them. Rescuing a child and getting rid of the one that is raping and beating him or her is satisfying, but it isn't going to stop it from happening over and over. We're working our way to the top slowly. It takes time, and it isn't always nice or easy. We don't ask for names nicely, is what I'm saying."

Seychelle's blue eyes stayed on Czar. Her palm felt hot, a brand burning her name into Savage's thigh. "If you get caught, you'll go to prison."

"Without a doubt."

"And doing this, any of you could get killed."

"We're very good at what we do."

"There are other things. Like the other night, in the bar. With that club. That wasn't about pedophiles."

Savage sat very still, unblinking. Blythe was in the room, calmly drinking tea and eating a pastry, looking serene. She wasn't involved in that kind of club business. She knew about the hunt for children. Sometimes she knew when Torpedo Ink was hired to try to retrieve a woman taken by the notorious Ghosts, who targeted other clubs by kidnapping the wife of a president of the targeted club and demanding compliance or they would torture and kill her. Blythe didn't know when the Diamondbacks asked Torpedo Ink to do them favors as a support club.

"There are other things we do, yes," Czar admitted but went no further. He didn't look away from her, his voice as gentle and as low as always, but there was no doubt his tone carried absolute weight.

"You're telling me I have to accept what you do, and trust that no matter what happens, no matter what I hear or how afraid I am, that if Savage does something I feel is wrong, you will hear me out and treat me fairly in spite of the fact that he has been with you since he was a child and you just met me."

"Yes."

"That's a pretty big leap of faith, Czar."

"I know it is, Seychelle. I know what is happening in your life right now has to feel enormous and frightening. I can only tell you that all of us are here for you. Every single member of Torpedo Ink. If you accept Savage, and that ring on your finger says that you do, then you're taking us on as well. When you take us on, you're swearing with your word of honor, on your life, that you will hold to the laws of the family."

For the first time, Seychelle's long lashes lowered, veiling her expression, and Savage's heart sank. She was too intelligent not to catch the meaning of what Czar was saying to her. He flicked his gaze to Czar.

"Is it club business or partner business if someone takes a contract out on my fiancé? Or on me, for that matter?" Seychelle asked. "Do we discuss that? Or do only the club members discuss it?" There was a distinct challenge in her voice. "Because, as far as I'm concerned, that is a matter between partners and is my business."

Savage tightened his fingers around her hand when she would have pulled it out from under his.

"Blythe gave excellent advice when she said she asks me only when she is prepared to accept whatever I tell her. My advice to you, Savage, is to never use the club as an excuse not to communicate with your partner, no matter how tough the subject. She's your number one priority. Her emotional well-being should be. Naturally, there might be things you want to protect her from, but those should be few and far between. We were talking this morning about Code finding out the chatter online. A contract was supposedly put out on Savage, Blythe."

Blythe gasped. "No. Who?"

Czar shrugged. "We have no idea. Code is working on it. We don't even know if it's real." He turned his attention back to Seychelle. "You're absolutely right. That is your business. It's difficult to define when we've never had partners before what is and what isn't. But Savage has clearly made up his mind that no matter what, you are the most important being in his world, and he wants you happy. In spite of whatever happened before you came here, had I told him he couldn't tell you, he would have walked out with you and told you anyway. I'm telling you that for two reasons. One, to point out how much you mean to him, and second, to point out what a pain in the ass he can be."

Seychelle's smile was thin, but it was there. "Why would anyone take out a contract on Savage specifically? That doesn't make any sense." She was trying, but her voice was shaky and her hand was trembling, pressed so tightly into his thigh.

"Told you already, baby." Savage brought her left hand up to his mouth and kissed her fingers, feeling that ring with his lips. He wanted to take her home and spend time making love to her his way. A long, long time. Worshipping her. Watching her come apart for him. Holding her close to him and reassuring her she would always be safe with him. "I'm not a nice man. You only think I am."

"Everything is happening fast, just as you said, Czar. There doesn't seem to be any way to slow it down." There were tears in her voice. Dripping.

Savage could almost taste those tears on his tongue. He

was asking so much of her. To accept the club and their rules. Their absolute rules. To accept him with his terrible needs that seemed to grow just being with her. With the various things happening within the club, especially to Alena, the monster was gaining ground—slowly, but gaining. They would run out of time. If what the club members all feared happened on or after the run, time would run out and his woman would be the one sacrificing when the real sadist in him came roaring to life.

She was expected to trust him. Trust Czar. Trust the club. If the circumstances were reversed, would he give his trust to them all? Hell no, not in a million years. She was intelligent enough to know what Czar was telling her. There were consequences for breaking club rules. Just like there were consequences for breaking his rules, only the penalties for breaking club rules, depending on what they were, could be permanent. Some women wouldn't get that. His woman would. She did.

Seychelle slowly put down the teacup. Very precisely into the saucer. "Thank you for the tea, Blythe. I really do appreciate the food and the talk. You both gave me a lot to think about." She stood up.

Savage cursed, his blood suddenly running cold. Ice-cold. He kept possession of her hand. "Thanks, Czar. Blythe. I know we interrupted your day."

"Anytime, Savage. The door's always open," Czar said.

"You're welcome to call me as well," Blythe added, to Seychelle.

Seychelle kept her smile, but Savage could see it was an effort. He took her out the door to his bike, very aware that Czar stood in the doorway watching. He knew Czar was right to warn her. Seychelle saw things others didn't. She had caught a glimpse of Shari Albright when he'd gone straight to her after he'd been with the woman, and Seychelle had been devastated. What if he took out an enemy and went straight home to her and she caught a brief sight of that? Worse, what if one of the others was with him? That would be a disaster.

"I'd like to take you back to our house, Seychelle."

He kept his voice very matter-of-fact as he straddled the bike and put her hand on his shoulder, indicating for her to get on behind him. She did so without protesting, wrapping her arms tight around him, as if for comfort, and resting her head against his back. The Harley roared to life, and they were on their way back.

Savage went over everything in his mind. What he could offer her. What he was offering her. It wasn't much on his side. She had every right to be feeling like she wanted out. He didn't exactly get that feeling from her, more like she was sad. He knew he'd blown it. He should have just told her straight up what she wanted to know, but he was afraid of the questions she would ask. His mind shut down, and he refused to think anymore. He wouldn't allow himself to know what was coming when they got to the house.

He dropped his gloved hand to cover hers, pressing her palm tight into him as he maneuvered the curves along Highway 1, wishing it was a longer ride. At least she hadn't demanded he take her back to her cottage in Sea Haven. He didn't believe in God or heaven, but he did believe in the devil and hell. He had the feeling he was going to be consigned right back into that place and his angel was going to be taken from him.

He backed his bike into a parking spot right in front of the house, not going around to the garage. He was afraid he would have to take her back to her house and he didn't want to face going into the garage and trying to talk her out of leaving him. The weight in his chest was tremendous. Her sorrow. His. She stood beside the Harley holding the helmet, just looking around her at the views, at the beauty of their home. He'd chosen a paradise for them. The blue waves crashing on two sides and forest protecting them on the other two sides.

She lifted her gaze to his when she handed him the helmet. There were tears in her eyes, and his heart clenched hard.

"You know this isn't going to work, Savage. It doesn't matter how much we love each other. I have no doubt that you love me just as deeply as I love you. It isn't going to work. Not like this."

He put the helmet carefully on the seat of his bike and stepped close to her. His little angel. He pulled her into his arms and held her tight. "I know. I know it won't work like this. We have to figure out how to make it work, Seychelle. We're both smart, and we're both willing to work on it. We'll do it."

She leaned into him, her face buried on his chest, so he couldn't see her expression. Ordinarily he wouldn't allow her to get away with that, but he didn't want to see whether or not she agreed with him. She *had* to be willing to work things out. She felt so sad to him, as if they'd already lost.

"Let's go inside, baby. Get comfortable. Find a place to talk."

She stepped back and looked up at him, her eyes searching his face. He let her see him stripped naked. Raw. Vulnerable. It wasn't a comfortable position for him, but if he was going to keep her, it was the only thing he could give her that might make her stay long enough to find a way to make it permanent.

Seychelle nodded and allowed him to take her hand. They went through the front door into the living room, and he took her straight to the coziest chairs in front of the stone fireplace. She curled up in one of the chairs facing the floor-to-ceiling window that gave them the sweeping view of the crashing waves.

"How are we going to fix this, Seychelle? Because we have to fix this."

"Do you realize how much you're asking of me, Savage? Did you even hear what Czar was saying to me? What he was implying? He wasn't just saying that you might get killed, he was saying I could as well. It was a threat. A veiled one, but still a threat."

What was he supposed to say to that? Seychelle was

never going to be a threat to them, and she would never be put in that position because Savage would never allow it. "This is my fault. Czar was concerned."

"Clearly. There's so much more to your life than I ever understood, Savage. I just went into this relationship blind. I thought I had my eyes open, but I didn't. I was already so in love and ready to give you anything that I didn't stop to think who you are, what the club is, and I should have. You know me. You know everything about me. The same isn't true about me with you. You asked me to give you my trust, and I did blindly. How is that possible now?"

Savage didn't have an answer for that, because if she knew who he really was, she wouldn't trust him. He didn't like the direction this conversation was going. This was exactly what he'd feared.

"You always say you're not a good man. I've heard you say that dozens of times. You even believe it, Savage."

It was the fucking truth, but he wasn't going to point that out to her, not now, not when he wanted to keep her and he was so close to losing her.

"I want you to tell me about your life. Your childhood. How you got the way you are. And what you've done that has made you not so nice and why people want to kill you. I want to know the real Savage. The man you're very reluctant to show me. That man. Tell me about him. Tell me what you do for the club that can get us both killed."

Savage closed his eyes. There it was. The one thing he'd been dreading all along.

FIVE

Savage couldn't sit still. He was out of his chair and pacing the length of the room, right in front of that wall of glass showing the wild, turbulent waves crashing just in their view. That matched his heart. The pounding of the blood rushing through his veins. Not hot. Cold as ice.

It all really came down to this moment. His life. Survive or die. Czar hadn't been talking to Seychelle. He'd been talking to Savage. If he wanted this woman, if he really wanted to share his life with her, he had to share *all* of him with her. At the same time, Czar warned him not to let her in so far that if she knew too much and she didn't accept him, she wouldn't live through it. Walking that fine line was hell.

From the beginning, Savage had told himself he'd be all in. He'd give Seychelle 100 percent. Devote himself to her happiness, and he'd meant it. He had.

But this . . . Telling her the truth of who he was. The things he'd done. Give her those things and expect her to look at him with love and not revulsion . . . no. Already he had confessed to her that he needed sadistic sexual practices. He had to see her in pain in order to be sexually aroused. That was bad enough to have to admit to, but the rest of it, telling her how he'd become such a monster and then going on to give her even more of his fucked-up life. He'd have to admit to his many kills—so many—and the way he turned off his emotions. She would think he was a psycho. She'd leave him for certain. It was too much to ask anyone to accept.

He had to be careful. He'd already given her part of his past. She knew some of it. He could give her more. Talk about what happened to him. Talk about the assassination work for his government. He just needed to sidestep what he knew she couldn't live with or handle right now. She was too overwhelmed. He'd work up to the worst—if he ever had to tell her.

Seychelle sat patiently while he paced back and forth like a feral animal. He felt like one. He could feel her eyes on him. Watching him. He glanced at her. Those eyes of hers. All blue. Serene. Not judging him. Seychelle never seemed to judge him. That brought him up short. He turned to face her. *He* judged himself. She didn't judge him. He didn't necessarily like the man he was. He didn't even like the things he did. He thought they were necessary. No one stopped monsters. He had to do it because no one else did. That was the ugly truth. He accepted it and he did the job. He didn't have to like it, he just did it. And those monsters needed to know what they did to those children they preyed on. How it felt before they left the world. Didn't they? Scarlet had raised that question in his mind just recently. He always believed they should know.

He looked at Seychelle a long time. Drank her in. That beautiful, angelic face. Those little tiny scars no one else ever saw, but he did. They were his. She'd traded her life for his without hesitation. She'd given herself to him and she was more than willing to do so again, to walk through the fires of hell with him, live in hell, but he had to strip himself bare and let her see the real monster in order for her to agree.

"You're shaking your head, Savage." Her voice was gentle.

"Once I put this shit in your head, baby, there's no getting it out." He didn't mean to, but he whispered the truth to her. He found himself on his knees in front of her, his arms around her thighs. "I tell you what you want to know, even a little bit, it never goes away. I don't want that for you."

Her blue eyes were steady, moving over his face with such love it made his heart ache. Her hand cupped the side of his face, her thumb sliding along his jaw just once, sending little darts of fire through him. Savage laid his head in her lap, finding her left leg with his hand. He needed the solace of the scars he could feel beneath the soft material. She'd sacrificed her perfect skin for him. Given him that. Maybe she could give him more. Maybe.

"You're sure you want this, Seychelle? It could rip us apart. You knowing these things about me. They aren't pretty. None of it's pretty."

"This is what can be the glue that holds us together for all time, Savage. You have to believe that. I have to know you inside and out. What and who you really are."

"What if you despise that man? What then, baby?" He couldn't look at her. Losing her was too close.

"What if I love you more than ever, Savage? What if you love me more than ever? What if our bond is so strong, so unbreakable, no one can ever tear us apart?"

She had an answer for everything, but then she was an angel and she'd never visited hell before. She was about to begin her descent.

"I talked a little bit about this to you earlier, baby." He didn't hide his reluctance to expand his explanation. "Sorbacov took us from our parents when we were just kids. I was a toddler. Two, three, I don't know. My two older sisters and Reaper. They murdered my parents right in front of us. Sorbacov stood there with this half smile on his face and his gold pocket watch in his palm while his soldiers killed my mother and father and took us from everything we knew. I'll never forget that smile as long as I live."

Seychelle's fingers were on his scalp, massaging in the way that she did. Soothing him. Keeping him grounded. He was grateful for that. He rarely allowed himself to go back to that place and those times.

"My hair is blond and really thick. Worse, it's curly. It grows in spiral curls all over my head. It has since I was born. Let's just say I was unusual enough that I caught the eye of Sorbacov. He was a fuckin' pedophile who loved little boys. Really young boys. And I had a headful of blond curls. My father ran a military school, and by all accounts, he and my mother, who was a linguist and scientist, were listened to by most of the very prominent people in the region. They opposed Sorbacov's candidate for the presidency, so they had to be removed. The fact that I had a brother and two sisters—all the better."

The bitter taste in his mouth was all too familiar. He knew he was going back there in spite of his determination never to do it. He tightened his grip with one arm around her thigh and with the other began a slow slide up and down her left leg, trying to ground himself.

"They took our clothes and threw us down into a basement. There were chains on the wall. There were other children, all naked, and they were filthy, had wounds on them, all over their bodies. There were three factions down there. Czar was the youngest and only had a couple of kids with him, but Reaper was insistent we choose him. It was terrifying down there. I didn't understand what they were telling Reaper and my sisters, but pretty soon men came and dragged my sisters up the stairs. Then they came for Reaper and me. Sorbacov was waiting. I could hear Reaper screaming. I could hear my sisters screaming. Sorbacov kept smiling that smile and petting my hair. He told me I'd better be nice to him and do what he wanted or he'd make my brother and sisters suffer. Then he raped me over and over."

He didn't look up, but he knew she wept. His woman. He had known she would. She had compassion. Empathy. It was a long time ago, but he was still that toddler. He'd been taken back to the basement, bloody and naked, to find his brother in bad shape. His sisters were thrown down the stairs, both of them, twisted, bloody and broken. Dying. He told Seychelle. Whispered it against her thighs. How they died. Who killed them. The pedophiles who delighted in torturing and murdering little girls. He forced himself to continue.

"Sorbacov got bored with his toys. He liked to see them hurt. He had friends who really loved to hurt little girls and boys, so he invited them to party with him. They had whips. They would take turns tying us up and taking the skin off our backs, me and a little girl, and then they'd rape us. All three of them. Sorbacov and his two friends. I was a little older by that time. Czar had begun to recruit more members and teach us how to survive in that hellhole. The basement was divided into three factions, like gangs, and even down there we had to work to survive. No matter where we were, it was always a fight."

He reached up and pressed her hand deeper into his skull, telling her silently she needed to continue her scalp massage. Immediately she complied, her fingers working her magic, easing some of the terrible tension building and building until he thought he had a volcano inside of him.

"The problem was I wouldn't cry in front of them, and they wanted me crying. They wanted me screaming. I fought back. Every time, I fought back. Knowing they would beat me more or whip me more, I still fought them. They thought that was great fun. I didn't realize for a long time I was adding to their enjoyment. By the time I knew, I didn't care. I was getting stronger. I worked out in the basement. Pull-ups. Push-ups. Push-ups with the girls—Lana and Alena—on my back. Every exercise Czar could think of, we did."

"All of the children?"

It was Seychelle's first question, and he welcomed the break. He lifted his head and got to his feet, reluctant to leave the solace of her warm body but knowing he needed to get water. He could barely talk with his throat raw.

"Only our group. You couldn't trust anyone but those in your own 'family.' Even then, the others weren't trustworthy with one another. Czar kept our group very small. He insisted we work out every day, no matter what. He taught us survival skills, like throwing little rocks through small holes until we were so good, we could throw a knife accurately and hit a target. We could blow homemade darts and hit a target. There were a lot of things Czar taught us that he didn't pass on to everyone, nor could we let anyone know we could do them."

"Why?"

Savage took his time, drinking the water, thankful it was cool on his burning throat. All those kids. He remembered every one of them. They'd tried to save them. Tried to talk to them. Tried to convince them that Sorbacov wasn't a nice person and anything he said was a lie. The children were just too scared and wanted so badly to believe an adult was going to save them.

"They needed to believe everything Sorbacov said to them. Even when he gave them to his friends. Even when they came back broken, bloody and so bruised and swollen. He petted them and told them it would be all right. Said he was proud of them for doing what he said. They would be rewarded. They needed to believe him, so they did."

"Honey," she whispered.

He turned his face away from her and stared out at the turbulent waves he felt such an affinity for. He fucking hated the pedophiles who had run that school. The ones Sorbacov had deliberately recruited. The most vile, depraved humans the man could find so he could watch in delight.

"One traded favors with Sorbacov. He was older, an asshole. None of the kids were safe with him. One lied and taught her group to comply in order to curry favor. We couldn't get them to see what was happening. We had to hide what we did. We couldn't chance them telling Sorbacov. It was sick how he treated them, but they would do anything for his food or his pats on the back, including betraying one another."

"Savage."

"We actually attended classes to learn what we needed to know to be better assassins for him. The instructors were sadistic. We were expected to learn various subjects, and the punishments were severe if we didn't get the material immediately. We helped one another the best we could. The other children were defeated and looked to Sorbacov, complaining and crying, but of course, that didn't stop them from being punished. They would tell on each other for any infraction. Sometimes he would give one or two of them food. We were all starving. We always shared food. They wouldn't."

"I can imagine all of you were in a state of terror all the time."

He frowned, wondering if that was true. He had been terrified at first. Then filled with pain and anguish when his sisters had died and he'd experienced rape and torture and the brutality at the hands of adults. Somewhere, that had quickly changed to anger. Anger had grown to rage. Rage to determination and the will to fight back.

"I just know it was impossible to trust most of the other children, and we could never let them see what we were doing. Even though we were just little kids, our skills with using homemade weapons grew over time, and we perfected our psychic talents. We spent a lot of time beat-up, cold and miserable, so we practiced a lot."

He had opened the door in his mind, and those memories were playing in his head. The fists hitting him. A male dragging him by his hair into a room with two other men and two little girls, both with blond curls like him. That had been the first time he'd experienced pleasure, a mouth on his cock while he was instructed in using the whip. The pleasure had been a bright fire streaking through his body, lashes of fiery flames like the red droplets falling to the floor. Nothing had ever felt so good. He hadn't known it could.

The man behind him, helping him wield the whip, had whispered to him how good it was when one could use a

whip, how arousing it was. Did he see how good it felt? He
was praised. Petted. The girl sucking his cock was forced to
take him deeper while the whip cracked and someone else's
tears flowed, and that bright, hot flame inside began to burn
because he'd experienced pleasure instead of pain for the
very first time.

Savage admitted it to her. "I was nine or ten, I can't recall
what age I was. After that, they would get me daily and take
me to a room with girls. Sometimes I was raped and
whipped, used by two of the most brutal men, other times I
was taught to whip females while girls sucked my cock, giving me so much pleasure I could barely stand it. Always,
they praised me and whispered to me how great it was to be
aroused like that. How good it felt, and it did feel good. So
much better than hurting."

He could barely look at her. "I wanted those times. I
looked forward to them. I willingly and even eagerly learned
those lessons." He rubbed his pounding temples. "I never
once considered that they were making me like them, that I
would end up a sexual sadist, craving the things I was taught
as a child. I only wanted the brutal rapes to stop. I wanted
the pleasure, not the pain."

"Savage." Seychelle's voice was gentle. Compassionate.
"Any ten-year-old would prefer pleasure over pain."

"I looked forward to those sessions, Seychelle. It was the
only time I wasn't getting hurt. I should have been looking
at the kids I was hurting. But somehow, it was me against
them. They were the ones ratting us out to Sorbacov, so
somehow that justified in my mind what was happening to
them. I don't know why I didn't go to Czar or Reaper. Why
I didn't tell them how mixed up I was. I couldn't sleep. I was
barely eating. Sorbacov was still giving me to his friends.
There were beatings. Rapes. The lessons. I was getting good
at learning how to assassinate the enemy. Top of the class at
all things ugly."

He risked a look at Seychelle when he told her that particular truth. He would have to confess more about that later,

things she really wouldn't want to hear and wouldn't be so sympathetic about. Her lashes were wet, her hands folded in her lap, knuckles white. She held her fingers so tightly together, but she didn't react.

"They brought in other boys and started teaching them the same way, only I was one of the ones they wanted to fuck up. They wanted to use me for the whipping boy. They wanted to fuck me and have me go down on the boy while he whipped the girls. No way in hell was that happening. I took that whip away and I beat the holy shit out of the kid with it. He was about four years older than me, and I laid out an intricate pattern on him, so the adults thought it was funny and cool. They praised me over and over, celebrating, treating me like I was one of them, someone special."

Savage detested telling her. Detested remembering what that felt like. That high. That euphoria. That rush. Even for one moment wanting to be like those animals. Not understanding the difference. He should have known, even at that age. He should have known. He shook his head, his body reacting, rubbing his arms to settle the blood moving through his veins far too fast. His breath came in a harsh rush, and he deliberately slowed it. He was the master of calm. Of pain. Of control. He had to be.

"I was rewarded by absolute inclusion. I chose the girls to be trained, and I got to train them for the others. I decided who would be whipped, while they were pleasuring me or one of the other men. If the boys were there, I showed off my patterns while the men played with them. There were times when Sorbacov would suddenly show up with a few of his friends and they would drag me up to the room and tear the skin off of me while his friends used me brutally."

He fell silent. Remembering. There was no way to forget, as much as he would have liked to. He had the scars on his body. The brands burned into his flesh. Front and back. No escaping. It was there for the world to see.

"You know they were grooming you, Savage. That's classic grooming. A horrific way to do it, but still, treating you like one of them, giving you pleasure and then ripping it away from you, hurting you as much as possible without explanation so you wanted that pleasure. Dangling it just out of reach so you'd do anything to get it back."

He nodded. He knew that now. At nine and ten and eleven he'd had no idea. Only that he'd rather feel pleasure than pain. Now he knew what grooming was. He knew how it worked. It didn't make him feel any less guilty for having participated.

"They knew what they were doing, except they underestimated me. They should have known when I pulled the whip out of that boy's hand when he was so much older. They didn't even consider that." He paced across the floor. Back and forth. Memories spilling over, crowding far too close. "I had Czar and Reaper, and they were keeping us human. We weren't, you know. We were just surviving, trying to stay alive in the worst possible circumstances. Alena and Lana were just babies. At least I thought of them that way. They were ours to protect. We couldn't, of course, but we all tried. This one day was so bad. So bad."

He shook his head, rubbed his arms as if he could remove the blood from where they'd taken his skin. "They nearly killed Reaper. Broke Czar's arm, a couple of ribs, they beat him so bad. The girls were a mess. Really bad shape. All of us were. I don't think I had any skin left. Reaper and I couldn't get down to the dungeon. We couldn't walk. We were crawling. The girls . . ." He broke off, shaking his head. "Alena. So little. Lana. What the fuck is wrong with people, Seychelle?"

"Come here, honey," she whispered. She had moved to the wide couch, and she sat the way she did in her bed, her back to the arm so he could lie facedown, his head in her lap, arms around her hips, his body beside her.

He didn't hesitate to unbutton her jeans and give himself the comfort of her bare skin. He needed it. She didn't stop him. She never did. Seychelle always seemed to know when he needed her strength. He breathed in her scent, that faint fragrance of wild strawberries and honey that somehow always transferred to his tongue. Her fingers right away were on his scalp, massaging, taking away the demons that were in his head, allowing him to breathe when his lungs had been raw and burning.

Her belly was wet, all that silky skin. He hadn't known his face was wet—but she had. She'd seen. She simply had moved to the couch and used her soft voice to beckon him, like the angel she was. She never made a big deal out of anything. His woman. He rubbed the scruffy bristles along his jaw over her belly and took her in with another deep breath.

"You're my fuckin' world, you know that, woman?"

She didn't respond, she just continued to massage his head with those firm strokes. He felt love in every single one. Caring. She took care of him. He mattered to her. There was an intimate feel to the way she touched him. It wasn't sexual, although there was a kind of sensuality to their connection. It was more the intimacy of intense caring. She shook him every time she touched him the way she did. She had from the very first time he ever met her.

"I just knew I didn't ever want to be like them. I didn't want anything about me to be like them. Everything about them was wrong. I vowed I wasn't going to cooperate with them ever again, no matter how many times they took the skin off my back. I was used to pain. I was used to rape. They couldn't break me. I knew they couldn't."

He rubbed his face over her belly again, mostly to get rid of the moisture leaking down his face. Fuck that. Fuck them. He had sworn he would never give them the satisfaction of seeing him broken.

"They aren't here, Savage," Seychelle reminded him gently, her fingers whispering over his temple and then his scalp in that way of hers that told him far more than words ever could. A declaration. "I'm here. It's just the two of us. We can both break into a million pieces, remember? That was our promise to one another. We'll find every piece and put us back together. I'll do that for you, and you do that for me. We're safe with each other. I give you my tears. You can give me yours."

He rubbed his jaw along her soft belly once more. The bristles left faint red marks, his marks, along with those wet trails in the silk of her skin, but she never once stopped him. He kissed the marks and dipped his tongue in her belly button, closing his eyes, savoring the taste and texture of his woman. The closeness of her.

Safety was relative. He didn't want her to know that even surrounded by his brothers and sisters, even as they grew, toughened by the thousands of drills they'd done down in the dungeon to strengthen their bodies and build muscle—push-ups, sit-ups, running in place or around the room, all with one of them on shoulders or back—that still hadn't saved them. They'd practiced martial arts, every kind of hand-to-hand combat skill they were taught, day in and day out. They still weren't safe.

"When they wanted my cooperation to train, they would take Reaper to another room and torture him until I did what they said. I became the Whip Master, and they burned that into my skin. Permanently. They knew it would shame me when I faced the others. I was a teen by that time. Absinthe and Demyan—he was Absinthe's older brother—would whisper to me that I was the best at what I did. That I liked doing it. That no one could be better, ever. It was the only way I could get by. It sickened me to train those girls. At the same time . . ."

Savage lifted his head, his blue eyes twin hot flames. Shame. Guilt. "I got off on it. I would get so fucking hard. I would have to take them one after another. They would beg me to, and I would tell myself they needed me to help them through it. It was part of their training, but it was still self-gratification any way you looked at it."

She didn't look away from his gaze, but in true Seychelle fashion, there was no judgment. "Honey, you insist on being so tough on a young boy. They held your brother hostage, hurting him mercilessly, and you were trapped doing their bidding. If that was part of the training, what would happen to Reaper, and those girls, had you not followed through?"

"That's true, Seychelle, but I *enjoyed* it. I didn't want to. I tried not to be aroused. I tried not to like what I was doing, but I did. I couldn't hide it. There was no way to hide it." He buried his face on her belly and let her comfort him when there had been no comfort as a child. Especially once he'd been a teenager.

"They were afraid of me. Sorbacov and his cronies. The instructors at the school. Reaper and I were different; we'd grown too powerful. Reaper made his first kill when he was five, creeping through a vent to get to one of the worst of the instructors. We had to be so careful, and we couldn't kill too many too fast. We had to take only the very worst and spread the kills out. Months apart. A year. Try to make them look like accidents. Never use what we'd learned at the school. Czar planned. The others helped, were lookouts or created illusions. Whatever we needed. But for the most part, Reaper or I were the ones that made the earlier kills. I think that began to show on our faces or in our eyes, whether we wanted it to or not."

He was trying to prepare her for the worst of him. That side of him that was even more of a monster than he had to show her in the bedroom. Wasn't that bad enough to have to confess to? Wasn't it bad enough to have to tell her he'd been raped and tortured as a child? That he'd crawled through vents and killed the men who had done their worst to all of the children in the school, not just the survivors?

"Why did I have to be so fuckin' good at it, Seychelle?" He could hear the whispers of Absinthe and Demyan telling him he was the best. No one better. He would be huddled in a ball, hating himself, wishing he was dead, knowing the only thing that kept Reaper alive was his ability to use that whip. His expertise. He detested himself for being aroused every time. For participating to keep those he cared about alive when others suffered at his hands.

"I got so I didn't know right from wrong. The lines just kept blurring, no matter how hard I tried to live up to the code. If they didn't take Reaper, they threatened one of the girls. I got so good at it. And so good at the assassination work. Too good. Sorbacov loved sending me out. I was his golden boy. I always got the job done, and he liked it messy. Bloody. Not at first. At first, he wanted accidents so no one could trace the deaths back to him. But then he wanted his marks to suffer and know they were suffering because he'd decreed it. I excelled at making them suffer. In fact, Seychelle, I was the best in the school, so once again, I was the golden boy, the Master of Pain. Had that shit burned right into my skin declaring me so. It wasn't just about my ability with a whip or a fucking flogger. The things they taught me there to do to the human body . . ." He trailed off.

He waited. Anger building. That red swirling up in him through the black. She remained silent, her fingers on his scalp, moving to his temples and then down to his neck, where his muscles were in merciless hard knots. That didn't deter her. Nothing seemed to. He wanted to knock her hands away. He wanted to shake some sense into her.

"What the fuck is wrong with you, Seychelle? Do you not understand what I'm telling you? Why they took a red-hot iron and burned that title into my back? When Sorbacov wanted information, I got it for him by taking his enemies apart. Enemies of the state, he said. I kept them alive until they told me everything he wanted to hear and then some. Do you know what I felt when I did that? *Nothing.* Absolutely nothing. What does that make me? If you were thinking of running away from me because I stupidly fucked up over not telling you why someone might want to kill me, then baby, you might consider this a much better reason."

What was wrong with him? Was he deliberately trying to drive her away from him? At the same time, he was holding on to her hips with everything he had. He had thrown one leg over her thighs, pinning her down, his head on her belly. She wasn't going anywhere, even though he was deliberately shocking her. Angry. Raging. Showing her the worst of him. Letting her see glimpses of the true monster inside him. *Because he still did that shit for his club.* He wouldn't admit that to her, because he knew she wouldn't be able to handle it.

She remained silent. Damn her. Her strong fingers continued to work on his neck muscles, a deep massage. He couldn't look at her expression. He rubbed his chin on her belly, kissed her soft skin and then nipped her with his teeth. She didn't so much as flinch. He soothed that little nip with his tongue.

He felt the breath move in and out of her while he traced his name on her belly and then on her thigh over the thin material of her jeans. "Seychelle? For fuck's sake. Did you hear what I said to you? Do you know the things they taught me? The number of ways they taught me to hurt people?"

Her fingers moved over his temples. "Does it matter how many ways they taught you to kill, Savage? They taught a child to kill. They taught a child to need to see whip marks on a body in order to be aroused. They trained you. Groomed you. It doesn't matter if you enjoyed it. Of course you did. How could you not? As for going out and assassinating targets for Sorbacov or your country? I imagine that was the only thing you could do. And it might have been the only thing that you could take pride in doing sometimes."

That right there was one of the many reasons he was so fucking in love with her. How could she hear the absolute wreck of his life, the things he'd done, and not condemn him? Not judge him? There was too much compassion in her. He sat up, feeling guilt for not giving her the truth of what he did for his club, but certain she was still too fragile—or he was. She hadn't made up her mind about Torpedo Ink. He knew she was wary of them.

She stroked her fingers down his face and removed them, leaving him feeling a little empty. He shifted his weight to allow her to get up. He was heavy and knew she couldn't have been too comfortable.

"You find out everything you needed to know? We done yet?" He sat on the edge of the couch, watching her closely.

"No, we're not." She wandered over to the window to stare out at the crashing waves. White water sprayed dramatically over dark, hulking boulders into the sky. "You haven't told me when you started taking on the pain for your brothers and sisters in the club or how long you've been doing it. Why they don't know and why it's so important to you that they continue not to know."

He went very still. There was no hiding from Seychelle. He'd been a fool to even try. From the very beginning he'd thought he was going to be able to, but he should have known the moment he'd cradled her in his arms and she'd known about Shari, the bitch who had followed him from San Francisco and he'd made such a mistake, using her for a second time when he made it a rule never to do that. Seychelle had known. She'd seen right into his mind. Czar had been right. He knew she would eventually see everything Savage didn't want her to see. Czar always knew these things. He needed time. More time. It was always about time.

Savage came up behind her, close, inhaling her scent. That special fragrance that was all Seychelle. Wild strawberries. Honey. Just smelling her hair, her skin, soothed him. He ran his thumb slowly down her spine. "We talked about this."

"No, we actually didn't, Savage. You glossed over it. I get that you're worried I'll blame the others when things get rough." She leaned back, letting him take her weight.

At least she understood that there would come a time when it would get rough. He could teach her so many things. He could give her body so much pleasure —and he would— but there would come that day when he would need so much more, and she would have to provide that for him. She already understood that he was gathering the rage and pain from his brothers and sisters and keeping it like some dragon, hoarding an obscene treasure he couldn't rid himself of alone.

He wrapped his arms around her waist as she put her head on his shoulder, a spear of despair striking straight to his heart. "You know what I'm giving you isn't something to romanticize, Seychelle. No matter how sensual and good I can make it for you, it still isn't right to have to hurt the woman I love in order to get off—to put welts on her body to be aroused. To train her body to like that shit. It's fucked up. It's always going to be fucked up. It isn't something I want for you—or for me either, for that matter. I tried to find ways to get away from it, especially once I laid eyes on you, but even Absinthe and Scarlet can't make this go away."

Seychelle laid her hands over his. She didn't try to hide the slight trembling, the indication of nerves, but then she was honest in their relationship. In her feelings. "I've never asked or expected you to be different, Savage. I made the choice to be with you as you are. I may take time to learn, but I will."

There was no blame in her voice. No expectation of blame. Simply acceptance. He closed his eyes and buried his face in her neck because he knew how bad his needs could get—she didn't. But she would.

He pressed his lips to her temple. "I want you to always remember, it's my choice to take on whatever I do of the others' rage, anger, pain, emotional distress, whatever I choose. They are completely unaware. I never take it all from them, just drain enough that they can deal. It isn't something they ever asked me to do, and if they knew, they would be upset. If what I have to do to get rid of it ever is too much for you, I always want you to remember the blame lies with me, not them."

He had to spell that out to her. He had to let her know that what happened inside him, that merciless, brutal volcano holding the demons would erupt and let them out and it would get bad. But that was on him. No one else. He waited. She remained silent. Waiting. So Seychelle. So patient.

"If there was one child in that school of nearly three hundred who Sorbacov despised, it was Czar. There were many older than he was, but it didn't matter. Czar's strong. He has a will of fuckin' steel. No matter what Sorbacov did to him, or had done to him, and I swear once, they broke nearly every bone in his body, he never wavered. Never broke. Czar just doesn't. He makes you believe. Sorbacov, I think, came to believe he was the enemy, his own personal demon."

"Why didn't he just kill him?"

Savage tapped out a rhythm on her shoulder with his fingers unknowingly, the code from his childhood when they sent messages to one another, the code Czar taught them. "Sorbacov liked games. Puzzles. And he didn't like being bested. He wanted to win. That meant he had to actually *win*. With Czar, he thought he could by threatening Czar's birth brothers. Sorbacov was certain he could break Czar through rape and torture. Sorbacov thought he could force Czar to give in, and he could bring one or more of the brothers to the school. Czar never gave in, although Sorbacov cheated and brought Gavriil, one of Czar's birth brothers, there once or twice. Sorbacov claimed Gavriil had brought it on himself. Czar somehow made Sorbacov send him back to the other school."

Savage caught her hand and tugged her around, taking her through the house to the master bathroom so he could walk her through to the wide grotto. He bent to turn on the taps. "You have to remember, Czar was just a kid, but he developed a way for us to fight back. He taught us to practice psychic talents. He devised ways to hone our skills with weapons we didn't even have. He gave us hope, but most importantly, he gave us a code of honor and taught us to have a moral compass. It might not feel that way to everyone, but he kept us human when they wanted us to be killing machines."

He found the shimmery bath crystals he'd purchased from Hannah Drake Harrington's Floating Hat shop. The crystals turned the water a deep purple and shimmered with a bluish undertone. He caught at the hem of her top. "Arms up, baby." Seychelle complied, and he pulled the little top over her head. Her bra followed. He turned her around so he could examine her nipples. "You sore at all?"

She shook her head. He lifted an eyebrow and tenderly ran his finger over those tight buds. Little goose bumps rose over her skin and she shivered in reaction. He couldn't help himself; he leaned forward and licked first one and then the other before drawing each breast into his mouth and sucking gently, giving each one equal attention. She cradled his head in her arms, her breathing changing to a ragged pant.

Giving herself. She did that for him without reservation. He lifted his head and found her mouth. Took it. Took everything. God. Her kisses. They were sheer magma, flowing through his veins in a slow burn straight to his belly, spreading through his body and reaching his groin. His woman. Nothing like her. He lifted his head, licked at her soft lips.

"You're so fuckin' beautiful, angel."

Savage sat on the edge of the tub to test the water. He wanted it hot for her. Steam was rising, but he didn't want it so hot it was uncomfortable. "The point I'm making about Czar is this: we needed him. Sorbacov wanted him dead. Not just dead, baby, but before he died, he wanted him suffering as much as possible. I was so little the first time I realized we would never make it without him and he was in such pain. It radiated off of him. Not just physical, but mental. He took everyone on. Not just us, but the other kids too. The ones he knew he couldn't save. He knew so much, still does. He's scary with what he knows. Anyway, it started back then. I was about four or five when I started trying to take it away from him. Just a little bit. Just enough to help him out. I didn't know what else I could do. Then little by little when the others were at their worst. I would practice all the time."

He reached up and unzipped her jeans. "Hands on my shoulders, Seychelle. I don't want you falling." She was trembling again. She knew. She'd given herself to him. Committed to him. He'd told her everything, and she hadn't run screaming from their home, so that meant their life was really going to start. Tonight. He was free. She gave him that, and she knew it. She was nervous, but she wasn't running. His woman. Courageous.

"And you've been doing it ever since."

He nodded. "After so many years, like you with your gift of healing, I can't seem to stop. It's a compulsion. Fortunately, I had trained myself to just drain away a small amount. It's more difficult when we're all together and everyone is upset, like at a meeting. Then I'm getting bombarded. Won't lie, babe, on my own, that rage can build up and take me there. Don't want you to blame anyone but me when I'm fallin' over that edge and it ends up on you."

Her hand cupped the side of his face. She waited until he lifted his gaze to hers. "We do it together, Savage. We give that gift to them together. They're your family. You take their pain on for them because you love them. You're mine. I take it from you because I love you. That's only ours, no one else's."

His heart nearly shattered in his chest. She meant it. That was the thing. Seychelle would give herself to him. Sacrifice herself for him. Give him her body and her tears. She would give him the freedom to be unashamed of who he was. He needed to be a better man for her. To live up to her. He needed to give her the world because she fucking deserved it.

He pulled her jeans and lacy panties down slowly over her hips, unwrapping his gift. He leaned in and inhaled the scent of her and then licked, liking the way her body jerked in reaction. "Step out of your jeans, baby," he said softly, holding her steady by her hips. "When you take your bath, take your time, think of me. Of us."

Deliberately, he slid his hand between her legs to find her clit, brushing his finger and thumb back and forth gently. Circling. Flicking. "Do whatever you want, Seychelle, bring yourself as close as you want, but you can't get yourself off. Promise me, baby. No cheating. I give every orgasm. I want you shaved clean and I'll bring you a robe and a bottle of water. You have to be hydrated." He pressed a kiss to her already-bare pussy lips and then stood up to help her into the deep bathwater. "Tonight, I'm going to show you something very, very special."

He watched her nipples tighten and the goose bumps rise all over her skin. Yeah, she liked the idea almost as much as he did.

SIX

Savage found himself smiling as he lit several candles, preparing the room for Seychelle's first time with the flogger. She was in the grotto, surrounded by the jets, those voracious bubbles teasing her sensitive body. He'd deliberately told her she could touch herself as much as she wanted, but not to bring herself off. Knowing Seychelle, she wouldn't have ever considered touching herself until he put the idea in her head.

He loved introducing her to new pleasures, watching her eyes light up, that slow, almost shocked surprise creep into her expression. The dazed delight. Seychelle gave him permission to be himself. She hadn't once asked him to be anyone else. He didn't have to hide the fact that he loved the things he did to her.

He had high solid metal stands that looked like pyramids wrapped in copper, four of them. Two were by the bed, one on either side but several feet away from it. When he lit the tall, dark honeycombed candles, the flames cast shadows along the walls and over the bed. The other two copper stands were on either side of the couch he'd had his brothers make but then put in storage and never brought out until he found the house. The pyramids were on either side of the couch, so the tall, honeycombed candles he lit threw shadows across the railing and windows. The candles were specially made, looking exactly like a honeycomb but black. When they were lit, they dripped red molten wax, so that it ran in either tears or little rivulets through those octagon-shaped holes. Both the bed and the couch had four-by-four posts with metal rings attached to them. The posts were anchored solidly to the floor.

Savage wore only a pair of soft black pants that enabled his hard cock to stretch. He was aching already, and it was going to be a very long night for him, but well worth the wait. This was really the start of their life together. Their real commitment to each other.

Seychelle was open-minded. Willing to try. Willing to think whatever he proposed might be sexy. Sex and pleasure began in the mind. She let it begin there. Her first reaction wasn't an automatic shutdown. She thought about it with the idea that whatever they did together would be sensual, that he would somehow make it that way for her.

There was no sound, but her scent drifted to him through the open doorway. Wild strawberries and honey. His blood grew hot, rushed to his cock, filling him, stretching those scars to a painful ache. Just knowing what he was going to do brought him to a sexual frenzy.

Seychelle entered the room, her hair in a messy knot on her head, dressed only in a short silken robe that scarcely covered her bare bottom, adding to his ache. She looked so beautiful she took his breath. The room was cool, and he could see her nipples pebbled beneath the thin material. Her breasts were generous, and as she approached him, they swayed invitingly, drawing his attention. She was aroused, the fragrance, that combination that haunted him, teased his senses. Her breathing was heightened. Her eyes bright. She looked a little nervous, and that was always intoxicating to him.

He swept his hand down the side of her face. "You look beautiful, Seychelle." That dimple. Those tiny scars no one ever noticed but him just above her eye, the ones she'd gotten for him in the accident, saving his life. She was his love. She always would be. In her state of arousal, she was even more beautiful than usual.

Kissing the pulse beating so rapidly in the side of her neck, he took her wrist and led her over to the long lounging couch that was positioned right next to the floor-to-ceiling glass wall. The couch was narrow and faced not the view but lengthwise, toward the middle of the room, allowing him to walk around three sides of it.

He slipped the silk robe from her shoulders and watched the little shiver that went through her body. Goose bumps were already rising on her skin—those endorphins telling him she was so ready for this. He ran his fingernails lightly down her back, from her neck to the base of the curve of her buttocks.

"Lay down on the couch, baby."

Savage watched the shadows play lovingly over her body as she obeyed him. She was freshly shaved, just as he'd instructed, and the sight of her naked skin sent hot blood pounding through his veins. He watched her crawl up on the couch, and his cock jerked hard. She was naturally sensual without knowing it. The firm cheeks of her bottom swayed as first one knee and then the other moved, as she crawled like a cat up the long couch toward the post he was certain she hadn't noticed.

"That's good. Stop right there. Lay down on your back, Seychelle." He kept his voice low. Velvet soft. "Spread your legs wide for me. I want to be able to see your greedy little pussy." He liked the little shiver that went through her. The blush that covered her body when she parted her legs and found his gaze glued to the slick, wet lips gleaming at him.

Deliberately, he dropped his hand on her scarred left leg and rubbed slowly, back and forth in a mesmerizing caress. "Keep your legs just like this for me, baby." He brought his gaze up her body to her face. "I like to see how much you want me."

Her breasts rose and fell with her ragged breathing. Her lips were parted. Eyes were so blue they looked like flowers pressed deep, surrounded by those feathery lashes. The scent of strawberries and honey was tantalizing in the air. Savage ran his hand up her leg and slid his palm inside her thigh to feather his fingers close to her heat. To that secret well of special spice, the aphrodisiac that was waiting for him. Her hips jerked, but she stayed in place.

"Good girl." He brought his hand slowly up her body, to her bare mound, where he would mark her for the first time. Just the thought had his cock so hard with need he could barely contain himself. He was finally free. After a lifetime of total restraint, she had allowed him to be free. This woman. Fuck. *His* woman.

Her tits were beautiful. Full. All woman. He found it amazing that she didn't realize how much he loved the way she looked. He fit her nipples in the palms of his hands and kneaded and massaged, watching her breathing heighten. She loved breast play. She had from the beginning. He was gentle with her nipples. She was already slightly sore from the play they'd done a few days earlier, and he was careful just to intensify her pleasure.

"I love when you work my breasts and nipples." There was a distinct invitation in her voice. More, there was a bit of a plea.

"You do love clamps, don't you, baby?"

The tip of her tongue came out to moisten her lips so that they glistened at him. His cock jerked, wanting to push deep.

Seychelle nodded slowly. "Not the clover clamps. Those are scary tight, but the other ones are so sexy and give me just the perfect amount of . . ." She trailed off.

"Bite," he supplied and bent to lick at her right nipple. "You loved the clover clamps, and they were beautiful on you." He slid his hand down her body to curl a finger into her slick heat. "Tell me you didn't love them, baby. How they tightened when you moved. That bite that just kept growing." Every word brought more scorching heat to his finger. He smiled wickedly. "Your brain hasn't caught up with your body. You do like them, angel. Maybe a little too much. That's what you're asking for, but I have to say no to you this time. I don't like ever saying no to you when you ask me for something sexually, but . . ."

Savage kissed his way back up her body to her breasts so he could pull first one nipple gently into his mouth and then the other. She'd said she wasn't sore, and she hadn't winced, so the lotions were doing the job, but he wasn't taking any chances with her. There was plenty of time for nipple play later; now he wanted to introduce her to other pleasures.

"I'm not taking chances getting you any sorer." He stepped back and looked down at her. "Don't pout, Seychelle, you're going to love everything we do. And I do have another lotion that has a kick to it for your nipples. It's not my teeth or clamps, but it will feel fuckin' good, I promise. You're so ready for this, Seychelle."

On bare feet, he walked with measured steps away from her, over to the long row of drawers built into the wall on one side of the room. Savage went to it and slowly opened the first of the drawers, where he had stored his personal whips. His heart began to beat faster at the sight of them. His cock pulsed and jerked, hot blood rushing, spreading through his body. He opened several drawers and looked at his high-intensity floggers.

He had so many. Some that delivered a mixture of sting and thud with the thick, dense leather. Another favorite was an eighteen-tailed round braided flogger that delivered a hell of a sting. The floggers went up in intensity from there. A big round braided one made from bull was dangerous in his hands. He had a latigo leather flogger. The stiff leather tails were each a half inch wide, thick and heavy. Seychelle would most likely never be ready for something like that.

He pushed those drawers closed and selected the galley whip, the flogger falls in thick and thin leather strips. The braided coiled handle that fit like a glove in his fist. It was an expert tool in his hands, and yet even for a beginner like Seychelle, he could produce streaks of flames that would light up every nerve ending and set her body on fire.

The ocean provided a backdrop of turbulent music as it rushed toward the boulders and crashed against them in a wild display of white foam and a wall of blue water. Nevertheless, he turned on his playlist, the dark, moody music that went with the shadowy world that he thrived in. Dark, sensual purples, reds and blacks. The candles were black but wept red wax. His woman laid out for him, knowing he was bringing her into his world. Letting him live free. Letting him live unashamed. He'd never loved her more, and he could honestly say that until that moment, he'd loved her so damn much he would have thought it was impossible to improve on that.

Savage approached her and paced around the couch, a slow perusal of his woman, taking in the sight of her, devouring her with his hot gaze, letting her see how much he wanted her. Letting her see the flogger in his hand, the falls dangling from the handle. He took her left hand and brought it over her head to the side where the loop was built into the couch. "I'm going to put your wrist in here and wrap it once. You can pull loose. I'm not securing you this first time because I want you to see that you can trust me."

"I do, Savage. I'm not afraid."

He was silent. She was afraid. That wasn't the entire truth, and he needed her to always give him the truth, especially under these circumstances. He secured her wrist, making certain it wasn't too tight and she could easily pull it loose if she needed to. All the while he held her gaze. As he moved down to secure her ankle, her lashes fluttered, and she bit her lower lip.

"I'm sorry. I *am* nervous. Excited. Wanting this. But very nervous."

"Good girl. You have to be honest, baby. Every single time. You can't bullshit with me or yourself. You're done, you have to say so. It's okay to be afraid. To say *slow down*, or *stop for a minute and let me catch my breath*. Talk it over. That you need reassurance. We're partners in this. Use the traffic signals—red, yellow, green. We talked about that, remember?"

"You need this."

"I'll teach you to need it with me, if that's your choice." His heart practically stopped. It had to be her choice. Let her choose him. He didn't deserve her, but let her choose him anyway. He was giving her an out again. He would every time.

"You've always been my choice. This is my choice, Savage. I'm not going into it with my eyes closed or with rose-colored glasses. I know what I'm getting into. I'm nervous, but I'm also excited. I mean that. I am."

He had to take her at her word. He walked around her, slowly, anticipating, his cock nearly bursting with greedy lust while his heart was bursting with love for her. She lay on the dark-blue couch, looking like a sacrifice. Her hair was just as wild and untamed as the sea outside their home. Her skin was pale and unmarked, waiting for his expertise, the signs of his possession, the promise of her love for him.

He reached down and took her right wrist to guide it into the loop that was at the bottom edge of the couch and slipped her hand into it. She lay quietly while he wrapped her ankle with the leather loop, leaving her completely open to him.

"I can feast on you. It feels like far too long since I've had that opportunity."

Savage leaned down and brushed kisses over her breast, his tongue swirling over her nipple, licking and then sucking at it. He fucking loved her tits. He loved her body. Her heart. Her soul. Everything about her. The fact that she lay spread-eagled for him and let him slip her ankles and wrists into restraints and never hesitated should have shocked him, but it didn't. This was Seychelle.

There was that scent of hers, the heady, potent fragrance that was on her skin and in her hair. When he kissed her, he could taste the wild strawberry mixed with honey, so subtle, but it was there, right along with the fire in her mouth. He could kiss Seychelle for the rest of his life and never get tired. Never. He lifted his head and traced her lips with his. Breath to breath.

"I love you, baby. More than life. Thank you for having the courage to love me the way I am."

Savage closed his teeth over her bottom lip, that temptation that drove him insane more than once during the day, and bit down slowly while his finger circled her clit and then flicked and thrummed, while another finger slid deep in and out of her. All the while, his eyes never left her blue ones. It was a fucking mind fuck to watch the way her pupils dilated and her breathing changed, going ragged, her hips rising to meet his finger, her channel so hot and slick and tight. He let go with his teeth and licked at the little wound. Kissed his way down her stubborn little chin and took another bite before standing up again.

"Savage." She nearly wailed his name.

He smiled at her. She thought she was close now. Wanting release. He hadn't even gotten started. "Have a little patience, baby. We're taking things slow, remember?" She had to be ready. So hot. So needy. He had to take her up slow. Keep her on the edge.

He caught up the bottle of lotion he'd put on the floor beside the couch and poured some in his hand. "You like attention to your tits, and I don't want to take any chances with clamps making you too sore, especially when the run is coming up and we may need to use those for our fun instead of anything else. I'm giving you something special here."

He rubbed his palms over her nipples, coating them in the lotion. It would go on cool at first. Soothing even. The heat would start slow. Very slow. Then the lotion would begin to tighten her nipples, and as it did, the burn would begin. He knew it wouldn't be too intense. The stuff was edible. Practically anything Preacher came up with for them to use was edible, but this lotion was extremely popular.

Preacher was a genius when it came to making them sexual lubricants. He had a vivid, wicked imagination.

Savage stood then, towering over her. Very, very gently, he trailed the tails of the whip from her throat, over the curve of her tits, those gorgeous hard little nipples standing so erect for him, down the valley between her breasts and then along her belly. Her eyes followed him, those big blue eyes so adoring, and a little fearful. That added to the excitement. She looked beautiful. Her tits rising and falling rapidly, nipples hard little peaks. The leather falls trailed lower, to her bare mound, where he wanted to put his name someday.

His cock nearly went into a violent frenzy at the thought of it. He gave himself permission to enjoy the flood of near euphoria overwhelming his senses. It was the first time in years he could be who he really was, and the freedom was incredible. Insane. He was soaring. Flying high. He glanced toward the drawers by the windows, where he kept his whips. The real ones. *Not today*, he reminded himself. That would come another day. Hopefully, a long time from now, when she was ready. For now, he had this.

The gallery whip in his hand felt like a part of him, an extension of his body. Hot blood ran like volcanic lava through his veins at the thought of Seychelle and the pure canvas of her body. His hand tightened on the handle of the flogger. Already he could see the slick heat on her bare pussy lips for him. Waiting. Anticipating. He bent and licked at those hot little drops, relishing her taste. A shudder ran through her entire body, her hips jerking. She moaned.

"So good, baby. You look so beautiful." He settled at the end of the couch, between her open legs. "This is why you're stretched so wide for me. So I can do dirty, sinful things to you, like eat you alive." He grinned at her as he trailed the leather falls lightly over her thighs and then dipped down to lick up her left thigh and stop just at that burning entrance. "But there is one little rule, Seychelle. You know how I am about those rules."

"Savage." Now there was a little demand in her voice.

"Tone, baby. You're in a bad position to give me attitude. The rule is, you don't get to make a sound. I give this to you, you take it quiet. You start makin' noise, we stop." He gave her another wicked grin. "Let's see how quiet my woman can be."

Seychelle was never quiet when it came to orgasms. Never. He wanted her on the edge. Desperate. So ready. He took one more look at what was his, and then he kissed his way to her bare pussy lips and began tormenting her. Devouring her. He used his tongue as a weapon, enjoying her taste, wanting to eat her morning, noon and night, reveling in the fact that she was his and he could.

His girl began making those little delicious noises that turned him on even more. Only his angel could make moans and kittenish mewls sound like music. They started off soft as her hips bucked and her pussy pressed tight against his mouth, and then she was thrashing wildly, and her voice began to rise, just as he'd known it would. He immediately lifted his head, wiping his face on her thighs, grinning wickedly as he met her eyes.

"Savage. No. You can't stop."

"Told you the rules, wild one. Can't help it if you chose to be loud."

"You set me up."

He had, but he wasn't admitting a thing. He stood up, stepping to the side to study her writhing form. "Baby, it's all right, you're going to get what you want. I'll let you have it." He brought the flogger down gently across her thighs. A whisper of leather. On her heightened nerve endings, it felt like a lick of fire, like his tongue. "Feel that?"

He sent the heavy falls thudding just a little more forcefully over her inner thighs, allowing them to reverberate through her body. She cried out, her hips lifting to meet the falls.

"You're so ready, baby. Feel that thin line of fire? Now, Seychelle. For me." He didn't wait in between strikes, twisting the flogger so the thinner edges struck over her exposed pussy, lashing with several streaks of fire.

Seychelle screamed as the coiled tension in her body exploded into a powerful orgasm. Savage flicked at those bright pink stripes with his tongue and then sucked on her inflamed, swollen clit while the brutal waves rushed over her like a terrible tsunami refusing to stop. It just built and built through her body, rolling through her. Savage lightened his touch, easing her down, but kept her body coiling tight again, needing more, with several lighter licks and flicks of his tongue. He petted and soothed her shivering body with his palm, occasionally running his fingers over the stripes, sending another small lick of fire through her.

Her entire body shuddered. "Savage. I need more. That was crazy, but I need more. It feels like my whole body is hungry for you. I need you right now."

He pressed a kiss on those fiery little streaks. They were beautiful and bright against the pink under all that gleaming wild strawberry and honey spilling out of her for him.

"I'll give you what you need, baby." He slipped the loops from her ankles, trailed the leather falls of the whip up her body to her throat while he slid her hand from the right loop.

Eyes dilated, her desperate gaze followed him as he moved around the couch to the left side. Her breath came in ragged little pants, sending her breasts jolting with each rush of air pushed so abusively through her lungs. He removed her left hand from the loop that held it. Hot blood rushed through his veins in anticipation. Stark lust mixed with raw love made a tight pressure in his chest. His cock had never been so hard or so full.

"I want you to stand, angel. Face the window this time, and the post. There's plenty of room for you to stand. Spread your legs past shoulder-width apart. That's right." She was so perfect. She did exactly what he told her. "The couch will be right behind you." His voice, usually controlled and velvet soft, sounded a little hoarse to his own ears. He cleared his throat and watched his woman obey him. That alone put more steel in his cock. Or maybe it was just looking at the perfect canvas of her back. His heart began to pound, a fucking drum of pure need. Of anticipation.

This time he caught her wrists and gently tied them together and then pulled them above her head and hooked them to a ring attached to the post. Outside the waves crashed in time to the beat of the music pounding in the room, and the drum of his pulse as his blood hammered in time through his heavy cock. He crouched low and attached the tie from the edge of the couch to one ankle so she couldn't move her leg and then did so with the other.

Savage stepped close to her, put a comforting hand on the nape of her neck and kissed her rapidly pounding pulse even as he very gently brushed the whip up one side of her inner thigh toward her heated center. "Trust me to give you pleasure like you've never known, Seychelle. You'll learn to love the way the fire brings you alive. Every nerve ending in your body will feel the rush. You'll be aware of me. Centered on me. Know my cock is going to make you come apart. Shatter you. Bring you back and do it all over again."

As he whispered to her, he rubbed the whip over her inflamed clit and used his other hand to cup her breast. She gasped, her head falling back on his shoulder as he tugged and rolled her heated nipple. Her hips moved on the whip handle helplessly.

"Give in to this, baby. You have to want this. Give yourself up to it and to me." He pressed his body against hers so she could feel the hard length of his cock tight against her, so she could feel his breath rising and falling with the same passion running through her body—that same intense connection they had from the very beginning. "Surrender totally to it.

"You say yellow if we need to slow down. Red if you have to stop. You say red, it's over. I won't be upset. You understand me, baby?" He caught her chin and turned her face so she was looking into his eyes. "You say red, we're done, and I'm cool with that. We've come this far, and this is good." He kissed her gently.

He had never instituted a warning system in his life. No safe words. He hadn't lived that lifestyle. But he hadn't had a woman he loved, and he hadn't felt the incredible euphoria of being completely free to be who he was. He hadn't expected that, and he didn't want to take a chance of loss of control. Not with Seychelle. Never with her. This kind of freedom was intoxicating—and therefore dangerous.

"Say you get me, angel."

She nodded. "Yellow if I need to slow down, and red, we stop."

"Good girl. Say you want this, Seychelle. I need to know before we keep going." He turned his hand so that it was his knuckles sliding against her heat, not the whip. Her pupils were so dilated, her body so hot, and when he used his hand between her legs to rub her clit, her pussy lips were soaked. She was ready, but he had to hear her consent. She had to be with him fully on this or he wasn't going to take them forward.

"I want this, Savage. I do. I'm afraid, but I want it." Her entire body shook with need. His knuckles were coated with her honey.

Savage pulled his hand free and licked at his fist and then kissed the sweet spot between her neck and shoulder that always made her shiver with need. His tongue touched that spot. Flicked it. His teeth nipped and then bit down, claiming her. A little moan escaped.

"Remember, baby. Tears are sweet to me. But I don't want to hear screams unless they're all about pleasure." He whispered the command and then stepped back from her, taking a deep breath as he allowed himself to really take her in. That sight. Her naked body tied for him. Open. Vulnerable. A willing sacrifice. Giving herself to him.

Her ass was gorgeous. Round. Two perfect globes. He flicked the flat falls across them with a gentle stroke, letting them land in a light thud, warming her. She jumped but settled immediately. He added a little weight the second time, letting the falls fan out. This time they left faint pink stripes.

He slid his hand between her legs to caress her pussy, to feel her wetness. He pushed one finger inside her and instantly was surrounded by her hot, tight, very needy channel. She moaned again and tried to ride his finger.

Savage stepped back, sucking the cream from his finger, his heart pounding, his cock jerking. "You liked that, didn't you, baby? You need that bite. That streak of fire. Once it gets in your blood, it consumes you. You want to feel it more, don't you? Do you need more?" His voice was a dark temptation whispering like velvet over her shivering body.

He could see the endorphins working, the goose bumps everywhere. She was breathing very rapidly, hips unable to stop moving, and she was so wet he could see the gleam on her pussy lips.

He slapped the falls harder against her ass, causing a distinct burn this time, and she gasped, shocked as the pain and fire rolled through her, crashing together until she couldn't tell one from the other. He plunged fingers into her heat, curling them, stroking her most sensitive spot while his thumb slid over her swollen clit. He snapped the whip a second time with the same intensity, laying a line of streaks above the others, over the curve of her sweet ass. She gasped and rode his fingers, grinding down hard. Honey spilled hot all around his fingers.

"You like that burn, don't you, baby? It makes you feel so alive. So connected to me. It's more intense than anything in the world. Do you want to stop, or do you want me to take you much further?" He pulled his fingers free and rubbed her clit soothingly. Her pussy lips. The insides of her thighs with the handle of the whip. "Do you want the burn? The pain? The fire? Do you want to shatter for me, Seychelle?" His voice was that same low, wicked temptation.

He had his arms around her, one hand on her breast, pulling and tugging on first one nipple and then the other while his teeth teased her shoulder.

"Don't stop. I don't want you to stop."

It was a whisper, but he heard. Surrendering to him in

that way she had, giving him total control. Total power. She gave herself to him. Trusting him. The rush of hot blood to his cock was brutal. Vicious. Beyond all expectations. He kissed the nape of her neck, his fingers whispering over the curve of her breast to give her courage.

He stepped to the side and swung the galley whip, increasing the strength behind the strike to bring a careful, precise smack just below the curve of her ass. Her entire body went rigid as fire streaked through her. She cut off a scream, and he slid his hand between her legs to help mingle pain with pleasure. The sound turned to a needy moan.

Quickly, he placed three more strikes, thudding the flat whip tails against her rounded flesh with two of them and landing the other across her thighs before stroking her clit and letting her ride his fingers with her jerking hips. She was already beginning to accept the stinging needles of fire as they lanced across her body, pain turning to bright hot flames rolling through her. Instead of dancing away from the heat, she pressed her ass outward toward him—just barely, but she did it, even while her forehead dropped against the post.

Savage was tuned to body language, and his angel was nearly there, her breathing so ragged. She was struggling to assimilate the pain with the sizzling pleasure. There was no separating the two at this point—he knew from experience. He dragged his fingernails from the nape of her neck down her spine and then over the lash marks.

"You're so ready."

"I need your cock, Savage." She tried to rock back into him.

"Not yet, baby. We're not nearly done. There's more. You need to climb higher for me." He rubbed the red streaks, listening to her moans. It was music for him.

She nodded. "Yes. Please, honey."

He found himself smiling. She'd asked him so nicely. "Then surrender to it, baby. Give yourself to the fire." He lifted his hand and flicked his wrist, sending the falls thudding over the backs of her upper thighs, right under her ass. Her entire body jolted with the strike. He didn't slow but continued up her body, the crease, the smooth rounded curve under her ass, and then over, sliding up her back, careful of her spine but leaving gorgeous stripes first on the left and then on the right side, all the time watching her closely.

When a light sheen dotted her body and she threw her head back, he moved up to her, wrapping his arm around her, one hand thrumming expertly over her clit while his fingers plunged in and out of her, his other hand tugging and rolling her right nipple. "You need to let go, don't you? It's crashing through you, isn't it, baby? That's the fire. It's rolling so hot and wild you can't stop it. You need to let go."

Her head fell back on his shoulder, and her eyelashes were wet. He looked into her eyes and smiled at her. "Your fuckin' pussy is so hot, baby. It's a fuckin' wildfire. Let go for me. Give that to me." He bent his head and took her tears, simultaneously stroking and flicking with his fingers in her scorching-hot pussy while the climax roared through her, taking her in a wild, violent perfect storm of blended, confused sensations. The whip fell over and over in much harder stinging strikes, urging the orgasm into continuous crashing, thundering, rolling waves, each building on the last.

Her entire body bucked against him, her soft little sobs intermingling with her cries of bliss. Savage tossed the whip on the couch. She might have fallen if he hadn't held her up with one arm around her waist, keeping his body tight against hers so she felt every inch of him against those lashes. He splayed one hand on her belly and then lower to feel the brutal spasms rolling through her body.

"It's all right, baby," he soothed. "You're just flying high. I'm right here with you. Breathe for me." He rubbed her shuddering body gently, his other palm covering those hot streaks over her ass cheeks. "Relax for me now. Just breathe."

When she took a breath, Savage reached down and unhooked first one ankle and then the other before reaching up to unhook her wrists. At once she slumped into his arms. He took her weight. "Eyes to mine, baby," he commanded. She needed an anchor.

Seychelle lifted her lashes and made an attempt to focus on his face. He leaned in and sipped at her tears. He'd take them over diamonds every time from his woman if she gave them to him honestly. These were honestly given, and they were for him. He kissed his way down her cheek to the corner of her mouth, pressing his body tight against hers so she felt his raging cock nestled against those ferocious stripes.

"Gotta get my cock in you, woman."

A ghost of a smile touched her mouth even through her tears. That got him right in the heart. He lifted her. When he did, her bound hands slid down his chest and found his diamond-hard cock. Just the brush of her fingertips ignited a storm of fierce lust in him.

Savage carried his woman to the bed, making it as far as the side before putting her belly down over the edge, presenting that beautifully striped backside to him. Adrenaline rose with a hot dark lust mixing into a ferocious need to own her.

"Don't move, baby, stay right there."

Looking down at her, at those vivid stripes on her back, with her ass and pussy presented to him while she waited submissively, he felt the ultimate surge of power, of control. Soft little sobs still intermingled with needy whispers begging for more. She tried to muffle both by pressing her mouth on the comforter. She didn't wait long. She turned her head, pushing out her ass a little desperately, seeking his cock.

He caught her hair in his fist. All that thick honey-colored hair, and deliberately yanked her head back, forcing her to arch her back. He dragged his nails down the streaks, all the way from her ribs over the beautiful curves of her ass cheeks to her thighs, lighting streaks of fire all over again.

She hissed and bucked. He swatted her hard. "I said,

don't move." His hand slid between her spread legs. "So slick for me. You like this, our dirty, sinful lesson. You liked this one a hell of a lot." He whispered the truth to her even as he lodged the thick head of his cock into her entrance. "Didn't you, Seychelle?"

So fucking hot. An inferno. His heart pounded, and he felt her heartbeat right through the walls of her feminine sheath. She was burning him alive, and he wasn't even all the way inside of her.

She tried to push back, to impale herself on him, but he held her still. "Such a greedy little girl." The marks on her skin inflamed him. Drove him wild.

"You did like it, didn't you, baby?" He rubbed his hand over the hot marks on her rounded ass. The stripes were so beautiful to him. Bright and fiery, standing out so starkly against her perfect skin. "It feels like fire burning right through your pretty little pussy, doesn't it?" She was so beautiful to him. Perfection. He wanted to savor this moment. To hold it in his memory as long as he could.

Sliding one hand around her throat, he tipped her face to the side so that her eyes met his. Confusion. Lust. Need. Acceptance. Complete, total acceptance. It was all there in her beautiful blue eyes. He bent his head to kiss her. Slow. Lovingly. Giving her that. Then he drove into that scorching-hot sheath, hard. Deep. Brutally. Taking everything she offered him. Claiming her the way he needed to. Savagely. Just like his name.

Fire streaked up his legs, roiled in his belly, rushed through his veins like hot lava and burned behind his eyes until he saw in black and red. He pounded into her. Rough. Vicious. He alternated between tracing those gorgeous lines on her ass with his fingernails and gripping her hips and losing himself in mindless bliss.

"Savage." Seychelle's ragged voice was pleading.

Her sheath coiled around his cock. Hot. So fucking tight. Like a damn vise. He pistoned into her harder, right through a million fiery, wet tongues intent on sucking him dry. He'd never felt anything remotely like this in his life, and he wasn't ready to give it up.

"Let go, baby."

"It's too much." Her voice was a strangled plea.

"Everything, angel. Give me everything," he insisted. He was merciless. He needed her to give him everything she was. "For me."

He smacked his palm hard over those perfect stripes on the curve of her beautiful, rounded ass, and she detonated. Exploded. A powerful, twisting, biting fist gripped his cock with such scorching heat he nearly lost it. He swore for a moment his vison went black and his legs wanted to go to rubber. He refused to give up paradise, his iron will fighting his body's response.

She took everything away. His fucking past. The memories burned into his brain. Into his bones. Into his skin. She was like some laser, removing every bad thing and replacing it with fucking nirvana. He planted one hand on the mattress beside her hip and rose above her, getting a different angle, one that allowed him a deeper, merciless drive. Her body gripped his so tight, never wanting to let him go. Welcoming him. Wanting him. Loving him, no matter that he'd unleashed that beast in him and she saw all of him.

"Again," he ordered. "Again, Seychelle." He rubbed her upturned bottom gently. She was breathing raggedly. Panting. But she was moving on him, pushing back into his relentless feral rhythm.

She shook her head. "I can't, Savage. It's too much. I can't."

"One more time for me, baby. With me this time." He lowered his voice to pure velvet. Coaxing her. Needing her to know she'd give him whatever he wanted from her. He watched his thick cock moving in and out of her. Disappearing into her body. It was sensual. Sexy. Dirty as hell when he was big and she was small and her body had to stretch for him. That just added to his power trip, his need to dominate, the rush the stripes on her thighs and ass gave him. Her willing sacrifice. "One more time," he pushed. "Tell me what you need. Say it, baby."

"I can't."

He was pushing her too hard. She'd given him so much already, and she had to be confused. He fucking loved her with every breath he drew. He raked his nails down those stripes and instantly felt the flood of liquid heat surrounding his cock. Fiery hot. Her body coiled tight. Seychelle giving herself to him.

"I've got you, baby. I'll always have you." He whispered the reassurance even as his hips surged into her over and over, driving her body forward with every forceful assault of his cock.

Once more he changed his angle, hitting her sweet spot, his finger on her clit, pushing her over the edge again, feeling her body clamp down on his cock like a fucking vise. His cock jerked hard—so hard it was painful. The scars stretched beyond limits, and still his cock jerked and pulsed, his spine bending, his legs shaking, as pleasure unlike anything he'd ever experienced shot through his entire system.

He felt as if lava were boiling in his balls, readying to blow from a volcano too long held suppressed. There was a madness rising in him, and for those few moments, with his release roaring through him, Seychelle forcing every last drop from his body, milking his cock with a determined ferocity, insanity reverberated through his mind. He lost every memory of the past of anything or anyone who had come before her. There was only this beauty. This madness. This agony and ecstasy. There was only Seychelle.

He had no idea of the passage of time or how long he lay over the top of her, soaring, flying higher than he'd ever been. His blood thundering in his ears so he couldn't hear anything but the reassuring sound of his wild heart competing with hers. It took a while for the blackness to recede from around his vision. For air to find its way back to his body.

Savage moved down her body and pressed his forehead

to the base of Seychelle's spine, breathing hard, trying to find his way back into his skin. She'd shattered him. He had known all along she had the capacity to break him wide open. He was so damn vulnerable with her. If his enemies had any idea the way he felt about her, they would take him down so easily. He would do anything to keep her safe. Anything at all.

Her little body shuddered under his. She was confused. Upset. Flying too high. About to drop too low. She desperately needed care. He rubbed his face along the curve of her beautiful ass, right over the stripes he'd made, before he gathered her into his arms and lifted her fully onto the bed.

"Let me take care of you, baby. I need to rub lotion onto those marks. There won't be any bruising, I was careful. I'm going to lay you facedown, on your belly, and I want you to stay that way for me while I work on you."

He had already set up for her care. The soothing lotion for her skin was in the tray right next to the packs of washcloths and towels he had set under the bed to clean her with. He was a man who believed in being prepared when it came to his woman. He was very gentle as he washed between her legs. He'd been rough. More than rough, and he examined her for tears. For any damage. He was a big man, and he'd skated the edge of control with her. Okay, he'd been totally out of control. Fortunately, it looked as if he hadn't done any damage to her sweet little pussy. Still, he made certain he applied the soothing, healing cream, which was absorbed into her tissues immediately. She mewled like a little kitten, but she didn't pull away.

"Was I too rough, Seychelle? Are you sore, baby?" He kept his voice very gentle, as gentle as his hands, as he lifted her and placed her very carefully in the center of their bed.

She kept her face averted from him, her fingers slowly curling into fists on either side of her head, pulling the comforter into the center of her palms as she did so.

Savage picked up the bottle of lotion and began to rub very gently along her ribs while he waited for her answer.

Those marks were the lightest and would bother her the least when he touched them.

"You weren't too rough, Savage. I wanted you to take me exactly the way you did." There was a little break in her voice. "I needed you to."

She kept her head tilted away from him even when she made her little confession. Her hair was all over the place, the thick honeyed strands like falls of silk, hiding her expression, but he knew her all too well now. She was confused with her body's reaction—with her mind's reaction.

Savage was careful of the darker red stripes on her ass, the ones that made his cock want to stir all over again. He soothed those lines tenderly. "Let me finish here, baby, then I can hold you. We'll talk this out. I know you're feeling a little confused right now."

He moved faster, still keeping his touch as light as possible while rubbing the lotion in. "I don't want any bruises on you. It had to feel like you were going to bruise a couple of times, didn't it? Tell me how these made you feel when I was lashing you." He rubbed the ones along the curve closest to the heat of her pussy and then leaned down to press kisses over the dark streaks.

Her legs moved restlessly. She didn't answer him. He let that go while he rubbed the lotion into the stripes along the backs of her thighs. When he was finished, he moved up in the bed until he was the one with his back to the headboard and he could pull her into his arms. He still had the front of her to cover in lotion, those small strips, but holding her was much more important. She needed it, and so did he.

She resisted, just for a moment, and then he had her cuddling close to him, burying her face against his chest. He could feel the shaking of her body as she wept silent tears.

"Baby, what did I tell you about your tears?" He stroked a caress down her hair, his palm taking in the entire back of her head.

He felt the twitch of her lips, and she tilted her head just enough to give him a watery smile. He knew she'd smile at his demand. "You. They belong to you. I've got to warn you. I think I turned the water works on."

He bent his head and sipped at the ones on her face, his tongue following the path to the corners of her mouth. *Bog*. There was no possible way to love a woman more. None. His heart felt like it was coming out of his chest. He cradled her head to him so gently. Even tenderly.

"Never loved another woman in my life, Seychelle. Only you. Never will again. Not saying you're getting a bargain, baby, but I swear to you, you're it for me. I'll do whatever it takes. Talk to me, angel. That's how this works. You have to tell me how you're feeling."

Her gaze started to shift away from his, but he shook his head. "Look at me. We're in this together. Remember? I'm right here." He brushed kisses on her mouth, her nose and both eyes. "We talk it out."

She nodded and took a little breath. "I don't understand why I'm like this."

He could hear the tears in her voice and see them in her mind. He stroked gentle caresses down the back of her scalp. Stayed silent. Waiting for the dam to burst.

"You knew I was like this, didn't you?"

He wasn't certain if that was an accusation or she was happy about it. "I suspected you would react to the things I needed from you, Seychelle." He pressed kisses up her shoulder to her ear. "I didn't know, but I suspected. I hoped. And yes, I tested you."

A little shiver went through her body, and she pressed a fist to her mouth to muffle the sound of her crying.

Savage slid down the mattress onto his back, lifted her and turned her into his chest so that she sprawled over the top of him. She tried to fight him for a moment, but he was strong and much bigger.

"Settle down, baby. Let me hold you while we talk this out. You have questions, and that's natural. I want to answer them for you. Put your head on my chest and relax." He cupped the back of her head, urging her to do just what he said.

"I don't understand. How can I be like this? The whip really hurt, but the more it hurt, the more I wanted you. The more I had to have you. The sensations got all mixed up in my brain—pain and pleasure, until it just burned so much all I could think about was needing you."

His heart lurched, and damn him to hell, but his cock jerked. He ran his palm down her spine, careful this time to avoid those marks on her back. It took control, but he did it. "Baby, this is a good thing, not a bad thing. We both wanted this. If you didn't like it, we'd be in trouble. I took you further today than maybe we really should have gone only because I'm trained in this shit and really, really good at what I do, and you love me enough to trust me to take you there. The combination allowed us to go this far fast." He spread kisses over her bare shoulder. "There's nothing wrong with you, Seychelle. I took you there."

"I do love you that much, Savage, but I didn't expect to react so . . ." She trailed off and heat rose under her skin. Confusion reached her eyes all over again.

"Tell me," he encouraged. "It's just the two of us, angel."

A little smile tipped the corners of her mouth, and she looked mischievous. His cock reacted with a hard jerk. Growing hot. A little too hard.

"I don't think I'm all that angelic at the moment, Savage. The thing is, eventually when that whip hit my skin, and it hurt, it also felt like a streak of fire straight to my . . . um . . . straight right there to my sex."

Savage laughed. He couldn't help it. *Bog*, she was beautiful. A joy. Perfection. "Your pussy, baby. Although I'm claiming it. So, when the whip landed you felt a streak of fire going straight to your sweet little pussy."

She nodded, albeit reluctantly. Her fingers played nervously in the sheets, and he caught them, threading his fingers through hers—calming her, rubbing their combined hands along his hip. Establishing that they were together always. In everything. Good or bad.

"I just kept getting more turned on, but it didn't make sense, not when it hurt so much. There was all this heat. My blood was pounding through my entire body, but mostly through, you know, *there*, and I couldn't stop needing you. All I could think about was you. Having you inside me."

She was whispering. Even after he'd been a maniac, a fucking psycho, with her, she still couldn't say "pussy." "Are you embarrassed because you wanted me, baby?"

"I just didn't think it would be like that. So consuming. I felt almost crazy, like I'd do anything for you just to have you inside me. That's scary, Savage. I'm not that woman."

"Giving up control is always scary, Seychelle. Trust is essential in a sexual relationship like ours. What you're giving me is a power exchange, and I'm not going to lie to you, sweetheart: for me, you handing me that kind of control, that kind of power over you, is a rush. For a man like me, it's better than any drug ever manufactured. Having you submit to me, seeing my marks on you, knowing you're giving me that willingly, that's the ultimate."

He nuzzled the top of her head and then held her eyes, needing her to see that he was more serious about this than anything else. "For me, babe, that rush can get out of control when I'm in a bad place. It's absolutely essential that you know your limits and that you call me on my shit. You stop us when you're done. You put your entire trust in me, Seychelle, but I have to put mine in you. I have to know that when I'm in that black hole you're going to be the one to keep both of us from going to a place we can't get back from."

Her gaze moved over his face, and then one hand came up and cupped his jaw. She was so gentle his heart felt like it might burst in his chest.

"I'll get us out, Savage. You absolutely can count on me." There was utter resolve in her voice.

Savage wrapped his arms tight around her and just held

her for a long time, even though he knew he still had to apply the lotion to the faint stripes on the front of her. Right at that moment, he needed the closeness between them as much as she did. She was strong. She was courageous. He believed her. She would pull them both out of the fire when it was needed.

SEVEN

"Babe, wake up, just for a minute."

Seychelle groaned. She refused to open her eyes. She had no idea how many times he'd already woken her up, but it had to be a million. She wasn't moving. Savage might be the hottest man in the world, but she was exhausted. And her body was super sore. If he wanted her, she was going to be a lifeless rag doll.

"Go away, Savage. If you don't, I'm going to find Sabelia and have her teach me some kind of hex to put on you to make body parts start dropping off."

She could have sworn he laughed, but then there was cold air on her body. He flipped her onto her belly, and the flat of his hand smacked her very sore bottom several times. Hard. Very hard. She yelped and threw her hand back to cover her bottom.

Savage caught her wrist and easily brought her arm to the small of her back, all the while peppering her bottom with more slaps. It felt like fire raining down.

"Asshole," she muttered into the pillow. "You are *so* going down." She was visiting Sabelia today. *If* she could ever move again.

"Are you seriously going to pretend you don't like this?" He leaned down and pressed a kiss into the small of her back. "If you didn't like it, your adorable little pussy wouldn't be wet and ready for me."

"Savage, I like you too, and my adorable little—um— vajj likes certain parts of your now-not-so-adorable, er . . . oversized and overactive . . . um . . . thing, but I'm too exhausted. Go away. And don't spank me anymore, please. Whether I like it or not, I don't honestly know, because I don't honestly know if I like *you* or not. I just want to sleep. So *go away.*"

He burst out laughing, the sound rich and masculine. She loved the sound, and she couldn't help opening her eyes just enough to look at his face as his weight settled on the mattress right next to her.

"My *thing*? It's my cock, baby, and you're very, very fond of that particular portion of my anatomy." He took her limp hand and stroked her palm over the swollen denim of his jeans.

She groaned, her eyes on his. "Are you always hard? Maybe that thing is broken. There's no turn-off button. That's the trouble. I need a remote so I can just turn that bad boy off when it gets stuck on."

He rubbed her bottom gently. "You have to learn to actually say *cock*, Seychelle. *Thing* is not going to cut it, although I have to admit, it's cute as hell. And makes me hard."

She gave an exasperated groan. "Everything makes you hard. Whatever wasn't working before I came along is totally fixed now." She brightened. "I fixed you. Now go away. I'm sleeping. I don't even think you're real. I'm just dreaming." Deliberately, she closed her eyes.

His hand kept rubbing her bottom gently. "Your car's in the garage. The keys are on your dresser. Tank is full, the oil's been changed, new fluid and windshield wipers."

She started to turn over, but he put pressure on the cheeks of her bottom, holding her in place, and it was too much trouble. She really was exhausted, although it was so sweet of him to take care of her car—and she was elated to have it back.

His hand was mesmerizing. "You need to pay attention, Seychelle. This is important. I don't like leaving you alone. I'd rather you stay here at the house, where I know you're safe, or keep you with me at the clubhouse, but you have to get your things. You're going to need clothes for the run. Whatever you want to bring with you."

She didn't think now was the right time to engage in an argument about her objections to going with him. She was too sleepy, and he seemed tense. "I'm listening."

"I've left a list of suggested clothing. Things you might want to bring. We travel light. We're on the bike, but we'll be gone a few days. Go to your house in Sea Haven. I'll have one of the prospects on you. When you're ready to leave here, text me. I'll let you know when he's here waiting to follow you. Don't leave until he's with you. Understand?"

"Of course." She wasn't going to object, although now that Joseph Arnold was gone, she was certain she was safe. Savage was the one with the hit out on him. "I've been thinking about this security thing. I'm happy to oblige you. But I do think you need to have a couple of your brothers with you at all times until the threat against you has passed." She did her best to muffle her voice in the sheets, because she didn't want to sound like she was laughing. She knew what his reaction would be.

There was a long silence. "Babe."

That one word. Another long silence. She dared to look up at him from under the sweep of her lashes. He was weighing his words carefully. She buried her face deeper in the pillow.

"You do recall that I told you I am a trained assassin."

"Ummm. I was thinking about that, Savage. Your skills might be rusty." She was really tired and not at her best, but she could mess with him as long as he couldn't see her face. "I think you should promise me that you won't go anywhere without someone with you just so I'm not so nervous all the time." She pushed just a tiny quiver into her voice. Not a lot. He'd know then.

Savage continued rubbing her bottom soothingly as he bent his head close to hers. "Baby, you know I'd give you the fucking moon if you asked for it, and the brothers do usually ride with me, but I don't want you going around worried. There's no need. I've got all my skills and I'm on alert. Let's keep the focus on your safe . . ."

He trailed off, his lips against her ear. Suddenly, his teeth were there, biting down on her lobe, and she burst into laughter, the sound muffled by the mouthful of pillow.

"Ow. Ow. Ow." She pushed at him, still laughing. "You deserved that. And you are getting kind of old. Who knows if your mind is going? I haven't seen you practicing your ninja skills. Shouldn't you have one of those obstacle courses set up in the backyard to keep you in shape?" She patted his stomach. It felt like iron, but she acted like he might have a little pouch.

"You weren't saying I was old last night." He nuzzled her neck, pushing her hair out of the way so he could have better access.

"Go away. You're waking me up, and I was having a blissful dream about . . . umm . . ." She closed her eyes and subsided into the pillows again. "Best not to rile you up again."

"If you were about to say another man, that's not permitted, even in your dreams." He gave her a very hard smack on her bottom and looked satisfied when she yelped. "I really do prefer you just stay home today and wait for me to take you to your cottage."

She resisted rolling her eyes. "I need to go into Sea Haven and do some shopping. Women things. Might need to stop by the Floating Hat and get a hex or two as well." She hoped to make him smile again.

"It can't wait until we get back from the run?"

His hand on her bottom was bringing every nerve ending

screaming back to life, centering her awareness to his mesmerizing touch.

"Birth control. Feminine products. Things for women.
Hexes for controllers for on and off switches. No, honey.
Can't put those off."

His palm followed the curve of her cheeks, fingers just
barely brushing her slick heat. Her sex clenched, wept for
him. She closed her eyes and let herself savor belonging to
him. He was clearly struggling with the thought of leaving
her alone. He'd told her from the beginning he wanted her
with him, and he'd kept to that.

"On and off switches?" He bent his head and pressed a
line of kisses from the small of her back along several of the
faint stripe marks still visible over her bottom. "You can't be
talking about the part of my body you love best."

The whisper of his fingers slid through her wetness again.
Her sex clenched in reaction. Nerve endings lit up. It felt
good to just lie there with him stroking her so gently. Those
little caresses, asking nothing of her. Just being so sweet.
Teasing. She loved it when he was like this with her. When
they were just happy.

"Well, I did kind of fall in love with that particular part of
your anatomy, it's true. So many things to love about it. *But*—
and that's a big *but*—it's very demanding when I want to
sleep. I'm a woman who loves my sleep. A remote might be
just the thing. You can control my comings and goings, and
I'll control your . . . er . . . ups and downs."

He laughed—a real laugh—and her heart turned over.
Her stomach did that looping roller coaster that did her in
every time. Love was intense. Overwhelming. The slow
burn was even better than the rush of a firestorm. His breath
on her neck, the soft laughter melting her heart. She was so
in love with him.

"Seychelle," he whispered right in that spot where her
shoulder met her neck, sending shivers down her spine.
"You're so fuckin' beautiful inside and out. I swear there's
this light in you that shines so fuckin' bright it pushes out

the demons in me and makes me feel like a human being. You make me feel like I'm a man, not a monster walking this earth."

Air was instantly trapped in her lungs. She couldn't breathe. A lump formed in her throat. She closed her eyes tight against the sudden burn. Savage kept his face buried tight against her sensitive skin, the bristle along his jaw rasping like sandpaper, causing every nerve ending to rise to the surface in electrical shock.

"From that first moment when you shoved me out of the way of the truck and you took the hit for me, when you opened your eyes, you saw right past the monster. You never saw him. You always saw the man. Even in the hospital room, I let him out deliberately. I let him taunt you, so you'd be afraid and run from me, but you kept looking past him and seeing the man."

He kept whispering to her, choking her up, so she couldn't breathe. Couldn't speak. His arm had curved around her hips, locking down the way he did, holding her so tight sometimes she wondered what he was doing—until now. Until this moment. Now she knew why he lay facedown on her belly, arms around her hips, locking her to him.

"Honey." One hand managed to move to his head—the head he kept shaved. No thick blond hair for him. He wouldn't ever be that little boy again. She couldn't imagine what he would do if he ever had a son with blond curls. "You've always been that man. That sweet, loving man. Mine. I'll always see you."

He shook his head. "Why do I need . . ." He shook his head again and then lifted it to look her in the eyes. "No, *crave*. Have to hurt the woman I love, adore, respect and admire the most in the world. Why do I need that in order to be aroused? I can't stop thinking about what I want to do to you next. I love what we did last night. I want more. I've never felt so free. At the same time, when we're not having sex, I look at you and wonder how you can be with someone like me. I used to not care what I was. I really didn't. Now, when I watch you sleep and you look like a fuckin' angel, I want to put a bullet in my head or drive off a cliff for what I'm doing to you, for where I'm taking you."

Her heart accelerated. Savage was capable of doing either one of those things if he decided he wanted out. She forced her sore body to move, turning enough that she could frame his face with both hands.

"You aren't thinking straight, Savin Pajari; clearly you need me to set you right. You *are* a man. *My* man. *My* choice. You don't ever get to take that away from me. I'm not such an angel that I don't enjoy what we're doing. That's part of the reason I have such a difficult time with coming to terms with our relationship. I still don't understand the *me* part of it. Stop condemning who you are. Let it be. We're going to have real issues, Savage. Relationship issues. The sexual part is something we seem to communicate about fairly well."

He leaned forward and kissed her. He smelled and tasted delicious. He'd taken a shower, and she was certain she had morning breath and smelled like sex and more sex. Maybe stale sex.

"You haven't seen the real monster yet, Seychelle. When he comes out, even my brothers tend to tread softly. I can barely control him. The things he will want to do to you terrify me."

"They don't terrify me," she said truthfully. "You and the monster are one and the same. He's simply another side of you. You don't fully understand him. He's actually a good part. He's filled with rage because he took that on for others. What does that make him?"

He sat up. "Don't baby. Really. I go to fucking underground fight clubs where you can fight someone to the death. The only reason I don't kill someone with my bare hands is because my brothers pull me off. And it takes more than one of them to do it. That person is no saint, and you can't ever deceive yourself into thinking he is. He knows you. Knows your weaknesses. Knows you love him. He'll seduce you into giving him more. He'll take and take from you. You can't let him do that, and if you think he's a fucking saint, you will."

She actually heard a note of very real fear in his voice. His face was an expressionless mask, but his eyes were hard, two blue ice chips. Glaciers.

She stroked her fingers over his features, the bones, his eyes, nose and mouth. "He may think he knows me, but he must have forgotten how protective I am. How extremely loyal. I love my man. He asked me to be strong enough for both of us when the time came. I will. It won't matter what is happening or what he tries; I only know one thing. Savin 'Savage' Pajari is my choice, and I will never let him down. When he needs me, he can count on me. The rest of the time, Savage, if I'm on board, even then when things seem out of hand, just feel the freedom and let go. Trust me to say *enough* when it is for me. When it is for you."

She meant every word. There was utter resolve in her mind. In her heart. It wouldn't matter how erotic or sensual Savage made anything sound; if she could tell he was pushing past where they should be going, she would put a stop to it. Even if it felt like the most sinful paradise ever. She was resolved to stop it.

Savage stared at her for a long moment and then nodded his head. "Lay back down. You deserve to sleep in if you want. I've got to get moving. Tell me your plans, baby. Make it something easy, like get in and get out."

"Honey, you asked me to just get what I needed, and I'll do that. I'll be as quick as I can. I can give you a list of the stores in town I'll go to ahead of time, if that will help. My house. The Floating Hat. The pharmacy. And maybe one of the clothing stores, depending on what your list says. That should do it. After, I'll go back to my house . . ."

"You'll come straight back here. I'm taking you to Crow 287 tonight. We're meeting Czar, Blythe, Steele and Breezy for dinner. You deserve a fun night out."

Her stomach knotted. She didn't know anyone that well, but she wanted to. She wanted friends. She'd moved to Sea Haven with the idea that she'd make an effort and actually have friends. He was making it easy for her. She knew if he was with her, if she got in trouble, saying or doing the wrong thing, he'd get her out. It was a chance to dress up. Crow 287 was Alena's restaurant, and it was reputed to have great food. Hard to get into. She'd wanted to go. Alena had brought her food when she had broken up with Savage, but she wasn't able to eat. Not even the heavenly scents had enticed her to eat.

"I love the idea. What time? I need to know so I'll be ready."

"I told Alena we'd be there around seven. Lana and Tessa are watching Czar and Blythe's kids for them tonight."

"Oh, that could be fun for Tessa," Seychelle said. Savage's fingers hadn't stopped moving. So unhurried. Just that light whisper of a touch, creating the slowest of burns. He circled her clit but never actually brushed it. She widened her legs to give him better access, but he rubbed the cheeks of her bottom with that same gentle circular motion and drew his fingers down over her burning sex in those leisurely caresses that seemed to ignite smoldering embers along her nerve endings.

"Alena and Lana both really like her. They've taken her to Blythe's a couple of times for bullshit things just to get her used to going over there, but like Czar and Blythe indicated, she disappears into Darby's room. She'll do okay. I think they want you to talk with her again. That voice of yours goes a long way to help. I know, because I'm under your spell."

His fingers glided up between her cheeks, painting her wetness there as if he was using a fine paintbrush. She stayed relaxed because he didn't change his slow assault on her senses. It almost felt like worship.

"Are you under my spell? I thought I was under yours."

It would be so easy to tell him she'd stay right there in the house and go without the things she needed and wanted just to please him, to alleviate his worry, but that would set a precedent. She didn't dare do that with Savage. She knew he would take advantage, whether he wanted to or not. He was the type of man who wanted control, and he would take it if she gave it to him. Bedroom, okay, she loved that, but outside of that, she had to stand strong. Be herself. He'd fallen for Seychelle, not a shrinking violet.

"If I were Maestro, you would be wearing no panties and a plug to dinner tonight. Your dress would be his choice and very short."

"Really?"

"Really. He would be strict with his woman. Very. And you'd be meeting him in the men's room. Or alley. Who knows? I don't like the idea of strangers seeing my woman. Torpedo Ink is one thing, watching out for you, but no strangers. Wouldn't like that, babe."

She found herself smiling. "Since I'm not overly fond of the idea myself, I'm grateful you aren't like that. And men's bathrooms don't appeal to me at all. How do you know Maestro might do that?"

His hands felt so good, lulling her into a state of harmony with the sound of the ocean, the waves rushing toward the bluffs, the storm from the night before long gone. His touch made her feel languid, as if she couldn't move a muscle. Beautiful. Decadent. Loved.

"We all know each other's proclivities."

Her lashes fluttered. Of course they would know. She wasn't going there. She wasn't going to think about that. "I promise to be careful, Savage." Her voice was soft. Aching with love. With need for him.

"You mean everything to me, angel. Anything happens to you, and I'm not going to be okay. I can be violent. Really violent. I'm not a good man. You know that. Nothing can happen to you."

His hands hadn't stopped moving on her skin. So gentle. Tender even. The pads of his fingers slid through her wet entrance, circled her needy clit and then moved back up to push deep, making the breath leave her body in a little ragged rush. Two fingers curled, stroked right over that spot that nearly made her convulse and then were gone that fast, making their way up the curve of her bottom, between her cheeks.

"Nothing will happen to me, honey."

"Keep Hyde close. Do what he says when he says it. He's looking out for you."

"Mmm-hmm." She could barely think when his mouth replaced his fingers and he kissed his way over her cheeks and licked as gently as his fingers had brushed her sex. There was suddenly so much heat. An inferno coiling tight. Then his mouth was exactly where she needed it, sucking lightly. His tongue added pressure. Just a little more and she could get off.

Savage lifted his head and rubbed his face on the backs of her thighs. "I want you thinking of me all day, baby. The way I'm going to be thinking of you. And don't you dare get yourself off. That's for me to do tonight." He pressed a kiss to the small of her back again and stood up, pulling the covers over her.

"Savage." She wailed his name. "Are you honestly going to leave me like this?"

He gave her a wicked grin. "That's exactly what I'm going to do."

She glared at him before closing her eyes. "I'm definitely visiting Sabelia at the Floating Hat and getting a hex for you. I'm just not certain what yet. Go away. You were cute before, so I put up with your nonsense, but now you're just annoying."

"Told you before, you can't call me *cute*. It ruins my image."

She could tell he was a distance from her, probably over by the door. She caught the sheet in her fist, surprised that she didn't want him to leave. She liked being with him so much.

"Right now, Glitch is outside, watching over you while you're sleeping. When you're ready to go, let me know and I'll send Hyde to relieve him. Text me often, angel, and if I text you, answer me. You don't, there's going to be trouble."

"What part of *go away* don't you understand?" she muttered.

He shut the door very quietly, but she heard him laughing as he left.

—

Seychelle loved her car. She didn't care if Savage thought she needed a different car, her little MINI Cooper was just perfect. It was small and could fit in the narrow backstreets of Sea Haven just as easily as it could zip along the highway. Dressed in jeans and a modest T-shirt, she felt more like herself, with the exception of the ring on her finger. Maybe she shouldn't have said yes so quickly. She needed time to come to terms with what she was learning about herself and whether or not she could fit in with Savage's club.

She accepted Savage for who he was. She was drawn to the danger in him. She needed that from him. If she was honest with herself, she craved that bite of pain sexually. She needed it or she wasn't aroused. Savage shocked her, showing her just how completely he could dominate her body. Not just her body—he possessed her. He took her over. She'd lost count of how many orgasms she'd had, or maybe it was one long, continuous one that went on and on forever.

She both loved and hated that whip he'd used. She craved more. At the same time, she wanted to run and hide from the truth of what that said about her. Savage had known all along. Deep down, she'd known too. She didn't want more though. She had to put the brakes on. What if it got beyond her ability to tolerate the pain and she said stop and Savage didn't? He got off on seeing those stripes on her body. She knew he wanted more of them. Welts. He hadn't really marked her, not the way he wanted. Not the way she wanted. Could she take it?

Her Bluetooth came to life, announcing Savage with "Wrong Side of Heaven" by Five Finger Death Punch. "You're driving erratically, Seychelle. What's wrong?"

"I don't drive erratically. I'm a great driver." She was highly insulted.

"You've crossed into the other lane several times. Doesn't matter if no one else is on the road, baby. And you're speeding. Slow down."

She glared into the rearview mirror at the motorcycle following her. "Fine. I thought you had some kind of meeting. Go meet."

"Behave yourself." He disconnected.

Seychelle counted to ten and then slowed, pulling her car to the side of the road, letting it roll forward for a bit before it came to a full stop. When it was at a stop, she got out and rounded the hood as if she was going to look at the engine. The engine was sideways in the car, between the two front tires. Still, she took her time and went back to look through the back seat as if she might find a rag.

"What's wrong?" Hyde asked. "The car just got out of the shop. Mechanic went through it personally. It should be golden."

Seychelle smiled at him. "The car *is* golden. The problem isn't the car, Hyde. The problem is the informer riding behind me. If you insist on telling Savage every little detail, that's just fine. But don't include your opinions on my driving skills, because opinions don't count when you're snitching. Stick to actual facts."

Hyde grinned at her. "Touchy little thing, aren't you? The actual fact is you were driving all over the place. You clearly weren't thinking about your driving."

"Just for that, I'm going to go to ten shops, all of them for lingerie. Then the Floating Hat. Hopefully, Sabelia will be there. I'll ask for a little conference with her about hexes. The men of Torpedo Ink are getting out of hand." She stomped back to the driver's door, slid behind the wheel and glared at him again. "Keep up."

There weren't ten stores in Sea Haven that carried lingerie, and if Hyde was anything like Savage, he couldn't care less if he was in a store where there were bras and panties. He'd most likely enjoy himself.

She went to the pharmacy first and got everything on her list. She was a very efficient shopper, ignoring Hyde as she marched past him, her chin in the air. He just grinned at her, his thumb flying on his phone, clearly checking in with Savage, reporting one store down. She was supposed to be checking in, but really, why should he get reports from both of them?

The boutique was next, a store she tried to stay out of because she really was a believer in a minimum amount of clothing. She didn't go to that many places. She didn't need a closetful, but she did love beautiful dresses and nice underwear, and the boutique had all her favorite brands. She couldn't help indulging in a few very sexy sets of underwear as well as lingerie.

There were two super-cute dresses she couldn't resist. One she thought Savage might like; the other was strictly for her. It was purple and blue, the purple handkerchief hems falling short and the blue ones a little longer. Both dresses were sleeveless. She always wore the sweaters her mother had knitted for her, so she didn't worry too much about being cold, even on the coast.

Hyde took her packages from her and stowed them in the back seat of her car. To her dismay, as she made her way up the sidewalk toward the Floating Hat, the last stop she had, Brandon Campbell stepped in front of her, purposely stopping her. He wasn't alone. Shari was there as well. Shari from the bar. Shari, who had had her mouth all over Savage's cock. Just great.

"Seychelle," Brandon greeted. He looked around her as if expecting to see her with someone. "You alone?"

She looked around as well. "Looks like it, Brandon." She didn't point out Hyde, who was leaning casually against the storefront not six feet away from them. He didn't appear to be paying them any attention, but he had his phone out, which was bad news for her. "How have you been?" The two were blocking the sidewalk, impossible to get around unless she went into the street.

"Just fine. You look good. Have you met Shari Albright? She's a good friend of one of your male friends." He looked smug.

"I have so many, that really doesn't tell me much. Hi, Shari. We did meet at the bar last week. It was a little crazy. Nice to see you again. Brandon, how nice that you and Shari know one another."

Shari gave a little indignant sniff. "Don't think for one minute, Brandon, that I don't know that you've been chasing after her . . ."

Brandon turned toward her. "Enough, Shari. Don't say another word."

Seychelle found the pitch in his voice amazing. It seemed to hit just the right note with Shari. She blushed and stepped back, ducking her head.

Brandon leaned down, his head over Seychelle, mouth close to her ear. She tried not to pull back, but his cologne seemed overpowering. "Shari has something she needs to tell you. It's important, Seychelle, so it would be good if you could just take a couple of minutes and hear her out. This isn't easy for her."

Seychelle couldn't imagine what Brandon and Shari had cooked up between them, but she definitely wanted to find out. She gave another quick glance toward Hyde just to reassure herself he was close. He was in the same exact spot, looking bored, staring at his phone.

"Of course."

"Just give me a minute. She needs a little courage." Brandon took Shari's arm and walked her a few feet from Seychelle, not noticing she glided a few steps after him.

"You're a beautiful, sexy woman, and you know every man wants you, especially Savage. You know that, Shari. You feel sad for this woman, and upset that she just doesn't understand that he's using her. She doesn't hold a candle to you. But you can never talk to me like that again, you understand? I'm the only man that can help you get what you want."

"I'm sorry, Brandon. I really am."

"Go to her now and talk to her. Say exactly what we talked about last night and make her understand the truth."

Shari nodded. Brandon smiled down at her benevolently. Seychelle backpedaled quickly so that she was standing beside Hyde, looking into the window of the store three doors down from the Floating Hat. Shari and Brandon came right up to her.

"I really wanted to apologize to you for my behavior the night you were singing at the bar," Shari said. She even attempted a smile and then looked over her shoulder at Brandon, who nodded encouragingly. "What I was really trying to say to you, and doing it very badly because I knew it would hurt you, was that Savage is two-timing you with me."

Seychelle saw Hyde's head come up, and she shifted her body to put herself squarely between Shari and her guard. Glancing at the reflection in the window, she could see he was busy texting like crazy.

"He is?" She squeaked it.

Shari nodded. "He put me up in the hotel in Sea Haven, and he comes to me every single night. He needs certain things that you just can't give him. It isn't your fault, it really isn't."

"Like what? I don't understand."

Hyde took a step along the wall of the building, sliding just a step closer. She wanted to kick him. Her phone vibrated in her back pocket. She knew exactly who was calling, and she ignored it.

"He requires a blow job. Not just any kind. I don't know how to put this. A certain kind," Shari said.

Seychelle regarded Shari with her most innocent expression. "You think Savage needs a certain kind of blow job?"

She canted her head to one side, her eyes wide with wonder. "I don't know what you're talking about, Shari."

Shari pounced on that triumphantly. "And that's *exactly* why Savage put me up in the hotel and is paying for my room. Because it doesn't matter if he's supposedly with you—you can't give him what he needs." She nodded her head, her eyes boring into Seychelle's. "He comes to my room every night and gets exactly what he wants. That's what I'm trying to tell you. To explain."

"Tell me." Deliberately, Seychelle knitted her brows together.

Shari stepped closer. "You're just a girl. An innocent girl. Savage needs a woman. He wants to fuck your face. Use you. He wants to shove his cock down your throat. He doesn't want to treat you with kid gloves, like you're some little doll that can break if he holds you too hard."

Seychelle forced herself to breathe evenly. She'd started this by engaging with the enemy. She should have just kept walking. The truth was, Savage had never once asked her to give him a blow job. She'd suggested it. Had wanted to. He'd let her stroke him. Touch him. Explore. But he hadn't wanted her to get on her knees and suck his cock, not ever in the months she'd spent with him. She didn't believe he was going to Shari, or that he was paying for Shari's hotel room. He was with her every night, so he couldn't be with Shari. Still, she didn't understand why he didn't want her mouth on him when he'd clearly had other women give him that particular thrill.

She widened her eyes innocently again. "Wow, Shari. I didn't realize just how generous you really are. You're so right. I don't have a clue. Are you volunteering to give demonstrations? Maybe on Brandon? Or better yet, Savage? He'd probably really get off on that, wouldn't he? You could show me. I have some friends that don't have a clue either. We were talking about it the other day, how no one ever tells you anything and you have to learn on your own. You're so absolutely cool. No wonder Savage is paying for your room. Maybe the others could learn too."

Reflected in the window in front of her, she could see Hyde texting away, and she knew Savage wasn't enjoying the conversation as much as Hyde seemed to be. That wasn't going to go over well, if the vibrations coming from her phone were anything to go by.

Shari's first reaction was a dull red flush of sheer anger creeping into her face, her mouth gaping open and closed. She looked at Brandon, who scowled at her and then nodded at Seychelle. Brandon looked like he was going to have some kind of stroke or seizure.

Seychelle's phone vibrated so hard she thought it would shake the flesh off her sore bottom. She slid it out of her back pocket and read the text from Savage. Yeah. She'd been ratted out.

What the fuck are you doing?

Well, I bought a book on learning the true art of giving blow jobs, but it isn't very good. It has pictures, but the instructions aren't clear. Especially the deep-throat parts. I thought while I had an expert available, I might get tips.

That ought to keep him quiet for a few minutes. Snickering to herself, she turned her attention to Shari, who clearly was thinking over her proposition.

"I don't know if Savage would want his little innocent to know all about me," Shari hedged. "The suggestion might have to come from you."

Did you really just tell that hideous woman you wanted her to demo on me in front of you? You aren't going to be able to sit down for a month.

Seychelle wanted to laugh. She couldn't imagine the look on Savage's face, or Hyde's, the little snitch.

She can't be too hideous if you had your cock down her throat. I notice you're overly fond and proud of that particular part of your anatomy. You wouldn't just stick it anywhere into anyone, would you?

Seychelle frowned and pushed a tiny thread of innocence

into her voice to make it all the more believable. She was going to have to end this conversation immediately before it blew up in her face. "Yes, you're right." She glanced at her watch as she shoved her phone in her back pocket. "I'm so late. You've given me so much to think about. Thanks, Shari." She let her gaze slide to Brandon. "I'm so glad the two of you have found each other. Enjoy the beautiful day." With a little wave, she hurried down the street toward the Floating Hat, knowing Hyde, the snitch, was following her.

Her phone vibrated. It wasn't pleasant or gentle. It should have been. It wasn't like the vibration could actually change. It was in her imagination. She tried not to laugh as she considered ignoring his majesty, but she was too intrigued to see what he'd said.

Hyde reached around her to open the door to the shop. The little hats swung, and bells sang merrily. "You're so badass," he commented, as he waved her inside. "And total trouble."

She grinned at him. No one had ever called her *badass* before. She liked it.

She glanced down at the message from Savage. **We're talkin about this when we're home. Stay the fuck away from her. And stop buying books.**

She caught up a basket and began going to the familiar tables to pick up the items she needed. This was her favorite store, and she knew where everything was. But she couldn't resist answering him. She knew better, but she also knew she was driving him crazy.

I did watch a few porn films to learn technique.

She added several items to her basket, moving quickly through the store. Tea. One could never have enough tea, and if she was going back and forth between houses, she would have to stock up at both places.

What the hell? Did you get off?

He was such a perv. She should have known he would ask her that. Sabelia was at the counter checking out a customer, but she looked up and waved. Seychelle waved back.

It depended on the film. That wasn't true. And she wasn't going any further.

You don't need books or porn when you have me to ask. We talked about this. Why didn't you ask me?

He could type so fast. She was *so* not going to tell him that reason. She already felt so inexperienced around him. She bit down on her bottom lip hard. How was she going to answer that? This had gone from fun to suddenly embarrassing, and it was her fault. She'd opened a can of worms. Did she want him to know about her nights alone in her house when she watched over her parents, trying to learn about sex when she felt absolutely nothing at all? Nothing. She was cold. Lifeless. She always felt so dead inside.

Then her dating life. That had been a disaster. Kissing. Ugh. Letting a man touch her? That had been worse. She definitely didn't want that conversation with him. She'd found porn and tried various types, hoping something, *anything*, would appeal to her. That's when she'd discovered what her body responded to. It had been rather humiliating finding out watching a man do certain inappropriate things to a woman made her body come alive.

Savage had discovered those things for himself, or at least, he was discovering them. She still wasn't certain she wanted to know how far she—or at least her body—was willing to go. Her head screamed *no*. Well, that wasn't exactly true either. She was just confused about what she should be feeling. She knew for certain she loved Savage and she wanted to be with him. The rest of it, she still had to work out in her mind. She also knew she couldn't let him consume her, and he would if she didn't stand up to him. Fortunately, Seychelle's nature was simply to go her own way when she wanted. She might be a pleaser, but only to an extent. Then she totally pleased herself.

She was next in line at the counter. "Sabelia, it's so good to see you. How are you?"

"Doing good. You?" Sabelia's gaze jumped from Seychelle to Hyde, who was at the back of the store, seemingly not paying attention, his gaze on his phone.

"Great." Seychelle put the heavy basket on the counter gratefully. "I love this store. Everything about it, especially the way it smells."

Sabelia smiled, a genuine smile, something Seychelle realized was rare. The smile lit up Sabelia's pale face. Her thick black hair had been pulled back into a simple ponytail, taming the wild silk and accenting the beauty of her bone structure.

"I love it too. It's my favorite place to be. I never mind working late hours. Hannah lets me study here. She's the best boss." As if it embarrassed her to admit it, Sabelia began to hastily ring up the items in the basket.

"I don't suppose you're learning any great hexes you can put on a man to scare the crap out of him?" Seychelle asked, mostly to make her laugh. Hannah would lift an eyebrow and ask her what she was referring to. Sabelia would pretend to consider it. "Maybe give me a few lessons." She glanced over her shoulder. Sure enough, the snitch, Hyde, was texting away.

"What kind of hex?" Sabelia asked, a smirk on her face, instantly dispelling her previous embarrassment.

"Remote control for certain body parts." Let Hyde text that one to Savage.

Hyde coughed, and both women immediately acted concerned.

"Would you like a drink? I can get you something very special that will help with that," Sabelia offered solicitously.

Hyde stepped back until he was pressed against the wall, shaking his head. "No, thanks. I'm good."

Seychelle's phone vibrated with alarming force, as if Savage were coming through the very tower to shake it himself. She tried not to laugh. Whatever Hyde was telling him was not going over so well. Between intimidating the prospect with the idea of hexing anyone and needling Savage, she was actually having fun. She took her time pulling her phone from her pocket.

"I don't have a hex for that yet," Sabelia said, "but I've got a pretty good one involving toads I might consider sharing."

"Really?" Toads sounded *way* better than making any mistakes with remote controls. She really wanted to keep Savage's body parts working. "I'm leaving for a few days but would love to talk when I come back."

Sabelia nodded. "You got it. Lana's interested as well. We should get together at her place. No chance of getting interrupted. It would be fun."

Savage wouldn't get upset if she was with Lana. It did sound fun, even if she really didn't learn a thing. Girls' night.

"I'd love that, Sabelia. Thanks." She took the gold, glittery bag with the strong handles off the counter. "I'll be in touch and we can set something up." She glanced down at her phone.

Hyde thinks you're a wildcat. I agree with him. Get away from Sabelia and her hexes now. You're in so much trouble already.

Hyde took the bag from her. She leveled her gaze at him, giving him the stink eye. "You know, you didn't have to rat me out for every little thing."

"Actually, I did. If I didn't tell him, he'd beat the crap out of me. No one wants a beatdown from Savage."

She eyed him for a long time. "Even so, you were having too much fun with the details."

He grinned at her. "Yes, I was. Hell, woman, if anyone can give that man trouble, it's you." He sounded totally pleased. "You look so angelic, who knew you could kick ass and take names. Did you get everything you need?"

She nodded. "Yes, I think that's everything." He dropped the keys to the MINI Cooper into her palm and started toward the driver's door. "Wait, Hyde. I did forget something. I had another package in the Floating Hat. I set it down on the floor when I was talking to Sabelia and was going to tuck it in the larger bag. She packaged the tea separately for me. It will just take a minute."

"It won't. You'll talk to her for an hour. I'll get it. You stay right there."

She wasn't about to leave her designated spot, not with Shari and Brandon on the loose. "I promise. Right here. I'm knee-deep in concrete."

It was a beautiful, glorious day. She spread her arms wide and just basked in the coastal afternoon. The sun had come out and the wind had died down, leaving the sea sparkling like a million jewels had spread across the water. She leaned against her car, smiling, happy she'd had a day just to shop. It occurred to her to text Savage and ask him if she had time to visit a couple of the older people she always kept an eye on, but she really wanted to look good for their date, and she was sore, so she definitely wanted to soak in the bathtub.

"You were the singer in the band the other night, the one with the beautiful voice."

The voice jerked her out of her reverie. It was admiring and a tiny bit familiar. Seychelle straightened and found herself staring into green eyes. It took a minute before she registered where she'd seen him. He was one of the Diamondbacks who sat at the small table near the band when they played. They'd been outside in back when Shari had screamed how Savage belonged to her. The two Diamondbacks had heard everything she'd said.

"Tony Ravard." He held out his hand. "You have a beautiful voice. The next time you're singing, my brother Leonardo wants to hear you sing." He indicated the older man sitting in a pickup truck parked across the street. He looked to be pushing forty. Maybe a little younger. Definitely harder and edgier than Tony, or at least he looked it.

"Seychelle Dubois." She took his hand. What else was there to do? He seemed sincere enough. He was wearing a vest with his colors on it. Jeans, a tee and his vest. He didn't look as if he was there for trouble. His older brother wore

Diamondback colors as well. He didn't get out of the truck, for which she was eternally grateful.

"Heard a rumor you were hooked up with Savage from Torpedo Ink? That true?"

She pulled her hand away from his and studied his face. "Why is everyone suddenly so interested in my dating life?"

Tony's gaze was steady on hers. "Savage has a pretty rough reputation, and I'd say it was earned. Maybe everyone's looking out for you."

She didn't answer him. What was there to say? She didn't want to give these men any advantage over Savage, and she had no idea what they were after.

"You know if he plans on going on the run this weekend with his club? You going with him?" Tony kept watching her, as if he could somehow get her to answer him if he stared at her intently enough.

Seychelle looked beyond him to the building he'd just come out of. A real estate office. She even knew the couple who sold homes and properties. They were a wonderful older husband-and-wife team and very successful at what they did.

"Are you buying a home here?" She was very uncomfortable with the way the conversation was going. She wasn't about to talk about Savage, her relationship with him or anything to do with his club. Fortunately, she really didn't know anything about his club.

"Looking," he said vaguely. "You have an amazing voice. There's something very soothing about it. I almost felt you could reach right into all of us and control our emotions. That's how beautiful your voice is. Torpedo Ink is lucky to have you singing in their band."

Her phone vibrated, and she pulled it from her back pocket. Savage. Of course. She glanced across the street. Hyde was just outside the door of the Floating Hat.

Babe, get in the car. Be casual. Just drive away. Hyde will catch up.

"I'm not sure what to say to that. Thank you for the compliment, but I'm just a regular singer, nothing special. I don't actually sing with the band all the time, just every now and then, when I feel like it. They're unbelievable musicians, and it's a privilege to sing with them." She glanced at her watch. "It was really nice to meet you, Tony, but I've got an appointment I can't miss. I got a little carried away with shopping today and let the time get away from me."

Deliberately, she gave a little laugh and indicated the packages in the back seat of the MINI Cooper, even as she pulled open the door to the driver's seat. Slipping in, she immediately started the car, not wanting to take a chance that Tony might stop her. He looked for a moment like he might step up to the window, but then he backed to the sidewalk. He lifted his head and looked down the street.

As she pulled the MINI Cooper onto the street, she noticed two more Diamondbacks, both in jeans, wearing their cuts. They were on the other side of the Floating Hat. Two others were across the street from the tea shop. Hyde was surrounded and alone. Should she just leave him? She drove up the street and around the corner, where she pulled over.

Hyde is cut off from his bike, surrounded by Diamondbacks. I could go back and do the innocent act, get him into the tea shop or something.

Seychelle found herself holding her breath. She wasn't cut out to be a biker babe. She had absolutely no idea what one did in these circumstances.

Drive on home, Seychelle. Lana and Alena are in town at the moment, and they will handle this. Don't want the Diamondbacks to know you're with us yet.

They were asking questions about us. About the run. Whether I was going with you. He talked a lot about my voice and controlling emotions with it.

For the first time there was a long pause before Savage texted back. **Get home, meaning the big house. A couple of the boys will pick up your protection and I'll meet you there.**

EIGHT

Savage paced back and forth, seriously pissed that he'd let his woman go into town without him. He'd been uneasy from the moment he'd left her. He knew something was wrong. Hell, every member of Torpedo Ink could feel the tension winding tighter between the Diamondback and Venomous clubs, and they were caught in the middle. The Diamondbacks wanted to get something—anything—on Torpedo Ink to make certain they were in their pocket.

Members of the Diamondbacks came to the coast occasionally and checked in with Czar. They frequented the bar with their old ladies on the nights the band played more often than they had before, but they didn't make their presence known in large numbers. They didn't want law enforcement to suddenly sit up and take notice that something might be up, such as a war between two clubs.

Savage really didn't like that Seychelle was anywhere on the Diamondbacks' radar. It was bad enough that Torpedo Ink had to worry about Alena, but now with this new play, he was extremely worried. So was Czar. Neither could figure out what the reason could be.

The comment about her voice controlling emotions had

to have come from Brandon Campbell. No Diamondback would have figured that out on their own. They wouldn't even believe in psychic gifts, and if they did, they wouldn't admit it out loud. He had known from the beginning that Brandon was going to be a vindictive little shit, but Little Miss Trouble just didn't listen to him. She smiled and went her own way. Why was Brandon getting involved, and how had he? He wouldn't just walk up to a Diamondback and give him that kind of information, not without them laughing their asses off at him.

He heard the garage door and motorcycles peeling off, going back up the drive. He glanced down at his phone. His brothers had seen his woman safely home. He listened to doors opening and heard the rustle of bags as she came through the side door carrying the things she'd purchased. He should have gone to help her, but he enjoyed the sounds of her coming home, knowing his woman was in the house.

Her scent drifted into the bedroom. A delicate wild strawberry that settled the tension swirling in his gut. He stood, feet apart, one hand on top of the thick wooden post at the end of the bed. It was solid. His brothers, when they made furniture, always made it solid. There were no half-assed measures. His fingers unerringly found the rings embedded in the wood, deep, nearly impossible to pull out. Definitely no half-assed measures. He didn't have to look to see where the rings were. He knew.

Seychelle came through the doorway, looked up and saw him. Her face lit up. That look. It clawed at him every time. Wrecked him. She put her packages in the corner and smiled at him, her dimple showing, the corners of her mouth turning up in that innocent, genuine smile. The blue in her eyes went sea blue. Sapphire. It was impossible not to see love there. Soft. Shining for him.

"Hi, honey."

He could hear love in her voice, stroking over his skin. His heart clenched hard in his chest. He had never expected to have her.

"Is Hyde all right? I hated to just leave him there."

Seychelle. She would have waded right through the Diamondbacks, uncaring of any danger to herself to help out a man she barely knew. It was no wonder she twisted him up inside.

"He's just fine, baby. Lana and Alena were headed to the tea shop. They took care of it. Acted like they didn't even notice the Diamondbacks until they had Hyde safely on his way. Flirted a little and then went into the shop. No problem."

She started toward him and he held up his hand to stop her. "Strip. Everything off, Seychelle. Then go outside to the verandah facing the bluffs and bend over the rail and wait for me. Have your legs spread wide. Farther than shoulder-width apart."

She halted in the middle of the bedroom floor, looking a little shocked, but at the same time, he could see the flare of excitement in her eyes. It was impossible to hide that from him. He'd seen it that first time in the alley, when he'd taken her cigarettes and he'd spun her around and turned her toward the wall, lifted her skirt and slapped her bottom. She'd obeyed him. She'd let him spank her without calling out for help. And she'd been aroused. He'd known then that she was far too compatible for a man like him. There was no way he was going to be able to resist her.

Seychelle frowned. "I don't understand."

"You understand perfectly. You're just going to add more strikes onto your punishment—and this is a punishment. You're not going to be feeling good after this, baby. You did a lot of bad things today. No more back talk. I suggest you make up your mind to get it over with."

His cock hurt like a son of a bitch. They were leaving early in the morning, and she would have to ride on the bike, something she wasn't that used to. He'd been thinking of ways to make the three days of the run hot as hell for them without being too obvious to anyone outside Torpedo Ink. He didn't want to break the rules Seychelle and he had set up between them, nor did he want her humiliated. Still, to know she was feeling his marks, that he could possess her his way without others knowing what was transpiring between them, promised to heighten their pleasure even more.

Seychelle reached down and unzipped her boots, her gaze darting up to him several times, as if to make certain he meant what he'd said. He didn't look away from her, keeping his gaze both steady and stern. He fucking loved this, and she had to know. He'd told her so many times. He'd warned her every screwup would result in punishment. Hell, he had all sorts of instruments of punishment, most of them to help ease her into his world. He told himself that, but he knew better. She did as well. If her heightened breathing and color were anything to go by, she was nearly as turned on as he was.

She removed her top and bra, spilling her gorgeous tits out into the open. Her hands dropped to her jeans, and she peeled them from her hips and down her thighs, along with her panties. There was only one lone pink stripe on her mound, so faint he could barely make it out. When she turned and walked out of the room, there were a few other faded stripes on her bare cheeks and the backs of her thighs, but they were mostly gone. He'd been careful her first time not to make the session too overwhelming, although he knew it felt that way to her.

This would be a painful reminder to stay the hell away from Campbell, and it had to be. The run could cut their time down to nothing, and Seychelle had to be ready. She was nowhere near that, nowhere near taking what he would have to dish out. He wasn't certain what he would do if time really did run out on them.

Savage didn't follow Seychelle right out onto the main porch for a few reasons. He wanted the cool air to seep into her body. That would heighten every stroke of the cane as it lashed across her flesh. She would worry endlessly about someone driving up and seeing her stretched out naked on their verandah. Every second would seem like an hour to her. He wanted to see if she would stay there waiting for him in spite of what she would perceive as a danger. The longer she was there, the more she would be convinced that someone would come—and she had every reason to worry.

Torpedo Ink members came and went all the time. No one thought to call first. They just showed up. If he was fucking her on the porch, they'd walk right up, either start talking or drop into a chair and put their feet up—unless it was Storm. He'd most likely get himself off. Savage almost wished one of his brothers would show up. Better here at the house than all of them on the run together for her first time.

There were going to be others around them when he fucked her. She'd be naked in front of them. He wanted her to see that others were naked, and no one thought anything about it, but it was better at home, where he could make her feel safe. He thought about texting one or two of the brothers to stop by but thought better of it.

Seychelle was learning about herself—about her body and what she desired sexually. She was confused and trying to accept her darker needs. She really didn't want others witnessing what went on between the two of them. She thought she could handle open sex in front of them, but not his punishments and not his whipping and not the other things he loved to do to her before he fucked her brains out.

Savage took his time changing into his soft drawstring pants that gave his cock ample room to expand before he took his favorite cane out onto the long, wide porch. The view was so much better with his woman draped over the wide railing, her ass in the air, toes barely touching the flooring, her tits mashed on the wooden plank while her head was over the side. Both hands held the decorative spindles tightly.

He stepped close and rubbed her bare cheeks. Her skin was cool, but heat came off her pussy in waves. She was slick, glistening with moisture. He ran his finger through her tight little slit and licked at the strawberry-scented cream.

"Guess you like the thought of your punishment, Seychelle. Were you out here thinking of all the things you did wrong?"

"I was speeding."

He continued to rub her bottom. His gaze went to her face. Her eyes. She was watching the drive just as he knew she would be. She was more worried about someone coming to the house than she was about her punishment. "You were. And you weren't paying attention to the lanes either, were you?"

She swung her head, trying to push back, looking indignant, but he held her down with a hand between her shoulder blades. "What was the one thing you did that you really know you shouldn't have been doing?"

He continued rubbing her bare cheeks, this time dipping his fingers into her heat to idly paint the liquid between her cheeks, back and forth in a mesmerizing glide.

Seychelle hesitated, her head dropping straight down, eyes turning toward the ground below them. A whistle was the only warning heralding the cane as it arced through the sky and then across her pretty little upturned ass. He knew exactly what that felt like. At first, nothing. Then a line of fire lighting up her world. It was never that first line of fire that really hurt, but the second wave as the burst of agony registered with the tissue and muscle beneath the skin.

He'd gone easy on her, careful of how much strength he'd put into his swing. She let out a wail, but she didn't try to move away from the railing. His heart pounded, went into overdrive. Every single day, he knew Seychelle had been made for him. He rubbed her cheeks, ran his nail over that stripe, adding to the fire. This one she might feel tomorrow, although it was fairly light. Any other stripes he put there he would make certain she felt but wouldn't last long on her skin. Not yet. This was new, and he didn't want the effects to last too long.

"I asked you a question." Voice still low. Almost a caress. He could see the goose bumps on her skin, the endorphins rising. She liked this. She hated it. She loved it. She was confused as hell. Just to make certain, he let his hand dip low and brushed her clit, circled, played, flicked. "Answer me."

"Brandon was there, and you didn't want me to go near him."

"Why?"

Again, there was that small hesitation. He didn't hesitate, and this time the whistle was much more pronounced, and the line of fire rose precisely on her sit spot, just above the line he'd just raised, so the two stripes touched. This one went from white to a fiery red, a bright line of sheer agony. He landed two more just like it in rapid succession, one just above the next so there was no space in between, yet he was careful he didn't repeat in the same place twice.

She sobbed. A real sob. Real tears. He knew the difference. She didn't try to cover up, and she didn't pull away. He immediately rubbed her sore bottom, his blood roaring through his veins, pounding through his cock, demanding more. Needing it now.

Savage gathered her hair in his hand and pulled her head up, needing to see her eyes. They were beautiful, liquid with tears. His tears. He took them, drinking them down, grateful to whoever had given her to him. Her eyes were soft with remorse yet filled with determination. She wanted to do this. He kissed her. He shouldn't, but he was proud of her courage, and they made their own rules.

"Why can't you go near Brandon, Seychelle?" he asked, gently letting her head down. He put his hand on her nape and let it drift down her back as he once more positioned himself in the best line to punish her.

"Every time he hears me use my voice to counter his, it's possible he can find a way to use that against me in the same way I can stop him from using his voice," she admitted with great reluctance.

His breath caught in his throat, and fear swirled in his gut. He knew the little bastard was dangerous to Seychelle, but only because he was a vengeful little worm and he would be plotting to get her back in some way. Savage hadn't known, hadn't even considered, that the man might be able to use Seychelle's voice against her in some way.

She *knew* that, and yet she'd deliberately used her voice in front of him to counter his commands to Doris and to Tessa. Twice. It was no wonder Campbell was after her. And somehow the little bastard had a connection to the Diamondbacks.

Savage took several deep breaths. He wasn't going to chance being out of control when he punished her, especially when she was being so brave and working her way into his world. "You deserve a hell of a lot of punishment for not informing me of the scope of danger he represented to you, but also for disobeying and talking to him."

"I know, Savage, I'm sorry. I really am." She sounded very sincere.

"I'm going to give you ten strikes with the cane, Seychelle. You aren't going to be very comfortable on our date tonight, but you earned every one of these. If you can't take it, what do you say?"

"You said I couldn't stop a punishment, Savage."

"Not when you aren't used to a cane, baby. I'm training you as I punish you. What's the word to stop this if you can't take it?"

"Red."

"You say it if it's too much. Don't hold out to please me."

"I'll say it." Her voice was small. Too small. She sounded scared.

"And remember the rules. No screaming. You cry all you want, but no screaming. You only do that when you're climaxing." He ran his palm down her spine gently, just to give her courage. His woman. Giving her that connection. "Don't tense up. Let the pain take you. Give into it. Surrender to it."

The cane whistled as he put a fraction more force into it, the sound a kind of music all on its own. The round rattan-filled stick slashed across her perfect bottom, leaving another much tighter line. The second and third followed immediately, almost right on top, before she could even register the fiery agony the cane could produce.

Seychelle's left leg kicked up, but she pressed her toes back to the floor of the porch, her sobs softer than they had been with the warm-up round he'd given her.

"You're doing so good, baby." He pressed two fingers into her tight, slick heat and fucked her for a moment while his thumb stroked her clit. Pulling his fingers out, he licked them clean. "You taste so damn good."

Three more strikes fell in rapid succession. He laid them out, descending toward the bottom of her round cheeks. Each should have been a little harder, but he kept them the same. The cane was one of his shortest and easily controlled, but he knew that even though he was using a lighter stroke, it burned like hell. The seventh strike had the most force so far, and he landed it just under her buttocks. She cried out and instantly jammed her fist in her mouth to muffle the sound.

"Good girl," he praised her. He didn't wait. Eight and nine landed up high on the back of her thighs. Ten was right across her sit spot again, the hardest yet.

He dropped the cane and used both hands to rub the dark, angry marks. They were incredibly arousing to him.

"Savage." There was an ache in her voice, even as she was crying. "I need . . ." She broke off.

He waited, but she didn't say it. She didn't ask him. He crouched down to use his mouth, catching the wild taste of strawberry honey that belonged to him. "You're so fucking wet, baby. You need me, don't you?" He sucked at her clit and then flicked at it with his tongue. "So needy. You loved the cane. Now you need my cock, don't you?"

Her breath hitched. She pushed her dripping pussy into his face. Her bottom was blazing hot. Striped for him. "Please, Savage. You have to . . ." She broke off again, another sob interrupting. "I know not with a punishment, but . . ."

He stood again, stroking his aching cock. He was so full

he was afraid he might burst just looking at her bent over the rail, her fiery bottom presented to him. "Tell me what you need, baby. Anything. I'll give it to you."

"Savage." Breathy. A plea. A little sob.

He hated waiting. He lodged the broad head of his cock into the tight slick opening but refused to move. She had to be the one. He couldn't take it further. She had to ask him. He was losing his mind, but the taking would be all the sweeter. He knew that. He rubbed those stripes, the ones darkening by the moment. Ran his fingernails over them even as he rocked his body gently.

"You have to fuck me. I can't stand it." The plea came out in a little rush. "Hard, Savage. You have to fuck me hard."

He caught her hips and drove into her just the way she asked him to, burying himself to the hilt. He was a big man and strong. Her silken sheath reluctantly gave way, seizing his cock, the friction so good he threw back his head and roared as he took her, his body hammering into hers over and over. That scorching-hot fist of silk twisted around his cock, grasping at him, a merciless vise that sent jolts of lightning up his spine.

Her breath came out in little raspy cries that tore at his heart when his body was going up in flames. She was burning him from the inside out, not just his cock but every fucking organ he had, including his heart and soul. She lit them on fire, detonated them, so they blew apart like bombs, scattering pieces of him everywhere.

Looking at the stripes his cane had put on her made him hard as fucking titanium, but she melted him inside. Turned him into some kind of melting pussy instead of the sadistic asshole he knew he was. He bent his head before he could stop himself and pressed kisses down her spine while her scorching sheath drummed with her heartbeat, surrounding his cock with a ring of pure fire.

"Baby." He breathed against her striped skin. "I love you. Fucking love you so damn much."

It was heaven and hell to see those dark purple lines

across her cheeks. His cock was a fierce piston that drove into her like a relentless, powerful machine. Every slap of their bodies coming together only incited him more. That rush. The euphoria. The feeling of absolute control and dominance. He fisted her hair and pulled her head back, forcing her to arch her back while he worked her body.

She came on his cock over and over, crying out. Calling his name. Her body desperately trying to steal the seed from his. He forced control on himself, not wanting to leave the paradise that was her body, not when he had this. But then the tsunami struck, overtaking her in a series of powerful waves so that her sheath clamped down like a vise, strangling his cock, ecstasy and hell, forcing ropes of semen from him. Long, jerking pulses that rocked him, that sent shock waves through him, flinging him to that place only she could take him.

He stood for a while on rubbery legs, bent over her, wondering how they were both still alive. He had no idea how long it took to register the sound of the waves hitting the sea stacks or his own wild heartbeat. He felt her shudder when he pulled out of her very gently. He felt like shuddering himself, his cock was that sensitive. Unheard of for him.

Savage waited another heartbeat before he managed to pull the drawstring pants up, and then he reached for her, getting an arm under her knees and around her back to lift her. He cradled her in his arms, but this time Seychelle didn't curl into him as he carried her into the house. She didn't link her arms around his neck or nestle her head on his shoulder the way she had every other time she needed comfort. He could lose her. He'd known this time would come. It was inevitable. She was bound to be confused, embarrassed, even humiliated that she could find sex so pleasurable mixed with pain.

She'd recognized early that she had a dark side but had never considered that she could go as far as Savage was taking her. She also knew it wasn't nearly as far as they needed to go, and she was scared. She was afraid of herself, and she was afraid of him. She had reason to be. She had been slowly building up to this moment, terrified of what was inside her, trying to work it out but unable to reconcile who she thought she should be with who she was becoming.

Tears ran down her face, but she tried to be very quiet, to keep the fact that she was crying from him. He carried her straight through the house to their bed, and instead of putting her down, he sank onto the bed, holding her in his lap.

"Look at me, baby."

She shook her head. "I can't, Savage. Not yet."

"We're in this together, remember?" He kissed her neck and then the shell of her ear. "We can do this if we're together. We can figure anything out. You never put judgment on me. I don't put it on you. Look at me, Seychelle. Please."

A little of the tension eased out of her body, and one of her hands, the one in her lap, curled over his biceps. Her fingers shook a little, but at least she reached out to him. Her head turned, and he was looking into her liquid eyes.

"You're so fuckin' brave, woman. I know this scares you, baby, and yet you still hang in there with me." He brushed several gentle kisses on her lips. Asking nothing from her. Giving comfort. Needing her to relax into him. "I want you to listen to me very carefully. I mean every single word I say to you. I love you with everything in me. Just as you are. Exactly as you are. I'm taking you down this path, baby, but you don't have to go any further. We're good right here. Or we can back the hell up to where you're more comfortable. I'll be fine with that."

She frowned and shook her head. "Savage." A little protest. Weak. Resisting him but not really.

He had no idea what he was going to do when the bad times came, but he wasn't going to have his woman ashamed or hating herself. He knew what that was like. He loved her and wanted her happy. Being confused was one thing, ashamed was something altogether different.

"I'm a fuckin' sexual sadist, baby. That's what I am. I'm always going to be that, so I'm always going to look for the next level. A little pain turns you on, and that's a good thing for us, but this is my thing, not yours. We both know that."

He brushed his lips over hers several times more and then took the tears from her face, his belly in knots. He wanted her tears, but not from shame. Not from humiliation. Not unless she wanted that kind of thrill, which Seychelle wasn't into, and quite frankly it didn't do a damn thing for him, but he'd give her whatever the hell she wanted if it brought her pleasure.

"I think pain is my thing, Savage, and it scares me. It really does. I don't understand it at all. How could I like it? It hurt like hell at first. It was pure agony. Excruciating. I wanted to stay still so I could do it for you. I really love taking the pain for you. Seeing you get excited. It makes me feel . . ." She broke off. "But then suddenly something else happened. I suddenly was so turned on it was sick."

"Babe, I was manipulating you. Using my voice, my hands. That's what I do. I'm training you to like what I do to you, to confuse your body so you associate pain and pleasure together. You reacted exactly the way you were supposed to react."

She nestled into him. "I was already slick and feeling desperate for you."

She made the confession in a low voice, but she didn't look away from him. That was good. Her trust in him was back. He held her close to him, brushing soothing kisses along her cheek and shoulder.

"Because you were taking the cane for me. You could see how hard you made me, Seychelle. I made certain you knew you were pleasing me. You need to please me. That's part of your personality. A good part of it. Don't you think I know that? That I take advantage of that when I'm training you?"

"I wanted you to cane me. With each strike the craving got worse and I became even more frantic for you to fuck me. I thought I might die if you didn't. But it doesn't make sense when there was so much pain involved."

He stroked caresses over her hair, feeling like a dick.

How could he get her to understand what he did? He'd grown up doing this shit for years. *Years.* There might be a few better at it than him, but he doubted it. Was he going to be less than brilliant with the woman he loved? He was going to make damn sure she felt as much or more pleasure than he did, especially when she was taking a fucking cane or the lash for him.

"Seychelle, you're supposed to feel that way for me. Think about what I was doing to your body between every few strikes. I made certain you not only saw and felt what you were doing to me, but I kept you slick, kept you wanting me. I made certain you needed my cock and your body didn't know the difference between pain and pleasure. That's what training you to like pain and pleasure together does. It confuses your mind and body."

Her lashes swept down, and then she looked at him again. He could tell it was very difficult for her to meet his gaze. "I used to watch porn like that, and it was the only thing that would excite me." Fresh tears flooded her eyes as she made the confession in a small voice.

He could tell she was at her limit with looking at him while she admitted what she considered were her sins. He brushed more kisses over her lips, because she had no idea what true sins were.

"I need to put lotion on those stripes, baby, or you won't be sitting at dinner tonight. I'm going to put you down on your tummy, but we're still going to talk about this. Remember, it's just the two of us. Only the two of us, and we can say anything to each other. I tell you the most outrageous things. And I expect you to tell me your every fantasy. I want to know just what porn films you watched and what turned you on."

He set her off his lap gently, taking care not to put her down on her bottom. He had plans later to let those marks flare back into life, but not now. Now she needed care and to be surrounded by love. He reached for the lotion he kept beneath the bed.

"Just because you watch a porn flick and it turns you on, doesn't mean you want that particular fantasy to play out for real. You know that, right?" He was gentle as he rubbed the lotion into his marks on her round cheeks. The stripes had gone from bright red to a deep, beautiful dark red.

"Why would seeing it turn me on though?"

"Did you get off?"

There was a brief hesitation. "No. I bought that stupid toy. I told you, nothing worked until you came along. But I was aroused. Briefly."

He liked that nothing worked to get her off until he came along. He'd given her a lot of firsts. He was particularly gentle rubbing the lotion along the dark red over her sit spot. That was going to really be something while she rode behind him on the motorcycle. It was several hours with the vibration running up her legs and delivering a jolt of awareness along every nerve ending.

Savage bent his head and pressed kisses to the small of her back. "That should tell you something right there, Seychelle. You like a little bit of pain mixed with pleasure, but it isn't the same as wanting to please the man you love. I'm taking you on a dark path, and you're going down it because you know I need it. You're doing it for me. But you always have to remember we're a team. We have to be. Spread your legs for me, baby." The command was low, a velvet rasp. He was going to have to make a confession he'd made before, but she hadn't really been listening. She needed to hear him. She needed to believe him.

Savage rubbed the lotion on the vicious stripes the cane had put on the undersides of her cheeks. "These welts should make a man who loves a woman feel sick when he sees them on her body. When I see them, I feel a rush that's unbelievable. It's all mixed together. Love, unbelievable lust, control, power, dominance, all those things. I get so fucking hard and want to own you. Every single inch of your body. Your heart. Your soul. I want to know you'd sacrifice anything for

me. That every tear you shed, you shed gladly for me. That's
a gift you give me, and it's greater than anything else you
could ever hand to me. That's your love right there on your
face. Open and raw. Real. For me."

He bent his head and kissed the small of her back again,
and this time he lazily ran his nails very lightly down her
left cheek. Her body shuddered. With his other hand, he
cupped her sex, his finger circling her clit, then slipping into
her heat to curl against the sensitive spot on her wall while
his thumb strummed her clit. She was already getting slick
for him. Just talking about what he needed, just that little bit
of fire streaking through her.

"I do love you, Savage. I want to give you what you
need," she confessed, a little hitch in her voice.

"I know you do, baby, and that's good." He removed his
hand and licked hungrily at his fingers. She tasted like
heaven to him. He knew he was never going to get enough
of her in his lifetime. "But the thing is, we both have to remember that I have an addiction. I'm always going to be a
sexual sadist. I'm always going to want to push for more if
you let me. You have to be the one to put the brakes on. I
don't want you to get addicted too. We both can't go down
too dark a path. We can keep things good. It will get bad
when I cycle to the worst phase, and you'll have to rein me
in. When we're training or having sex, you don't go any
further than you want to go. When I'm at my worst, I'm
counting on you to stop me. I'm *counting* on you. I swear to
you, Seychelle, if I ever hurt you, I'll fucking put a bullet in
my head. That's the consequences of me going too far.
You're strong-willed. You want to please me, but you can
stand up to me or anyone else when you want to. Do you
understand what I'm saying to you? This isn't a game we're
playing here. This is our life together. You're a full partici-
pant. We do this together."

She turned her head. He could see one eye looking at him
through a fall of silky hair as she lay there quietly. He con-

tinued to rub the lotion into the welts on her upper thighs. "I'm strong enough, Savage. I do listen to you, whether or not you think I do."

"When I'm at my worst, I'll be at my most manipulative. I'll work your body until you're drenched. Until you'll beg me to fuck you any way, anywhere I want to. You'll be scared, and that will be part of the rush for me. All that power. All that dominance. I crave that shit, Seychelle."

He had to warn her. He needed her to hear him. He had to make her understand that if it was really going to be the two of them, she would have to handle the danger to them. If he hurt her, he really would kill himself. He'd never take that chance again. Never.

"I'm well aware." There was just the faintest trace of a smile, the flash of her dimple. "I study people, Savage. I read them. Do you think I wouldn't read my man? Every inflection? Every expression?"

"I don't have expressions. Stopped that shit when I was a kid and didn't want the fuckers torturing me to know it hurt. Wanted them to think I was a fucking psycho. I think I became one."

"No, you didn't, silly."

She sounded sleepy. He might have to carry her to the shower later, but she could have a small nap. He moved up the mattress beside her and wrapped his arm around her waist. "What got you the wettest when you were watching those porn flicks, baby?"

"I'm not telling you. You'll only use it against me."

"You like it when I torment you."

"Not so much anymore. I *used* to like it. Now I end up with a sore bottom."

He smiled. He couldn't help it. Her voice was low and sexy, although she didn't mean it that way. She meant to be sulky. Seychelle wasn't a sulky person. She had her head turned away from him. He nuzzled her neck and scraped his teeth back and forth, waiting for the goose bumps to come up on her sensitive skin before kissing his way up to her ear.

Placing his lips over her ear, he nibbled on her lobe and then licked.

"Your bottom could be a lot sorer if I spanked you for not answering me, now, couldn't it?" he whispered.

"If you did that, I wouldn't be able to go out to dinner with you and your friends."

Little Miss Sass with the smart comeback. He couldn't help smiling. She made his life fun when before, it had been nothing but a dark pit of rage.

"You would come with me. If you can't sit down, it's because you chose to put yourself in a position of getting punished." His teeth tugged at her earlobe. "They'd understand. Maybe not Blythe. She'd spend the evening sneaking you worried looks and giving me murderous ones. Then, when they went home, she would give Czar absolute hell." He sounded pleased because the idea of it was gratifying. "I'd like that, baby." He reached a hand down and rubbed her bare cheeks. Gently, but hard enough to let her know his hand was there.

"You really are the devil, aren't you? I'm not giving you a reason to spank me. I can't imagine how I'm going to walk straight tonight, let alone sit."

That made him laugh. "Then you have to tell me which porn made you the wettest. I'm getting turned on just trying to guess."

She gave him her grumpy sigh but didn't turn her head, refusing to look at him when he really wanted her to. "That doesn't surprise me. Everything turns you on, especially when it comes to me and dirty, kinky sex."

"We haven't actually done the dirty, kinky sex you like yet because you haven't asked me for it, Seychelle. You were supposed to ask, remember? I ask you for what I want, and you ask me for what you want."

He rubbed her back, right between her shoulder blades, because she was beginning to tense up a little at the idea of disclosing to him what kind of sexual acts had aroused her when she watched them.

"I'm not asking for this at all," she said, her voice muffled by the comforter, but there was just a trace of excitement there.

Savage slid his hand down her spine, massaging gently, rolling over those marks that proclaimed she was his. Her legs were already spread, but the moment his palm was on her bare cheeks, she shifted, spreading her legs even wider to accommodate his exploring fingers. His smile was wicked. He felt wicked as he cupped her sex. She was slick. He began a slow, intimate massage designed to smolder. Burn slow. Take embers and fan them. Make them into roaring, leaping flames.

"There were two that were crazy. Both were outdoors. I don't know if the outdoor thing was part of it, you know, the cool weather, maybe someone coming up on you, sun setting behind you, I don't know, but both were pretty cool settings. One, the girl was naked, and she'd just gotten out of a hot tub, so she was damp—you could see the little beads of water running off her skin. He tied her spread-eagled, faceup on this lounge similar to the couch you have in our bedroom, with rings everywhere. Her legs were split so wide open and her arms were very wide apart. He had a crop. The crop was leather, and the end was flat like a tongue."

"I am familiar with a crop, baby," he assured her.

"He began hitting her with it very hard, on her breasts and nipples, over and over until she was screaming. He began spanking her . . . um . . . down there."

"Pussy," he supplied. She was so wet. Drenched. He plunged two fingers deep and her silken muscles were so tight they tried to strangle him, tried to drag him in and milk him. Yeah, she liked the idea, although she was afraid of it. "He spanked her pussy with the crop."

"Yes. Until she came. And she did."

"The second one?" he pushed while she blissfully rode his fingers. She was drifting on a sea of bliss, heading toward an orgasm. He pulled back, pressing hard on her clit to stop her. "The second one, Seychelle. Tell me." He slid his fingers between her cheeks, painting until that sweet, tight little star was just as slick as her pussy. He began to put pressure there.

Seychelle tensed. Resisted. He smacked her bare ass right over the darkest red streaks, bringing those fires to roaring. She hissed at him, her hips bucking hard, driving his finger deeper into her. He pushed two fingers into her pussy and pumped, using all three in rhythm.

"The second was outdoors, and it was more in the woods, like out back with the trees. She was naked, but he wasn't. He put clamps on her and then a plug of some kind."

Her voice shook. Her body shuddered. She was close. Savage brushed her clit with his thumb. Strumming. Pumping. He bent down and kissed his way over her flaming cheeks, those dark lines that belonged to him. That excited him. That had every cell in his body roaring with life.

"He told her he had cut a switch for her and to get it. She did, and then she stood with her front to this tree and he switched her with that thin branch on one side and then she had to turn around and he pulled off the clamps. I could tell it hurt. Then he switched her on her front. I could hear others in the background and so could she, somewhere in the woods, and she stayed very quiet so they wouldn't hear. Then he had her turn around again, bend over, and he took her right there, in the open."

She talked very fast. All the while her hips rocked to his fingers, riding them, back and forth between the ones in her pussy and ass, his thumb giving her inflamed clit what she needed, driving her higher and higher. He used his fingernails, tracing those dark red lines so they came alive under her skin, pushing that fiery pain right into the building pleasure like a heat-seeking missile. She came apart for him, crying out his name, her silken muscles clamping down hard and then rippling over and over.

He eased her through the powerful orgasm, soothing her

with his voice. With his hands. With everything he was. He whispered he loved her against the small of her back. Kissed his way up her spine to her nape and then whispered he loved her there as well.

"Don't ever think I don't love you, Seychelle, or that I don't know the sacrifice you're making to be with me. I don't want you to ever feel shame. I had to come to terms with what they made me into. I don't want that for you. I don't want this life for you, not at that cost."

"I'm going to have moments of doubt, Savage." She sounded sleepy. Exhausted. "Not of my commitment to you or to us, but of understanding why I can like what is happening to my body or how far I want to take it. You have to give me that. You can't think, when it happens, that I'm pulling away from us. I told you I was in this with you."

"You won't sell your fucking house." He knew he sounded like a sulky child.

She didn't open her eyes, but she laughed. That laugh. That got to him every damn time. He slid up onto the bed as close to her as he could get, pulling her into his side, his arm tight around her waist. "Sleep for a little while. I'll wake you up when you need to shower and get ready."

He needed to find a couple of enemies of Torpedo Ink and spend time slicing them up just to find some balance. He didn't even know who the hell he was anymore. She was making him soft inside. Either that or making him worse. He couldn't be certain which it was, because he knew if anyone laid a hand on her, they were going to die a slow, agonizing death.

"Savage?"

"Right here, baby." He tugged at her hair. Her voice sounded so damn drowsy. Sexy. Wrapping him up in something he'd never had.

"Stop thinking about torturing people. Think about kissing me. I want to go to sleep with that in my mind."

There was that little hint of laughter in her voice again.

Shit. Now she was making his fucking dick hard. Again. Not that it had ever relaxed. "Stop making me worry that someone is going to try to take you away from me." He bit her shoulder and lay still, doing his best to think about kissing her without getting so hard he'd have to get himself off right there, all over those dark stripes that marked her as his.

NINE

"I had no idea the restaurant was so nice," Seychelle said. "I've never actually been inside of it."

"Why not?" Savage asked, guiding her around the tables in the dim lights like he knew the place intimately—which he did. Hell, he'd helped put it together for Alena. Master, Player, Maestro and Keys had done most of the plumbing, electrical and woodwork, but the rest of the members of Torpedo Ink had done the grunt work. The club was damn proud of it too. Proud of Alena. Crow 287 was a cut above most restaurants due to the fact that the main chef was a cut above most chefs.

"I mostly stayed in Sea Haven with my little group of seniors unless I was singing. It was always a bit of a risk to go anywhere for a prolonged length of time in public. And who would I go out to dinner with, Savage? Especially to a place as nice as this?"

She was wearing a beautiful turquoise dress, one that accented her glowing skin and brought out the color of her eyes. He knew she'd chosen the dress because her little bottom was too sore to have jeans rubbing tightly against it.

After she'd showered, he'd rubbed numbing lotion into those stripes, giving her some relief, but the cane could cause muscles to ache deep inside, not just on the surface. He'd been careful not to put too much strength in his strikes, but she'd felt every one of them.

Seychelle hadn't complained. Not once. She never did. She just looked at him with love in her eyes and, sometimes, that laughter that got him going. Other times it was the slight hint of a mixture of complete calm and the little chin lift that told him his little angel was going to give him trouble. She was going her own way regardless of how much trouble she might get into. He loved that about her too—unless her safety was in jeopardy.

He led her to the "back room," which was really more of a space behind an arched doorway kept open most of the time. It was normally reserved for Torpedo Ink if they were going to meet together to eat. Sometimes Alena had smaller tables set up for locals who hadn't been able to get in, or special parties. Czar was joining them with Blythe at Savage's request. He'd asked Steele, the VP of Torpedo Ink, and Breezy, his wife, to come along as well. Not only did Seychelle deserve a nice outing, but so did Breezy and Blythe. Both had kids, and evenings out were rare.

Savage really wanted Seychelle to become comfortable around the others and to feel as if she had friends of her own. Blythe was sacred to all members of the club, level-headed and calm in any situation. She was accepting and nonjudgmental, although he doubted she knew about his need to put stripes on his fiancé's beautiful, round ass.

Breezy was born into the life. Another club, the Swords, which treated women as property, had been a nightmare for her to grow up in. She'd nearly lost her life and Steele's son before Torpedo Ink had been able to rescue the child. Savage hoped Breezy would be able to help Seychelle maneuver her way through the rules of club life.

He knew Seychelle had hoped Ice and Soleil were joining

them, but the couple was busy. Ice had a jewelry order he had to fill, and his wife was helping him. He hoped Seychelle would enjoy meeting Breezy.

Savage pulled out a chair for Seychelle. He'd called ahead and asked Alena to use chairs at the table with thicker padding covering the seats. He knew she had them. She didn't always use them, preferring the plainer wooden ones, as they were beautiful and easier to keep clean.

Seychelle settled carefully onto the chair he held out for her and glanced up at him with a rueful little frown. "I think this one is going to linger a little longer than anything else you've ever done."

He couldn't help smirking. "Good. You'll remember to keep far away from Brandon Campbell, won't you? You're going to really love riding on the motorcycle, baby. It's a long trip. In tight jeans, rubbing over your sweet little pussy and your sore ass, we might not have to think too hard about how we're going to get things stirred up. That's going to be a constant reminder to keep away from that asshole."

"Very funny." She squirmed a little in the chair.

Savage couldn't tell if the thought turned her on or made her uncomfortable. She was frowning again. Thinking. Deciding whether or not to tell him what was on her mind.

He glanced at his watch. The others would be arriving any minute. If she had something she needed to get off her chest, she'd better get to it. Darby came in with a fresh loaf of hot bread as well as breadsticks. She greeted both of them cheerfully and then hurried off.

"Savage." Seychelle slathered butter on a piece of the bread, her gaze carefully avoiding his. "I've really been giving a lot of thought to this run the club is making tomorrow." She took a small bite of the bread and started chewing as if her life depended on it.

She kept avoiding his eyes, although she was very smooth about it, concentrating on adding more butter to her bread since the slice was so warm the butter was melting fast. Savage waited her out. She thought she was safe, sitting there looking innocent and sweet, the way she did. His little angel, as if he hadn't known all along his Torpedo Ink sisters had scared the holy hell out of her and she'd made up her mind not to go with him. They'd had this conversation more than once. As far as he was concerned, it was over. Not to mention, Czar had specifically decreed that Seychelle needed to go. He'd never done that with an old lady before. Czar knew things, and it made Savage uneasy that the president of their club had been so adamant that Seychelle attend the run when all of them knew things could go to shit very fast.

She sighed. "I think it would be better if just this once, I stayed behind. It would give me more time to feel as if I fit in. I could learn the rules and get to know everyone. We'd have our rhythm down better. I wouldn't always feel as if I was out of sync."

He waited in silence. She tried the ploy of taking another bite of bread, of chewing, but he didn't budge. Finally, she heaved another sigh and lifted her long lashes and looked at him.

"Already told you, babe, not leaving you behind. Told you the rules when we go on a run. You don't leave my side unless I put you somewhere, and then you stay there until I come get you. You do exactly what I say, when I say. I don't think that's so fuckin' hard to follow. You fit with me. You don't have to fit with anyone else."

She was quiet another minute, but she'd given him that little chin lift that always made him want to smile, definitely made his palm twitch and cock ache. His little rebel was about to make her point.

"With that many people around, someone is bound to be ill, Savage. You know what I mean. A serious illness. I won't be able to help myself. I'm a healer. I won't even know I'm trying until I'm doing it, and it's always an exchange. You'll be angry and I'll be sick, and then what?"

"We already talked about this, Seychelle. You're at my side. The moment you feel someone is ill, you tell me, and I get you out of there. I've told the band members, and they know to get you out of there. The club will surround you any time we're out in a crowd. I've thought about how to handle it."

"I thought we established that we had a partnership, Savage. That means we talk things out. You can't just decree something, and I do it."

"We set the rules down first thing, baby. I told you there were certain things I needed from you, and you agreed to that. But, just because you seem to think this is important, I'll tell you why you need to come with me. You're a runner, Seychelle. You hide from life. You know you do. You stay in your little house, locked up safe, until you can't stand it anymore, and then you go out looking for something wild and crazy to do that could get you in real trouble. You had a genuine stalker in Joseph Arnold. Just because that wasn't bad enough, you've got Brandon Campbell fixated on you. I have no idea who else might have you on their radar, but you just go through life, making an appearance, doing something crazy and then hiding yourself away again."

Color swept up her neck into her face. "What's that got to do with anything?"

"Babe. Really? You're impulsive. A fighter at all the wrong times. You'd take on anyone if they were hurting someone else, but I'm not certain you'd fight that hard to protect yourself. You can't stop yourself when someone is really ill from trying to heal them. Angel, you're a fuckin' mess without me."

That little intriguing dimple that sometimes made an appearance showed for a few seconds and then was gone. Her lashes had veiled her vivid blue eyes, and then she was looking directly at him. There was stark, raw love staring at him. His heart clenched hard in his chest. So damn hard he thought it was possible he was having a heart attack. Could someone love a woman that much?

"Those are not legitimate reasons for me to go on a run with you when I'm terrified I'll do something wrong and you'll be the one to get hurt because of it, Savage." She reached for his hand. Her fingers were actually trembling. "I hate making mistakes. I know this isn't just about fun. I know something big is up."

"Those fucking sisters of mine. I should kick their asses for scaring you."

"It isn't their fault. The entire club thing scares me. I have to get used to *our* life first before I take on club life. It's all so overwhelming."

Savage closed his fingers around hers, his thumb sliding over the back of her hand in soothing caresses to reassure her. "Seychelle, I want you to seriously hear me on this. I am Torpedo Ink. I am the club. You have to trust me to take care of you, baby. I know this scares you, but I swear to you, you just look to me and I'll let you know what to do. The others will too, but it's really me you have to trust."

He brought her hand to his mouth and nibbled on the ends of her fingers and then bit down slowly, watching her eyes go wide. Her lips parted, but she didn't protest. Her breath came out in a long rush, and she squirmed a little on her chair. He sucked her fingers into the warmth of his mouth to ease the sting.

"You're so used to being alone all the time, Seychelle, but you have a family now. If we had the time, we could get married, and you'd have a little more confidence."

She burst out laughing, that dimple of hers making an appearance, just like he knew it would. "Are you crazy? I'm already so overwhelmed, and you're already so damn bossy, the last thing I need is to be your wife. I'm rethinking that part of our arrangement."

Steele and Breezy arrived, Breezy taking the chair nearest the wall, Steele sitting across from her. He smiled at Seychelle. "Sorry we're late. We got the boy down, no problem, but Breezy changed three times before we got out of the house. She seems to have a difficult time making up her mind what she wants to wear when we're going out."

"Why don't you just choose for her?" Savage asked.

"Yeah, baby, why don't I do that?" Steele nudged his wife.

Breezy giggled. Actually giggled. "There were extenuating circumstances. Every time I put something on, Steele seems to need to take it off, sometimes quite aggressively."

"See," Seychelle said, pointing one finger she managed to get out of Savage's grip at him. "There you go with your *why don't you choose for her?* advice. You would choose for me if I decided I didn't like something at the last minute and annoyed you by changing."

"Babe. Really? If I wanted you to wear something for the evening, I'd just ask you to and you would."

"I might not."

She gave him her chin. He wanted to pull her across his knee right there, she was so fuckin' cute.

"Yeah, you would. And now we're havin' one of those absurd conversations we get into that I'm never certain how we got there."

Czar and Blythe arrived. Czar pulled back the chair beside Seychelle for Blythe and then took the one next to Savage.

After greeting them, Seychelle turned to Breezy. "What do you think? Are men bossier after you marry them?"

Steele laughed. "Was I bossier before or after we got married, baby?" He nudged Breezy's shoulder.

She gave her contagious giggle again. "You've been bossy since the day I met you, but yeah, you got bossier after we got married. For sure."

"Definitely bossier after you get married," Blythe weighed in.

"What the hell, woman?" Czar asked, not even trying to hide his grin. "I am the epitome of a politically correct partner. I believe in equality all the way."

Blythe rolled her eyes. "You're the epitome of bullshit right now, and lightning is going to strike you any minute. Why are we wondering about our men being bossy after marriage?"

"I'm considering my options," Seychelle said. "Long engagements are making more and more sense to me. Perhaps even so long they last until I'm like in my nineties with this one."

Blythe nodded solemnly. "I concur. Especially since Savage is so completely wrong over so many things. Think about it, Seychelle." She leaned close. "He doesn't even like tea. Imagine first thing in the morning when you're *dying* for a cup of tea and he completely ignores your need and decrees coffee is the only solution to mornings." She gave a delicate shudder. "It could happen."

Seychelle hit her forehead with her free hand. "I hadn't thought of that. That would be awful. A real disaster."

Breezy gasped. "They're kidding, right, Savage? You do drink tea."

He shook his head. "Nope. Used to. Drank it all the time." He rubbed the back of Seychelle's hand and then let go to pick up a slice of the new batch of fresh, hot bread Darby brought to the table. He buttered it, aware of Czar and Blythe both staring at him as if he'd grown two heads.

"That was before. Blythe and I don't agree on much, and she got pissed at me over something I said very early on to Kenny. Poisoned my tea."

Breezy gasped again and swiveled in her chair to look at Blythe with wide eyes.

"Not enough to kill me. Just made me sick. Never could look at tea again without turning green." Savage took a healthy bite of the hot, freshly baked bread.

Seychelle's gaze cut to Blythe and then looked back at Savage. Breezy and Steele both eyed her as well. Steele narrowed his gaze and turned to the president of the club.

Czar shrugged. "My wife certainly has knowledge of the kind of herbs that could make someone sick if she wanted to dose someone's tea. It's always been common knowledge that Savage and Blythe disagree over just about everything."

"Maybe so," Steele said, "but Savage is full of shit."

Breezy looked to Blythe. "Is he lying?"

Blythe raised an eyebrow. "Maybe. But then, why would he?"

Steele scowled. "You did not." He made it an absolute

statement. He ruined the certainty by looking to Czar. "She didn't. She wouldn't."

Blythe gave him a placid smirk. "Savage, would you mind passing the bread? It looks delicious."

Savage immediately passed her the small platter of hot bread while Steele and Breezy studied Blythe's face. Steele continued to look at Czar and then shook his head again.

"If Blythe really made Savage sick, we would have heard about it." Again, he spoke with complete assurance.

Savage rolled his shoulders, drawing attention to the fact that they were massive and covered in muscle. "It was early on. We'd just met Blythe, and Reaper was protective. We thought it best to let it go. And I was being a dick."

"No surprise there," Czar said. "Besides, I gave her a fitting punishment."

Blythe blushed. "You did not. You *tried* to, as I recall. Savage totally deserved what happened to him, so there were no punishments allowed. Remember that, Seychelle: no matter how bossy they get, you have righteous justice on your side."

Seychelle lifted her chin. "I'm going to attend classes with Sabelia, and it's very possible Hannah Drake might actually help oversee them. Sabelia is going to give a few of us lessons in . . . um . . . *properly* . . . throwing a hex when needed. Not the kind that make body parts drop off—that would be just eww—but you know, the toad kind. You two should think about coming."

Czar sat up straight, his eyes suddenly twin ice chips staring at Savage. Steele did the same.

"What the hell, Savage? Your woman is totally causing an uprising. I thought you, of all people, would have some semblance of control over her," Czar said.

Seychelle lifted her chin. "He has none. Zero." She waved her hand, and her engagement ring sparkled under the lights. "Fiancée, yes. Wife, no. While I can, I plan on holding as many rebellions as possible. Now that I know Blythe can serve poisoned tea and Sabelia can teach us to bring on the toads, the women will be a force to be reckoned with."

Savage sat back in his chair and regarded his woman. She was laughing again, that little dimple coming out, showing itself to the others. He thought of it as his and realized she didn't laugh that often around other people. He was happy she'd chosen to go along with Blythe's teasing everyone.

Her gaze suddenly met his, and the impact was physical. He shook his head. "You do like to get yourself into all kinds of trouble."

"Sometimes I like the consequences," she teased.

Breezy managed to get her hands on the bread, although she made a face when she took it. "I may as well put this directly on my thighs. All those exercises I'm doing aren't helping. Steele doesn't have to do anything. He can eat all kinds of calories and never gains an ounce. I look at food, and I gain weight. It's so unfair."

"Bread is my nemesis," Seychelle commiserated. "I try to be strict with myself, but I have a really hard time passing up fresh-baked bread. And I especially love to bake it. It makes the house smell so good."

"If it's warm," Blythe added, "you have to put butter on it. What's the use of having fresh-baked bread without adding salted butter? And then you just wasted the entire night's run and your spin class on top of it."

Savage raised an eyebrow. "Are all women like this? Sometimes when I hear Seychelle talk this way about herself, I want to punish her until she realizes it's plain bullshit to think that way. Then they all do it."

Czar shrugged his shoulders. "Yeah, Blythe stops for a little while and then goes right back to it. I think they're all raised to be hard on themselves. They look for what they think are flaws and then just see those. Even when they don't have them, they just make shit up."

"We don't have them," Steele said with a solemn face, "so we can't possibly understand when anyone slightly subordi-

nate to our good looks and intense sexuality feels under-
mined and inferior."

Czar and Savage gave a small nod of approval.

There was a small silence. Breezy turned to Seychelle.
"You were saying the Floating Hat was giving classes on
hexes? Do you have information on specific nights yet? I'll
need to get a babysitter, but I'm definitely in."

"Count me in for certain," Blythe said.

"You got it," Seychelle said. "I'm thinking remote control
and body parts along with the toad class sounds good."

Savage noticed she shifted in her seat and winced a little.
He reached into his pocket and found the bottle of Tylenol.
His fingers closed around it, but he didn't pull it out. What
the hell was wrong with him? She was supposed to be feeling his punishment. She was supposed to remember never to
go near Brandon fucking Campbell again.

"All in," Breezy affirmed again.

"These women are out of control," Steele groused, picking up his menu.

Another round of laughter went up. Savage found he was
more than happy that he had brought her to dinner. He kept
possession of Seychelle's hand across the table, his thumb
brushing across the back of it. She was seeing that she could
fit with Torpedo Ink.

"That man Brandon Campbell," Blythe ventured as she
looked over her menu and then put it down. "The one at the
Floating Hat, Seychelle. He had Tessa with him, and you
talked to her. How well do you know him?"

Seychelle stiffened, tried to pull her hand away from Savage, but he clamped his fingers around hers and kept brushing his thumb to show her he wasn't upset with her. He had
no idea where the line of questioning was going, but he
didn't want her clamming up every time the bastard's name
was mentioned. They needed information on him.

"Not particularly well," Seychelle said. "He owns a house
across the street from Doris Fendris, one of my senior
friends. Why?"

"He signed up for a massage at my spa. I have someone else dealing with all the clients, and honestly, I might not have recognized the name before I went into the room. He asked a lot of questions about you. Too many. I don't gossip about others and certainly not about any member of Torpedo Ink, so I just told him we were friends and left it at that. He clearly wasn't happy with my lack of response to his inquiries."

Blythe traced letters on the menu and glanced up at Czar as if she knew he wouldn't be too happy with her. "I had the feeling he was trying to use his voice on me to get me to answer his questions. He kept trying different octaves, and sometimes I could hear them sort of knocking at my brain, like he was working to get in."

Czar's eyes moved over her face. "Baby. You should have told me."

"I know, honey. I was going to, but when I got home from work, Jimmy was sick with the flu and you were dealing with club stuff, and by the time you got home, I was so tired I just fell into bed and went to sleep. Then life got in the way until I saw Seychelle tonight."

"Has that little bastard been back since?" Savage asked, mainly to take the spotlight off his woman and give her a chance to take a breath. He kept up the slow caresses on the back of her hand, keeping their connection.

"No, and I put him on my blacklist. He can get a massage from one of the other therapists, but I'm always too booked," Blythe explained. "None of the others know Seychelle, so even if he asks, they can't answer."

"What kinds of questions did he ask you about Seychelle?" Steele persisted.

"Was she really with Savage? How long had she been dating him? Did she sing at the bar regularly? Was she going on the run with Torpedo Ink?"

Savage stiffened. "He asked that? If she was going on the run with us?"

"Yes. I didn't answer any of his questions, but he had an

hour massage and he would talk about other things and suddenly throw in a question out of nowhere," Blythe said.

"Why would Brandon ask if Seychelle was going on the run?" Czar mused aloud. "He doesn't belong to a club, does he, Seychelle?"

"Not that I know of," Seychelle said, "but I honestly don't know him very well."

Savage frowned. "One of the Diamondbacks talked to Seychelle in Sea Haven today, Czar. Came right up to her and asked about her voice, said something about her controlling others with it. No Diamondback would ever think about having psychic gifts. If they did think it, they wouldn't talk about it, not out loud where someone might overhear them. Campbell had to have put that shit in his head."

"Tony asked me if I was with Savage and if I was going on the run with him," Seychelle confessed. "There was another, older man in the truck. Tony introduced him as his brother Leonardo. Both wore Diamondback colors."

"What the fuck is going on?" Savage whispered aloud.

"They were at the bar the night I was singing," Seychelle said. "Brandon and Tony from the Diamondbacks. I didn't see them together, but they were both there that night. I saw each separately."

"Yeah, I don't like any of this," Czar said. He put a hand to the back of his neck and rubbed. "We need to figure this shit out, Steele."

Darby approached the table. "Packed full tonight. Hope you had a chance to look at the menus. We need to get your orders in fast." She leaned one palm on the table in front of her father, smiling at them. "Seriously, packed. Starting with you, Steele, what will it be?"

She lifted her hand to scribble the orders in a kind of shorthand, going clockwise around the table, taking the orders from them all. When she raised her hand, a pen was in her fist, but she left behind a folded piece of paper she slid partially under her father's bread plate.

"I'll have a server get in here and refill your water glasses and grab your beers. How many?"

All three men wanted beers. Blythe raised her hand, but both Breezy and Seychelle passed. Seychelle shifted again, and Savage caved. Under cover of the table, he shook a couple pills out of the bottle and passed them to her.

Seychelle looked down at them and then lifted her lashes.

"Take them." It came out a growl. A command. He was turning into a damn pussy.

She swallowed the pills with water while Czar removed the note his daughter had left behind, smoothed it out using his cloth napkin, as if wiping spilled water up. He glanced down at the paper and then just as carefully folded it, pulled out his wallet and placed it inside before he spoke very quietly.

"We have a little problem developing in the kitchen. Pierce has come to visit Alena again. He hasn't come alone. Darby thought it was possible we were being watched. Alena said Pierce was with her while she was using a small torch making a dessert and he remarked that now he knew why she was nicknamed Torch. She remembered that when she first met him, she'd told him she had a road name and so did Lana. She'd forgotten. He seemed to believe hers had to do with her chef skills. Now he's insisting she go outside with him. She's stalling him but can't for long. There are at least two Diamondbacks out back. Trade and Lion both are there." Pierce was a Diamondback who'd dated Alena and then was caught cheating on her. Trade and Lion were two Diamondbacks close to the chapter president.

Czar looked around the table, swearing under his breath. "This changes things. I thought Alena was in the clear. She told me Pierce had no knowledge anyone ever called her Torch."

"Easy enough to forget," Blythe said gently.

"Alena is in a lot of danger," Czar bit out between his teeth. "It's coming at us from every direction, and I don't know why." His gaze jumped to Seychelle's face.

Savage tensed. He felt Czar's rage. It spread like a cancer through the man, that feeling of losing too many, of trying over and over to save them and failing. Alena was theirs. She'd come so close to dying so many times, and they weren't losing her now.

Anger. Rage. Hatred. Those emotions could destroy one from the inside. Shred your soul. Dehumanize you. Make it possible to do terrible, vile things and feel absolutely nothing. Make one need to do them. For so long no one had ever looked out for Czar. Physically, yes, but not for his emotional well-being.

Savage had realized early on that they would all lose Czar if he didn't have help, the kind of help only someone with Savage's strange talent could give him. As a boy, he'd looked up to Czar. He'd recognized they needed him. If anyone was going to lead the way to freedom, it was going to be Czar. Savage had practiced for hours every day until he could draw the terrible fury from Czar. He had to do it slowly so no one would know or suspect. He had to be careful. Eventually, he got so good at it, he was able to take on the rage of the others until he couldn't stop. Now, it was as much a compulsion for him to take on the anger of the Torpedo Ink members as it was for his woman to reach out to heal sick people.

Savage lifted his gaze to Seychelle's. His woman. She would be the one paying the price if he did this. If he took this on his shoulders. He knew he would. It was Czar. He had to, and yet there was Seychelle, and she wasn't close to being ready to take on his sadistic repercussions. Damn it. Just damn it. He had committed to getting the club through the run and what was necessary to clear them with the Diamondbacks. That would already be a weight on him.

The only way to stop himself was to get up and walk out. Abandon Czar. The man he respected most in the world. Looked up to. Owed his life to. Loved. Taking on his rage was the only way Savage knew to show his love for the man.

Taking on the fury for the others was his way of showing love. He had always done it, and he didn't know how to stop.

Seychelle smiled at him. *Bog*, so damn sweet. She saw what he was already needing to do. What he could never stop himself from doing. She simply nodded her assent. She knew what it would mean for them both, but she gave him the green light. Put herself squarely in his corner. Made herself his partner all the way, even knowing ultimately it would be her pain. Her tears. Her suffering. First Czar. Then Savage. Then Seychelle. A fucking chain.

Savage reached across the table and took her hand as he inhaled. As he opened himself up and took on the brunt of Czar's rage, allowing him to think clearly and precisely the way he always did when he planned out how the club would handle saving one of their own.

The fury was almost too much to contain at first. Savage was always astonished at the depth Czar was capable of feeling for all of them. He'd started so young and he'd continued for so long. He felt responsible for every child brought into that school of torture and death, no matter their age, and many were older than he was. Czar still carried that responsibility. That was his personality and his nature.

Savage took more care than he ever had, to bleed that rage from Czar slowly. Czar knew his secrets now, and he wouldn't like that Savage was helping him, but it was what he did. What he would always do. The dark rage swirled into Savage like a ferocious wind, ripping and tearing through him in the way that it did. Wrath was a repulsive, ugly emotion, one that fucked a person up inside, twisted the brain into so many dark paths that eventually it was difficult to find a way out.

Czar stood up slowly, pushing back his chair. "Ladies, if you'll excuse us, we have a little work to attend to in the kitchen. Just helping Alena out. This won't take long."

Savage and Steele followed his example, rising as well, pushing their chairs up to the table. Savage brushed a kiss along Seychelle's temple. "Be good, angel. We'll be back soon."

Seychelle nodded. Czar walked boldly through the restaurant, Steele by his side. Savage moved deeper into the long, rectangle room, going to the farthest corner, where it was nearly impossible to see him and really impossible if you weren't in the room. He opened a door she hadn't known was there and slipped out into the night.

A chill crept down her spine. Something really was wrong, something to do with Alena. This was what Savage had been worried about all along. She looked at the other two women. Breezy was Steele's wife. She knew. Whatever it was, her husband had shared with her ahead of time. He had made certain she wasn't blindsided. Blythe definitely knew. Whether she had asked the right questions or Czar had volunteered the information, she was the only one unaware of what the powder keg was. Must be club business. She was definitely not included. Clearly, no one had expected this business to affect their dinner out, but it had.

She reached for the bread, the same sadness that had invaded before she and Savage had begun to work things out settling over her. Blythe leaned toward Seychelle and laid her hand over Seychelle's nervous fingers, stilling them. "They'll be right back. There's nothing to worry about. Alena will be fine. I think Pierce actually cares for her. I don't know why he would keep coming around to warn her if he didn't. She told me he's been asking her not to go on the run. To just stay here and work the restaurant and to always be with someone."

"Why would he say that to her?" Seychelle asked, knowing Blythe was misinterpreting her sudden change in mood, although she was worried for Alena. "That's a little worrisome. Do you think he's warning her that someone wants to hurt her?"

Breezy sighed. "I don't know why anyone in the Diamondback club would want to harm Alena, but clubs are unpredictable. Right now, the Venomous club is trying to take over parts of Diamondback territory. They just keep chipping away at it. Just tiny pieces, but the Diamondbacks will appear weak if they let them continue. If that happens, all hell will break loose. No one sees how that can have anything to do with Alena. Or you, for that matter. Nothing the Diamondbacks are doing or saying or even asking of our club is making sense."

Blythe nodded. "Pierce has been coming around and texting Alena quite often since his mishap with her. It came out that he was cheating with Tawny Farmer. She was a woman who used to hang around our club quite a bit. She made trouble all the time. Now she's with the Diamondbacks. Pierce seems to want Alena back. Tawny is just plain trouble."

Breezy buttered another piece of bread. "Tell us about this Brandon Campbell, Seychelle. Why is it he's so interested in you? Savage went absolutely still when his name first came up, and you looked like you might bolt from the table."

Seychelle sighed. "Brandon has a psychic gift enabling him to use his voice on others, to get them to do what he wants them to do."

Breezy nodded. "Some of the Torpedo Ink members have gifts like that in varying degrees."

"Brandon's is pretty developed, and he uses it on women. He likes to make women think they are totally inferior to him and that they need only him. I think his ultimate goal is to see if he can drive them to suicide. He craves power over them. He had a woman, Sahara Higgens, bright, pretty, successful in her own right, and he totally separated her from her family, got her under his thumb and managed to turn her into a shell of a human being. She was very close to taking her own life when I happened to meet her."

Seychelle pressed her palm into her thigh, trying not to be nervous. Savage would be really angry if he knew the extent of Brandon Campbell's capabilities. To be fair, she hadn't known—not until she had stupidly challenged him when he came to her home with Doris after she'd broken up with Savage early on in their relationship.

"I got Sahara away from him. It took some doing. I had to sneak visits to her because I knew he had influenced my friend Doris to report any visitors or activity to him. I had to be careful using my own voice to counter his. If I went too fast, I could have done irreparable damage to Sahara. In any case, the bottom line is, with Torpedo Ink's help, I got her out of there. Brandon already had another victim, this one very young, still in her teens."

"The girl Lana is helping," Blythe said.

Breezy was the vice president's wife. She knew everything happening in the club. "Yes, Tessa, she's coming back nicely. Lana told us you were able to use your voice to take her away from Campbell."

"Lana helped as well. It became about her being so young, but he knew it was me taking away his prey. That's how he views them, and already he was watching me. He'd asked me out before he'd gone after Tessa, and I turned him down. I'd seen him a time or two walking along the headlands by my street. He didn't have to do that. He did it on purpose. That was before I met Savage. I didn't respond to his voice, and that intrigued him, I think. At least at first. Then it was a matter of pride. I took something he valued. Then it was a challenge. He came to my house with Doris, trying to turn her against me, showing me he could manipulate her."

She looked around the restaurant and lowered her voice. Mostly, she didn't want Savage to know. "I made a terrible mistake that day. I wasn't going to see Savage again. I felt empty and lost without him. I was so angry that Brandon would dare come to my house with Doris, that he'd take advantage of an older woman who had so little joy in her life."

She shook her head, trying not to think about that moment when she'd made the decision to show Brandon that she was quite happy to bring him all the way down. If he wanted to go to war, she was more than happy to oblige. He'd tried his voice on her several times. He'd used it on Doris and, like an idiot, Seychelle had countered his influence right there, right in front of him, opening herself to him. It wasn't a lot, but it was an in.

She should have backed off there, but she hadn't. "I knew better, but he was so sure of himself. So positive that he could take Doris back anytime he wanted, and I'd be afraid of him. Like a lot of men, he believes males are superior to women in every way and his talent is stronger than mine, just because he's a man." She shrugged. "I wasn't at my best. I was missing Savage and upset that he'd been with another . . ." She broke off.

Breezy and Blythe exchanged a long look. Seychelle was fairly certain they knew what happened. Blythe did. All of Torpedo Ink probably did. They seemed to be in each other's business. That was difficult for her. She was a private person for the most part. She'd grown up alone, and she tended to spend long periods of time by herself. She'd come out of her shell for brief singing gigs, and then she'd crawl back into her house and pull her armor around her.

Shifting uncomfortably in her seat reminded her of Savage's punishment for even engaging with Brandon. Going near him. Strangely, the aching pain on her bottom felt comforting, as if Savage was there with her. As if he cared enough to tell her in a physical way that she wouldn't ever forget that Brandon Campbell was a man out for revenge, and he was plotting to harm her—and he was. She'd given him a far more powerful tool, if he knew how to wield it, than she'd admitted to Savage, and she wasn't looking forward to telling her man she'd done that. And she had to. She just didn't know how.

"I knew better, but when he tried to use his voice on Doris, to turn her against me, I made certain to look him right in the eye, something a man like him can't take. I let him see that I wasn't meek. I wasn't afraid. He hadn't conned me or made me submit to him. I also let him see his voice didn't work on me, and that every time he tried to find a path inside my brain to make me submit, I turned it back to find a path inside of his."

Blythe sat up very straight. "Wait, wait." She tucked a stray strand of hair behind her ear. "I'm struggling to understand what you're saying. I know that several of the club members can use their voices for various things. I'm not certain I realized that your gift was that different or that someone else could in any way compromise you through it."

Seychelle wasn't happy going into detail. Anything she said to these women would get back to their husbands. As president and vice president of Torpedo Ink, the men would expect their wives to tell them anything that could eventually impact the club—like Seychelle's screwup. Savage needed to hear it first.

A shadow fell across the table, and she looked up. Tony Ravard stood looking down at them, his green eyes moving over Seychelle with a look she couldn't quite interpret before it touched on Blythe and Breezy. An older woman was on his arm. Seychelle knew her, had been to her house numerous times and knew she frequented the bingo hall. She was a widow, very sweet, a member of the Red Hat Society and friends with Inez and Doris. Seychelle often had tea with her at the Floating Hat and played cards at her house. Never once had she associated her with Tony. Not one single time, but she should have. They shared the same last name.

Seychelle stood immediately, a welcoming smile lighting her face. "Eden, how lovely to see you." She hugged the woman and kissed her on the cheek. Looking at Tony, she couldn't help laughing. "You even told me your last name. Ravard. No wonder you looked familiar. Your eyes. Blythe, you must know Eden Ravard. This is Tony, her son. This is Breezy and Blythe, my friends." Tony wasn't wearing his colors, but she wanted Blythe and Breezy to know exactly who they were dealing with. "Tony and his older brother, Leonardo, are members of the Diamondbacks."

"Yes, of course," Breezy said. "Shark and Lion, right?"

Seychelle looked at her sharply. Of course Breezy would know the names used in the Diamondback club. Breezy seemed to know everything about the various clubs.

Tony nodded. "Mom wanted to come over and say hello," he said. "I hope we're not interrupting."

"I saw your friends leave and thought we could visit until they returned," Eden said cheerfully. "Is that all right?"

Seychelle's heart dropped when she saw Blythe and Breezy exchange another long look. She would have said yes in a second. Eden was a dear friend and very sweet. That was all she saw. Tony was Diamondback. That was what they saw. That was what Savage would see. She wasn't certain how she was ever going to fit into the Torpedo Ink club. She waited for Blythe to make the decision. She'd been up front with them; that was the best she could do.

TEN

"We'd love to have you join us," Blythe said, her smile genuine. "Please do sit down, Eden. Tony, I don't think we've met before."

Tony Ravard helped his mother into Czar's chair, and he took Savage's former seat directly across from Seychelle. She had to, once again, manage to slide onto the padded chair without wincing. Her bottom wasn't nearly as sore as she had anticipated, but she definitely felt those stripes on her cheeks. It didn't help that Tony seemed to be watching her very closely the entire time.

"I knew you had several children, Eden," Blythe continued. "We talk so much when you come in for your therapy massages, but I think I pictured them as teens. You're quite young-looking, and I have teens, so I suppose I wish them on everyone."

Seychelle found herself laughing with the others, even though she was nervous that Savage might strangle her when he saw Tony sitting across from her, staring at her so intently.

"I have a stepson, and four sons," Eden said.

The way she said *stepson*, with a small shiver in her

voice, had Seychelle's head going up alertly. Eden had mentioned she had several children. She'd included the stepson
in her telling how many. This was the first time Seychelle
had caught that little tell that she might be afraid of her
stepson. A little chill went down Seychelle's spine. That had
to be the connection Czar and the others were looking for.
Brandon Campbell had to be Tony Ravard's half brother.
That was Brandon's connection to the Diamondbacks. And
what would she do if Brandon suddenly walked in and sat
down? Savage would *kill* her for certain.

"What's wrong?" Tony asked, his tone low, almost a
whisper. "You're suddenly very pale."

Seychelle picked up her glass of water. "I think the
thought of raising all those boys is quite frankly daunting."
She raised the glass. "To you, Eden. And Blythe. Breczy,
you too. I'm going to be a cat lady, myself. I don't have one
yet, and so far, every time one sees me it runs the other way,
but I'm holding out hope." She took a sip while the others
laughed. Tony did as well, accepting her ridiculous explanation. Savage would never have let her get away with it.

She took out her cell phone and, under the table, stared at
it. For all she knew he could be up on a roof with a sniper
rifle, protecting Alena. Or in a tense standoff with Pierce. If
she sent a text, she could get him killed.

"I highly recommend being a cat lady," Eden concurred.

"Mom," Tony objected. "I'm sitting right here, and I took
you out to the restaurant of your choice. I had to bribe our
way in."

"Who did you bribe?" Breezy asked, signaling Darby,
who was two tables away, looking a little harassed. "Sorry,
babe, but we need clean water glasses and more bread. They
aren't joining us for dinner. They're at table six."

"Thanks," Darby said. "Coming right up."

"My cousin. He has a standing spot, and I told him mom
really wanted to come out tonight, so he was kind enough to
let me take his reservation."

"Originally, Crow 287 never took reservations; it was

first come, first serve," Eden chimed in. "I wanted to eat here every night, the food was so good."

"I know what you mean," Seychelle agreed. "Just smelling it puts ten pounds on my thighs."

"There's nothing at all wrong with your thighs," Tony said.

There was a small silence while Eden looked at her son with her mouth open. Blythe and Breezy started laughing.

"I can't believe you said that," Eden said. "Are you staring at her thighs?"

"Yes," Tony admitted without one ounce of remorse. "Any man with a grain of sense would be staring at her thighs. They're perfection."

Seychelle clutched the phone. She should have texted Savage. There was no stopping the lobster-red blush that started at her thighs and swept up her body like a tidal wave.

Where R U? R U getting yourself killed?

What's wrong?

Nothing. Tony Ravard and his mother R sitting at table with us. Stepbrother is Brandon Campbell unconfirmed but fairly certain. Just a gut feeling. Sometimes that happens to me but nearly always right

There was a small waiting period as if Savage was giving that some thought.

U handling this? Need me?

Her heart shifted just a little in her chest. Just knowing Savage would be willing to come to her if she needed him made her world right. She already felt so much better just letting him know the Diamondback had joined them at the table. She wasn't going behind his back. The thigh thing was probably a joke, and she could handle that. If Tony took his joke any further, his mother would most likely box his ears publicly. Seychelle wasn't telling Savage about that joke for any amount of money. She knew Savage would take that remark very personally.

Deliberately, Seychelle rolled her eyes. "Don't worry, Eden, I'm wearing a dress. He can't see my thighs. He's just trying to get a rise out of everyone."

Breezy groaned. "Is this what we have to look forward to? You might want to take note of that, Blythe. Kenny is already giving you trouble, and I noticed Benito was driving everyone right up the wall. I think I'll be very strict with Zane, not that it will do any good with Steele for a father." She smiled at Eden. "Those are the various boys in our families."

"It just gets worse when they get older and move out on their own," Eden said, "because you can't boss them around so much." But there was love in her voice and even more in her eyes when she looked at her son.

Tony laughed. "Mom, you boss me more now than you did when I was a kid."

"Only because I want you to find a good woman, settle down and give me grandchildren. Is that too much to ask?"

"All the good ones are taken. Every time I see one, someone else has gotten there before me." Tony's gaze went back to Seychelle.

"You have to move faster, Tony," Eden said. "I can't live forever, you know. You aren't setting the best example for your brothers."

"Does she hound them for grandchildren too?" Blythe asked.

Seychelle was aware Blythe was deliberately taking Tony's attention from her, and she was grateful for it. On the other hand, if Tony was seriously just attracted to her and his attention had nothing to do with his club, that would be a great relief. She didn't believe that was his interest, but she hoped. It would be for the best. She settled more comfortably, used to talking with Eden about her sons.

⤛

Savage stood in the shadows of the kitchen, watching Alena as she prepared dishes quickly, turning them out almost magically. Each seemed a work of art as she pushed them on a belt that sent them to Delia Swanson, the woman she'd hired to help. Delia had owned a diner for years, had been hired to

work in the grocery store in Caspar, but one week there and
she'd changed her mind. She liked the comfort of the kitchen
and the smell of food. Alena was overjoyed to have scored
Delia. She was fast and efficient, and she could fill in cooking,
finishing the plates or even waitressing. Delia was currently
living in one of the two apartments over the bar in Caspar.
Bannister, a regular at the bar, lived in the other one. He
seemed to have developed quite the crush on the woman.

Czar and Steele were on the rooftop outside watching the
two Diamondbacks who had accompanied Pierce Franklin.
One sat on his bike, looking bored, staring at the restaurant
and occasionally shaking his head. The other paced restlessly and kept looking at his watch. The one on his bike was
known as Trade, and the one pacing went by Lion; both Diamondbacks were close friends of Pierce. It was rumored
they had served on a SEALs team with him.

Pierce stood to the side of Alena, giving her plenty of
room to work. He wore his Diamondback colors like a second skin. His gaze followed her every movement. As often
as he'd been with Alena, watched her work, watched her
glide and move so gracefully, Savage didn't understand how
a man as astute as Pierce didn't see the killer in her. Maybe
he didn't want to.

"Did you give any thought at all to what I asked you,
Alena?" Pierce kept his voice low, but Savage heard him.

"Of course I did." Alena shot him a quick look. "You're
not cut out for marriage. How would that even work? We
have an open marriage? You go on runs and fuck anyone you
want to and I stay home? We both go and it's a free-for-all,
with neither of us getting upset? If that's the case, why
bother getting married in the first place? Come on, honey, I
appreciate the gesture, I really do, but you know the first hot
chick offering to blow you, you're going to take her up on it."

She sent him a lazy, sexy smile. "You know how I know
that? I've got skills. Mad, wicked skills. Blow-your-mind,
take-off-the-top-of-your-head-and-make-you-forget-your-
own-name kind of skills. Not too many women can do what

I do. That's a fact, and you know it. But you still went far down the ladder and had someone like Tawny put her mouth on you. That can only mean one thing, babe. You aren't all that discerning when it comes to sex. You take anything, including the bottom of the barrel."

All the while she talked, she finished more plates of food. They were perfect, but Savage could feel the red-hot rage working through her. Swirling deep. This man cut her to the bone. He'd gotten to her. She'd let him in. Alena didn't let too many people in. Pierce might be trying to make up for it in his way, but he'd betrayed her like so many others had in her past.

Savage looked at his phone, the text messages his woman had sent to him. She was sitting in the dining room with a Diamondback. Coincidence? He doubted it, but he wasn't going to say that to her.

Alena's in a bad way, sorry baby

He needed to warn her. Apologize to her. He was collecting more rage for that wide, deep pool he stored and guarded like a mythical dragon until it all became too much and erupted like an explosive volcano.

We're in this together

He knew Seychelle would understand what he meant. He opened himself up and allowed Alena's very justified anger to find its way to him. That would only make the time he had to prepare Seychelle shorter. She took it in her stride though. She had no idea how bad it could get when he was raging. He really did think it would be better to have one of his brothers there, maybe two of them, that first time. Just to be safe. Just to ensure that Seychelle was safe. They would have to have another discussion. She wouldn't like it. She didn't want anyone witnessing what he did to her, but it was far better than him harming her.

Savage felt terrible for Alena. She had developed a tough outer shell. She looked the part, giving Pierce a cool, sexy look with a sweep of her long lashes and a sensual half smile from her full, pouty lips. She looked a little amused as he stood there in her kitchen acting like he was trying to save a woman when she refused to need saving. But she was soft inside. So vulnerable. All of Torpedo Ink knew it, even Destroyer, their newest member. They could see past her façade into the real Alena.

"That's bullshit, Alena. Yeah, I go on runs, and I take what's offered. I use club girls and patch chasers; I always have. You know you were different. I didn't make any bones about that. I just wasn't sure what it was. I'd never felt the things for any other woman that I felt for you. Give me a fucking break here. I was sorting things out, trying to work through it. You were pulling away from me, and don't pretend you weren't."

Alena sent him another look from under her long lashes as she sent plates spinning down the belt toward Delia. "Maybe. But I didn't get on my knees for other men, Pierce. And what about that video you just had to have? You begged me for it, right out there on my back porch." She indicated the back door.

Her eyes turned ice blue. Her voice hissed at him, glacier cold. "I told you I was trying to get the restaurant up and running and couldn't get help. You didn't care. You made me feel as bad as possible so I'd give you what you wanted, and you wanted that video so you could give it to your friends. You know how many of them have had things to say to me? Asked me for a little taste every time they see me?" She shrugged. "Not that I give a damn, but sooner or later, they're going to say it in front of one of my brothers. You know what will happen then. Our clubs will explode. A lot of people on both sides will die, and for what?"

Savage moved closer, careful not to draw attention. That was the million-dollar question. What did the Diamondbacks really want with Torpedo Ink? They were a club made up of assassins, but that wasn't anything the Diamondbacks could possibly know. Research wouldn't gain them anything. Torpedo Ink were phantoms, sliding in and out of the

shadows. No one saw them until they wanted to be seen—
and then you were dead.

Pierce shoved both hands through his hair in obvious
agitation. "I'm trying to make things right, Alena. The fucking video wasn't my idea. Plank, my president, doubted my
loyalty to the club. He said you were pulling me in too deep.
The idiotic thing is, Plank has always used me to get information he wanted from other clubs by having me get close
to a woman. He sent me after you. He wanted me to get information on your club. When you weren't forthcoming, he
thought it was because I wasn't trying hard enough, not because you were loyal to your club."

Alena sent him another quick look from her ice-blue
eyes.

Pierce held up his hands in surrender. "I could lie to you,
but I'm not. He did send me after you, but I found I wanted
to be with you. It was the first time in my life I wanted to be
with a woman. That never happened to me before."

Savage could understand the mixture of anger and panic
in Pierce's voice. He'd felt the same when Seychelle had invaded his thoughts and become such an obsession.

"You weren't in our club. I knew you weren't ever going
to leave your club. Plank was pissed I was getting zero information from you, and you were so elusive, never committing to me. I wanted to shake you half the time, Alena."

"The video, Pierce."

"Plank wanted me to get the video to prove my loyalty to
the club. It was a shit move. I knew it when I asked for it, and
I should have told him to shove it."

Again, Alena's blue eyes cut through Pierce, and then she
pulled something that smelled delicious out of the oven. "He
is your president. Very hard to do when your president
makes it an order. Still, you could have warned me."

She flashed him a little smile before turning her attention
to the savory meat dish. Savage knew that smile. Alena was
a wolf in sheep's clothing. "If I had known you were going

to give that video to all of your friends, it would have been unbelievably memorable and made you a sexual god."

Pierce swore under his breath as he watched her fix several more plates and then pull out warm bread, put the loaves in baskets and send them to Delia. "Are you going to be able to take a break and go outside with me? Just give me ten minutes. It's important."

Alena glanced at the clock and then the stack of orders. She sighed. "You're not getting a blow job, Pierce, not after Tawny's filthy mouth has been all over you. You need to be scrubbed raw until you bleed, and I don't know if that would work to get those germs off you. But you need to talk, I can give you five if it's really that important."

"I've got this," Delia said, not looking at Pierce.

Pierce held the screen door for Alena, allowing her to precede him. Savage used the small back door they'd built into the kitchen alcoves for just such emergencies. Czar and Steele were already in place, patiently waiting, knowing Pierce would lure Alena outside. She had indicated she would go outside where his brothers waited, using herself as bait, to see what the Diamondbacks wanted with her.

Pierce took her elbow and rather than taking her close to where the other two men sitting on their Harleys waited, he steered her away from them, thankfully, close to where Savage was concealed in the shadows.

"Listen to me, Alena, since I only have five fucking minutes to convince you, I'm trying to save your life here. I know I screwed up. I'm serious about marrying you. At least let me tell everyone you're mine. Stay away from the run. Stay home from this one and be visible all the time. Don't be alone. I want you out in the open with people around you at all times. At night, stay with friends. Stay at Czar and Blythe's. Be where people are."

"Why?"

"I've already said too much. Enough that can get me fucking killed. Just do this for me. We can talk later, when you have more time."

"I have no choice about the run, Pierce, but I'll buddy up. I can promise you that. I'll be very careful. Thanks for the warning." Alena looked up at him for a long time. "I let you in, and that's on me. I'm usually very cautious."

"I've got a job I have to do for my club."

She shrugged. "I get it. I have my own club. It's just that you should have told me. I would have understood." She gave him another half smile. "Be careful yourself, Pierce. I don't want you getting in trouble because of me. Torpedo Ink will look after me."

He opened his mouth as if he might say something else, shook his head and then leaned down as if he might kiss her. Alena turned her head, so his lips brushed her cheek. She stepped back. This time, Savage felt her pain, hurt, but not anger. He'd taken the anger away from her. She watched Pierce go to his bike and then ride off along with the others. They waited until they could hear the roar of the pipes on Highway 1 before Czar and Steele joined them and then Savage slung his arm around Alena.

"I'm sorry I forgot I told him about being called Torch, Czar. All of us were at the bar that night. It was when Plank's brother-in-law grabbed Anya and tried to hold her as a shield. I don't think anyone was paying much attention, me included. It was a shit night."

"Doesn't matter. He put it down to you being a chef. He refuses to see you any other way than a woman serving a man. I wonder why. He appears so much more intelligent than that." Czar gave her a long look. "You've always been good at hiding in plain sight, Alena. You waited for him to see you, and he didn't."

"I gave him every opportunity."

Savage hated that her voice choked with hurt. He wished he could take that for her too. He dealt in rage. Anger. "Alena, that makes you superior to him. You know that." He brushed a kiss on top of her head. He was still going to kill the bastard one day, just not soon. They had to let whatever the Diamondbacks were going to do play out. In the meantime, all of them were guarding Alena. Surrounding her and keeping her safe.

"He had the balls to come to you and warn you," Steele pointed out. "That was a big risk he took."

"He did do that," Alena said. "That was to make up for the video distribution, I'm sure. I've got to get back to work. Enjoy dinner and thanks for the backup."

Savage trailed after his president and vice president, making his way from the kitchen, down the wide hall and through the dining room. He heard Seychelle's laughter. He'd know it anywhere. Blythe and Breezy chimed in. The sound of another woman and a man's laughter joined them. Czar paused for a moment in the archway, giving Savage just enough time to draw in a deep breath at the sight of Tony Ravard, another fucking Diamondback, staring at his woman as if he wanted to devour her.

Savage knew the older woman, Eden Ravard, seated at the table laughing with Seychelle. He'd never put it together that she was Tony Ravard's mother. He swore silently to himself. He couldn't shove a knife down Tony's throat and drag him out of the restaurant with his mother looking on.

Tony Ravard was known as Shark, another SEAL and brother to Lion. He had two other brothers in the Diamondbacks. His other brothers were both in other chapters. They had also served in the navy, the SEAL program, returned, moved and then joined the Diamondbacks. It seemed it was a family tradition. Savage had been in their mother's home more than once, and he'd never seen a single photograph that would indicate Eden's sons were in the club.

Seychelle looked up and instantly gave him that smile that was for him alone. Soft. Loving. Ripped his heart out on the spot. Settled his need to kill Tony right there.

"Hey, honey. Look who found us."

Savage stepped around Czar and Steele and went right up to Eden, taking her hand the way he did when he was in her home, ignoring her son. "Ms. Eden." He kissed the back of her hand as if she were a movie star.

"Savage." She beamed at him. "This is my son Tony. Tony, Savage. Savage has saved me twice now. He's . . . wonderful."

"That's not quite accurate, Ms. Eden," Savage said. "And I have met Tony, although I didn't realize he was your son."

Tony stood up, vacating Savage's seat immediately. "What do you mean, Savage saved you, Mom?"

She laughed. "I was being dramatic as usual." She smiled at Czar and Steele. "The girls can tell you. I have a real flair for drama. I should have been an actress."

"You would have won several Oscars," Seychelle agreed immediately.

"Mom," Tony persisted, helping her out of the chair. "What do you mean, Savage saved you twice?"

"The first time, Seychelle came to check on me. She brought me groceries and cleaned the house and changed my bedding. I wasn't feeling too good. I'd been sick for a week."

"Where was Aunt Nina?" Tony interrupted.

"You know how she is about sick people," Eden said in a low voice.

"So you called Seychelle. How does that translate to Savage saving you twice?" he persisted.

"The silly kitchen sink had sprung a leak about a month earlier, and I wrapped a rag around it, but it didn't hold and got worse. I was in bed and didn't see, so the pipe just disintegrated, and water flooded the kitchen. Seychelle turned off the water. Savage was outside mowing the lawn. He came in and cleaned up the water in the kitchen and then put in all brand-new pipes while Seychelle took care of me."

Tony stared down at his mother and then looked up at Savage. Savage did his best to look like a killer. Shit. This was why he didn't go out in public. Shit like this. Ruining his image. Tony was struggling to equate what he knew of

Savage, a man who had a reputation for torture and killing, with one who mowed lawns and fixed sinks for little old ladies. He kept a groan from escaping.

His gaze shifted to Seychelle. There was amusement in her eyes, and if she dared laugh, he was going to put her over his knee right there in the restaurant in front of everyone. He had to reestablish his reputation fast somehow.

"And the second time?" Tony's voice sounded strangled. Rough. His arm was around his mother. His head turned toward Seychelle, but his eyes were on Savage.

"Oh dear," Eden said. Her hand went protectively to her throat. "I had a little seizure, honey, nothing bad. It wasn't a bad one. I fell and hit my head. Seychelle was with me. We were playing cards with Doris Fendris and Harriet Meadows. Hearts. I had a great hand. Then I had the seizure and hit my head on the corner of the table."

"She hit it pretty hard," Seychelle confirmed. "I asked Doris to go to the kitchen to get warm water and Harriet to bring me towels. Then I tried to keep her from hurting herself until she stopped having convulsions."

There was a small silence. Seychelle touched her forehead, up high on her right side, near the hairline. She rubbed the little area for a moment as if it ached.

"When I came too, Seychelle was lying next to me, her head bleeding profusely, and Savage had a cloth pressed to my head and was holding me. He yelled for Doris. For a minute I thought Seychelle had had a seizure too." Eden sent Seychelle a little smile. "There was spilled tea on the floor, and we both had slipped in it. As I said, my seizure wasn't that bad, a very mild one. I was up, and really didn't even have a headache like I normally have afterward. I got to have Savage pick me up. It was very swoon-worthy." She batted her eyes.

"Why didn't you call me, or one of the others?" Tony demanded.

The smile vanished from Eden's face. "You and Leonardo were in Ukiah at some big meeting with your club. I never disturb you when you're there. You know your brothers live too far away to come when I have one of my little episodes."

"You could have called Brandon."

Eden pressed her lips together and looked stubborn. She didn't reply. It was very clear she didn't want to call him. That certainly cleared up any doubt that Brandon was related to the Ravards and Seychelle's "gut instincts" had been right.

"Brandon?" Savage echoed, just to confirm.

"Brandon is my half brother. His mother is Nina Campbell, Eden's sister," Tony said. "It's a long story."

Seychelle cleared her throat delicately, bringing the attention to her. "I see your mom at least once a week. If you leave your number and maybe your brothers' numbers on the kitchen counter, if there's ever an emergency, I can call one of you immediately."

"I would appreciate that, thank you, Seychelle," Tony said. "It was nice meeting all of you," he added as he walked his mother back to their table in the main dining room.

"Tony seems a very pleasant man. I had no idea Eden's sons were members of the Diamondbacks, or that she had a stepson she clearly doesn't like. Well, I guess, technically, he'd also be her nephew. I massage her on a regular basis," Blythe told Czar once the two visitors had cleared the room.

Savage took the chair Tony vacated, reaching for Seychelle's hand. "Everything all right, babe? You look a little pale."

"I didn't see any evidence of Brandon in her home anywhere, Savage, and I've been going there on an average of once a week for months. There aren't any photos of him, but then I didn't see any photos of her sons in their Diamondback colors either. Eden has never said a word to me." Seychelle almost sounded hurt. "She talked about them being in the navy, but never in a club."

"Wouldn't Inez have known?" Breezy asked. "Wouldn't she have warned Seychelle?"

Darby arrived, pushing a small cart. She began to place various dishes of food in front of each of them.

Blythe stopped her daughter before she could leave. "Honey, this firefighter you're seeing, Asher Larkin, the one I talked your father and the club into leaving you alone about so you could date in peace. That man. Is his aunt Eden Ravard? Is he a cousin of the Ravards? The four brothers who are all in the Diamondback club?" Her voice was very mild. Soft. Low.

Darby took a deep breath. "Yes. Asher's mother is Reggie's, Eden's late husband's, sister. He has nothing to do with the Diamondbacks though." The last came out in a defensive rush.

"But you didn't disclose that information, Darby, and you put your father and the club in a bad position. That wasn't right, and you know it," Blythe said. "Withholding such an important piece of data could have gotten someone hurt or even killed just because you were being selfish. You wanted to see that man, and you didn't trust your father enough, after all he's done to prove himself to you, to make the right decision. I thought I taught you better than that."

Darby stared at the floor. "I'm sorry."

"I'm not the one you owe the apology to, and in our home, we never apologize unless we know we're sincerely sorry and we're willing to pay the ultimate price for forgiveness," Blythe said. She indicated the open floor of the restaurant with her chin. "I know you have a lot of work to do. You think on whether or not you really are sorry and what could have happened to your family before you ask anyone for forgiveness."

"Yes, ma'am." Darby blinked back tears and pushed the cart away.

There was a small silence. Breezy looked over at Blythe. "I have no doubt you can handle those teenage boys without Czar's help. You didn't raise your voice at all, but you definitely said everything that needed saying."

"Knowledge is important. *All* knowledge. She knows

that. It isn't a small thing she did. This is no little infraction," Blythe said. "Czar and all of Torpedo Ink need to know who they're dealing with at all times. If they have an enemy close to them, they have to know that. Even a potential enemy. Asher may be dating Darby, but his family are the Ravards. That equals Diamondbacks. If he overhears something he shouldn't, that could put Czar or any one of the members of Torpedo Ink in jeopardy. She knows better."

"Blythe really could have poisoned Savage's tea," Steele said, awe in his voice. He sat back, regarding Blythe with new respect.

She picked up her fork, avoiding Czar's gaze. "I should have waited until we were home. I'm sorry, honey."

"It was club business, not just personal, Blythe," he said gently. "What you did was right. While we were attending to Alena, she put all of you in jeopardy."

"But I did lose my temper." She pushed her food around on her plate.

Seychelle nudged her. "That's losing your temper? I threw a mug at Savage and was really upset that I didn't hit him in the head. I'm still kinda upset I didn't hit him in the head." She squirmed around on her chair and sent Savage a very intimate smile.

He grinned at her, his cock stirring at the thought of those stripes on her bottom.

A faint smile tugged at Blythe's mouth. "Savage might make me want to throw things," she admitted. "Actually, in the kitchen, a time or two, around the knives, it was touch-and-go there."

"Hey." Savage paused in the act of putting a forkful of food into his mouth. "How did I get into this conversation? I was staying very quiet over here." He winked at Seychelle, telling her he was proud of her for getting the conversation off Darby's scolding.

"Blythe has been known to throw things at me," Czar admitted. "I'm actually the calm one in the household."

Steele and Savage both snickered derisively. Breezy

coughed behind her hand, and Blythe looked around, gazing up at the air. "I'm expecting lightning to hit you any moment, Czar, for that whopper."

Savage was grateful he'd thought of bringing Seychelle out to dinner. She seemed to have a good time. Breezy and Blythe both had her laughing, and he appreciated the musical notes floating around the table going up toward the ceiling. Sometimes when the others laughed, he could see their notes as well, but mostly, it was Seychelle's notes.

He sat back in his chair after he finished his favorite dish on the menu, and drank the dark, bitter coffee. He didn't need sweet in it. He had sweet seated right across from him. He had no idea how he'd gotten so lucky. Just looking at her sometimes hurt. He spent the rest of the evening waiting to get back home, mostly because he knew she was worried about something and he wanted to be alone with her.

The moment they were in the car and on the way back, he asked her. He wasn't a man who believed in waiting too long to get things out in the open.

"What is it, baby? Something's on your mind. Didn't you enjoy yourself? I know it was awkward having Ravard and Eden show up, but everything turned out okay. Pierce didn't bring him. He really was just bringing his mother to dinner. It was a coincidence. They do happen."

"I'm not so certain, Savage," Seychelle mused with a sideways glance at him. Her fingers plucked nervously at the material of her dress. "It's possible his cousin the firefighter asked Darby if we had a reservation for tonight at the restaurant. I was shopping for a dress. I had it with me when I ran into Tony. Shoes, dress, the entire outfit. Asher could have passed the information on to Tony if he'd asked him to do it."

"Why would he? Do you think he's that interested? He has to know you're mine. You're even wearing my ring." Savage tried to keep the edge out of his voice as he reached over and took possession of her hand, his finger running over her ring. He liked it on her finger, liked it proclaiming to the world she was part of him.

"We aren't the only ones with psychic abilities. It's arrogant to believe we are. Brandon has his voice. The thing is, Brandon's mother is Eden's sister, Nina. Eden is Tony's mother. If Brandon got his psychic talent from Nina because it runs in that family, it's possible Eden carries that same talent. Do you see where I'm going with this? Tony was in the bar the night I sang and tried to keep everyone at the meeting feeling calm. I didn't see who went in the back room. You did. Did any of Tony's brothers attend the meeting? Tony was in the bar, sitting at a table near the band."

Savage hit the remote for the gate. Her voice trembled when she asked him. She wasn't looking at him, so he could only see part of her face, but she sounded scared.

"Are you afraid the Ravards or the Diamondbacks want me dead, Seychelle? This all started when you overheard the phone call with Czar, and you've got that same look on your face. You can't be worried like that, babe."

She began pulling at her hem now, folding the material between her fingers. She really was upset. Her teeth bit down on her full lower lip, and she just stared out the window until he parked in the garage and shut off the engine.

"We're home and safe, Seychelle. Tell me what happened to scare you."

"Can we get in bed first? I always feel safer talking in bed with the lights off, and I'm tired."

He'd give her the damn moon if she asked for it. He went around the hood of the car, but she was already out. He slowed her down, making certain security hadn't been breached. Now that he had Seychelle to protect, he flipped through the camera screens and checked each entry point. The alarms would have come to his phone if any window or door had been penetrated, but security remained intact.

Seychelle didn't turn on lights as she hurried through the house, straight to their bedroom. For some reason, the bed seemed to be a comfort to her, sitting in it, back to the headboard. It wasn't the same as the one in her cottage in Sea Haven, but he'd tried to make certain it had a similar feel to it. He wanted her to feel as if she could talk about anything—and he liked lying on the bed with her, just the way they did in her cottage.

She reached behind her in an effort to get to the zipper, but it clearly was a struggle. He came up behind her and moved her hand.

"After we talk about whatever is scaring the hell out of you, I want to hear more about this book." Savage unzipped her dress slowly, letting his nails trail lightly down her back and then over the stripes on her bottom and thighs. They were dark, just the way he knew they would be, in stark contrast to that flawless pale skin.

He wanted to lighten the moment, help soothe her, distract her just a little to allow her to calm enough to talk to him. She was really on edge.

She stepped out of the dress and stood for a moment in just her low heels and panties. "I really made a mistake with Brandon, Savage. It might have been me that caused all the trouble." She looked at him over her shoulder, her eyes dark with pain. With fear. "I could be the one that made them come after you."

He ran his hand down her back, that beautiful, silken back. There was possession in his touch. Comfort. "Get ready for bed, baby," he reiterated. "I can assure you, no one in other clubs needs much of an excuse to want to kill me. You take on too much. Give that to me. I've told you before, you hand over those things to me and I'll take care of them for you."

She bent to slide her shoes off before walking to the master bath. He couldn't take his eyes from her. She didn't pull the door closed, which pleased him. Her natural inclination was to not only close the door but lock it. She was trying to do the things that made him comfortable. He didn't like closed doors, and he couldn't tolerate locked ones—which is why she couldn't have even locked that door if she'd wanted to. In turn, he gave her time alone in the bathroom before barging in. It was a compromise he could live with and hoped she could as well.

When he finished brushing his teeth, she was already in bed, looking smaller than usual, her back to the headboard, hair in that messy knot that always got him right in his heart. Her face was scrubbed free of all makeup, not that she ever wore much. He padded to the bed barefoot and naked, watching her gaze stray to his cock. She definitely liked his cock. She could so easily center an ache there, especially now, when she wore those stripes on her skin.

He put a knee on the bed and crawled up to her, dragged her legs straight by her ankles, wrapped his arms around her hips and laid his head on her belly the way he had so many times before. It was one of his favorite places. Immediately, her hands dropped to his scalp and began that slow, soothing massage he loved. No one ever put their hands on him. He had been astonished that first time when she'd touched him, and his skin hadn't reacted adversely to the feeling of flesh against his. Instead, there were sparks. Embers flying. Flames licking over him.

"You're safe, baby. Just tell me whatever it is. Give it to me." He murmured it to her, rubbed his scruff along her belly and kissed the slight pink marks.

"This is going to sound crazy, but it's a theory."

There was hesitation in her voice. She had good instincts. Really good instincts. Savage wasn't going to put anything she said down to hysteria or craziness.

"I'm listening." He drew circles on her hip with the pads of his fingers, deliberately soothing her. She was used to their interaction in bed when they talked. Already the tension was leaving her body.

"Brandon knew from the first time he ever heard me talk to him, when he asked me out and I turned him down, that I had the same talent he had. He tried to use his voice on me to make me go out with him, and I countered him. I thought he was sleazy and just used his voice to get dates with women who didn't want to go out with him. It occurred to me that maybe he even took it further and made women want to have sex with him. That seemed a real possibility.

Then I found out about Sahara from Doris, and what she said about her didn't add up for me, especially since I'd already encountered Brandon."

Savage remained silent while her fingers moved over his scalp and down to his neck. He had bulging muscles everywhere. He was a big man with a lot of bulk, but that didn't seem to matter. Her fingers were strong when she dug into the knots, slowly easing the tension in him.

"He recognized I was a threat to him—or maybe I'd be of use to him—long before I did. Then you took an interest in me. You're Torpedo Ink. His half brothers are Diamondback. Savage, he isn't Diamondback. That says something right there. A man like him would want to be. He's arrogant. Truly vain. Very entitled."

Savage turned that over and over in his mind. She was right about Brandon. The man was vindictive and cunning. He would be furious that his brothers were accepted into the largest badass club in the U.S. and overseas, but he couldn't get in. He had to have tried. If he tried and was turned down . . .

"The Diamondbacks didn't accept him into the club for a reason. He has four half brothers in that club, so it would stand to reason he would get in easy. A man like Brandon would be royally pissed to be told no. And he'd look for a way to get back at them." There was speculation in his voice.

"He would," she agreed. "He would need an edge. Suppose his talent is stronger than Tony's. Or Leonardo's. Or all his other brothers, if they have any talent. It's possible to steal a talent, Savage. It can be done."

"How would that be possible?" Savage kept any alarm from his voice. There was alarm enough in Seychelle's voice. In her body language.

"Bending and twisting voices isn't that difficult, Savage. I can do it. It's gathering strands of pitches, much like a musician takes the various sounds he hears and puts them together to form a song. Brandon's talent may not be as strong as mine, but if he managed to steal his brother's or even several of his brothers' talent, should some of the others have it as well, he could become quite powerful."

"There was a man we ran into," Savage admitted. "The international president of the Swords club. He was pretty fuckin' powerful, and it was a few voices that brought him down in the end. Voices." He repeated the word softly. "So I'm in his way because I'm standing in front of you."

He didn't move his head from her belly, but he turned it, settling his chin on her soft skin, feeling the firm muscles contracting with the weight.

Seychelle bit her lip, eyes worried. "If he thinks he could command me, take my voice, take my talent away from me and use it for his own, then yes, I think he'd go so far as try to get rid of you. He could wreck the chapter of the Diamondbacks his brothers are in. If he managed to get in another chapter, he could do the same thing and continue to do so over and over for as long as he could control it."

Savage breathed a little easier. Control. That wasn't Brandon's strong suit. "This entire thing that the Diamondbacks are worried about could be Brandon stirring up trouble because he didn't get into their club. That's really what you're saying. If he's doing the same thing, talking to someone in the Venomous club, using his voice to persuade them to keep going after the Diamondbacks, he's going to start a war. Maybe that's his ultimate goal."

She nodded. "And he probably either put out the hit on you himself, which I doubt, or he persuaded someone else to do it. I hate that I'm responsible, Savage. I really hate it."

He loathed that she sounded like she might cry. It made him want to go find the fucker right then and show him why he'd earned the name Savage. Instead, he kept his voice gentle. They had no proof of anything. It was all speculation.

"You're not responsible. I told you, Seychelle, everyone other than you pretty much wants me dead. I'm used to it, and I don't much give a damn. I'm still alive. Brandon Campbell is a cunning little weasel. If you're right, then he's contracted with someone in the clubs. Code will find out who is coming after me. It isn't open-ended, baby. He got a specific hit man. We'll find him. In any case, we could be way off."

"Don't you think it would be so much smarter to skip this run? Between all the dire warnings to Alena and now this with you, maybe Torpedo Ink just shouldn't go this time."

She shifted her weight subtly, and he couldn't help smiling, knowing her bottom was uncomfortable sitting so long in one position. He kissed her belly. "We have no choice. Don't worry about the run. And you're our ace in the hole. Brandon can't go on it, so we'll have your voice, if needed, to calm everyone the fuck down."

She sighed. "I don't want anything to happen to you." She shifted a little more when his hand moved over her thigh, close to her heat.

"Nothing is going to happen to me." Murmuring it almost absently, he covered her mound and bare lips, needing to distract her. "So wet for me, baby. I love that you're always so ready for me."

"I want you so much. Every time I moved on that chair, it felt like your marks on me were igniting a wildfire, Savage," she admitted in a whisper.

His gaze met hers. Her eyes were deep blue with need. He loved seeing her like that. His. How the hell had a man like him gotten so damn lucky?

"Tell me about the book."

He wanted her burning for him. All night. All the next day on the ride to the run. She had to be half out of her mind with frustration. With need. She would find it difficult to be around all the other clubs, the parties, drugs, alcohol, the open sex. Torpedo Ink would surround her, protect her, and he would do his best to shield her, but he knew what was going to happen. There would be a lot of rage swirling among his crew, rage that would inevitably end up in his gut, growing like a monster in him. He would need to bleed some of that off. He would need her.

Color swept up her body to her face. "That book. Seriously? Can we please just forget the book?"

Effortlessly, he pulled her down the bed and flipped her over, so she was on her belly. Jerking her legs apart, he wrapped one arm around her hips again, and then anchored her with one leg thrown over her thighs. "We're not forgetting the book. I want to hear all about it. Why you bought it when you had me right here."

He shaped her left striped cheek with his palm, rubbing, massaging, then allowed his fingernails to ignite the fire all over again as he raked over the stripes.

She moaned and pushed back with her bottom against his hand, clearly wanting more. He didn't give it to her. "Talk to me."

"It was just a silly how-to book on blow jobs. A kind of illustrated book with instructions. It's not like I have tons of experience or anything, and I wanted to be good at it for you."

His hand went back to her bottom, rubbed, then his fingers were moving along her wet lips. He circled her clit. Lovingly. Tenderly. He applied a little pressure and heard her gasp. Her hips rocked. She tried to press into his fingers. Tried to grind down onto his hand. He kissed the nape of her neck and pulled his fingers back, giving her ass a hard swat, once again igniting those beautiful, dark, fresh stripes. She jumped and hissed, nearly forgetting about not making a sound unless she was orgasming. *Bog*, but he wanted a good reason to put her across his knee again. His cock ached. Jerked. Throbbed.

"You'll be good at sucking my cock, Seychelle. You don't need a book." He couldn't keep the amusement from his voice.

"How do you know? All those women you had before, that's what they did for you. You never once asked me, not in all the time we've been together. Shari told me you liked it a specific way and I wasn't capable of giving you that. I didn't understand what she was talking about."

"She meant I fucked her face. That's what I did to those women. I fucked their mouths. After I whipped the shit out of them, I fucked their faces."

Seychelle looked back at him, a little frown on her face. "I don't understand what you mean."

He couldn't help the smirk as he reached up to trace her lips with the pads of his fingers. That mouth of hers. So damn beautiful. Made for wrapping around his cock. "Of course you don't."

Seychelle stared up at him for a few more seconds, and then her long lashes veiled the expression in her blue eyes. Tension coiled in her body. She rolled out from under him, to the other side of the bed, sat up and was off and walking away to the bathroom. Back straight. Shoulders straight. Head up. She didn't look back. She closed the door. There were no locks on the door, but there might as well have been. She'd locked him out of her head just as sure as she wanted him away from her—he wasn't certain why, but he knew he'd just fucked up. He just didn't know how.

ELEVEN

Savage had to admit to himself that he was worried about his woman. The ride to their destination was long, and Seychelle wasn't used to being on the back of a motorcycle. He'd made it as comfortable as possible for her, and they'd stopped twice—something he would never have done for himself or anyone else.

Maestro and Keys had stopped with him while he went with her into the women's restroom, ignoring the shocked looks of the patrons of the restaurant he'd chosen. He applied the numbing lotion to her bottom while his brothers guarded the door. She hadn't complained or indicated that she was in pain, but he could see the relief in her eyes when he smoothed the lotion over her ass and the backs of her thighs.

He couldn't imagine what the vibration of the bike, mile after mile, was doing to her sore muscles. He should have rejoiced in her pain, but he didn't. He framed her face with both hands and kissed her gently before putting her behind him again. She hadn't hesitated. She'd just climbed back on and slid her arms around his waist, locking them tight.

Holding him. He was grateful for that, because she sure as hell wasn't talking to him much.

After leaving their bed the night before without saying one word to him, she'd taken a long bath. When he'd gone to her, she'd been asleep in the tub. He'd let out the water, carried her to bed and rubbed lotion onto her bottom and thighs before pulling up the sheet and wrapping his arm around her waist the way he did in order to fall asleep. In the morning, they'd hastily packed their things in the small compartments in his bike, pulled on their riding gear and joined the others for the long run starting in the early morning hours.

He detested that they were out of sync. He dropped one gloved hand to her calf as they made their way down the highway toward their destination. His brothers rode close, but this time, Blythe was staying home. Czar made the excuse that two of the children were sick. She wasn't the only wife not going. Most weren't making the run. Savage knew, even though she hadn't yet commented, that Seychelle had noticed the lack of women riding with their men. Her gaze slid over the bikes at every stop and then went up to his face.

Only Scarlet, Absinthe's wife, and Lissa, Casimir's wife, were along, and that was because both were worth their weight in gold when it came to fighting. Czar had made the decision to have the rest of the women stay home. He was concerned that whatever they were walking into might be too dangerous. More and more, Savage wished he'd left Seychelle home, in spite of his need of her and Czar's insistence that she come along. He knew the club needed him, and he would need Seychelle, but this one time, maybe he should have tried toughing it out.

Where Savage went, Seychelle went, especially in this particular shit show. He detested that he was putting her in such a dangerous position. Worse, she was hurting. Not the physical pain she was enduring; he would get off on that. He'd hurt her feelings last night. He wasn't certain just how, but he knew he had. He didn't like that at all. And she knew something was very wrong just by the lack of other wives going on the run. He played with the idea of turning back. Taking her home.

His woman wasn't oblivious. She'd heard about how "fun" the runs could be. Even though they'd said this one might be dangerous, they'd also told her it would be fun. Just the fact that Ice hadn't brought Soleil or Reaper, Anya, meant something. She was already upset with him, and the lack of other women wasn't helping his cause.

He reached for her hand and brought it to his thigh, pressing it deep into his muscle, half expecting her to pull away from him. She didn't. She pressed the hand at his abdomen tighter into him and left her other hand trapped between his thigh and palm. He realized she needed comfort. He didn't feel anger coming from her. He would know. More than anything, he felt that well of sadness in her. He'd much prefer the anger.

She didn't ask him to stop, even when she grew physically uncomfortable. She didn't try to communicate. Not once. Maestro called for a halt two hours later, and Savage knew he'd done it for Seychelle. She was so damn stubborn she wasn't about to ask for any special favors, no matter how tough the ride was on her. Maestro had noticed she was walking slow when she made her way to the restroom, and he took pity on her.

"That is one tough woman," Maestro said, glancing toward the restrooms.

The women's rooms were only about twenty feet away from the main parking area, but Savage was uneasy with her out of his sight. He should have gone in with her, but she'd objected to him invading her privacy in the bathroom and held out her hand for the bottle of lotion. That shouldn't matter to him, not when her safety was an issue. The others were pulling into the parking lot, but he didn't like giving her any space at all—so why was he?

Because he didn't want to face the fact that she knew things weren't right and he couldn't answer questions once again. He needed time to think. They were close to their destination now, and if he was going to take her home, he would have to turn around now.

"Yeah, she is," he agreed.

"Czar briefed us on the Brandon Campbell–Ravard connection she put together and the possibility that Campbell is behind the hit on you. You think she's right?" Maestro tipped his head back, studying Savage's face through his shades.

Savage nodded slowly. "Yeah. I think it's possible she's onto something. I think it's entirely possible Campbell's been trying to start a war between the Diamondbacks and the Venomous club, and along come Seychelle and Torpedo Ink. She's totally on his radar now. Her talent is huge, and he knows it. I'm in his way because he knows I'm her protection. He has to remove me. Torpedo Ink is a small club. He isn't looking at it like we're a threat as a club yet. Only me. If he's been working on the Venomous club for a while, all he's thinking about is removing any obstacles in his path and building his power base."

"And this shit with Alena?"

"I think that Plank is trying to get something to blackmail our club with." Savage shrugged. "I could be wrong, but he's nervous, and the club president shouldn't be showing his nerves to his club. Two separate things are going on."

"We're going to have to do a little cleaning," Maestro continued. "Maybe a lot." There was a hint of worry in his voice. "Just an observation, but your woman seems to be able to read more than you might want her to when she's touching you."

"Yeah." Savage rubbed the back of his neck. There was an itch developing between his shoulder blades as if a target had been placed squarely on him. "I'm very aware. She thinks she understands what I do for the club. Talking about it and seeing it are two different things."

Maestro took off his shades and lifted an eyebrow. "You expect me to believe that shit?"

Savage sighed. "I'm easing her into it. I'm hoping she

never has to know the extent of what I do. She knows I've had to kill and that I ask the questions, just not how. I'll shield her as best I can from that shit. I'm not easy as it is, Maestro, and I never will be. She's got courage. This is just the beginning, and she's getting thrown in when things are rough. I was hoping for time to ease her in, but we aren't getting it."

Maestro sighed. "Why didn't you leave her behind?"

Savage scowled at him. "You know why. I have to bleed off some of the fucking rage or I'll kill someone."

"There're going to be hundreds of willing women there, Savage. Any one of them will get on their knees for you. They always do."

"You want to cheat your woman, Maestro, you do it. I'm not disrespecting mine."

"Sparing her and disrespecting her aren't the same. In any case, I don't see that letting her have the upper hand in the relationship has done any of you any good. Your woman is in danger, and you have no idea how she's going to behave on this trip. None. She's a total wild card. All of them are. For all of her disagreeing with our lifestyle, the only one we can count on to obey when push comes to shove is Blythe, and that's shocking."

There was no getting around who he was. A fucking sadist who had to put whip marks on his woman to be aroused. To see tears on her face. To spank her ass until his handprints turned her bottom a deep hue. He glanced at Maestro. There was no getting around who Maestro was either. They were all products of their childhood. They'd tried to turn it around, tried to escape what they'd been shaped into, monsters some of them, but it was impossible, and in the end, they had to make peace with themselves or blow their fucking heads off.

"That's because Blythe totally trusts Czar and puts her faith in his word," Savage said. "That kind of trust requires time, Maestro. Keeping your fucking word, no matter what, including not cheating. You, of all people, know that trust is huge between a couple in our kind of relationship. This shit isn't easy, and I'm not going to pretend to know what I'm doing. I feel like I'm walking through a minefield, but she's worth it to me. I do know that she's going to get hurt and she's going to take on a lot of pain for me. I have to give her something back. I *want* to give her something back."

"What you're giving her by looking at her the way you do is a fucking target painted right between her eyes, Savage. I'm your brother. I stand with you, and I'll protect that girl with my life, but I hope to hell you and Czar know what you're doing this weekend."

Savage hoped they did too. Czar needed Savage there, and Savage needed Seychelle. Czar was positive they needed Seychelle there as well. He'd all but decreed she be there. That was unusual, but Czar had that weird talent that no one questioned. If he said they'd need Seychelle, then Savage wasn't going to argue—at least he hadn't been. Now, things were different. He should have talked to Seychelle about what was coming. He'd intended to do just that the night before, but then the Diamondbacks showed up at the restaurant. After that, everything went south at home.

More motorcycles had pulled into the gas station, and he found himself meeting his woman as she came out of the restroom. Any other time he'd be happy she was walking slow and gingerly, but he could only focus on the sadness on her face. That wasn't Seychelle. She lived in the moment. She would normally be looking around her, taking everything in, looking at him with joy and sharing the smallest detail.

His heart dropped. This wasn't okay. Not by a long shot. He wrapped his arm around her and drew her close. "Babe, I've got to talk to Czar. Shouldn't take long. Would you mind hanging with Maestro for a few minutes?"

Her stunning blue eyes searched his face, moved to the rest of his brethren, the few women, and then to where Maestro lounged beside one of the few tables outside.

"I'm good right here." She patted the seat of his Harley.

"Standing and walking around feels good on my sore bum."
She flashed a small grin at him, inviting him to share her
predicament.

Savage framed her face with his hands. "I should have
listened to you, baby, about the run. I was being selfish. I
never thought of myself as being a selfish man, but I'm beginning to see I have more of that in me than I ever realized."

She gave him a little frown. "You're always so decisive,
Savage. Why are you changing your mind about me going
with you?"

"I don't like what this is doing to us. Just give me a few
minutes, Seychelle. I'll be right back." He brushed his lips
gently over hers, trying to convey tenderness. Love. Trying
to tell her no matter what, he stood with her.

She nodded, and Savage dropped his hands and walked
away from her. He didn't like the fact that Lana, Alena,
Lissa and Scarlet sat at one of the small tables in the middle
of the grass and his woman was by herself on the sidewalk
near his bike. Deliberately, he didn't look back, but he saw
everything, and he carried that shit in his mind when he approached his president.

"Need to talk to you, Czar."

"Sure," Czar said readily.

Savage glanced at Reaper and Destroyer, the two men
guarding Czar. "Private."

Czar frowned, lifting his gaze beyond him to where Seychelle paced in front of the row of bikes and then nodded.
He gestured along the walkway. "What's up?"

"I want to take Seychelle back home. I'll leave her with
the other women and your brothers, the ones looking out for
them, and I'll meet you before midnight. I can take Maestro
with me."

"What's wrong, Savage?"

"I don't know, but something. Something huge, Czar. I've
got a bad feeling, and I don't ever ignore my gut. She's not
happy. She didn't want to come in the first place. We're not

in sync, and for something like this to work, we need to be. She shouldn't be here."

Czar stood at the corner of the building, once more looking at Seychelle. "Ordinarily, I would say you would be right to leave her home, but you're going to need her, Savage."

Savage felt a sudden rush of adrenaline, the onset of his vicious temper. He turned away from his president, pushing down the swirling rage. "I wish everyone would quit telling me what I'm going to need. The truth is, only I can say what I'm going to need, and when. I do have some self-control, and over the years I've actually used it a time or two."

"That's true. I can't argue with that. On the other hand, we have enemies coming at us from all sides again. We don't even know who half of them are, Savage, and it's your job to find out."

"That's another reason she shouldn't be here. Do you really think she isn't going to find out what the fuck I do to get that information? She had nightmares even after I took tremendous precautions after questioning Arnold. She'll be right here with me. It isn't like I'll be able to go somewhere for a night before I see her. It's best if she's home waiting for me."

Czar was silent for a few moments, his gaze still on Seychelle. Slowly, he shook his head. "That isn't going to work this time."

"It's my body. My head. I can hold it together," Savage snarled. Seychelle was his woman. Czar had the right to dictate club business, but this was stepping on relationship business. "Seychelle is in over her head, and both of us know it. She's hanging on by a thread. You all but threatened her when I took her to your home. She's a smart woman, and she caught on to what you were saying about club business and who she could trust and who she couldn't. I'm telling you straight up, she isn't ready for this. I want to take her home. You can count on me. I wouldn't ever let the club down."

Czar's eyes were a deep, penetrating blue, like twin ice picks. "I never thought you would, Savage, but you put your claim on her, and that made her Torpedo Ink. She's needed. Not just by you, and you will need her. I absolutely know that you will, but the club will need her too. So no, this isn't just about your relationship. This is club business."

Savage balled his fist and stepped toward Czar. "Like fucking hell, it is. Seychelle is *my* business. You don't get to dictate to me what I do with my woman."

Reaper and Destroyer moved closer, feeling the threat to Czar. It poured off Savage. Czar didn't move. He just looked at Savage, waiting.

~

Maestro sauntered across the grass to Seychelle's side. She flicked him a quick look from under her lashes but kept striding back and forth. Lana and Alena followed him at a much more leisurely pace. Seychelle could tell by the stealthy looks they were exchanging and the quick glances they were sneaking at Czar and Savage that what they were really after was information.

"Are you going to stop wasting energy?" Maestro demanded. "Stand still, for fuck's sake, Seychelle."

Of everyone in the Torpedo Ink club, Maestro reminded her the most of Savage. Sometimes Destroyer did as well, but he rarely spoke, so it was difficult to assess his personality.

"Did you want something?" Seychelle asked, coming to a stop in front of him but where she could keep an eye on her man. He seemed very tense. Angry, even, which didn't make sense when he was talking with Czar. Just looking at him, anyone could see the danger pouring off him, warning anyone coming close to him to stay away. She wasn't the only one to think that; Czar's personal bodyguards had moved in protectively.

"What's got Savage so upset that he's threatening Czar?"

"Is that what he's doing?" Seychelle asked, going for wide-eyed innocence. He definitely looked threatening, not that Czar was backing down.

"Yeah, I'd say Savage was getting close to decking him."

"Isn't there some kind of rule against decking the club president?" Seychelle lifted one eyebrow. Savage would have yanked her to him and delivered a smack to her butt. The moment she was sarcastic, he would have known she was giving him crap.

Lana and Alena overheard. They had walked right up to them, uncaring whether or not the conversation was private.

"I see you didn't waste any time causing trouble," Lana pointed out. "I was afraid this might happen. A rift between our top enforcer and our president. All over little old you. That must make you feel powerful."

Seychelle sent her a vapid smile. "You have no idea. I lay awake at night and plot how best to get Savage riled up against the president of his club just to cause trouble. It gives me such a rush."

"Lana," Alena cautioned. She waved a dismissing hand, as if that would clear the air between all of them. "Stop acting silly. She doesn't mean anything, Seychelle. What are they fighting about?"

"I wouldn't know. Savage told me to stay put and he'd only be a minute. That was a little while ago. I could tell the exchange was getting heated, but I have no idea why." She turned her gaze back on Lana. "You know, I'd really appreciate it if you didn't pretend to be my friend when we're in Sea Haven, around all the ladies having tea. You told me you thought I was so good for Savage, and now you act like I'm poison for him. I don't mind someone despising me without reason, but being two-faced is difficult to take." Seychelle thought she might as well throw down the gauntlet. What did she have to lose?

Lana's face flushed under Maestro's sudden, penetrating scrutiny. "It's hardly like that."

Seychelle's eyebrow shot up. "Really? Because it feels exactly like that. An attack on me every time you get anywhere near me. You didn't want me here. You still don't."

"No, I don't think it's a good idea."

Seychelle looked at all three of their faces. "None of you do. So what exactly do you think Savage should do when he needs to get rid of his rage? Beat someone to death? Or are you all three advocates of him cheating on me?" She thought she might as well put that out there and find out just who was supporting Savage and her as a couple and who wasn't.

Maestro and Lana both frowned at her and then looked at each other. Alena looked at her boots. She understood what it felt like to have someone she thought was with her exclusively betray her.

Lana shrugged. "Cheating isn't the same as making sure Savage is taken care of properly in a bad situation."

"You clearly don't think I'm capable of doing what perfect strangers do." Seychelle tried not to think about the amusement in Savage's voice or the smirk on his face the night before when she'd asked him questions about giving blow jobs.

Lana shrugged again, her face a mask of indifference, showing she didn't believe Seychelle capable of meeting Savage's needs.

Alena's breath hissed out. "Lana." That was a clear reprimand.

Seychelle flicked her gaze to Maestro's face. Like Savage, he wore a mask, but his eyes held compassion and also an emotion that told her he didn't think she should be there either. She turned away from them without speaking again. She'd known she really didn't have friends or allies in Savage's club in spite of him telling her she did.

Torpedo Ink remained their biggest problem, and she knew it probably always would. She would have to find a way to come to terms with it if she was going to remain with him, and that meant she would have to convince him to allow her to stay separate from them as much as she could. She ignored the pang of hurt. She'd wanted to be part of his family, but truthfully, she was used to being alone. She had a good life without the club. She liked her older friends, and they kept her busy. She didn't want to be used for her talent and have the members of the club support her partner cheating on her.

"Seychelle." Maestro's voice was gentle.

She didn't turn around but kept up her pacing, eyes on Savage. He was, thankfully, heading her way. "What is it?"

"No one meant to hurt you."

"I told Lana I preferred honesty, and I do. It isn't always easy to hear what people think of you, especially the family of the man you love, but better it be honesty than lies."

"You're misinterpreting what we're saying."

She shook her head. "No, Maestro, I don't think I am. You want Savage to be with another woman, not me. I'm not good enough to get him through a bad time. I think that's clear. Torpedo Ink is a closed club unless the woman is a fighter like Scarlet or Lissa. There's no respect for someone like me. I think that's obvious. I feel a little sorry for you. You're going to find a woman and you're going to blow it so bad with her. Your lovely little family isn't going to help you either, because she isn't going to fit into their image of what she should be."

Before he could answer her, Savage was there, his strong fingers wrapping around the nape of her neck. "You ready to go, baby?"

Seychelle shrugged, her heart sinking. She had been hoping the argument with Czar had been about the two of them turning around and going home.

Savage turned them toward the line of Harleys. Already, the others were on their bikes. "Thanks for looking out for her, Maestro," Savage said.

Maestro didn't answer, and Seychelle didn't look at him. Maybe Maestro really thought getting rid of her was the best thing for Savage after all. Was it? She had never considered that. All along, she thought she was good for him. What if she wasn't? What if his club knew better than she did? Better than Savage?

Ordinarily, Savage would have read her silence and immediately asked her what was wrong, but he didn't. He simply walked her to the Harley, handed her the helmet and waited almost impatiently for her to put it on. He seemed upset.

"Honey." She needed to clear the air between them.

"Not here, Seychelle. We can't get separated. We can talk at the campground." His gaze avoided hers.

"More club business?"

"If you want to put it like that." He slid onto the bike with his casual grace, and the Harley roared to life.

Seychelle took a deep breath, got on behind him, wrapped her arms around him and pressed close, closing her eyes against the burn of tears. Why did it feel as if every time they made any progress, the world found ways to tear them apart?

Seychelle had to be somewhat intimidated by the number of clubs represented, so many bikers together, a sea of them. Just the sheer volume of laughter and conversation as they made their way through the campgrounds. Music blared, the parties already starting. They parked their Harleys in long rows in the area they'd claimed and then, as was their usual routine, took a walk around to orient themselves so they would know which clubs were camping where. Torpedo Ink members had learned from the time they were young to keep maps in their heads. Even in crowds or in the dark, they didn't get lost.

Savage knew he'd been too abrupt with Seychelle at the gas station when she'd asked him about his conversation with Czar. She hadn't even asked him. Just as if everything was okay. He should have taken the time to reassure her, but he was so angry with Czar insisting she had to be on the run when there was unspecified danger to all of them. Czar wasn't willing to risk Blythe, but he sure as hell was willing to risk Seychelle.

Seychelle stayed one step behind him, moving in unison with him, staying in the center of their club members, but that was only because they surrounded her. Not because she wanted to be there. She held herself away from them. Savage was tuned to her, and she was very stiff, avoiding looking at any of them.

Her fingers tightened in his belt loop. "You do realize that the only women from Torpedo Ink here are Scarlet, Lissa, Lana, Alena and me."

Savage knew he was in trouble just by the dead calm in her voice. Seychelle was quite capable of taking that cell of hers and finding a way to call an Uber or getting a passerby to drive her all the way to the coast just on her big blue eyes alone. He was treading on thin ice, and he knew it. She might give him what he wanted sexually, but he had to fight for what he wanted outside of it.

Savage nodded, glancing at her set face. There was no lying to her, putting her off by telling her the flu was running through all the women and they had to stay home. She was intelligent, and he had to give her a partial truth.

"Yeah, babe. At the last minute, the club decided we could be in a lot more trouble than we first thought. Lana, Alena, Scarlet and Lissa can handle themselves in a fight. I needed you with me or I wouldn't have brought you. I was going to talk to you about that last night, but other things came up. We were in a hurry this morning, and I just didn't think about it."

"Mmm-hmm," she murmured.

Yeah, he was in trouble. She'd flicked a quick glance at Scarlet and Lissa. That was trouble right there. She *really* didn't like the fact that she wasn't privy to club matters and yet some of the others were. How did he explain that Scarlet and Lissa were told things when, technically, they wore the same jacket she wore? Shit, he was really fucked. That hurt she was feeling? Traces of anger were beginning to thread through it. Never a good sign when they were out in the open and he needed to keep his woman under the radar.

He kept walking, keeping her moving, weaving his way

through what appeared to be the chaos of bike clubs. He was used to the sights and scents, the loud music and conversations. The roar of the bikes and the greetings of old friends. He nodded to several acquaintances as he made his way through the crowd, his club surrounding Seychelle, although they just appeared as if they were walking together.

He realized, for the first time, how many women watched him with hungry eyes as he walked through the crowd, seeing them through Seychelle's eyes. She was a couple of steps behind him, her hand still in his back pocket, allowing him to scan the crowd and lead the way, ensuring her safety. He'd never paid attention before to the women or the way they looked at him. Maestro was right. There were quite a few making it obvious they were more than willing to be with him in spite—or because—of his rough reputation. It didn't seem to matter to them that he had a woman with him.

He'd lost Seychelle once already over using another woman when things were rough. He wasn't chancing it again, but . . . He sighed. Things could get very rough this weekend. Was it possible Maestro was right? What was the definition of cheating?

Seychelle pulled her hand from his back pocket abruptly and suddenly stopped, turning around in a slow circle. She started walking in the opposite direction. He caught her around the waist, jerking her none-too-gently back to him. The only thing that had allowed him to keep her with him was the fact that the club had kept her surrounded.

"What the fuck, Seychelle?" He let her see that he was pissed. "I thought I told you not to wander off by yourself, and the first thing you do is take off."

She tilted her fucking chin at him, her eyes so dark he thought he saw pure fury in them. He could *feel* her fury. This wasn't like anything he'd ever experienced with Seychelle. She had spurts of temper, but not like this.

"I didn't realize I needed your permission to make certain I knew where the bathroom was, Savage. I think I'm all grown up." She flung that right in his face, uncaring if anyone heard her or not.

"That's why Lana, Alena, Lissa and Scarlet are here," he snapped.

"Yeah, well, Lana and Alena aren't happy I'm here, so I'm not about to ask them to escort me to the bathroom every time I have to go."

Yeah, she was royally pissed. He'd never seen her so angry. She wasn't going to back down. Not for him. Not for the girls. Not for the club. He looked over her head at Alena and Lana. Seychelle hadn't bothered to be sweet and nice, keeping her voice lowered to spare them her anger. For that matter, she didn't bother to hold back at all. Czar and the rest of the club heard. Ordinarily, there would be some smirking going on, but not now, not under these circumstances. The danger factor was too high.

He'd obviously fucked up huge again. Shit. Had she caught his thoughts? It was entirely possible. He'd been thinking about other women blowing him. The images had been there in his mind. If she'd been looking, she would have seen them. That wasn't good coming on the heels of whatever the hell he'd done the night before or the fact that she knew he was keeping things from her the other women knew. The club knew. This was turning into a shit show.

"All right, babe, we'll scout out the bathrooms nearest the campsite. Fatei marked them for us," he said, doing his best to appease her. She had been touching him. Her hand had been in his back pocket.

Seychelle was spoiling for a fight with him. Looking for a reason to leave. She'd been too quiet ever since they'd left that gas station. Different. Holding herself away from him. Not her body, but her mind. There was that space he couldn't quite bridge. Something had happened while he'd been arguing with Czar.

He glanced over her head to Maestro. Several times he'd checked on her and he'd seen Lana, Alena and Maestro with her and he'd been reassured. Now, he wondered what had happened, especially when Maestro sighed and shook his head. That wasn't a good sign. He tapped a code on his chest.

Maestro tapped two words back. *Shit show.*

What the fuck did that mean? Even though Seychelle didn't want to take his hand, Savage shackled her wrist and began walking in the direction of their camp, forcing her to go with them. Short of an all-out struggle, which for a moment she seemed to actually consider, Seychelle went with him. He tapped the question on his chest. He didn't like the answer he received. His brother and sisters, rather than making Seychelle feel as if she was wanted, had made her feel as if they didn't approve of her for Savage. That hadn't been their intent, but they didn't feel she was capable of handling what might happen. She'd taken it wrong. It had been delivered in a clumsy manner.

Savage cursed under his breath. He was fighting to get his woman to accept Torpedo Ink, and they were making it much more difficult for him.

Czar moved up to the other side of her, giving Lana and Alena an inquiring lift of his eyebrow. Neither woman met his eyes.

"I know this is stressful, Seychelle. I wouldn't have asked Savage to bring you along if I didn't think we'd really need you again. I appreciate you coming. I know you didn't want to be here. It's difficult when you don't know the rules, but we'll look after you."

"Maybe you should look after Savage. It appears he needs it more than I do."

"I can understand you're worried about him," Czar said, feeling his way. "But we'll watch his back, and when he's in trouble, you'll be here to see to him."

"I'm told the help he needs when he has too much rage is in plenty of supply here, Czar, and I'm not needed at all. In fact, I'm a liability to him." There was frost in her voice. Pure ice. She kept walking, head up, not looking at any one of the club members walking close to them.

Savage turned his death stare on Maestro and Lana. It

was a shit thing for them to do to make Seychelle feel she wasn't worth anything.

Czar's head snapped up. He looked at Savage as if Savage had lost his mind. Savage shook his head. He would never tell his woman that. Not in a million years, and Czar should know that.

Before Czar could ask, Seychelle went on. "It appears you don't need many of the other women, Czar." Her cool blue eyes raked the president. "Nor did you have any problem telling the ones you chose to bring what to expect."

Shit. Shit. Shit. She didn't care in the least about throwing shit in Czar's face. Her jacket might say PROPERTY OF on it, but she didn't know exactly what that meant, and that was on him—not that she would have cared at that moment. She was looking for any reason to leave. One wrong misstep, and there was going to be a battle to end all battles; he could see the determination on her face.

She gave another twist to her wrist to try to get his fingers off hers. He tightened them, not willing to let her go. For all he knew, she might take it in her head to run. She definitely didn't want his hands on her. She wasn't fooling around either. Seychelle was her own person. He had a feeling if she could have, she would have marched right out from under the club's watchful eyes and gone back to Sea Haven on her own.

He glanced at Czar's set features. Czar read people better than anyone he knew. He had a gift for it. Right now, he was reading Seychelle. Like Savage, he was concerned that their little songbird was contemplating flying her cage. Czar sent Savage a look that clearly asked what the hell he'd done. Then Czar glanced over his shoulder at the two women with that same look on his face. They both squirmed as well. At least they knew Czar wanted Seychelle along. If he'd demanded she be there, their petty interference hadn't been a good idea, and both of them knew it.

Savage remained quiet. He just wanted to get to their

campsite and be alone with his woman. He needed to know what had been said to her. He needed to tell her what Czar had said to him. They had to be united as much as possible. She had to be hurt and scared. She needed to lean on him, and he had to show her she was his priority.

TWELVE

Hyde and Glitch had secured the campsite Czar had ordered, one in deep cover, one they could protect fairly easily. They'd scouted the site weeks earlier when they knew they were going to join the Diamondbacks on the run.

Once Czar had realized what might happen on the run and that Savage would most likely have to use his skills to extract information for the club, Czar wanted to give him as much comfort for Seychelle as possible. They both knew she might be needed every evening rather than just one. Their camping area was in the very corner under trees, with the rest of the club surrounding them on three sides. They had plenty of room, including a picnic table and an area where they could sleep privately, as well as a small firepit of their own if they wanted to use it.

Savage set up their gear while Seychelle watched him, keeping the picnic table between them at all times. She pulled off her gloves and heavy jacket, tossing them onto the table before undoing the tight weave she'd put in her hair. The wind had picked up, and as fast as she pulled her fingers through to tame the wavy platinum-and-gold hair, it got away from her and went wild, just the way he liked it best.

The other members of Torpedo Ink claimed various spots to set up their private quarters around them but at a far enough distance to give them privacy, something that was not ordinary by any means. He didn't bother to tell Seychelle that, nor did he think she would care, not the way she was looking at him.

Once he had everything exactly where he wanted it and could get his hands on weapons anywhere in their campsite, he turned his attention to his woman. She had watched his every move, noting where every item was kept, alternating with scanning around to check out those camping beyond Torpedo Ink. That was much more difficult, because Czar had claimed a bit of territory for them to make it harder for any club to get to the women in the center. He was just as worried about Alena as he was about Seychelle.

The second Torpedo Ink chapter based in Trinity had surrounded their chapter, adding an additional protective ring. Originally their own club, the chapter was made up of men and women who had attended one of the schools Sorbacov had run. They had been trained as assassins to be used as assets for their country. Like the original members of Torpedo Ink, their families had been murdered. They had petitioned to join Torpedo Ink as a second chapter. The original members had voted them in.

"Babe, do you want to go first, or do you want me to?" Savage asked as he lifted the cooler onto the picnic table. "Czar had me so pissed I couldn't see straight this afternoon, and I didn't even notice you were upset. I should have." He pulled out plates and put bread on them. "You want cheese or ham and cheese? I can fire up the grill if you prefer something hot."

"I'm good with cheese. In case you've forgotten, I don't eat meat."

She was actually talking to him. That was a really good

sign. She came around the picnic table to climb up onto the other side to get out the condiments to help him.

"Yeah, babe, I remember. Wanted to make sure you were paying attention." He didn't forget details like that.

"Why were you so angry with Czar?"

"He didn't bring any of the other women. You didn't want to come, and you were really uncomfortable. Contrary to popular belief, I can actually control myself and go without someone who is not you blowing me for a couple of days. I wanted to take you home and then come back. Czar, instead of acting like a brother, acted like the president of the club and insisted you stay. He said it wasn't only me that needed you, whatever the fuck that means."

He slapped the thin slices of cheese on the bread and handed her the plate. "He was adamant. I told him I thought it was bullshit when he wasn't risking anyone else's woman."

"But you didn't defy him," Seychelle said, her voice very low.

His gaze jumped to her face, fury rising for a split second. He shoved it down. The anger was at himself. She didn't sound judgmental. That was on him. He hadn't told Czar to go fuck himself as he wanted to do. Like he'd been doing since he was a toddler, he followed his decree. He put his woman squarely in the path of whatever danger they were in. He couldn't even be angry with Czar. It had been his choice to go along with his president's ruling.

"No, I'm so used to always doing what Czar says because he has this sixth sense. Just the way we developed our psychic abilities, he developed his until they were razor-sharp. He sees things, knows things. He's never steered us wrong."

"Did he say why he thought I needed to be here?"

Savage shifted his weight onto the table and shook his head. "I don't think he knows. It was that way when we were kids down in the basement. I remember this one time there was this little girl. She was with another faction. We all kind of liked her. Lana and Alena were summoned upstairs, and so was the girl. They were going to be given to some asshole friend of Sorbacov who loved using the crop on little girls before he raped them. It wasn't the first time Lana and this girl had taken the crop. They were so small, but Sorbacov didn't care. Alena had never had the experience. We wanted to kill the fucker. Anyway, this girl said she was the new girl and took Alena's place."

Savage made himself a second ham-and-cheese sandwich and found a cold beer. He offered one to Seychelle. When she declined, he handed her a cold bottle of water.

"Keep going, honey. What happened to the girl?"

"She hit her head, which, honestly, we were grateful for. She couldn't see any of us in the room. We killed the asshole before he could hurt Alena. When we tried to tell Czar that we should find something to trade to the other group for her, he thought it over and then said no. He was like that sometimes; he wouldn't take kids we wanted to bring in with us. He said it was too risky, that she didn't fit with us. She never knew we even asked, but we all felt bad. The group she was with lied all the time and traded favors upstairs with the guards and instructors. Sorbacov owed someone a favor, and he gave her away. We never heard what happened to her."

"Has Czar ever been wrong?" Seychelle asked.

"Not that I know of. He says plenty of times, but when we've compared notes, none of us found when he was wrong. He's gotten us out of some bad messes just by having the right people in place when shit goes down."

"So you're saying I could be one of those right people." She took a drink of water, her blue eyes fixed on his face.

"You're the right person for me," he said.

She winced visibly. "Some of your brothers and sisters don't think so."

He'd been afraid of that. She'd said it straight up to Czar when they'd walked through the grounds earlier. He hoped Czar was delivering a much-earned lecture to Lana, Alena and Maestro right that minute. They had no right to undermine Seychelle's confidence. It was a damn good thing he wasn't alone with them right now. Maestro had all but admitted that he and Lana had told Seychelle she wasn't right for him. They hadn't meant it that way, it had just come off that way, whatever the fuck that meant.

To keep the adrenaline pouring into his system under control, he jumped off the table to retrieve two gas lamps. Lighting them, he hung them in the sprawling branches of the tree that spread across the campsite. Crouching beside the firepit, he began to build a fire for them.

"That's a load of crap. Are the girls giving you a hard time? I thought they'd dropped that and decided to be your friend." He didn't look at her. He didn't want her to see how upset he was.

"Why is it everyone seems to be under the impression that I can't handle your needs, Savage?"

He looked up at her from where he was crouching down beside the firepit. "I don't know, baby. They don't know you, and they haven't taken the time to get to know you. It isn't their business either. We made a pact, an agreement between us. What we do together is between us." He gestured around their campsite. "I asked for a private site, and they did come through for us. The brothers are protecting us, but we're shielded for the most part."

Seychelle took her time studying the borders of their site. She could see Ice and Storm moving around if she really tried. There were bushes between them, but not that many. Destroyer had a bedroll set out just down from them and in front of Czar. They were a fairly good distance from each other and from Savage's campsite. On the other side was Maestro and Keys. It wasn't easy to see any of them, and Savage knew they would avoid Savage's camp unless expressly invited.

"I thought I was getting to at least know Lana," Seychelle said. "She really was against me coming here. There seems to be some kind of idea that it's perfectly all right for you to use other women while you're away from me."

Her voice was very matter-of-fact, but he heard the underlying note of uncertainty. His gaze jumped to hers. She had the water bottle in her hand, halfway to her mouth. Her teeth were biting down on her bottom lip.

Savage stood and went to her. "Is that what they think?" He took the bottle from her hand and set it aside before sitting on the table.

She hopped off the table and immediately paced away from him. "You know they do." She rubbed at her temples as though she might have a headache and began to pace around the campsite.

"Do you care what they think, Seychelle?" He kept his gaze on her.

She didn't answer immediately, but her agitation was growing. His woman. She was pacing slow. Savage tried not to let the monster in him react. She was going to have enough to contend with on this trip. She already did. They were working through problems, and she was facing one hell of a punishment—which she knew and was probably thinking about right at that moment. Still, watching her move in those jeans, knowing his marks were rubbing, setting her ass and thighs on fire with every step, woke the beast in him.

There were all kinds of assholes who could wield a single-tailed whip and tear open skin, leaving a bloody mess and horrific scars, but very, very few could wield that same whip, raise long, bright welts in complicated patterns and never once break the skin. That was skill. Especially if they did so while sheer fury raged through their bloodstream.

The minute he laid eyes on Seychelle, he'd begun putting hours into practicing again. He wasn't about to slice open her skin. Welts were just fine, vicious ones when he was at his worst—he accepted that it would happen, but he refused to go beyond that. He was honest enough to admit he looked forward to seeing her skin covered in the hot, complicated patterns he could create, knowing they would stay for days, knowing just how much pressure he could wield before that whip would break the soft tissue of her skin.

Sometimes he woke covered in sweat, no longer dripping

from nightmares but with his cock raging with hunger. Images of Seychelle tied to the post, tears running down her face, begging him to take her, her body so needy, while he circled her, whip in hand, looking for one more hit, one more rush, before answering that need for both of them, pounded through his brain.

He had given himself hard limits with her. *Hard* limits. He wouldn't cross certain lines with her, no matter how far she was willing to go for him. He wasn't willing to go there. Not with her. He wouldn't be able to live with himself if he ripped her skin open and then got off on it—and he would. He'd be beyond aroused. They'd wired him that way. No matter what he'd done to try to undo the damage, it hadn't worked. He didn't need to go that far. He didn't even want to. But everything else—and there were so many other things that his little innocent had no idea of, in spite of her foray into darker porn.

"No." Her gaze flicked up to his. "Maybe. I don't know. I thought Lana and I were becoming friends. It was disconcerting to realize she doesn't respect me."

"Why are you way over there?" He patted the tabletop. "Why aren't you over here with me? We're working things out. Just the two of us. You're getting more agitated instead of calmer. Why is that, baby?"

She paused in her pacing. "I'm not." She flushed. Even she had to hear the lie in her voice. "Okay. You're right. I am. I don't know why. I do know why. I broke a lot of rules, and you're not going to let that go, are you?"

"No, babe. I'm not. But you wouldn't want me to."

Her chin went up, and her eyes flashed at him. "I had every right to be super pissed."

"Yes, you did," he agreed gently. *Bog*, she was beautiful in her righteous anger. She was working herself up. "Absolutely, you had every right to be pissed at Lana, Alena and Maestro. Czar too. For all I know, the whole fuckin' club." He leaned toward her, his eyes holding her captive. "But not at me. You were pissed, and you disrespected me in front of everyone."

In the yellow light of the two lanterns and the crackling fire, he saw the flush spread up her neck and into her face. "I was just so angry with Lana. I did think of her as a friend, Savage."

She looked at him, and he flinched inside at the hurt in her eyes. He wanted to shake Lana until her teeth rattled. "I know you did, baby. I'm sorry she hurt you. I'm certain she does consider you a friend. She separates things in her mind in a way she shouldn't. We're all damaged. That doesn't give any of us the right to hurt others, and we can't use it as an excuse, but that's the reason she doesn't get that what she said to you was wrong. Czar is setting her straight, and she's going to feel like an utter ass."

"That won't make any difference to how she made me feel," Seychelle pointed out. "Alena is supposed to be her sister. Pierce totally betrayed her. The things she said to me had to have struck a nerve with Alena too, but she didn't even think of that. Not for a minute."

Savage nodded. He rubbed his hand on his thigh, watching her try to move in the jeans. She was very uncomfortable after riding all day with the denim rubbing on her sore bottom. She was about to get a lot sorer. She knew it. He knew it. His cock *really* knew it. Most likely, so did her pussy. She squirmed a little, but she wasn't quite ready to give either of them the outlet they needed.

He had no idea when he looked at her, like now, with the strange light shining on her, giving her hair a glow that always made him think of her as his angel, that he would actually feel a physical sensation of an emotion. Love welling up. It was stronger than the terrible rage that was always present in his belly. That well that was inside, churning, waiting for a way to burst its way out. Her love smothered it, just covered it like a blanket.

He experienced the emotion nearly like a panic attack,

with his heart pounding and his mouth going dry. He felt a little light-headed. He didn't understand why his fellow Torpedo Ink members couldn't see she had changed his life completely. He'd been ready to drive off a fucking cliff. There was nothing for him. Nothing. It wasn't like he hadn't tried to find outlets or pursued ways to "cure" himself. He was intelligent. In the end, he accepted that he wasn't going to live much longer. And then Seychelle had virtually saved his life and his sanity. She brought him laughter and even joy. She also found what was left of gentleness and tenderness. Both those emotions were growing in him. He didn't know if that was a good thing or a bad thing. He was supposed to be a badass, but his woman had a way of turning that around.

"Baby, come here to me." He said it softly. Letting her know it was time. She'd feel better. She would. A release of tension. Letting it all go. The anger and hurt. That slow buildup of sexual tension between the two of them. He would feel better as well.

She shook her head. Held up her hand as if he were moving toward her, not the other way around. "They were horrible to me. I really don't like them."

"I know they were, Seychelle. If you come here to me, you know I'll make you feel better. I can't do that when you're all the way over there."

"You're going to punish me," she repeated.

"Not for anything you said or did to any of them. You had every right to say whatever you wanted to, although I will say, you were wearing my ring and my jacket, and I'll have to answer to Czar for your disrespect in front of the club. They would overlook it, but it was in public, which means another club might have overheard."

Seychelle froze. "I don't understand, Savage."

"I'm responsible for anything you do, baby—you know that. We talked about that. Czar is president of Torpedo Ink. In public, especially around other clubs, he is always held in the highest regard. I don't start a fistfight with him at a gas station, and you don't call him out when we're walking through the campsites, where other clubs can hear you. It's no big deal. You didn't say much, and if he chews me out, I'll take the hit. He deserved it, and he knows it."

She bit her lip and then raised her gaze once more to his. His heart stuttered in his chest. He loved her so much. "I should have taken you home, Seychelle. What happened with Czar was on me as much as it was on you."

She shook her head. "No, it wasn't. I knew better."

Seychelle regarded Savage in the flickering light thrown from the firepit. Her heart began to accelerate. Her mouth went dry. Her hands shook, and behind her eyes there was a curious burning sensation. He looked powerful, very intimidating as he sat there on the picnic table, his muscles moving subtly beneath his thin tee when he leaned toward her. His eyes were that pure glacier blue that made her heart pound and turned her blood to molten heat.

She had known better than to call out Czar as they walked through the other clubs' campsites. She'd been so angry at all of them. The more they'd walked through the various clubs, the more the tension had risen in the members of Torpedo Ink. They'd hidden it well, but she'd felt it.

She realized she was the only woman who really couldn't be considered a club member. She'd heard about Scarlet and Lissa and their skills as assassins. They could be fully patched members if they chose. They fought as one of them. They were treated as one of them. They had all the information as one of them, unlike Seychelle, who once again, just like the night she sang at the clubhouse, was clearly being used by the club but was uninformed.

With every step she took, she felt the danger increase—not to her, and surprisingly not to Alena, but to Savage. He knew it too. They all knew it. Every single member of the club. Yet he walked calmly like the sacrificial lamb, as if no one were going to try to kill him. They were all part of that club. She was the outsider. No matter how hard she tried to get close to him, no matter what she did for him, with him, Savage didn't seem to trust her enough to confide in her. Just the people he surrounded himself with.

She had wanted to strike at them all, especially Czar. In that moment, she despised every single club member. Lana had pointed out that she wasn't good enough to take care of Savage's needs, and just like that, he had an image of a woman down on her knees, his cock in her mouth. She'd wanted to kick him hard in that particular portion of his anatomy. So yeah, she thought Czar deserved her snapping at him. Lana and Maestro deserved her contempt, and even Savage, now that she remembered what had been going through his mind.

She narrowed her eyes at him and remained a distance away, even though everything in her wanted to go to him. She was almost desperate to go.

"Angel, you're going to feel so much better once we take care of this. You're just dragging it out now." He drew his thighs apart. "Seychelle. Babe. The only way to make this right is to come over here to me."

"They all know someone here is going to try to kill you, Savage. They act like it doesn't matter at all. They act like it doesn't matter if you cheat on me. Nothing seems to get to them because it isn't happening to them." She paced in front of him, back and forth, the tension in her coiling tighter and tighter.

He remained silent, just watching her.

Did she need him to ground her? Sometimes when he was holding her firmly, giving her orders, she wasn't thinking. Right now, her brain was all over the place, looping like mad. She wanted to throw things. At him. At his club. She honestly didn't know what she wanted—or needed. Only that she hated that he could look so in control when he knew someone was going to try to kill him and she was a mess. Why was he always so in control?

Finally, he sighed. "Seychelle, come here." He pointed to the spot between his legs.

He had that damn voice. Low. A kind of caress that brushed over her skin like the velvet rasp of his tongue. She shook her head, because her brain said no, even when her body said yes. She even took a step toward him, blood thundering in her ears, attempting to drown out the noise that refused to make any sense looping in her brain, making her want to yell at him.

"Baby, you're only making this harder on yourself. You know you want to come here to me. You need me. It's written all over your face. You have to do it, angel. I can't do it for you. It's always your choice, you know that."

She took two more steps toward him before she stopped herself and considered, one hand pushing against her trembling lips.

She both hated and loved him for giving her a choice. She didn't want to make decisions. She wanted to bury her head in the sand like an ostrich, not see what was right in front of her, because if she did, then she'd know why she was there. She didn't want to be with Savage for that reason—to be used. She wanted to be with him because he loved her. Because she was part of him. Because he couldn't bear to be away from her.

Right now, she needed to know she was loved. She needed to feel the emotion from him surrounding her and comforting her. She'd felt him considering whether or not he should turn to other women for his precious blow jobs. Just for that moment, that he would even consider such a thing after what happened the last time, after breaking them up, the time apart, how miserable they both were, she was devastated all over again. How could he? How could he even contemplate such a thing?

"Babe, you're shaking, you're so upset, but you're not talking to me. Are you angry?"

Was she? Mostly, she was hurt. And so frightened for

him. But yes, she was angry at him as well. She nodded slowly.

"Take another step closer and lose the top. Did I hurt you? I know the club hurt you. Did I hurt you? Tell me how I hurt you."

She took the step before she could stop herself. Her hands automatically had gone to the hem of her T-shirt, and she pulled it off. The evening air felt cool on her overheated body. She stood facing him in just her lacy bra and jeans. Her nipples felt like twin flames in spite of the breeze, or maybe because of it. Maybe the coolness emphasized the hot blood flowing in her veins.

She nodded again. "Yes. You hurt me. Twice. Last night and again today. I don't care about the others anymore." She didn't. She was done with the club. Finished. They weren't going to be part of her life.

"Come here to me, Seychelle, right here." He pointed between his legs again. "You need to take off your boots. I can't make things better unless you're right here."

He was using that voice, the one that crawled inside of her head, the one that wrapped around her heart, the one that stroked her sex until she was weak and so slick with need, she blindly followed his every command.

She found herself standing between his thighs, caged there, shaking, feeling a little desperate but unable to articulate what she wanted or needed from him.

Savage curved his palm around the nape of her neck, urging her close to him, so close she felt the heat of his groin press tightly against her bare stomach. His mouth was gentle on hers, his lips brushing back and forth.

"I'm sorry I hurt you, baby. We'll talk about that after. Straighten it out. I never want to hurt you. We should have cleared things up last night. From now on, let's make a pact that we won't go to bed hurt or angry. We'll talk it through."

He kept brushing his lips back and forth over hers. He didn't really kiss her, but the promise was there. It was sweet. Not fire. The fire was smoldering between her legs. A slow burn that kept building for no reason other than he reached behind her and unhooked her bra. His gaze dropped to her breasts as he tossed her bra on the table. The way he looked at her body, so hungry, so filled with an obsessive craving, almost as if he couldn't wait to get his mouth and hands on her, brought that flame between her legs up another fiery notch.

"You with me, baby?" he murmured against her lips. His hands dropped to her jeans, opening them, pushing them off her hips, sliding them over her generous curves, taking her panties with them. "Push them down the rest of the way and step out of them, Seychelle. Boots all the way off, and step out of your jeans."

It was a relief to get the material off her sore skin. The night air soothed her almost as much as being close to Savage did. She stripped off her boots and the rest of her clothes, folding them while he stayed very still, his eyes hooded and watchful.

"Come up here, Seychelle." He patted his lap.

She caught her lip between her teeth. Did she really want him to punish her? Why did she need to be punished when he was the asshole? He'd been thinking of other women. He'd dragged her to this hideous place with people who didn't want her here. All of them knew exactly what was going to happen here with the exception of her. So why should she crawl willingly into his lap and let him smack her? Hard. Right over the top of those stripes on her sore bottom.

She took a step back and looked up at him, letting him see her anger. Her defiance. The confusion in her eyes.

"I know you're upset, baby. I can't make things better until you let me." His voice was low. So gentle. He held out one hand to her. "I love you more than life, woman. I'd do anything for you. Anything. You name it, I'll do it."

She lifted her chin. "Would you get on your bike and ride out of here with me if I asked you to go?" She gestured to the club members that were at their campfires in a semicircle around Savage and Seychelle, but giving them plenty of space.

"Yes. You know I'm needed here, so you would never ask me to leave without a good reason. So the answer is yes, Seychelle, if you asked me to take you out of here, I'd do it in a heartbeat."

That was not the answer she'd expected or even wanted to hear. She let him see despair clawing at her belly. "Saving your life isn't considered a good reason, is it?"

He trailed a finger from her chin, down her throat, between her breasts to her belly button. "No, princess. I don't die so easy, and we came here knowing someone was going to make their try." He patted his lap. Lowered his voice so that he was the devil. Sin. Temptation. Her savior. "Come here, baby. Let me take care of you."

She knew she was going to give in to him, not for him but for herself. She needed him. She needed to fly away from the thundering chaos in her head. She crawled up his body, using his arms to pull herself over him, and draped herself over his lap. He sat on the table, rather than the bench, so she found herself staring at the planks of wood that made up the table-top. Her breasts floated free, the evening air tugging at her nipples. He rubbed her exposed cheeks and then pushed her thighs gently but firmly a hand's width apart.

"You really broke a few of the rules we set up between us, didn't you, baby?"

"Yes." She had. She disliked his entire club, and she really hadn't liked him very much. So she'd been deliberately as disrespectful as possible to him. She knew that would set his teeth on edge, but more, if anyone was watching, or cared, he would look as if he couldn't control her—and Savage was all about control. "I disrespected you in public."

The way his palm moved over her bare cheek felt deli-cious. The stripes from the cane hurt, but in a good way now, and the way he rubbed sent heat deep. A fist of pure desire formed in her belly.

"You chose to do that in public. Fought with me in public,

didn't you, Seychelle? And worse, disrespected the president of our club."

"*Your* club," she clarified.

"*Our* fucking club," he stated clearly.

Goose bumps broke out all over her skin. She *had* chosen to do that. She would debate with him in public. Tease him. Argue points with him. But it was wholly against her nature to fight in public with him, especially with his club members around him. What had gotten into her? That was so unlike her. She would walk away before she would ever do something like that.

"Yes," she whispered. It didn't make sense. Nothing made sense to her anymore, with the exception of being with Savage, and that made absolutely no sense at all, yet right at that moment, he made the only sense to her. She needed him—needed this to ground her. That was how confused she was.

He rubbed her bare cheeks again. His knuckles slid between her legs, and a jolt of pure heat became a dark fist in the pit of her stomach. She knew she was slick. Already growing hot in anticipation. She had given up trying to figure out why she was the way she was. She only knew her body responded to the things Savage did to her.

Savage leaned over her, his mouth close to the nape of her neck. "I told you, and I meant it, that Czar deserved the things you said to him. I'll take whatever he wants to dish out, not you. This is only for disrespecting me in public. Whatever you're upset with me for, and I know there is something, we talk about in private."

She sent him a smoldering look over her shoulder but didn't dispute what he said. She'd agreed to his terms when they first got together. In any case, she *needed* to feel his hand on her.

"This is going to be intense because of the bruising from the cane. You can cry, but no screaming, Seychelle. If you need to take a break, you can slow it down, or stop it by giving me red or yellow. You get that, baby? I want you to know you can stop this."

"It's a punishment," she said stubbornly. "You said there was no stopping a punishment."

"We're not alone, baby, and you took a severe punishment already. We're being flexible here. So you can stop this if it gets to be too much. It's your choice."

Savage was careful to make everything her choice. She knew it was far more arousing to him that she *chose* to let him do the things to her body that he did. He wanted her to give her consent every single time. In essence, it was giving herself to him—giving him her trust every time. He seemed to need that from her.

The first smack on her left cheek was an explosion of fire that raced up her spine and down her thighs. It hurt like hell. Savage usually warmed her up first, with a series of gentler strikes. He told her how many times he was going to smack her bottom. This felt different. She didn't know if it was the cane marks and the deeper bruising or the way he didn't let up, his palm coming down hard on her buttocks, activating those terrible, fiery stripes.

He'd said *intense*. He might as well have said *excruciating*. She couldn't stop the tears. She'd been determined not to cry, to give him that, when she knew he wanted her tears, but she couldn't help it.

He paused, rubbing her bottom. "Relax into this, Seychelle. Surrender to the pain. Let it carry you away. You're tensing up." His voice was softer than ever, his palms spreading the fire around, until that fist in her belly grew darker and thicker. His thumb brushed her clit, and her entire body shuddered with hunger. She was drenched instantly, hungry for him. "Relax for me, angel. You like this. You need it."

She couldn't help responding to his voice. To that dark lust growing in her belly. The flames his thumb produced as he flicked and teased. Then he was smacking her again. Hard. The backs of her thighs. Her sit spot. The curve of each cheek. Again and again. The pain at first was agony. She was certain she would have to call out her safe word, but then she found herself drifting away. Floating on the pain. Letting it take her somewhere far away.

Tears came, but it didn't matter; it was more of a release than sobbing because she hurt. She was floating somewhere in a space she didn't recognize. The screaming in her head calmed, and all around her she drifted with stars. Deep in her core, the throbbing and heat came together into a swirling pool of molten liquid. She saw it burning bright in the middle of a vortex of stars, a bright, hot volcanic pond that glowed orange and red as it splashed high into the air, threatening to explode.

Her breath came in ragged, desperate pants as Savage rubbed her blazing cheeks, massaging in deep circles she felt all the way through her entire body. He slipped one finger into her wet, clenching pussy while his thumb brushed her throbbing, inflamed clit. She pushed back against his hand and he gave her a second finger.

"I don't know how you can be so scorching hot and fucking tight, woman."

Seychelle moved against his hand, tried to ride his fingers since he didn't move them, just thrust them into her and then went still. Only that thumb stroked her clit, but not enough. A touch, no more, just enough to make her want to scream at him for more attention. Abruptly, he pulled his fingers free and licked them.

"On your feet, baby."

His hands went to her waist, and he guided her gently to a standing position between his thighs. She was unsteady, her body shaking, trembling, barely able to stay upright. She caught at his thighs to keep from falling.

"Savage."

"You needed that, didn't you, Seychelle?"

She sank her teeth into her lower lip, tears still streaming down her face. Her bottom was on fire, but he was right: she had needed him to spank her. To ground her. Now she wanted his cock buried in her. She wanted to feel him moving in her, claiming her. She nodded, lifting her gaze to his.

He was staring at her with his blue eyes, dark with lust, watchful. Cold like a glacier. Merciless. Possessive. His fingers bit into her hips as he pulled her in tight against his body so that the tips of her breasts pressed tight to his chest. It felt as if twin matches had lit flames to her nipples, and a moan escaped before she could stop it.

He leaned forward and sipped at the tears on her face, licking at the tracks, first on the right side and then on the left, before he pulled back to look down at her. "I love how you look right now. I fucking love it, Seychelle. I want you to kneel down, right there. Right where you are. I think it's time you learned how to suck my cock the way I like it, baby." Savage opened his jeans and then slid off the table. He fisted the thick girth in his hand and lazily pumped, his eyes dark with lust. "Another lesson in dirty, sinful sex."

Seychelle had always loved his cock. It was large and impressive, velvet over steel. The crown was broad, and whenever she touched it, satin soft, it leaked those pearly drops that always made her want to lick them off of him. There was a thick vein running the length of his shaft and scars that wrapped around the entire shaft, making him look even more intimidating. She knew part of the reason he liked rough sex was because his penis needed enough stimulation to be able to feel through that scarring.

She'd dreamt of taking him in her mouth. She'd wanted it for so long. His hand was heavy on her shoulder, urging her to her knees. Her mind was suddenly filled with images of another woman, her mouth greedily devouring him. She could hear others surrounding her laughing. Pointing and laughing. She could hear Savage laughing too. The images and voices whirled together into a terrible blurring kaleidoscope of sound and vision.

Savage rubbed the head of his cock along her lips, murmuring something she couldn't hear above the jeering laughter. He stroked her cheek, then her jaw. His eyes flashed that cold blue that sent shivers down her spine.

"Seychelle." His tone. Commanding.

Now his hand spanned her jaw. Pressed. Opening her mouth. He rubbed along her lips, and she tasted him. The laughter grew louder. The images in her head flashed brighter.

"Red." She whispered the word. "Red." She said it louder, trying to be heard above the noise in her head. She sank back on her ankles, away from him, extending both arms, hands up, palms out to defend herself. "Red, red, red. Red, Savage, red."

THIRTEEN

Few things shocked Savage, but the sight of Seychelle, obviously frightened, crying real tears, backing away from him on her knees, frantically whispering her safe word over and over, managed to throw him. She literally was crawling away from him, looking terrified, as if he were a monster about to attack her. When he took a step close to her, she shrank back even more, her hands going up to protect herself, and her safe word got louder.

"Seychelle, baby, look at me." Savage crouched down, putting himself at her level, trying to connect with her. "Angel, you're safe. You're with me. You're always safe with me. Let me hold you. Come here to me."

She blinked rapidly, her tear-wet lashes fluttering, her eyes bouncing all over the place, pupils dilated, as if she was so terrified, she was looking for a way to escape, to run from him. He softened his voice even more, stilling, not moving a muscle.

"Angel, you mean more to me than anything on this earth. You have to know that. See me, Seychelle. See *me*. This is Savin Pajari, your fiancé, your man. Say my name. Say it, baby. Tell me who you belong to." He kept his voice low. Not in the least demanding. Velvet soft, letting it caress her nerve endings. He didn't reach for her. He did nothing that could constitute a threat to her.

Savage willed her to look at him. Seychelle was already conditioned to obey him, especially when she was naked and vulnerable. Her gaze jumped to his face, moved up to his eyes and was instantly trapped there. Good. He kept his focus on her, knowing once she looked into his eyes, she wouldn't be able to look away.

"That's it, baby, you see me now. Savin. Say it." Deliberately, he used his birth name. He rarely gave it up to anyone, even her. She knew it. She whispered it to him occasionally, but only when he made love to her. When they stared into each other's eyes and it was more intense than he had ever imagined loving a woman could be. She would whisper *Savin* in that soft, breathless voice and turn his heart upside down.

He wanted her to see his love for her, not his domination. Not Savage the biker, although he knew she loved and trusted him as well. Just at this moment, she needed to feel safe, totally safe, and he didn't know what was scaring her. She was upset with Torpedo Ink. The club. The members. With him. Something was off-kilter.

Her lips parted. Formed his name, but no sound came out. Her eyes darkened. That blue went to sea blue. Sapphire. Terror receded just a little but was still there. She wrapped her arms around herself. Her entire body shook so much he was afraid she would topple over sideways before he could get his hands on her. It took a tremendous amount of restraint to hold himself back.

"Say it for me, baby," he encouraged. "I need to hear you say my birth name out loud. Not too many people I trust with that name."

She blinked again. The terror in her eyes faded to fear and confusion. A little frown took over. That frown turned his insides to pure mush, not a good thing when he was surrounded by enemies and his club counted on him to be their enforcer. It didn't matter. Nothing did in that moment but Seychelle.

Her fingers came up to dash at the tears still streaming down her face. Her hand was trembling so much he wanted to capture her hand in his and hold it still, but he didn't move, afraid of ruining the little progress they'd made.

"Savin." She whispered his name.

The moment she said his name out loud, even though it was a mere thread of sound, barely heard, the fear receded almost completely to leave mostly confusion. Her lashes fluttered more. The teal blue stared into his eyes.

"That's right, Seychelle. Keep looking at me. Keep seeing me." He inched closer. An inch. No more. Testing the waters. She didn't flinch away from him, and he breathed a sigh of relief. She recognized him. Knew who he was.

"I see you," she acknowledged, sounding hesitant. Her gaze didn't waver from his. She looked more confused than ever, but she didn't move away from him when he edged closer.

He took advantage, even from his crouched position, gliding right into her, pulling her into his arms, cradling her into his chest and rising into a standing position to carry her to one of the camp chairs he had placed beside the firepit. The fire had died down to embers, but that didn't matter to him. He settled into the chair, cradling Seychelle in his lap. She had never, not one time, used her safe word. Not during all the things they'd done together. She hadn't appeared to even come close. She might have thought about it, but she hadn't even formed the word.

Now? At the thought of sucking his cock? She'd bought a how-to book on the subject. She'd even discussed it with Shari, the bane of his life. He thought it would make her happy. Of all the things he could think of to do, new and different for her, on the run, he thought they might make a little instructional video of their own. Nothing like what he'd ever done with any other woman, just theirs alone, the two of them. Shit. He'd thought she'd fucking like it.

He tightened his arms around her, rocking her gently, one palm to the back of her head, holding her so her face was buried against his chest, muffling her sobs. They were genuine. Heartbreaking. What the hell? She was crying all over again. This had nothing to do with her spanking.

"Fuck, baby, you have to talk to me. I thought this was something you wanted to do. You never have to do this for me. Never. There's a million other things we can do we'd both enjoy." He kept rocking her. Something had been off since the night before they left. They'd talked about her sucking his cock then too. Then he'd been thinking about something similar when she'd gotten so upset as they were walking toward the campsite earlier.

"Angel, you don't think I'd ever risk losing you again to have someone else give me a fucking blow job, do you?" He caught her hair in his fist and very gently tugged to try to get her to lift her head so he could see her eyes without being rough. "You're going to have to look at me sometime, Seychelle. We have to talk about this."

He needed to just shut the hell up and let her cry it out. She'd talk to him when she was able to. He was a fixer with her. He wanted to make everything better, and he definitely didn't want Seychelle running from him—not here, not when they were surrounded by so many other clubs. He didn't want her ever feeling insecure about their relationship. He thought they were past that. *Bog*, he fucking hoped they were past that.

Savage tightened his arms around her and kept rocking, dropping his chin on top of her silky hair and letting her cry herself out. It took a good fifteen minutes before she managed to get control and then another five before she found the courage to lift her gaze to his again.

"I'm sorry, Savage. I don't know what got into me."

He bent his head to sip at the tears on her face, following the trail to the corner of her mouth before he pressed a gentle kiss on the trembling curve of her lips. He brushed caresses back and forth, taking his time, letting her know he wasn't in the least upset with her and they had all the time in the world. When he lifted his head, he casually reached for his jacket, the one lying just at fingertips' reach on the table, and pulled it to him so he could wrap it around her shoulders and back, enveloping her completely.

"Take your time, Seychelle. Nothing you feel is wrong. There's nothing wrong between us. You give me everything and more. This is a little glitch."

Her eyes moved over his face, then went back to his eyes and she shook her head. "It isn't though. It really isn't. I screwed up. I screwed up, and it could have cost me you. I could have gotten you killed. What if *I'd* killed you?"

Her eyes filled with tears again, and her slender arms slid around his neck, fingers linking at his nape. She pressed in, as if she could melt her skin into his. Damn if her nipples weren't hot enough to do just that. Her generous breasts mashed up against his chest, and he felt every intriguing inch of her. He wanted to peel her back and yet mold her to him at the same time. He did neither. He stroked his hand down the back of her hair, a long, soothing stroke, while he continued to rock her.

"I told you, baby, I'm damn hard to kill. We came prepared, knowing they were going to start shit with me. I've got you to balance me out." Amusement crept into his voice because in spite of what was happening at that moment, she centered him.

"This isn't funny, Savage," she objected swiftly, sounding a little more like the old Seychelle, *his* Seychelle. That little snippy voice she sometimes gave him when she was about to lift her stubborn chin and her eyes flashed that gorgeous blue flame at him.

He pulled back a couple of inches just to see if she was going to give him those things. Yep. She was. Her eyes glittered at him fiercely, like twin gemstones. Relief swept through him. He smiled down at her, his first genuine smile in quite a while. The knots unraveled in his belly.

"Believe me, I'm taking this threat very seriously; we all are. That's why you're here. Czar insisted, or I would have locked your ass up in a basement somewhere with all kinds of bondage equipment surrounding you to keep you hot, anticipating my arrival home."

That got him a raised eyebrow. "Funny how your answer always has some sexual innuendo in it. You can't think with your cock, Savage. I'm very serious about getting you killed. I did that."

She was so serious, back to sounding distressed, that he continued to rock her and pet her hair, stroking caress after caress down those unruly waves. "I know you're serious, angel. You scared me is all. Seeing you feisty helps me breathe a little. You're going to have to give me that. Now, you good enough to sit back and talk to me about what you think is going on? I can build up the fire in the pit and get us something to eat and drink. You put on a sweater or my jacket and curl up in the chair while I see to our fire and food, unless you're not good yet."

She lifted her chin to meet his eyes again. This time her gaze was soft with love, turning his heart over. She gave him a tentative smile. "I'm good, honey. You do the fire. I'll find a sweater and see to the food."

Savage was extremely happy when she made the first move to lean back in and kiss him. It wasn't a full-on kiss, but it was enough to tell him she wasn't terrified out of her fucking mind, afraid he was going to hurt her.

"Honey, you have to let go of me so I can get out of your lap." She nuzzled his chest. "I feel very safe sitting here with you, but I don't think we're going to get anything done."

He found himself reluctant to let her go. She'd never, not once, freaked out on him like that. He swept the pads of his fingers over her face, searching her delicate features carefully for any sign that the trauma was still with her. "You sure you're all right now, Seychelle?"

She nodded. "Absolutely. If you're worried, we can sit here and talk, Savage." She snuggled closer to him. Her bottom slid over his cock, the one thing he was trying to avoid. He didn't want to think about sex with her right now. They had to figure this puzzle out, not have mind-blowing, carnal, out-of-control, explosive sex like they did every time he touched her.

His answer was to lift her off of him, although he made it clear he did so with obvious reluctance. He didn't want her to think he wanted her away from him. She was a little unsteady on her feet, and twice he noticed out of the corner of his eye, while he worked on the fire, how she caught the back of a chair or the picnic table to steady herself.

Savage would have preferred she keep his Torpedo Ink colors on her, but she folded them neatly and pulled on a long sweater that fell to the backs of her thighs. Shoving her feet in a pair of flip-flops, she made them sandwiches again from the various supplies Hitch had put in a cooler for them. She added chips and beer for him, sparkling water for her, and then sank back into the chair he'd pulled close to the firepit for her.

He wanted his chair as close to hers as possible. There wasn't going to be any escape from this talk for her. He'd zipped up his jeans but left his shirt off. Around them, the rest of Torpedo Ink did what they always did on a run. They'd spread out in pairs, getting a feel for the mood of the various clubs and the underlying tension that ran beneath the party atmosphere. They would collect information as they went. They were adept at knowing what the smallest hint of gossip might mean.

"What happened, Seychelle? No more bullshit. This started before we left. You got upset and refused to talk to me. We had an agreement that we wouldn't do that." He poured command into his voice. He was no longer sweet and gentle but demanding.

She had been looking into the fire. Now she turned her head, and those blue eyes of hers fixed on his face. He knew better than to ever stare into a fire. Doing that made one blind, even if it was momentarily. The firelight played with the gold and platinum colors in her hair. He wanted to reach over and slide his fingers into it but didn't dare. Right now, he had to be in charge. She had to know he wasn't going to let her off the hook.

Seychelle took a deep breath and let it out. "You made fun of me just like she did. Just like Shari. She said something similar outside the bar that first night. About giving you a blow job, how I wouldn't know how to give you one the way you like it. She said it again in town in front of Brandon. Then, when we were talking about it, when I asked you what Shari meant when she said you liked a blow job a specific way, you acted so amused. Just the way she did. I said I didn't understand, and you said of course not. And that clearly amused you. Instead of talking to me about it and helping me to understand, you laughed at me. Like she did. Like Brandon did. Just because I'm inexperienced."

Inwardly he groaned. He could see the naked hurt on her face. "Baby, it wasn't like that at all."

She shook her head. "Don't, Savage. It was exactly like that. You were amused at my lack of understanding. Don't pretend you weren't. Lana and Maestro made a point of telling me that I couldn't give you what you needed but there were so many other women here that could. And today, with your club all around you, I was the *only* one that didn't have the information of what is going on here. Everyone else knows. Except me. I don't. You insisted I come here. Czar insisted. I wasn't given a choice, but I'm the outsider. You intend to use me, and so does Czar. I have no idea for what, but you clearly feel you need me here, both of you. It doesn't matter whether or not I know the entire truth of what is happening, even though I'm the only one who doesn't. Do you have any idea what that feels like?"

He didn't, so he kept his mouth shut. He could see the hurt on her face, feel it coming off her in waves.

"Then, while we're walking through all those fucking women who are staring at you with lust, many who have had their mouths on your cock, which I haven't, you start thinking about them blowing you. I had my hand on you. You can't deny the truth of that either."

She turned her face away from him, but not before he caught the sheen of tears in her eyes. "I'm so glad I haven't married you. I don't think you can give all that up, Savage, as much as you want to. There's just something in you that needs all those women fawning all over you. What I don't understand is why you insisted on bringing me along when I begged to stay home. You could have just come here alone. Your little club brothers and sisters would never rat you out. Not in a million years. I'm nothing to them. They made that so clear to me."

Savage frowned listening to her voice, that shaky, near whisper that told him Seychelle was on the verge of flight. She definitely didn't have any self-confidence when it came to this particular subject. Before he denied anything she said, he had to give it some actual thought. He *had* been amused. She was so adorable buying a how-to book on the subject of giving a blow job. What woman did that?

Naturally, she wasn't going to know the difference between a face fuck and a blow job—a crude cum dump or a woman giving pleasure to a man because she wanted to. He loved her innocence. He hadn't been making fun of it, but yes, he'd been amused at certain aspects. So he needed to own that and start there.

"We're going to take one thing at a time, Seychelle, because this is important. I should have insisted on talking to you last night instead of letting it build up until it turned into something monstrous. I wasn't laughing at you. I wouldn't do that. I like that you have an innocence about you. I like that I can teach you things, especially when they're things I want done my way. We have something special between us, our sexy-as-hell you-learn-dirty-sinful-lessons-from-me, and I love that. Was it amusing to me that you bought a how-to book on learning how to give your man a blow job? Hell yes. Did I think it was adorable as in I'm the luckiest man on the planet? Yes. That's the fucking truth, angel."

"Stop saying *fuck* and *angel* in the same sentence, Savage," she whispered. "You're going to go to hell if you keep that up."

He didn't dare look amused over that either, not if he

wanted to get through this conversation. He tortured and killed men. Saying *fuck* and *angel* in the same sentence was hardly what was going to send him to hell.

"As for explaining to you what Shari meant, I hated sounding like a complete dick, which I would. I've already told you what I was before I met you. When my rage gets to a certain point, I have to have a release, which I achieve through fighting, doing specific things for the club, or in a sexual way, which is whipping the shit out of a woman and then fucking her face. It isn't pretty, and she doesn't get a whole hell of a lot out of it, although I get her off with my hand."

"They must get something out of it if they keep wanting to come back for more." She kept her face turned away from him, eyes on the fire, as if those flames could give her all the answers she sought.

"Very few women ever want a repeat with me. There are a few like Shari who get obsessed."

"You mean like me."

"Not like you. You love me, Seychelle. You see me. You know me and everything about me. Even shit like this, where I look like such a fucking dick, you still love me. I can feel it. I hate that I hurt you. I hate that we have misunderstandings. As for thinking for one second that I could use another woman if things go south, instead of you, that was a suggestion one of the members gave to me because he was worried about you. It passed through my mind because I'm afraid this could be bad and you're not ready for me to be hard on you yet, but I know I couldn't have another woman touch me. If you had kept your hand on me a second longer, you would have known that too."

There was a long silence broken only by the sound of the crackling wood as it burned in the firepit. Savage kept his gaze fixed on Seychelle. None of this explained her visceral reaction to his command to suck his cock. That still didn't make sense. There was no one around them. It wasn't like she could plead he was deliberately trying to humiliate her.

"Baby," he kept his voice velvet soft. Very low, but commanding. "You're going to have to talk to me."

"I think Brandon managed to use Shari to plant a suggestion in me." Staring into the flames, she blurted it out without looking at him. "It took time to work, and you laughing helped to set it."

Savage frowned, studying her averted face. She was back to trembling, the shaking so extreme, he was afraid she might fall out of the chair. "You'll need to explain this to me, angel."

"When we were at dinner and Eden clearly didn't want to talk about her stepson, I realized she was afraid of him. Once I knew Brandon was her stepson, I started thinking about Tony and his brothers, whether or not they might have any psychic talents. The morning I ran into Tony in Sea Haven, he specifically said, *I almost felt you could reach right into all of us and control our emotions. That's how beautiful your voice is.* That implies he knows about using a voice to control other people's emotions."

"You didn't tell me that." He kept his tone strictly neutral.

"I did tell you, just not specifically what he said. I believe you had all kinds of grievances against me at the time, and I wasn't thinking too clearly. I certainly didn't have as much information, and I could be way off now. I just don't think I am."

She sounded sad. Alone.

Savage wanted to pull her into his arms, but he couldn't—not yet. "Keep talking, Seychelle. What kind of suggestion could Brandon have planted?" Twice she had indicated she thought she was responsible for someone trying to kill him. Was that why? He needed to know.

"Shari said I was too innocent for you. That you wanted a specific type of blow job. I don't remember the exact words. I should remember them when I almost always remember everyone's exact words. It's odd that I can't, and I've tried."

"Why did you panic when I wanted you to suck my cock? Was it Brandon's suggestion making you panic? Or something else? And baby? Look at me when you answer." He poured command into his voice. If she didn't obey him, he was going to force her head around so she had no choice.

Seychelle very slowly turned her face toward him. There was real fear there. "I know he planted a suggestion for me to be afraid of being humiliated, but I also am fairly certain that's how he plans to kill you. I think he put the hit out on you. Brandon would think he was so clever using a woman. You've established a pattern on these runs. You choose a woman, usually more than one, right? However many nights there are, you use that many women. You whip them and then they blow you. You've done it every run, right?"

He nodded wordlessly, keeping his gaze on her face, the hurt that was there, without her even knowing.

"What better way to kill you? He just needs to plant the suggestion in the right women, the women you'll choose. He has to get me out of the way. I'm too innocent, too naïve. Too terrified to suck your cock. I don't get the job done, you go to someone else. That someone starts out perfectly but then whips out a knife or a gun and you're dead. She would be the last person you would expect to want to kill you because, truthfully, she would have no idea she was about to kill you. She wouldn't remember she was given the command. After it was done, she wouldn't remember either. She would have no idea why she killed you."

"Shit, baby, you could be right about this," Savage said. He noticed, now that they were talking about things she was more sure of, like psychic talent, she seemed much stronger and more self-confident. "Campbell definitely believes he can get women to do anything for him."

She nodded. "That's true, but he believes he's superior to everyone. I have the feeling his half brothers' talents aren't nearly as strong as his. Mine is far stronger than his, yet he hasn't for a moment considered that could be the case."

"You said something about the possibility of him being able to find a pathway into your mind just as you could into his," Savage said, "if you used your voice on him."

She shook her head. "Not a pathway into my mind exactly. He could find a thread of sound to use. That's what I did to him to stop him from using Doris. That enraged him. I took two of his women from him, and then when he came to my home with Doris, I was so upset over losing you, I didn't recognize that he'd set a trap for me."

He stayed silent, willing her to continue. She was shaking. He wanted to get up and get her a blanket, or at least his jacket again, but she was next to the fire, and it wasn't cold. She was afraid. He couldn't imagine her being afraid of Brandon Campbell, but he was going to hear her out. He knew psychic talent could even the playing field very fast.

"For me, the way people speak are notes in the air. They have color to them. Everyone's do. Those notes are trails that are paths leading to that person's mind. You actually have the same talent. Most people have more than one talent, but the talents are varied and small surrounding the vast one. The main talent is usually not developed. Your voice commands people. It soothes at times. You use it on me, and I let you because our notes create this beautiful, unbelievable, wild music together."

She saw it, then. He wasn't the only one. Her notes. His. He rarely saw others, but sometimes. More so when he was with her, as if he was seeing the beauty of musical notes through her eyes.

"The point I'm making is that my talent is quite significant in this area. I recognized Brandon's ability when he asked me out and used his voice on me. I was angry that he would right away use his gift rather than just ask me out. At that point I didn't let him see that I had any talent. It wasn't worth it. At the time, I had no idea what he was doing to other women."

Savage would like to hunt the bastard down and do a few things to him. He stayed silent, willing Seychelle to continue. He could feel she was trying to separate herself from him, so he reached over and took her hand, prying open her fingers to bring her palm to his thigh. She didn't look at him, but she didn't pull away.

"He knew immediately I didn't react to his voice. Not everyone does. That must have intrigued him because he started watching me. I'd spot him sometimes on the headlands walking with a woman, kissing her even, but he would be looking at my cottage."

Savage didn't interrupt her to tell her Brandon wasn't intrigued with her because she hadn't succumbed to the persuasion of his voice. Savage had recognized certain traits in her the moment he was with her. Not only that she had a gorgeous, curvy body, but that she might be more likely to be open to his needs. Granted, he was the kind of man who was trained in spotting every type of characteristic in others, but that didn't mean someone like Brandon might not see those things in her as well. Savage didn't tell her because Seychelle still hadn't quite come to terms with her nature, and it would embarrass her to think anyone else might see into her darker needs.

"When I thought I'd lost you, Savage, I lost a part of myself. I felt broken inside. It was silly, really, because we were just friends. You'd made that clear. We hadn't been together intimately . . ."

"I have to stop you right there, baby," he said. "We were more intimate than I'd ever been with anyone. Ever. You knew it. I knew it. Both of us felt broken, and that was on me. I should have just told you what I was, but I was afraid of losing you, so I blew it before we even got started." He pressed her palm tighter into his thigh. He couldn't let her think she was the only one damaged by his careless behavior.

She flicked him a quick look from under her thick, dark lashes, and his gut twisted. Those blue eyes of hers did him in every fucking time. The smallest beginnings of a smile flirted with her lips, and that dimple on the left side of her mouth flashed briefly, making his heart turn over.

"I wasn't myself," she corrected. "I didn't pay attention like I should have. By that time, I knew he was upset with me. I'd gotten Sahara back to her parents and out of his reach. He came with Doris, and I thought it was to find where Sahara was so he could get her to come back. I also thought it was to show me he could control Doris, my friend, to subtly threaten me through her. That wasn't his intent either. I opened myself up inadvertently because I wasn't paying enough attention. By doing so, I put you in danger."

Her palm rubbed back and forth on his thigh, and she looked down at his hand covering hers, unable to meet his eyes, as if she was ashamed.

"Baby, I still don't understand." He didn't. His brothers had been watching over her at the time, since she wouldn't let him into her life. They'd even recorded the encounter for him. Savage had watched the recording several times and he'd been angry with her, but only because she'd been list-less and despondent, seemingly not interested in Doris's visit until she suddenly turned her head to look Brandon straight in the eye at something he said. The camera caught her look of absolute challenge. She had a *fuck you* look on her face. There was no mistaking it. Brandon wouldn't mis-take it. She had issued a challenge, and no way was that man going to back down.

"He used his voice on Doris all the time, having her tell him when someone was visiting Sahara and then later Tessa. He asked her details about you and me, and she told him, all chatty and innocent, but always on his side because wasn't he wonderful." She sounded sarcastic. "I should have known he was being too heavy-handed."

She sighed and looked up at him again. This time he read remorse. Her eyes were overbright, a beautiful gem-like sap-phire.

"He wanted me to stop him, Savage. He wanted me to shield Doris from him. That opened me up to him. He saw my notes and could trace them just as easily as I could trace his. That was what he wanted from me, a thread. He didn't have to be stronger. He just needed an in and I gave it to him because I wasn't paying attention."

"Baby, you can't think that way."

"He wants you gone. Out of his way. I really made him angry. I turned down his invitation of a date, and he's very vain. Then I interfered with Sahara and got her away from him. Then I did it again with Tessa. You're mine, Savage. If for no other reason, he'll try to take you away from me."

"Before you decide this is all on you, let's separate what we think is going on here. First, you think Brandon is the one who put out a hit on me. If he's using a suggestion buried in his voice, he wouldn't be paying for a hit, Seychelle."

"No, not unless that's his backup plan. What are the odds that I wouldn't come on the run with you, Savage? Even if he did manage to plant a suggestion through Shari, taking away my ability to give you a blow job on this run, he still has to believe you'll bring me with you."

Savage rubbed the top of her hand with his thumb. Yeah, that was true, but he had a well-deserved reputation for being a first-class bastard. "If he asked around about me, angel, he'd learn very quickly that I don't give two fucks about anyone but my club. I've never treated the women I've used as more than a face fuck. I've used them and walked away without looking back. He most likely would think I would fuck another woman right in front of you."

He didn't like admitting what a dick he was, but it was necessary if they were going to figure this out. In any case, he wanted to be honest with her. The strange thing was, and he'd never understood it, a few of the women did want a repeat performance, and others, having heard of him or even seen his treatment of the women on runs, because he didn't hide what he did, begged him to be next.

Her eyes widened, moved over his face as if searching to see if he was telling her the truth. "Would you really do something like that?"

"Before you?" He sighed. "I did a hell of a lot worse. I've never tried to hide what I am from you, Seychelle. If anything,

I've gone out of my way to be very honest, so you had every opportunity to walk away." He made a point of using the past tense. As far as he was concerned, they'd made a commitment, and it was solid now. She wasn't backing out, no matter how tough things got.

"I promised you I'm one hundred percent in with you, baby, all the way. I meant it. There will not be other women. I don't cheat. I expect the same from you." He caught her chin and looked her straight in the eyes. "I know ways to torture a man, learned that shit starting at an early age in that school I was in, and I'd apply every one of them to any man who dared put his hands on you."

She gave him a little half smile. "I guess I should have gotten an instructional manual on ways to torture and kill, just in case you go back on your word."

"I can teach you anything you want to know. You don't need books or videos on anything, Seychelle."

Her gaze drifted over the angles and planes of his face for a long time. He let her look until she nodded.

"He's got to have programmed more than one woman to vie to give you a blow job, Savage, and in the middle of it, or afterward, when you're not thinking too clearly, she's going to try to kill you." Seychelle was certain. "I'm a little insecure in that department, so wherever you're going, I hope you're taking me with you."

He didn't look away from her. That was an impossibility with what he had to do for the club. "Baby . . ."

"Damn it, Savage." She tried to pull her hand out from under his. At the same time, her legs, tucked under her, came down so she could stand, but he refused to release her.

"Stop it, Seychelle. You know I came here to work. The kind of work I do is not something I'm willing for you to see. So no, I'm not taking you with me. You're going to stay right here at our campsite with several guards on you and wait for me to return. When I come back, most likely I'm going to need you. You're going to know I haven't been with another woman."

"This is such bullshit. I hate this so much. I really do. I suppose all your brothers know what you'll be doing. Lana, Alena, Lissa and Scarlet will know what you'll be doing. Only I have to sit here by myself with guards around me, once again the outsider."

"I'm getting information we need, and I won't be polite about it," he said quietly. "Since when don't you trust me? Has Campbell really managed to mess with your mind to such an extent that you can't trust me anymore?"

She frowned and pressed her hands over her ears. "I keep hearing laughter and seeing images in my head, Savage. It isn't you. I told you, he got inside my head."

"We'll get him out. Before we do, I need to know if you think any of the other members really could be in danger as well," he said, suddenly alarmed. He had been thinking in terms of the hit placed on him, not on the other club members being in danger. All of them were dominant men, and most had fairly dark fetishes they indulged in on the runs.

"He'd be spreading himself thin," Seychelle said. "But I would warn them just in case."

Savage did, sending out a mass text, including Alena and Lana. He didn't know what they were into, and he didn't want either of them caught unaware.

"Brandon hates the Diamondbacks and wants to destroy them," Savage ventured. He used his own hand to rub her palm up and down his thigh while he puzzled out how Brandon could use his talent to wreak the kind of havoc with the clubs they were seeing. "How would he go about it?"

"He's using women," Seychelle said with confidence. "He just has to listen to his half brothers talking and he'd get the structure of the club. Who is important, who is married, who matters. Jealousies. Anything like that. He would be patient and collect the information over time. Remember, for Brandon, it's all a game. He likes to feel superior and powerful. He doesn't want you to know you're even playing the game with him until it's too late."

"Shit," Savage said. "He'd use their old ladies?"

"Once he knows who the wives are, he just accidentally bumps into the ones he wants to influence. He can do that at a coffee shop. Anywhere. He's charming. No threat. If it's a Diamondback, he'd be even less of a threat, because four of his brothers are Diamondbacks. It would be so easy to get all the data he needs to undermine very subtly the various club members' relationships."

"Such as Plank, the president, and Pierce, his enforcer," Savage ventured.

"Most definitely," Seychelle confirmed.

Now that he knew how and why, Savage sent a lengthy text to Czar explaining everything Seychelle had discussed with him.

"Now that we have that out of the way, baby, we have the rest of the evening to get that little bastard out of your head."

FOURTEEN

"I have to leave later tonight, and I want to know we're solid. I need to know you're with me all the way. I don't want to find out, after I've gone, that you decided to try to hitchhike home," Savage said.

Seychelle raised an eyebrow, trying to look as if she wasn't nervous, but then she bit her lower lip, completely destroying the image of her calm. "I was thinking Uber, not hitchhiking."

"I want you to tell me what you're most afraid of when you think about sucking my cock."

The moment he said the words, her eyes went wide with fear, but he pressed her palm tight into his thigh, his thumb continuing to stroke caresses back and forth over the back of her hand. He kept his gaze steady on hers. He hadn't asked her to actually do anything to him. His jeans were on and zipped up. She was in her own chair, and there was no command in his tone at all. He had deliberately kept his tone very conversational.

Her lashes fluttered several times, drawing his attention to their length. He waited in silence while the fire crackled and the flames burned orange and red.

"I don't want you to be disappointed in me. Or compare me to one of the other women and I fall very short."

He considered her fears carefully. "Does that sound like something I would do, Seychelle?"

She shook her head. "I know it's an irrational fear, but the moment you say the words to me, I hear laughter. I know that I'm surrounded by your club members and other women who have done this for you, and everyone is watching. You're laughing with them."

Savage really despised that she had feared his family, Torpedo Ink, would laugh at her. That he would. "You know where Campbell made his big mistake?" He kept his voice gentle.

She shook her head.

He reached out and slid his fingers into her hair. "He's done his research and he's been told I'm a sadist. Most sadists like to humiliate others. Because of my past behavior with the other women on these runs, he thinks I deliberately humiliated them. I didn't. I don't get off on that at all. The last thing I would ever want to do with the woman I love is to humiliate her. Planting a suggestion where I'm laughing at her because she chooses to give me pleasure by sucking my cock is absurd. I wasn't going to do anything remotely resembling what I did with other women with you. You wanted to learn, and I thought it would be a fun surprise for you, better than your book, something we'd enjoy together. Definitely *not* humiliation—that isn't my thing and never will be."

His woman was listening to him, and this time when he deliberately used the words *sucking my cock*, she hadn't tensed up or looked as if she might run. Seychelle was intelligent. Campbell might be able to plant suggestions, but she was too smart to be fooled for long. She was more than willing to work with Savage to undo any damage Campbell had done to her. She sat very still and let him continue to massage her scalp.

Savage had put her into intense situations, but he had

never humiliated her. Even now, when they talked about her coming on the run and he knew he would need her, once he had sounded her out about changing up the rules they'd put in place, when he realized she would be uncomfortable, he tried to think of alternatives. He let her think about that.

"How do we get those images out of my head, Savage? I want them gone. I get nervous when you ask me to do new things, but I always want to try them. I look forward to trying them. I wanted your cock in my mouth, although looking at you, I don't see how anyone can do that without choking to death. Still, you always are so generous with me, and get me off so many times when I try something new, so I suppose even if I didn't succeed the first few times, I'd still win in the end."

He wanted to smile at her telling him she might choke, but at the same time, he nearly groaned. Generous? Is that how she saw him? He was a greedy, selfish bastard half the time. More than half the time. It wasn't like he didn't see to her pleasure—he did. Over and over. But that gave him pleasure as well, and it was always on his terms.

"We just keep talking it out until you're not afraid anymore."

There was another long silence. Averted face. Biting lip. He rubbed his thumb along the back of her hand, and this time he made a little letter S over and over along the top of it. Waited until recognition hit and overrode the demons in her head.

"What if there was more to the suggestion?" There was real fear in her voice. "I've thought about that, and there could have been."

"Baby, look at me." His phone vibrated, and he knew that was Czar making the call, telling him he was out of time. Cursing silently, he pulled out his phone and texted back one-handed, fast.

Give me fifteen

"You would know. I have every confidence in you. You have to find that same confidence. You said so yourself:

you're stronger than he is. You're afraid for me, and that's what has you so shaken. You realized, somehow, that he planted the suggestion to be afraid of giving me a blow job, and that led you to the conclusion that someone here is going to try to kill me if they tried it. I think you panicked, Seychelle, more than you succumbed to his suggestion. You panicked thinking you might try to kill me."

Savage hadn't once changed the low, velvet tone of his voice. She responded naturally to that note. It always wrapped around her like a physical caress. Coupled with the way he wrote the letter of his name on her skin with the pad of his thumb, she calmed even more, her gaze finally lifting to meet his. Her lashes were wet, clinging together, making them dark and innocent-looking.

"I know something is very wrong with this entire situation, but I can't think clearly. There's too many other things in the way," she admitted. She looked at him with trust. With that look that said he was her white knight and he'd sort through all of them with her until she could find the truth. It was buried deep, a suggestion that Campbell had managed to plant in her head. "I hate the idea that he managed to get anywhere inside me. I need him out now."

Savage wanted him out as well. "No more than I want that, angel. Take a couple of deep breaths and clear your head so we can figure out what he's done. You're a thousand times more intelligent and a million times more talented. You know you are. He shook your belief for a moment, but you know better. We can talk this out. Think about what's actually happening in your head, Seychelle."

"That's possible," she admitted, her voice trembling. "I know, in the back of my mind, someone is going to make their try. I hear the laughter, the sound of women's voices. Your club is right there, Savage. Maybe it isn't me kneeling in front of you." She was frowning. Confused. "Another woman is in front of you, kneeling." Her eyes were closed.

Shit. That wasn't good. He didn't like where this was going. He could tell she didn't like it either. Her entire body had gone stiff. Those long, wet lashes lifted, and he found himself looking into horrified eyes. Accusing eyes.

The phone vibrated again. Cursing silently, Savage glanced down. **Sorry, Savage, out of time. Can't give you fifteen. Need you now.**

How could he possibly leave Seychelle like this? She was shaky. Vulnerable. Fearful of Campbell in her head. Already she was leery of his club and why she was there, other than for him. She knew that wasn't the only reason. Now she had sick images of another woman kneeling at his feet. The club laughing at her. She already didn't like or trust them. She didn't believe they would tell her if he fucked up—and they wouldn't. Reaper had nearly lost Anya over just such a thing, and it was Tawny who was trying to give him a blow job. This wasn't good at all.

He snatched up his T-shirt and dragged it over his head in one motion, jerking it down over his chest before catching up his jacket.

Seychelle's eyes went wide and dark as she watched him stomping into his motorcycle boots and shoving knives and a gun down into them.

"Wait a minute. Are you leaving? Now? In the middle of talking about this? Just when I'm talking about another woman?" She wrapped her arms around her middle, shivering.

He did his best to shut out the hurt in her voice. In her eyes. "Baby. We fucking put that topic to bed. I don't know how many times I have to reassure you that I don't want another woman's mouth on me. It isn't happening."

"We didn't put this to bed, Savage. This is different and you know it. I need your help to sort this out. Something's really wrong. You're my partner. I *need* you."

"Babe." He softened his voice and took a step toward her. Seychelle stepped back, the hurt in her eyes moving to her entire face. It felt like a fucking knife in his heart. "You knew I had to do some club business tonight. I'll be back soon. We'll sort this out then."

She shook her head. "I can't believe you'd do this. Leave me like this. You can't leave me when I really need you. This isn't something silly. I've never once asked you for anything. Not one single time. I need you here with me to sort through this. I'm scared."

"You don't need to be afraid, Seychelle. You won't be alone. I'll have guards on you. I'll be back as soon as I can."

"My God, you're really going. You're choosing them when I need you desperately." The pleading on her face disappeared. For the first time he couldn't read her. "This club of yours is so damned important to you, Savage. I hope it keeps you warm at night."

What the fuck did she mean by that? "I don't want you leaving this camp for any reason. You understand me? Not for any fucking reason. You have to pee, you tell one of the boys, and they'll get Lissa or Scarlet or both of them to escort you."

"Like I'm two."

"Like you're a treasure that no one is going to get the chance to hurt."

She just looked at him. He stepped into her, intending to kiss her, but she stepped back, holding up her hand. "Go, Savage. It's what you do. I know that. I knew it when I came here, what would happen. It isn't like I don't know what a fool I am. Just go, and don't rub my face in it right now. You said you aren't into humiliation, so please just don't."

"What the fuck is that supposed to mean?"

Reaper and Czar stood at the edge of the trees. "Savage, we need you *now*." That was Czar. His president talking. A clear order. He had to go.

"Don't you fucking move, Seychelle," he snapped and stalked away. Hyde and Glitch waited just behind Czar and Reaper. Savage pointed at them. "If one thing happens to her, so much as a scratch on her, I'll hold you two responsible. She isn't to leave the campsite. If she does have to use the bathroom, *both* Lissa and Scarlet go with her. If you can't get them, dig her a fucking hole right here and call it good."

He stormed off, glaring at Czar, for the second time in his life wanting to punch the man. "You couldn't give me fifteen minutes to straighten out something important with her?"

"I'm sorry, Savage, no. After you texted me that any of our people could be in trouble, and that Campbell may have gotten to some of the women in the Venomous club, it occurred to me that there might be a real connection between Tawny and that club. She admitted to trying to get information for the Diamondbacks from the Venomous club. It is entirely possible that Campbell and Tawny hooked up at some point."

Savage slowed his pace, allowing Czar and Reaper to move up beside him. They were moving steadily through the crowd. The sun had set, and as the sky darkened, the parties began in earnest.

"Seychelle thinks I abandoned her. Some really fucked up shit happened right before you got there. She was scared, and she asked me not to leave her." He looked at Czar. "She already thinks she plays second to the club, that she doesn't matter as much to me."

Czar shook his head. "I'm sorry, Savage. The timing on this entire thing is so wrong. I'll talk to her."

Savage raised an eyebrow. "She doesn't like you very much. She sees you as the enemy. She sees the club as her enemy. After what I just did, I don't know how I'm going to make it right."

"I fucked up big-time with Anya and she took me back, Savage," Reaper reminded him.

"Yeah, well, you don't have the kinds of things to ask Anya to accept that I've had to ask Seychelle to accept, Reaper. She didn't want to come. She knows most of the other women didn't come. It didn't help that Lana and Maestro all but told her she couldn't take care of my needs and she shouldn't be here. They all but told her she wasn't the right woman for me. She also resents the fact that Lissa and Scarlet know what's going on but she doesn't, even though she's here for the club to use her talents."

"Do you think it's wise to tell her?" Czar asked. "Because if you do, if she can handle that shit and you think she'll settle down, then it's best to just let her know things are going to be taking a bad turn here."

Savage thought they'd already taken a bad turn. Seychelle was only going to take so much shit before she was going to fight back. He was damn sure that battle was waiting for him. Just ahead, he could see Alena in her blue jeans and leather boots, Torpedo Ink colors and wavy fall of platinum hair. She faced them as they moved toward her. One hand was on the branch of a tree. She looked casual, but even from the distance, he could feel the seething rage pouring off her as she faced Pierce. Tawny was all over Pierce, deliberately running her hands over him, blatantly declaring ownership.

Automatically, Savage drained enough anger from Alena to give her the ability to hang on to the casual, indifferent appearance she presented. Four other Diamondbacks were close by, and two other women. She had somehow managed to walk right into a trap.

Alena stood still, her platinum hair falling around her face in a waterfall of waves, giving her more of an icy appearance than just the glacier blue of her eyes. She moistened her lips, her one sign of nerves, but she didn't take her gaze from Pierce and Tawny. Tawny continued to play with Pierce's zipper and run her hand up and down his chest. He didn't stop her but kept his gaze fixed on Alena, as if that would somehow keep her from noticing the woman practically stripping him right there.

"You trying to steal my man again, bitch?" Tawny asked, a challenge in her voice.

An arm snaked around Alena's waist. It was huge, all muscle and tattoos, an iron bar, and she was pulled back against Destroyer's large body. It was a little like smashing up against a steel wall. She recognized his scent immediately. He always smelled a little wild. Untamed. He looked it too. A dangerous, scary man she wasn't quite certain of, coming to her rescue. For once she was grateful and she'd take the help.

"Sorry I was a little late, baby," he whispered loud enough for the other two to hear. His voice had a growling rasp that told of a throat that had been damaged somehow years earlier. "I snagged a bottle of your favorite though."

He kissed the side of her neck, then scraped with his teeth, hitting the exact spot that sent little sparks lighting up her nerves. No one had ever managed to do that. She turned her head just enough to look up at him, knowing he was saving her pride. She *so* was going to owe him for this. She'd forgotten just how tall he really was.

"Thanks, honey, you're always so thoughtful."

"Just who the fuck are you?" Pierce demanded. "I keep seeing you. You wear Torpedo Ink colors, but I don't know you."

Destroyer lifted his head and looked at Pierce with flat, cold eyes. "I don't know you either and don't particularly want to. Right now, I'm going to have fun with my woman, drink some whiskey, fuck her hot, tight pussy because nothing feels better than she does. Nothing. Give her any damn thing she wants because a woman like her deserves it. Come on, baby. Been waiting all day to get a taste of you."

He lifted her as if she weighed nothing at all, put her over his shoulder and walked her right through the Diamondbacks and into the crowd. Savage wanted to laugh at the expression on Tawny's face. She despised that Alena seemed to get the men and attention no matter what she did. The expression on Pierce's face wasn't funny at all. He was furious.

"Destroyer just set himself up," he whispered to Czar.

Czar gave him a look that said he knew damn well what Destroyer had done. Destroyer's little sister had been Alena's age. She hadn't made it out of that hellhole they had been raised in. Her death had been particularly ugly. "Like we didn't have enough to worry about. Code is absolutely positive that Plank and three other Diamondbacks will be killed this weekend. Savage, you're going to have to find out how that's going to happen. I don't care how many of the Venomous club we have to go through to get the information, but we need it."

"And if that woman right there is the one who can provide it?" Savage asked, indicating Tawny.

"Then you need to get it from her." Czar was implacable.

"Fuckin' great," Savage muttered.

Plank and two other Diamondbacks arrived with two more women. It was clear that Czar was meeting the president of the Diamondbacks at the location and Alena just happened to stumble onto it.

"How are you going to play this?" Savage asked.

"Plank has to be made aware that there could be an assassination attempt on him. He's heard the rumor, and Tawny put it out there that Alena might be the one to make the try," Czar said. "Lion and Shark are both here. I wanted to make certain Shark was here at least. Plank's going to think I'm crazy when I tell him some of the women might be under the influence of a suggestion."

Maestro and Keys joined them, coming in from another direction. Keys grinned at Czar. "They'll all be afraid of demanding blow jobs even if they say they don't believe you."

Steele and Ink came up behind them. Ink gave a little shudder. "So much for thinking I might find the woman of my dreams."

"She'll take your fucking balls off," Steele said. "Wouldn't you be a pretty boy then?"

Reaper and Maestro dropped back to protect Czar while Savage and Keys stayed at his side. Savage didn't like having to be put in that position, but there was nothing else for it. He had to be the one to play this through. Pierce was once more in the spotlight with Tawny. The woman was trying to cuddle into him, whispering into his ear, pulling at him and pointing to the darkness where the music was the loudest.

"Czar," Plank greeted. "Got your message. Sounded urgent."

Czar nodded as they shook hands. "Yeah, this is going to sound so sci-fi and bizarre, but we have more than one source, and I didn't want to take any chances. There is a hit list for certain, you knew that going into this."

Plank swore, turning his head to look at his second-in-command, Judge, and then Lion and Shark, who were on either side of him. "I knew it. I fuckin' knew it."

"Someone has gotten to the Venomous club and slowly been destroying them from the inside out. He's taken them over, so he's running things behind the scenes but making it appear that it's business as usual," Czar said. "He gives orders, and those orders are followed."

"I'm not sure what you're getting at," Plank said.

"You, Judge, Lion and Shark for certain are on the list, as well as Savage. This is where the sci-fi part comes in. Some of the women here have been given a suggestion, much like a hypnotic suggestion, to offer a blow job, which is not unusual on a run. At some moment during the blow job, she will suddenly pull out a gun or knife and kill him. She won't remember the suggestion or even know she had that suggestion in her memory. That's not to say there aren't backup hit men waiting in the wings."

Plank stared at Czar as if he'd grown two heads. Then he turned that same stare on his brothers. "Holy fuck. If someone is capable of doing that, we could be in deep shit."

"Especially, Plank, if they were able to get to your wives." Czar delivered the bad news quietly.

Plank swung back around. "No way. No way could they do that. How? My old lady would never betray me. Not in a hundred years."

"I told you, she would never know. He'd meet her through a mutual friend like Tawny, have a casual conversation with him and he'd plant the suggestion. That's how it's done," Czar persisted.

Judge shook his head. "I don't see how. I've been to those

shows where someone is hypnotized. They have to volunteer and be agreeable to be put under."

Czar shrugged. "I'm just giving you the information we've uncovered in our investigation so far. That's what you asked for. It's still ongoing."

"Don't be so quick to judge," Lion interrupted. "I know it can be done. Planting a suggestion. You have to be really good, but it can be done."

Shark nodded. "Why go after the Venomous club, Czar?"

"I believe they're using that club because it's big enough and has enough chapters to undermine other clubs. It's chewing away at Diamondback territory. Venomous is making alliances with Headed for Hell. They can start slow, with patience, moving their pieces on the chessboard to get what they want. Did you take notice of how many pawns they sacrificed in Sacramento? They didn't care how many of the Venomous club members died. If the club presidents were concerned, that would never have happened. You don't treat your brothers like that."

Deliberately, Czar misled the Diamondbacks into thinking the enemy might be more than one person. They didn't know for certain if Campbell was working alone to undermine the Diamondbacks or if he had partners. That was what they were there for. Savage had to start extracting information. Unfortunately, their most likely informant was Tawny. None of them liked the idea of taking the data from a woman, but they needed it, and they needed it fast. Code was working overtime to get everything he could, but he was one man, and there were a lot of clubs to cover.

Savage could see Plank's dawning comprehension. "This has been going on for a long time. Shit. The slimy bastards. They're taking us apart from the inside. Making us doubt one another. Taking pieces of our territory and getting us to turn on our friends and allies."

"That's what we believe they're doing, yes, and oftentimes using the women to do it. The women have no idea it's happening. They're innocent victims." Czar wanted to reiterate that point. The Diamondbacks already didn't treat their women the way Czar felt they should. He didn't want to throw the women under the bus and have the men treat them even worse.

"How do you want to play this, Czar? You clearly have a plan."

Czar nodded. "We've got our people working, but we have to move faster. They've had time to put their assassins in the field. I want to know how many are here and who they are. We need names, and we need them fast." He jerked his chin toward Tawny, who was standing with a group of other women, laughing. Her gaze kept straying to Savage and Plank. She looked . . . greedy. Hungry. Pierce stood halfway between her and his president, but his gaze had followed Alena and Destroyer into the crowd.

Plank lowered his voice. "That bitch. She's doing a good job of tearing apart our club all on her own. She tried to start trouble between my wife and me. You think she's involved in this?"

"I don't know, but her name came up just enough times when we were listening in on the Venomous club to wonder who she was working for—you, them or someone else. In any case, I feel it's necessary to find out."

Judge cleared his throat. "Didn't want to bother you with this, Plank, didn't think it was worth it since my old lady brought it straight to me and we already had plans to take care of . . ." He broke off and then started again. "Tawny tried to get my old lady, Theresa, to help her get to you. Said she could do you and blame it on Alena, that she already sowed that seed. I could step up and take your place. Theresa told her to shut the hell up and never talk like that around her again. She came straight to me and told me what Tawny said. I assured her I'd take care of it."

"That fucking bitch was going to kill me and blame it on Torpedo Ink?" Plank demanded.

"That's what she told Theresa. And she was spreading that gossip, that Alena wanted to show everyone that she could be as badass as the men in her club, and everyone would believe she did it." Judge glanced at Czar.

The men of Torpedo Ink wore their expressionless masks. They simply watched the Diamondbacks. Savage could feel the fury pouring off his brothers in waves, but nothing showed on their faces. He did what he always did: he bled the rage from Czar first. Their president needed to be thinking with a clear head. Then he drew from the others in small increments, just enough to keep the anger contained and all of his brothers thinking straight. He buried the rage deep, where it swirled hot and dangerous but kept under cover, where he was used to containing it.

"What do you need from us, Czar?"

"We have a quiet place we can take anyone we need to interrogate already set up. Thing is, Tawny looks to be protected by your enforcer. We don't want to start a war with your crew. We've already got bad blood between our clubs because of what happened between Pierce and Alena. He had every right to make his choice. His bad luck to choose Tawny. Alena is locked down for the night. She's with Destroyer, and he'll watch over her. I give you my word we'll return Pierce's woman alive to him, but he can't be around objecting to anything we do to get what we need. Nor do we want that shit recorded. You want us to run with this, you have to let us do it without interference; otherwise, we've warned you and we've done our part. We'll step aside, and Pierce can get the information you need."

Savage could see that Plank wanted to let the Diamondbacks handle the interrogation. He despised Tawny at this point. Already she had cost them far too much and would continue to do so. Plank was aware he wasn't blameless. He had bought into the rumors she'd spread, and that embarrassed him. He was the leader of his chapter, and he was responsible.

In spite of the fact that Czar wanted the information for their own purposes and there was no way the Diamondbacks would get everything they needed from Tawny, nor would they share, Savage hoped Plank would insist they be the ones to question her. Savage knew what interrogating Tawny would entail. He would have to allow her to make her play for him, and the idea was sickening. He also didn't like what he would have to do to get information from her. They needed names, and everything Code had found out indicated she could provide them, at least give them enough to start the hunt up the ladder. Savage just didn't want to be the one to take her apart.

Before Plank could make up his mind, Shark suddenly interrupted. "Savage, you brought your woman, Seychelle, with you, didn't you?"

Savage froze. His ice-cold gaze slid sideways to land on Shark. A killer's eyes. There was an instant of recognition in the circle of Diamondbacks. A shift as Lion and Judge moved to close ranks on Plank and yet try to include Shark in their protection. They recognized a threat, and all Savage had done was look at him. He was still looking, unmoving, a shadow come to life, the assassin unmasked.

Savage. You have to stand down.

Tony doesn't get Seychelle.

Take a breath and let me handle this. You're too close to the end of your cycle, and you're pulling in too much rage from the rest of us. Trust me to do this.

"Tony." Czar kept his voice even and calm. "Out of respect, we don't bring your women into meetings, and we expect that you leave ours out as well. One of our women was already disrespected and continues to be so every time she meets one of you playing your silly video of her like teenagers, like you did in the bar a couple of weeks ago. We take that shit because we gave our word to Plank and we keep our word. Please don't take that for weakness. That would be a big mistake." Even issuing the warning, his tone didn't change.

"There's no need to bring other women into this," Plank agreed immediately, sending Tony a warning look.

"I wasn't being disrespectful of her," Shark said. "Just the opposite. I believe she could help all of us. She has a gift that might allow her to identify any of our women who might have the suggestion planted in them."

"How could she do that?" There was real interest in Plank's voice.

There was silence as everyone looked at Shark. Savage had never taken his death stare from him. Czar watched him closely as well.

He doesn't know for certain, and he's got a hidden agenda, Savage. I think he hopes Seychelle can identify something Brandon did to him.

She won't have to if he's dead.

You can't start a war here.

Watch me. She can't do what they want her to do. Putting out that much psychic energy would kill her. He knows it if he knows anything about psychic energy.

I'm betting he doesn't. Not really. Look at Lion, his brother. He's in the dark as well. They suspect something is wrong with them, but not what it is. I'm betting they're worried they're spreading this dissent among their brothers.

That would make sense and explain the sudden interest in Seychelle and her capabilities. Absinthe was somewhere close. So was Scarlet. Both had extraordinary abilities to ferret out truth. Savage wouldn't mind seeing the two of them interrogate Tony.

Tony cleared his throat. "I'll admit I don't know exactly how it works. But she can do it. I'm certain of it. She has that ability. They only brought a few women with them. Five. That's it. They have another full chapter with them from Trinity. Two women. They knew there was trouble, and they brought women capable of helping them in a fight. Seychelle is the exception."

Plank looked to Czar. Czar shrugged. "She's Savage's old lady. Where he goes, she goes. He doesn't leave her behind."

"I think it best if your people extract the information we need from Tawny. My people would kill her. I'll need one of mine observing."

"Absolutely not. We don't have witnesses. We'll give you information, that's the deal," Czar said, "but I won't compromise any of my men. And I don't want her man coming after any of mine because we weren't nice asking questions."

Pierce had walked closer to the circle. It was clear he had taken in quite a bit of the conversation. He wasn't happy about it. "I'm not her man and never have been. I'm doing a fucking job, keeping that bitch in line. Who exactly is Destroyer? Where did he come from?"

Czar turned his cool silver eyes on him. "He's Torpedo Ink, that's who he is. She'll live, but we will make it very clear that she will not go to the cops. We'll follow up on anything we get from her as soon as possible unless your men will take it from there."

Plank shook his head. "That's what I asked you to do."

"Consider it done." Czar signaled to his men. Maestro, Keys and Ink began stalking Tawny, a slow move, easing their way into the crowd heading toward the small group of women.

"Czar, I'd like to meet Savage's old lady, just have a conversation with her. Respectful. She sounds interesting," Plank continued.

"I'll see if I can arrange that. She's new to the life, and it was her first time on a long ride. She's exhausted."

Czar was already moving, Reaper and Savage closing in on him to cover him as they followed the others into the crowd. Behind them, other members of Torpedo Ink slipped in to shield them, more and more, building a wall until Czar couldn't be seen.

Just across from the spot Czar had chosen to meet Plank were two buildings and several trees. On the rooftop of the women's bathroom, Lana kept Plank in her sights, her hands steady, finger never leaving the trigger.

Sitting comfortably in the crotch of the apple tree, Scarlet had Lion in her sights, watching carefully that he didn't make a single move toward Czar.

On the roof of the third building, Lissa kept her rifle centered squarely on Shark. It was Gavriil and Casimir, Czar's two birth brothers and Torpedo Ink brethren, who were the biggest threat to the Diamondbacks in the group watching Czar fade away. The two Prakenskii brothers were like ghosts, able to slip in and out of crowds, shadows unseen, even when making a kill. They listened to make certain Plank wasn't double-crossing Czar and sending someone to kill him.

There was no way Seychelle was going to be able to sleep, not with Savage prowling around the craziness that was loud music, the sound of motorcycles, laughter and conversations vying for airspace with all the partying going on. In other words, to her, the night was chaos. There were many parties, not just one. Each party was loud and different and seemed to rival the one next to it. She was left alone in her little world of illusion and madness; the worst of it was, it was of her own making.

Seychelle paced around her little campsite there in the shelter of the trees and darkness. The fire in the pit was burning low and didn't throw light to the outer perimeter, so she could walk around in silence hopefully unseen, for the most part. Occasionally she could hear the murmur of voices. She knew a couple of the club members had stayed behind to keep an eye on her. She had pulled on her jeans and boots, put on a bra and T-shirt under her long sweater just to feel like she could make a run for it if she needed to. She'd even transferred everything she might need inside the built-in pocket of her boot.

She had asked for this life. She chose it when she chose Savage. Granted, she'd thought she was choosing him, not his club. Not this. He had said he wasn't into humiliation, and she believed him. He should understand how it felt to be used by an entire group of people who looked down on her—who didn't include her in their circle. They made it clear she was inferior to them. That was humiliation, any way you looked at it.

Why? She pondered that question as she paced. She didn't have fighting skills. Clearly, that was prized. Lissa and Scarlet were treated as members of the club. They were definitely in and privy to information. Blythe wasn't a fighter, but then she was Czar's wife. That might make her exempt from any judgment. Since all of them shared everything, it was possible Torpedo Ink looked down on her because she allowed Savage to use her the way he did sexually. It was more than possible that he actually discussed with them that she enjoyed it. That she begged him to take her over and over. If that was the case, and they thought she was really nothing more than someone they could use, that might explain why she was treated so differently.

She was in love with him, and Savage knew it. He knew she craved the sex and the experiences he gave her. He knew every button to push with her and how to keep her coming back to him when she was certain she should walk away. Seychelle forced herself to sit in the camp chair, where she pressed both hands to her face. She would have to live like this for the rest of her life, knowing she truly loved Savage. She was *in* love with him, but she wasn't altogether certain he was capable of loving her back.

He said he loved her. He looked as if he loved her. He touched her with reverence and love at times. But then there were other times like this. He knew she was scared and felt battered emotionally. Instead of talking to her and letting her know what was happening and what to expect, he kept her in the dark, knowing it made her feel alone, an outcast. An outsider. He had set their relationship up so that if she protested in front of his club, he had the right to punish her. She had the terrible fear that he might choose to do so in front of them. She knew she would never forgive him if he did.

Did he really know her at all? She had watched him so carefully, tried to take the time to get to know him so she could see to his needs. Had he done the same with her? After they had sex, he always cared for her. Always. She was up and out of the chair again, pacing back and forth, trying to think about the in-between times.

He had come with her to visit her friends. He'd been charming to them and, more importantly, he'd done badly needed repairs at his own expense. He wouldn't even allow her to help him with the money for materials. The homes might look nice on the outside, but there was always maintenance to do. The older people tended to put it off. After the string of robberies that had occurred in Sea Haven, most of them refused to allow strangers into their homes, even for repairs. It meant a lot to her that Savage would go with her and help them. He'd done that for her.

She pressed her fingers into her temples to try to stop the pounding headache. She could hear the roar of her own blood. The ache. She'd gone without him. Weeks. The pain of that separation had been excruciating. She hadn't been able to eat or sleep. In the end, she'd gone to him because she'd thought she could take living his lifestyle, but she thought she would be truly loved by him.

They'd asked each other the question about loving totally, intensely and wholly, and she had been truthful, telling him that was what she was looking for. She was a natural healer. When she was around sick people, she often couldn't stop herself from trying to mend them. Her body took on the illness. She already had damaged her heart. The doctor had warned her she didn't have long to live. Savage had promised to protect her during those times she was compelled to help others with diseases she couldn't possibly save, but where was he when she needed him? When she'd begged him to stay with her? He wasn't with her. He was with *them*. The club. His club.

She was only something to use when he needed her, and he controlled her with his voice and the promise of amazing sex because she allowed it. She chose that. She had to learn to choose differently in order to save herself. No one else was going to save her; one way or the other, she was going to have to do it. She didn't know if she could live without him, but then that was a choice as well.

FIFTEEN

"I'm telling you, Czar," Savage said, as they approached the Torpedo Ink camp. "The moment Seychelle touches me, she's going to know Tawny was all over me. What do you think is going to happen then? She was already upset that I left her. She'd asked me not to leave her and I did anyway."

"You tell her nothing happened," Czar said.

Savage stopped dead in his tracks. "Do you honestly believe she trusts me after the way I left her? She's an extremely intelligent woman. She knows damn well she was brought here for a purpose and it wasn't just because I need her with me. The club needed her at the bar, and now they need her again, but she isn't included in the reasons why."

"That's for her protection, Savage," Czar pointed out. "You just said it yourself. You don't have her complete trust. Until you do, it's too dangerous to her to know everything. If she were to get scared or angry and say something to the wrong people, where the hell would we be then?"

Savage knew Czar was subtly reminding him they'd eliminated all threats to members of the club. No one was eliminating Seychelle. He was in a hell of a position.

"Plank is going to insist she's introduced to him. You've got to get some of the rage pulled out of you. I know this blows, Savage—the timing, everything about it—but we're walking a tightrope. The Diamondback club is too big for us to take on. We'd be running for the rest of our lives. We have to get out from under this. Absinthe and Scarlet both know if someone is telling the truth, but they can't tell if a suggestion has been planted. We've got names of some of the top Venomous members from Tawny who may be in on the assassination plot. It's fairly ambitious to try to take out so many top members of one chapter at once. And they aren't the only chapter here." Czar rubbed his forehead. "I knew she was needed, I just didn't know why."

"I'm aware of the danger our club is in, Czar," Savage said and glanced at his brother. Reaper understood what he was trying to say. His features might be unreadable, but his eyes held sympathy. He knew what Savage would be facing when he tried to talk to his woman after all but turning his back on her. "I'm telling you, the chances of Seychelle helping us out aren't quite as good as you seem to think they are."

He stalked away from the president, the others, and past the two prospects, who looked relieved that he had gotten back. He made his way deeper under the seclusion of the trees where he'd set up the camp. Seychelle sat in a camp chair, fully clothed, including her boots, and a heavy sweater with a vest over it. Not the club jacket, he noted. There was a coffee mug in her hand. She stared into the fire instead of looking up when he arrived.

Savage had washed up before he came to her, but he needed to change out of his clothes. He knew they had Tawny's scent on them and probably drops of blood, although he'd been careful with her, maximum pain without too much damage. He pulled off his jacket and tee, watching her closely as he tossed them aside. She didn't even turn her head.

"You going to talk to me?"

"There's not much to say."

"We had something unfinished before I had to leave. Let's start there."

She tossed the coffee onto the ground and put the mug down with a little sigh. "Just give me the bottom line, Savage. What do you need from me?" She turned then and looked at him. Her gaze slid from him to the clothes he'd tossed aside and then to the jeans he was pulling on. Usually, Seychelle was an open book. Right at that moment, he couldn't read her at all.

Shit. She wasn't going to give an inch. He didn't blame her. If he'd been in her shoes, he would have walked away already. She'd closed herself off to him. That was walking away. He needed to get an explanation in fast before there was any physical contact.

"I want to tell you what went on tonight, and then we'll talk about the things that we should have talked about before I had to leave. That was fucked up, Seychelle, me leaving when you needed me."

She pushed out of the camp chair and paced away from him as he stomped his feet back into his boots and reached into his pack for a clean shirt. "I don't need to know what went on tonight. Really, Savage. There's no need to tell me."

There really wasn't interest in her voice, and that worried him more than anything. She moved restlessly around the firepit as if she couldn't hold still, skirting carefully around him, keeping a safe distance away. She neared the picnic table, and out of habit she leaned down and picked up his dirty clothes off the ground, her fingers smoothing over his jeans and tee as she started to fold them.

Savage saw the moment images pushed into her mind. She froze, her breath catching. Very slowly, she raised her eyes to his. He expected condemnation. Pain. Agony. A burst of anger. Something. What he didn't expect was emptiness. She looked at him as if she didn't know him. As if he were a total stranger to her.

She didn't drop his clothes on the ground the way he expected. She turned toward the picnic table and continued to fold them, only he saw her remove her engagement ring and push it into the pocket of his jeans.

His belly tightened into a thousand knots, but he kept his features as blank as hers. "Had to interrogate a woman tonight. That's one of the worst jobs there is. Her name is Tawny. She has a history with our club, which made it even worse."

She didn't look at him again but paced away dismissively, as if she couldn't care less what he said. She couldn't leave, and that was his only advantage. She had to listen.

Savage kept talking. "She despised every one of us. From our club she went straight to the Diamondbacks and began to make as much trouble for them as she did for us. Code learned that a hit was put out not just on me but on several of the Diamondbacks as well. It turns out other hits were taken out on top members of the Venomous club, which is the club all of us suspected was behind the trouble. Four other members of Torpedo Ink have hits out on them as well as me."

For the first time, she looked up, her eyes meeting his.

"Reaper, Ice, Storm and Alena are all on the list. That's a lot of people under death threats." He shoved his hand through his hair, suddenly tired. "This is such a fuckin' shit show. And no, baby, interrogating Tawny definitely doesn't mean she ever touched me in any sexual way. I can guarantee she never wants to see me again. I find her the most repulsive woman on the face of the earth."

He scrubbed his hand over his face, trying to wipe out the memory of the greedy, grasping woman as she tried to crawl on her hands and knees and wrap herself around his legs, her fingers on his zipper. There was no arousal, only disgust.

"Seychelle, please look at me. I know I hurt you when I left. I didn't know what I was walking into, so I couldn't tell you. But it's important to me that you believe me that I didn't allow this woman or any other to touch me, nor did I touch them in a sexual way."

Seychelle kept the length of the picnic table between them. The flames in the firepit had died down and barely reached her, but the light played over her face just enough to let him see that blank expression that tore at him. She wasn't giving him anything. She'd folded his dirty clothes and set them on the tabletop right next to her fingers as she leaned against the table, her hands gripping the edge as if for support.

Her lashes had lifted at his request, and her gaze met his. The blue was dark and shuttered. She'd left him. Seychelle might be standing there, but she'd left him. He could feel panic building. His chest hurt, pain exploding through him.

"It's important that you believe me," he reiterated.

"Why?"

He frowned, trying to understand her question. Of course it was important; how could she trust him if she thought he was fucking other women? "Why?" he repeated aloud.

"Yes, Savage, what difference does it really make? Does it change anything? Does anything change the dynamic between us? Nothing ever will change it. You'll come back and tell me how much you love me. You'll say I'm your entire world. You'll kiss me and we'll have amazing sex and every single thing will be exactly the way you want it to be. Everything. When I object, you'll sweep my objections away. When I say I need something, well, that's too bad, and if I'm upset, we start the process all over again. I've become that girl."

"What girl?" He didn't like where this was going. He had to hear her out. That was what Torpedo Ink did. They listened to one another, but what she was saying was damn hard to hear, mostly because when he went over it, she wasn't wrong, not from her point of view.

"The one without a voice. Without any life of her own. I live only to serve you and your club. I don't even know if they truly are laughing and talking behind my back about what a fool I am to do whatever you ask me to do. I'm even beginning to wonder how different I am from Sahara or Tessa."

She shook her head. "In the interest of full disclosure, Czar said to me that if there ever came a time that I felt I needed help, I was to call him. He said not to ever call the cops, that he would handle it. I texted him and told him I wanted out. We'll see if your president keeps his word and gets me a ride home. If he does, I'm packing my things and leaving. I don't want you to follow me or look for me."

Savage couldn't speak. The pressure in his chest was so severe he couldn't breathe. A roaring in his ears took away his ability to hear. Sweat broke out, trickled down his forehead, his chest. It was a weird sensation because mostly, he was numb. His mind shut down until all he could see was black. Screaming mixed with the thunder and pounding of his blood in his ears. He gripped his shirt with his fist and held on.

The red began to swirl through the black in his mind. The terrible chaos receded slowly as he fought for control. He inhaled. Exhaled. The hammering in his blood grew more demanding. The rush was hot with rage-laced adrenaline. It moved through his body in a familiar flow, pushing away panic, leaving him with total clarity as he took back control.

"I can guarantee you that's not happening, Seychelle," he bit out.

"It is if your president keeps his word."

"I don't give a damn what he says. You aren't leaving."

"What's going on?" Czar asked. "I received your text, Seychelle." He wasn't looking at Seychelle; his eyes were on Savage, assessing him. With him were Reaper and Maestro.

Savage ignored Czar. "Why is it always me fighting for us, Seychelle? You knew I'd be fucking up repeatedly. I made that clear from the beginning. You can take off the ring, but you don't get to run. That was always the agreement. We see it through. We make it work no matter what. I'm fucking up, we talk it out. You don't get to run. So no, whatever you've got going with Czar and my brother and Maestro, just know, it's going to turn ugly really fast."

Czar's piercing gaze swept over him and then slowly turned to Seychelle. "I understand you want to go home, honey. Tell me what's wrong."

Savage folded his arms across his chest and waited. Her hand moved from the edge of the picnic table to rest on top of the folded jeans. Once more, her lashes lifted, and this time she looked past Czar to take in Reaper and Maestro. There was no welcome on her face. Seychelle wasn't exactly a poker player. Her expression gave her feelings away. She didn't like them. She didn't want them there. She didn't understand why Czar brought them. Savage knew. Czar was aware Savage was already fighting that edge, and if anyone tried to take his woman, he would fall right off the cliff. When he detonated, he was going to take a lot of people with him.

"This just isn't going to work. I don't like it here, and I want to leave. I've already packed my things. I want to go." Her voice started out firm, but her gaze flicked to Savage and trembled at the end when she made her declaration.

"Answer me honestly," Czar said. "Are you in love with Savage?"

Her fingers fisted in his jeans. "That is beside the point."

"I think that's the entire point, Seychelle," Czar said, his voice calm. "Please answer."

She stuck her chin in the air. Savage had always loved that little gesture she made of sheer defiance. "You said I could come to you instead of calling the cops. I need to go."

"You need to answer the question," Czar persisted gently. "Are you in love with Savage?"

"Yes."

She opened her mouth as if she might argue her point, but she pressed her lips together and then pressed her fingers over her lips. She was shaking. Savage had the urge to go to her and comfort her, but he knew she would reject him. This sucked, especially since there were witnesses.

"Savage, are you in love with Seychelle? Not just love her, but are you *in* love with her?"

"Absolutely."

"Then we need to get down to business. Seychelle, what exactly is the problem? I know you've done everything you could for him, because Savage has been happier than I've ever seen him. You aren't happy. Why?" Czar sank down onto the bench beside the picnic table.

Seychelle flicked a quick glance at Maestro and Reaper. Reaper had taken up a guard position, turning his back to the drama to watch for intruders. Maestro, on the other hand, was paying close attention, frowning at the three of them.

She spread her hands out in front of her. "We don't work, Czar. Sometimes it doesn't matter how much you love one another, you just don't work. He's happy because I give him whatever he wants."

"Is that true, Savage?" Czar asked.

"Yes," Savage said without hesitation. She did.

"I'm not because he refuses to see that I have emotional needs as well as physical. If he doesn't see them, he doesn't have to meet them. I've gotten to the point where I feel as if I'm only being used, not just for him but for his club. It isn't just a feeling. It's the truth. I needed him tonight. There was no justification for him leaving. None. But he did."

"There was justification, Seychelle," Czar said quietly. "I assure you, he was needed to save lives."

"I don't have a clue what's going on. Everyone around me does, but I don't. Still, Savage is insistent that I do as he asks and use my talent to help all of you when I'm treated like an outsider." She shook her head. "I can't be that person anymore. I've lost who I am. It makes me feel weak, and I'm disgusted with myself. I've become someone I don't like very much."

Maestro shook his head. "A woman trusts her man, she

does what he says. It's that simple. She doesn't cause drama like this in the middle of one of the most dangerous runs we've ever been on, especially when her man needs her the most."

Savage wanted to leap across the picnic table and take his brother down, feel the satisfying thud of fists hitting flesh. He must have made a sound, because Reaper turned and Czar stood, but Seychelle was there before the men. She glided in between Savage and Maestro, one small palm on Savage's chest, but she faced Maestro.

"How dare you think you know me to reprimand me. You're the idiot that gave Savage the idea he should use another woman to give him a blow job when he was with me. That's called cheating, in case you're not smart enough to understand at least that much in a relationship between a man and a woman. You think you know so much, but you don't have a clue. It's too bad that you helped lose your *brother* the best thing he ever had."

"I fucking have not lost you. You aren't leaving me," Savage decreed. He all but snarled it, glaring at first her and then Maestro.

Seychelle was unfazed by Savage's glare. If anything, she was calmer than all of them. Distant. As if she had made up her mind, and all the questions and answers in the world weren't really going to make a difference.

She shifted her gaze toward Czar. "You were aware I needed Savage, that I asked him to stay with me, yet you insisted he go with you and the club. Why?"

"He was needed in his role to extract the information we needed."

"Every one of you is capable of getting the information you needed. Even him." She jerked her chin toward Maestro. "He clearly isn't in a committed relationship, and if he is, he doesn't give a damn about his woman. Why not have him get the information for you? Why insist that Savage put his relationship on the line? Was it some kind of loyalty test?"

She was magnificent. Savage would have thought he couldn't

admire or respect her any more, but she just stood up to both club members, the president and Maestro, who could put the fear of the devil into anyone. Seychelle certainly wasn't intimidated.

"No, honey, it wasn't a test of loyalty. I didn't realize what was happening to you. I still am not certain what was going on. He kept asking for more time, but Code had uncovered information that led us to believe members of our club and several other clubs were in danger. We needed the names of those in danger and also any others who might be able to point us toward who wants all of us dead. We have to shut this down." As always, when Czar spoke, he did so calmly, his eyes that piercing silver that seemed to look right through you.

Savage remained absolutely still, with the exception of one hand. He had to connect with Seychelle, and she had made that first move, giving him the opportunity. She came close to him. Put her hand on him. Right over his heart. He put his palm over hers. Gently. Barely touching her, trying not to be possessive. Trying not to make her feel like his prisoner. Just needing that connection. She didn't move her hand, and he closed his eyes and let the rush of electricity heat his blood and slide over his skin like armor.

"You're right that all of us were trained to extract information from prisoners, but Savage is without equal in this department. He's fast, and he can get the job done without killing the prisoner or harming them to the point that we'd have to kill them. In this case, Tawny, a woman, was the person we needed information from. That made it even more difficult. We needed his expertise. It was my call. There were so many lives at stake, and I had set up the meeting. I knew we didn't have a lot of time. I should have considered something might be going on and asked first."

Seychelle nodded her head and sighed, leaning back so her weight was partially on Savage. His arm slid around her waist to lock her to him.

"I was in trouble, Czar. Brandon Campbell planted one

of his suggestions in my head, and I needed my fiancé to help me. I never, not once, asked him for anything. I asked him to stay and help me. He didn't. He went off with you. He would again, every time, because he is Torpedo Ink. I will always come in second to the club."

"It isn't like that," Czar said. "This was my fault."

Seychelle shook her head. "It is exactly like that, and you know it. I didn't want to come here. He insisted I come."

"He wanted to take you home. I refused. I knew we were going to need you. I still think it's imperative you're here," Czar said.

Seychelle looked at him steadily. "It was obvious, just like the night I sang in the bar, that something was wrong. All of you know what it is, and you clearly brought me along because you need me to perform some task for you. I'm not a club member. You're using me. He uses me. What exactly am I getting out of this? Because I don't know."

"None of us really knew for certain," Czar said. "It isn't a matter of using you."

"Of course it is. Don't kid yourself. None of them like me for Savage. They've said as much, so don't try to tell me different. I don't like any of you. I don't want to help any of you. You treat me like an outsider and encourage my partner to screw other women. Hell, you're probably laughing behind my back. I don't know. I don't care. I'm tired, and I want out."

Savage tightened his arm around her, locking her to him. He bent his head and brushed a kiss on top of her hair, waiting for Czar to sort through the mess. She had a right to feel the way she did. He couldn't fault her on anything she said. Still, he wasn't letting her go.

"What do you think about all this, Savage? You've had time to assess it," Czar asked, his voice quiet in the darkness.

"Seychelle is right. I am Torpedo Ink, and I always will be. But I'm Seychelle's partner. She's my other half. I should have made certain she was safe before I did anything else. She's my first priority. I could have made that clear to you and taken the time to help her. If necessary, the club could have helped her."

Czar nodded. "Exactly. Relationships are difficult when you've never seen them before. We were raised without parents, Seychelle. We had no patterns to follow. We learn as we go, so mistakes are made all the time. You have to be patient, but Savage, you have to listen to her. She does come first."

"Why am I the only person not included when you tell everyone what's going on?" Seychelle asked Czar.

Savage's heart nearly stopped beating and then accelerated. Involuntarily, his arm tightened to the point she had to reach up and touch his face.

"Too tight, I can't breathe." She looked up at him. "It's you. Not the club. You're hiding something from me."

"We don't talk about club business," Czar said, backing Savage up.

"That's bullshit," Seychelle said. "You told Scarlet and Lissa. This has something to do with Savage and what he does."

Maestro made a sound of derision. "You're ready to run at the first sign of trouble. Do you really think we're going to put our lives in your hands?"

"Be fucking careful how you talk to her."

"Why, Savage? Are you going to beat me to death with your fists? You're right there on the edge. You need a woman. Your woman is running away. She was never strong enough to help you, and you know it."

"That's enough, Maestro," Czar ordered.

On some level, Savage knew Maestro was taunting Seychelle, trying to get her to fight back, to stand up for Savage and their relationship.

"It takes trust to allow Savage to take what he needs from me, Maestro," Seychelle said, looking at the club member. "If he doesn't trust me, then how can I possibly trust him?"

Maestro didn't respond. He of all people knew what she said was the truth.

She switched her gaze to Czar. "You had him bring me here because you wanted something from me, just like the night in the bar when you wanted me to keep the Diamondbacks calm for you, yet none of you trusted me enough to tell me what was going on. I have no intention of helping you out. None. Again, I don't trust you. It's impossible to put my faith in people who don't put it in me. So, Maestro, go ahead and think the worst of me, because, believe me, I think it of all of you."

Czar stopped Maestro from responding with one look. "You shouldn't, Seychelle. Not everything is always what it seems. The truth is, Maestro made the suggestion of another woman helping out Savage because he was worried about you. The club is protective of you," Czar continued. "He wasn't thinking in terms of Savage cheating on you. He was afraid of you getting physically hurt. He didn't want you leaving Savage because he got out of control and no one was here to help you."

"And yet we've come to this point anyway," Seychelle whispered. She didn't move away from Savage, rather gave him more of her weight, as if the world was just too much for her to bear.

Savage wanted to lift her into his arms and cradle her close. How many times could a man fuck up and hurt the woman he loved? Evidently, he could do it every damn day. He put both arms around her and pressed his mouth to her ear.

"I'm sorry, baby. I'm so damn sorry. I wish I knew what the hell I was doing."

She turned her face up to look over her shoulder at him, tears glistening on her lashes. "Me too, Savage."

They stared at each other for an eternity. Savage knew it wasn't going to end well. Either way, she was going to leave him. If he gave her what she wanted—no, needed—she would never look at him again. If he didn't, she would leave him. No matter what, he was going to lose.

"I can't live like this, Savage."

"You're not leaving, Seychelle. That's not what we agreed on. The deal was, we talk it out. We find solutions."

"Savage." There was despair in her voice. In her eyes. "You're the one who isn't talking, not me. I've been talking so much my throat hurts. I can't find a solution. If I could, I would have told you what it is by now. I can see that you need me. Do you think it's easy to leave you like that? If I don't go, I'll do something crazy. I know myself. This is self-preservation, Savage. I love you, but you need to be with me. With *me*. That's the only way I can be with you. Then we can be with them."

Savage walked her to the picnic table and sat on the table-top, pulling her to stand between his thighs so she was facing him. "You aren't going to like me much, baby."

"Savage, you're the one who doesn't have a lot of faith in me."

Czar stood up, drifting closer to her. "Seychelle, he's putting his life into your hands. That's what you're asking him to do. I hope you're prepared for that. The things he might say won't be easy for you to accept."

She lifted her chin, her blue eyes moving over Czar and then Maestro and Reaper, who had also moved closer. "Do you think I'm naïve? If it were easy, he would have told me a long time ago." She turned back to Savage, framing his face with both hands. "I'm counting on you to save us. Just do it, Savage. Trust me."

Savage shook his head. It was now or never. "That nightmare you kept having about Arnold? You asked the wrong question, baby. You asked me if I killed him. I didn't. You saw those images because they were real. I told you I question our prisoners to find out who has the children or who are the ones taking them. I don't do it nicely. I torture them."

She was very still, her fingers digging into his thighs. They'd told her straight up that he'd questioned Tawny and that pain had been involved, but it had been different with Joseph Arnold. She'd seen images, and they'd been gruesome.

Savage kept his gaze fixed on her face while she pro-cessed. It was her way to take her time. When Reaper started to say something, Savage shook his head. They waited. The wind blew, touched his face, ruffled her hair. She took a deep breath. At least she wasn't running.

"I'm not certain why Arnold would have to be ques-tioned, but if all of you believed he needed to be, then I would want to trust your judgment."

He forced himself to keep looking at her, not taking his eyes from hers. "I told you I was raised to be an assassin. I still do that work. I take out our enemies. I'll be doing it here."

She didn't look away from him, nor did she say anything. No one did. There was absolute silence. Her fingers bit harder into his thighs. She touched her tongue to her lower lip, and then her chin went up. "You knew before we came here, all of you knew, that you would be killing someone."

He nodded. His hand covered hers, his thumb moving over the back of it. "More than one person. Several."

"Just you, or will the others be doing this kind of work as well?"

"That will depend on the situation. Usually, it's me. Sometimes one of the others has no choice." He wasn't go-ing to incriminate any of his brothers or sisters.

She inhaled deeply and then stepped back, pulling her hands away from his thighs. "I have to think about this for a minute. Give me a minute. You know how I am."

He did. She needed to process. At least she wasn't telling him to go to hell and demanding Czar get her a ride home. She was surprisingly cool about Arnold now that she had time to think about it. He had to learn to give her the time she needed, and if he wasn't always able to protect her from the things he did, he needed to man up and talk to her about them so she didn't have nightmares like she had with Arnold.

Czar glanced at his watch several times but refrained from breaking the silence. Maestro and Reaper assessed

Savage and how close he was to the edge. They'd been through it with him many times and knew every single sign.

Seychelle came back to him faster than he'd thought she would. "You aren't going to name names because you aren't going to incriminate anyone but you." She looked at Maestro and Reaper. "You came here with the intent to kill some people who I presume are an actual threat to you, or you wouldn't want them dead. Can you give me your word that anyone you kill deserves it, Savage?"

"Would you take my word, Seychelle?" He pushed stray strands of hair from her face with gentle fingers, his heart turning over. She was such a gift, and he had come so close to blowing his chances with her.

"As far as I know, you've never lied to me, so yes, I would believe you."

"I would never kill an innocent. They would have to be a threat to you, me or the club, and that isn't an innocent in my eyes. Anyone else is someone we're after because they're involved in human trafficking or a pedophile ring. I neutralize any threat to any member of the club or anything such as this mess we're in now."

"The one I tried to talk to you about before you went off with Czar."

"That's the one," he confirmed.

"How long are you going to be the one doing this for the club?"

"Indefinitely." He made that a firm statement.

"I see."

He didn't like the quiet acceptance in her voice.

"What do you mean, you tried to talk to Savage about it before he left?" Czar said. "Why would that be what you were upset about? Why was that in any way affecting you, Seychelle?"

"Brandon Campbell, as you know, is related to four of the Diamondbacks," Seychelle said.

She moved away from Savage again. He couldn't tell if she did it because she needed to pace or if she was suddenly upset again that he had left her in a highly emotional situation. She pressed one hand to her temple as if it hurt.

"He's very vindictive, and I don't think he's very happy with the Diamondbacks for rejecting him when they took his brothers. He's the kind of man who would be happy to stay in the background and wreak havoc by planting suggestions, mostly to women. But you know all this—Savage texted you the information."

She skirted around the firepit and stopped in front of it, putting her palms out as if she was cold. There were only embers left, the flames gone. Savage could see the little shiver that ran through her. He immediately got up and went to her. "Baby, it's all right."

"No, it isn't. Brandon doesn't have near the talent I do, but I gave him an in when we were broken up, and he used it to plant a suggestion in me. If I hadn't come with you, you wouldn't have known those women were going to be used as assassins. They aren't the only ones. Brandon thinks he's so clever, but he isn't nearly as clever as he thinks he is."

Czar went to the other side of the firepit. "Can you tell if someone else has been tampered with? If they have a suggestion planted in their head?"

Seychelle shrugged. "That depends on the person. If they talk to me for more than a minute or so and I can get a rhythm, a vibration if you will—it's like a pathway into them—then yes, I would be able to see the discoloration and know he was there."

"What about removing it?" Maestro asked. "Is that even possible?"

Her gaze jumped to his face. "It's possible, but anything like that takes energy. Using psychic energy is draining and would be difficult depending on how long the suggestion has been planted and how resistant the subject is to the removal."

"So you're saying a long line of willing subjects is out," Czar said. "That would be too hard on you?"

"I don't know." She pressed her palms to her head again. "He's trapped in my head for the moment. I had planned to get rid of him right away, but then I realized I could extract some other thoughts he had when he was planting his suggestion to Shari. That's what I wanted to talk to Savage about. It was terrifying to have his thoughts in my head."

Savage definitely didn't like the idea of Brandon Campbell sharing any part of Seychelle, however small it might be. "Get him out of there."

Czar held up his hand. "I say she's right, we should discuss it."

"Why now?" Seychelle asked. "The time for that was hours ago, and it was supposed to be between my man and me. What are we doing here, Czar? Are you trying to resolve this issue because you need me to get Brandon out of other people's heads?"

"Yes and no," Czar answered honestly. "The most important thing I need to do is resolve the issue between you and Savage for both your sakes. I saw him when you two broke up. Alena saw you when you were apart. You both were a mess. Clearly, that isn't the answer, Seychelle. You know it isn't."

Savage dipped his head down, his lips against her ear. "Baby, I told you, I don't make the same mistake twice. I said I won't walk out when you tell me you need me, even if the club calls. I'll trust you to say so only when it's the truth. I told you the worst of me. The truth of why I'm here and why I didn't want you to know what I was doing here."

She lifted her chin. "What am I doing here?"

Czar stepped closer, his eyes piercing the darkness like two lasers. "That's on me, Seychelle. I told Savage it was imperative you come. Sometimes my talent is strong in the way I get these warnings I can't always interpret until the last minute. I had a very strong warning telling me you were needed for Savage. Without you, he was going to be in trouble, but more than Savage, without you, the entire club was going to be in trouble."

"Why couldn't you just tell me that? I would have felt part of something instead of an outsider. I'd be more inclined to want to help you instead of leaving you all to fend for yourselves. Doesn't that make a little more sense to you? You're all intelligent men. Or so I thought." She lifted her gaze to Maestro. "Most of you are. Why wouldn't you just tell me?"

SIXTEEN

A loud whistle cut the night. Savage tightened his hold on Seychelle but then turned her, thrusting her body behind his. Czar moved in front of her to stand beside Savage. Reaper and Maestro instantly took up positions in front of them. Torpedo Ink club members poured in from all directions, surrounding the president and Seychelle, allowing Savage freedom.

"Baby, stay right here with Czar. Don't you move unless he does. Do what he tells you." Savage leaned down and brushed the top of her head with a kiss and then moved into the shadows. Maestro did the same. Keys and Mechanic took their places.

"Bringing in company, Czar," Lana called. "Plank and five of his men have come to see you. Plank's old lady, Sylvia, is with them as well. Said you were expecting them."

"Keys, Mechanic, take Seychelle as far back away from the light as you can get her," Czar said. "Let me see what they want. Honey, go with them and stay quiet until I call you or Savage comes and gets you."

Seychelle nodded. Keys took her arm and led her to the

heavy brush that bordered the back of the campsite. "There better not be ticks," she whispered. "If there are, I'm collecting them and letting them loose in the Diamondback campsite."

Keys flashed a grin at her. "That's Tony Ravard. He goes by Shark. His brother Leonardo, who goes by Lion, is with him. Trade, Judge, Pierce and Plank."

Savage joined Czar and the others gesturing toward the picnic table. Plank sat down with Czar, but the president of the Diamondbacks was looking around the campsite. "Where's your woman, Savage? I wanted to introduce her to my old lady. Shark insists she could talk to my old lady and tell whether some bastard planted that suggestion in her. Shark and Lion said they want to talk to her first though, just to make certain she's the real thing."

"It didn't occur to you Savage might be busy with his woman?" Czar asked, his tone mild, even a note of amusement in it.

There was nothing amusing in the way Savage was looking at Shark and Lion. Both men clearly were uneasy, but they stood their ground.

"Yeah," Plank admitted. "But I wasn't going to have a good time. None of my men are either if we don't clear a few things up. Would you mind producing her, Savage?"

Savage didn't like any of the alternatives. If he did as Plank asked and Seychelle didn't cooperate, they would be in trouble. He'd look like a fucking pussy who couldn't control his woman. His club would really look bad. She was pretty angry with them all. She wanted to go home. They hadn't cleared everything up.

If she did help Plank, he'd want her to test every one of the women he'd brought with him. He wouldn't understand— or even care about—the danger to her. He'd only care about the danger to his men.

Czar tapped out a code on the table. *You have to go get her. We don't have a choice.*

They had choices. Czar just didn't like any of them. Savage turned, taking two steps away from the group. Lion and Shark shadowed him. He swung around.

"You don't want to be anywhere near me right now," he warned, his tone low.

"Know you're pissed, Savage," Tony said. "I can't say as I blame you. There was no way to get to you alone. Or to get to Seychelle. I wouldn't throw her under the bus so a few brothers could get blow jobs tonight, not after what she's done for our mother. We suspect there's something bigger happening here."

Savage kept walking to ensure they were a distance from any of the others. He folded his arms across his chest. "Start talking."

Leonardo immediately objected. "Just to the woman, Tony."

"Don't be a dumbass, Leonardo," Tony snapped at his brother. "Do you really think Savage is going to let us near her if we don't tell him what's going on? Or that she isn't going to ask his permission first and tell him everything we say to her once she finds out?"

Lion stared at his brother.

Tony glared at him. "Did you think you were going to shut her up after she helped us?"

"Hell no. What are you talking about? I just don't want any of this getting back to Plank. He'd kill us both, Tony."

"You going to argue all night or get to the point?" Savage said, forcing a bored tone.

"A while back Czar sent a club to us, the Demons."

"I remember." Torpedo Ink had retrieved the wife of the Demon president from the Ghosts. She'd been kidnapped so the Ghosts could horn in on a pretty sweet counterfeit operation the Demons had. It was nearly impossible to tell the difference between real money and the money the Demons produced. The Demons wanted Czar to run the money through Diamondback territory for a cut. Czar refused, but he'd put them together with Plank and had them make their own deal with him.

Tony looked around and lowered his voice even more. "The last two shipments never made it through our pipeline. The Feds were waiting on the other end. I personally handled one of the shipments. Lion handled the other. Someone has been ratting to them. They've got undercover Feds here. A team."

Savage kept his expression perfectly blank, but that added an entire layer of danger to what had to be done. Even interrogating Tawny could have gone all ways bad, and both of these men had known it and hadn't warned them.

"Can you identify them?"

Both men shook their heads. "They're meeting up with their informants on the run tomorrow."

"And you know this how?" Savage pushed.

Tony sighed. "We think we're the informants. We both separately received instructions on where to meet our 'handler.' It could be bullshit, but I've found myself in strange situations and don't remember how I got there. I've been suspicious that my stepbrother has been messing with my head. Then Leonardo mentioned he was having similar problems. When our shipments started going south, we knew we were in real trouble. We both suspected Brandon had planted some kind of suggestion. He's capable of doing it. He fools around with using his voice to plant suggestions all the time."

"You heard Seychelle sing," Savage said.

Tony nodded. "I suspected she had a very powerful gift. If she had developed it, she might be able to counter Brandon. He's a vindictive little shit."

Savage gave him a little half smile. "My assessment exactly. I'm surprised you haven't taken him out."

"It isn't so easy to take out family," Tony said.

Savage shrugged. That wasn't his problem. "You ever pull a fast one on Seychelle like this again, you'll never see me coming. Plank's going to want her looking at every woman you brought with you. That's going to be too hard on her. There's nowhere you can go that I can't get to you. Your brothers will never know it was me."

As far as he was concerned, it wasn't a threat he'd made, it was a fact, and he delivered it that way. A statement. Calm. In a low voice. Looking at them directly with killer eyes. He turned and walked away from them, heading to the woods, signaling for Keys and Mechanic to escort Seychelle to him.

She came straight to him, ignoring the Diamondbacks, her gaze only on Savage. He framed her face with both hands and filled her in on what the other club wanted—no, was demanding. He told her Tony and Leonardo's fears and what would happen to them if they were correct and anyone found out. "Just know you don't have to do this, baby. I know you don't like the club. You're not doing it for the club. Or for me. Quite frankly, I don't want you to do it. I'm afraid for you. It's your choice, Seychelle. You want out, I'll get you out."

Her eyes searched his. He was telling her the truth. He wasn't altogether certain if Leonardo Ravard would take it in his head to try to kill her if she discovered he'd been snitching on his chapter and the Demons to the Feds. Savage wouldn't put it past the man. "If you see it in either of them they want to kill you after you find something, if you do this, you tell me. Understand? That's the one thing I ask of you."

"You can't use me as an excuse to fight someone, Savage. I can feel the rage rising in you like some kind of tide."

"We're not in sync, Seychelle. You want to leave me."

"No, you're wrong. I've never wanted to leave you, Savage. I love you. Didn't you hear me? I love you more than anything. I don't love what's happened to me. I'm losing myself. That's not wanting to leave you. That's trying to save myself." She leaned into him and brushed a kiss across his lips. "We're in sync enough for me to know these two men are Eden's sons. I don't care about the Diamondbacks, but I do care about Eden. She loves them, and she's my friend. Let's see if I can figure this out. If there are Feds here, Savage, you and the others are going to have to be very careful."

He knew that already. She didn't have to give him the warning, but he was grateful she cared enough to do it. He wanted everyone to go away and leave the two of them alone to work it out together.

"Wish you were wearing your ring, baby. Don't like that you're exposed to either of them without it, or at least my jacket."

"I know who I love, Savage. There's never going to be another man for me."

"It just gives you another layer of protection. Tony, I have a little more faith in than his brother. Leonardo has been Diamondback a long time, and he knows they'll skin them both alive if they've ratted to the Feds, even if it isn't their fault."

"Stay with me." She took his hand and walked over to Tony, greeting him as she always did, as if they were old friends. She completely ignored his colors. "Tony. I wasn't expecting anyone this evening. I have to admit, I'm pretty tired, but Savage explained the problem." She glanced toward the picnic table where the Diamondback president and his old lady were talking with Czar, Lana and several of the Torpedo Ink crew. "We should move a little farther away."

"Thanks for this, Seychelle," Tony said. "I'm sorry to put you on the spot like this."

"I completely understand. It's a little scary to think Brandon—or someone else, for that matter—may have managed to plant a suggestion in you and your brother." She smiled at Leonardo. It was clear, to her, they were Eden's sons, not Shark and Lion from the Diamondbacks. She didn't see them any other way.

"I'm getting you a chair, Seychelle," Savage declared. "Don't start anything without me." He stalked away, indicating to Mechanic and Keys that they needed camp chairs as he approached the others. "Your men are talking with her now," he assured Plank. "Once they determine if she can help you, they'll ask her to come meet your old lady." He didn't look at the woman. He caught up the four chairs Mechanic handed him, along with a bottle of water for Seychelle, and hurried back to her.

He could hear her soft laughter. That was like his woman. She managed to put everyone at ease when she wanted to. Even Leonardo was giving her a faint, rusty smile. Once they were seated, she had Tony start talking to her. She asked him questions about his mother, about his childhood and home.

Leonardo became impatient and snarled at her. Savage nearly exploded out of his chair, but Seychelle held up her hand imperiously. "Leonardo, if you want help, you have to let me work. That means staying quiet while I work on your brother. You're next. A suggestion was definitely planted, but it wasn't by Brandon. Had it been by him, I could have gotten to it much faster." She sounded sweet, but there was a firmness to her voice. She didn't look at him, her focus remaining on Tony.

Savage was shocked. Someone other than Brandon had planted the suggestion in Tony? What the hell? That wasn't possible. How widespread was this conspiracy? He kept his gaze fixed on Seychelle's face. She frowned in concentration. He could see the exact moment when she cast her golden net as Tony was talking. She was very precise, focusing not on what he said but on the actual notes in his voice. When Savage looked closely, Tony's notes were maroon and gray, but the one single note she swept into her net and circled with her golden ones was a very, very faint pinkish purple.

A look of triumph slid across her face and then was gone instantly, and she was concentrating again. Leonardo seemed to realize she was onto something. He leaned forward, elbows on his knees, watching her closely. Within a matter of minutes, Seychelle frowned again, then she began to hum a few notes, shook her head, changed the notes and then nodded.

"Tony, do you remember when I told you about leaving numbers for me by your mother's phone? Did you?"

"Yes. In the kitchen. I listed my brothers and me and put our cell numbers beside our names and then pinned that memo to the corkboard she has up."

Savage watched as the golden loop slowly pulled those pinkish-purple notes away from the maroon and gray ones. She kept them safely in the net until they slowly faded away. Her eyes met Tony's, and she smiled.

"I believe you are just you again. Let me see to your brother, and I'll tell you what I found."

Instead of looking at Leonardo, she turned her gaze fully on Savage as she accepted the bottle of water. He could see she was extremely disturbed by something. Whatever it was, she wasn't going to tell Tony and his brother. She was waiting to tell her man. Savage found satisfaction in that. He reached for her hand.

"Do you need a break?"

She shook her head. "Let's just do this. I'm getting tired, and I want to go to bed. Once they leave, I can do that."

She began again, getting Leonardo to talk about his mother. That seemed a safe enough subject. She avoided the club he was in and his stint in the SEALs. She watched him closely as he spoke. His tone was lower than his brother's. She focused on his notes, careful to catch his exact rhythm until she was certain she had a direct connection and followed that faint pinkish purple back to the source, just as she'd done with Tony.

Savage couldn't help but admire her, watching that curious little frown, the determination. Worry flitted across her face, and once, her lashes lifted, and she looked across the dark grass toward the picnic table where Czar sat with Plank and the others. That made Savage uneasy. She cast her golden net and drew the pinkish-purple notes away from Leonardo.

He sighed with relief. "I feel much lighter. You're the real thing. Thanks, Seychelle. You can't say one word of this to anyone."

She rolled her eyes. "You're Eden's sons. That makes you

practically family. It wasn't Brandon. It was a woman. The same woman. You met her at a club you both frequent in San Francisco. She's of Russian descent. Really pretty. Between twenty-five and twenty-eight. Her accent is nearly perfect American. She has dark hair and eyes. You weren't together when you met her. Leonardo, you met her first. The suggestion in you has been there longer."

The brothers looked at each other with completely blank expressions. It was clear they had no memory of the woman.

"Do you remember the club?" Savage asked.

Leonardo nodded. "I go there once in a while."

Tony looked uncomfortable, not meeting Seychelle's gaze. "I do too. But I don't remember a woman like the one you're describing."

"She most likely planted the suggestion and also planted one to have you forget her," Seychelle explained. "She wanted you both to inform on your club."

"Why us?"

"She didn't care who it was, only that your club and the Demons didn't do what you were told. She works for the Ghosts. They kidnapped Plank's wife and also the wife of the president of the Demons. Both women escaped, and that angered the Ghosts."

"Is there an informant in the Demon's club?" Tony asked.

Seychelle looked at him as if he'd grown two heads. "How would I know, Tony?" She rubbed at her temples. "I've got a headache. You're both clear. If I were you, I'd steer clear of the De Sade in San Francisco for a while just to be safe. Let's go meet Plank's wife so I can rest." She stood up, and immediately the three men stood up with her.

Tony and Leonardo hastened to tell their club president that Seychelle could tell him whether or not his woman had been given a suggestion to kill him. Seychelle held back, walking slow, her hand on Savage's arm.

"This woman was originally after the Demons and Diamondbacks because they didn't fall in line when the Ghosts took their women. It was a retaliatory, vindictive move on the part of the Ghosts against both the Demons and Diamondbacks. Someone in the Demons has the suggestions planted as well. I don't know where this woman fits in with the Ghosts. I don't know the first thing about the Ghosts. But I do know that her vengeance has gone from those two clubs to seeing Czar dead. Somewhere she heard of him inside that club. She hates him with a passion. I'd be worried if you had visited that club recently, Savage. She could so easily use a Torpedo Ink member to exact her revenge against him. Has anyone else gone there?"

They were almost to the picnic table. Savage wanted to curse at the Diamondbacks and tell them to get the hell out of his campsite. He was done making nice with his unwanted guests. Who else frequented the kinky underground club? Every member of Torpedo Ink had fetishes. Shit. This wasn't good, and they couldn't talk freely.

Seychelle was all smiles, handling the introductions Czar made to Plank and Sylvia, his old lady. Tony and Leonardo sang Seychelle's praises. Plank seemed very annoyed at the delay.

"Yeah, I don't understand what took so fucking long," he groused. "You just had to talk to her for a couple of minutes," he snapped at the two members of his club.

Both seemed to freeze. Seychelle took his lousy temper in stride. "My talent doesn't work like that, Mr., er, Plank. I had to plant a suggestion in both of them, and they had to realize I had actually done it, and then I had to show them I could remove it. They didn't want me working on your wife if there was the potential of hurting her. I know their mother, so they have a little faith in me, but still, they told me they wanted to be very careful with Sylvia." Seychelle sent him another one of her sweet, innocent smiles.

She looked like the girl next door, the furthest thing from a biker babe she could possibly be. Twice, Savage noted Tony looking at her bare ring finger and he cursed under his breath. Plank was falling under her spell, the combination of her voice and her sweet demeanor. She was harmless, and after being introduced to Sylvia, she held out her hand, and Sylvia smiled and went with her. Plank didn't send his usual guards, and he didn't follow or insist Seychelle conduct her "experiment" right there in front of him.

Savage paced a distance behind them as if giving them privacy but watching over them. Tony did the same, while Leonardo held back but still took up a position to look out for his president's old lady.

"You're here with Savage?" Sylvia asked when the two women were alone in the shadow of the trees and brush of the forest that backed up to their campsite.

"Yes. He's mine. I want to kick him half the time, and the other half I'm super crazy about him." Seychelle's laughter invited Sylvia to share her amusement at herself, and Sylvia joined in.

Sylvia nodded. "I hear you. That's how I feel about Plank half the time. He makes me want to pull out my hair."

Seychelle leaned toward her and lowered her voice so Savage had to strain to hear her. "Does he know you're pregnant?"

Sylvia gasped. "How did you know?"

"It's part of what I do. The baby's perfect, but you should be seeing a doctor. Seriously. Why are you waiting?"

Sylvia cast a quick glance in the direction of her husband. "He's never said he wanted children. Never. Not once. He likes to pick up and go. I've been afraid he'd insist I get an abortion. I wouldn't do it, and I'd have to leave him. I don't think that would go over very well."

The entire time Sylvia spoke, Savage watched Seychelle's focus. The colored notes were faint to him, but evidently not to Seychelle. Sylvia produced a combination of reds and orange, but they were very shaded pastels rather than vibrant.

Suddenly, Seychelle leaned forward as she spoke, and when she did, she released her golden notes in those rounded tones, the ones that looped like tiny nets. "I think you will be very surprised, Sylvia. That man may be walking on the wild side. He might be rough and bossy, but he doesn't take his eyes off you. I believe he loves you. I don't think he's going to freak too much that you're having his child."

"I really hope there's no suggestion in me. Tawny has wreaked havoc in our chapter, turning everyone against each other. All the old ladies are suspicious of one another. They all think their men cheated. Even I thought Plank was cheating with her at one time, but he convinced me he wasn't." Sylvia looked down at her hands. "At least I let him convince me. I don't know. That's another thing. If I can't come with him on the runs, because I have a child, I'll always wonder."

Savage expected pinkish-purple notes in a stream, that faint mixture a telltale sign that the same woman had somehow managed to penetrate Sylvia's defenses, but instead, the notes were a dull grayish blue. Immediately, the golden net gently, with exquisite skill, dropped over those out-of-sync notes and pulled them into her loop, so she could follow them back to the source. All the while, she continued to nod her head and keep the conversation flowing.

"Blythe usually comes with Czar on these runs, but she will have someone watch the children while she comes. It's only for a couple of days. If your baby gets used to a routine like that, they don't think anything of it. In any case, if Plank didn't fall for Tawny's crap, I don't think he falls for very many temptations. He's not going to throw away what he has for something like Tawny."

The dull, grayish-blue notes were slowly extracted from Sylvia as she replied, this time with a smile on her face. "No, I think you're right. As far as I know, he never has cheated, and he's always been good to me. I don't know why I started having all these doubts about us. The entire chapter seems— unsettled."

"Sometimes it takes one person's influence to undermine everyone's happiness. I think they have mad skills in the meanness department." Again, Seychelle laughed softly, her tone an invitation to join her.

Sylvia complied, and Seychelle sat back, satisfied. "I

think you can safely go back to Plank and tell him you are clear, and no suggestion is in your mind."

"You're certain?"

"Absolutely."

Sylvia leapt up and threw her arms around Seychelle. "Thank you. I was so worried. I felt this heaviness all the time, and frankly, I was so nervous around Plank. And snappy. I feel so much better after talking to you." She turned and practically ran back to her husband.

Seychelle stayed in her chair. She looked exhausted. Savage went to her, lifted her out of the chair and sat her on his lap. She didn't protest but took the bottle of water he handed to her. "Drink, baby. You're done for the night. I don't care how many other women Plank wants you to examine, it can wait until morning."

She pushed her face into his neck. "The threat to Czar is immediate and huge, Savage. The hostility that woman from the De Sade club felt toward him came off her in waves, and she wasn't even making a suggestion to Tony or Leonardo that had anything to do with him. She was being vengeful to both the Demon and Diamondback clubs." Her voice was muffled. "I have the worst headache."

He knew she had expelled too much energy. "What do you mean by 'the threat to Czar is immediate'?" His gaze was on his president even as he held his woman. "Czar is surrounded by Torpedo Ink. No one can get to him."

"Torpedo Ink can get to him," she murmured tiredly. "If she got to one of them, they wouldn't know."

Savage wasn't as certain as Seychelle, but there was merit to what she said. Plank had his arm around his old lady, and the Diamondbacks were leaving. He whistled, the pitch low, alerting his club to stay after the other club was escorted completely off their grounds.

"You found a suggestion planted in Plank's woman, but you didn't let on to her or to Plank."

"There was really no reason to do that. She has enough to contend with. Let her be happy. It really doesn't make much difference, does it? Definitely Brandon planted that suggestion. He must have done it before boosting his power by stealing from his brothers—if he ever did. The suggestion was weak. I doubt if she would have carried it out." She yawned, her lashes falling.

"Drink more water, Seychelle." Savage pressed the bottle to her lips. "Once you do, we have to talk to Czar."

She sighed and did her best to rally, sitting up a little straighter in his arms and drinking the water. "Okay, Savage, I'm as ready as I'll ever be, but all this water makes me have to go to the bathroom. That has to be in the cards soon."

"I'll take you there as soon as we talk to Czar and the others. Can you wait that long?"

She nodded and started to slide off his lap. He stood up, shifting her in his arms so he cradled her close to his chest. "I'll carry you, conserve your strength that way. You going to put my ring back on your finger?"

Seychelle sighed. "We haven't exactly worked things out, Savage."

"We worked out that we love each other and we're going to talk shit out. That you're my first priority and I'm yours. We knew it wasn't going to be easy, baby. We both knew it."

"I didn't know I was going to have to contend with your club, and they weren't going to even attempt to be nice to me."

"Seychelle. It isn't like that," he denied. He was on dangerous ground sticking up for the members of his club. "One or two acting like assholes doesn't mean all of them act that way."

She went silent, turning her face into his chest but pressing close to him so he could feel her tits smashed tight against him. She felt light, almost insubstantial, in his arms. He carried her right to the picnic table where Czar waited, ringed by the others.

"I think Seychelle discovered why you felt a distinct threat and knew you wanted her here," Savage said without preamble. His gaze took in Lana, Alena and Maestro. He wanted them to know Czar had been certain they needed Seychelle and she had come through for them. Destroyer and Alena had answered the call when the text message went out that the Diamondbacks had invaded Torpedo Ink's campground.

"Sylvia definitely had a suggestion planted by Brandon, but she said it was weak. She didn't bother to tell Sylvia or Plank. She just removed it. The weird thing was what Shark and Lion had to say and what Seychelle found with them," Savage informed them.

He filled his club in on everything his woman had told him. There was a long silence. It was Code who broke it. "The Ghosts again. They do keep circling around us, don't they?"

"Why would this woman be after you, Czar?" Mechanic asked. "You go to the De Sade and get her hot and bothered and then dump her?"

Czar turned his penetrating eyes, laser-sharp, on Mechanic. "Got Blythe. I don't go to clubs, Mechanic. You should know that. I don't need other women. I would never risk my relationship with her for a couple of minutes with some woman that isn't going to be my everything."

"I get that, Czar," Mechanic said immediately. "In all honesty, I wouldn't be too happy if you were going behind her back."

"But Mechanic does pose a good question," Transporter said. "Why would this woman have it in for you?"

"Even if she's affiliated with the Ghosts, and they figured out that our club had something to do with taking back those women for the other clubs, and I don't see how that's possible," Steele mused, "why would her anger be centered on you?"

Czar looked to Code. "You listen in on the Ghosts as much as possible. You've got their supposed private investigators in San Francisco and Los Angeles. You found an office in Louisiana. I know that doesn't give you much to monitor, but has my name ever come up? Has Torpedo Ink ever been named specifically?"

"Czar, come on," Code said. "If your name came up, I would tell you immediately, even if it was in the middle of the night. As for the club, they've looked at us a couple of times, but only because we were a support club for the Diamondbacks and the one time they were after Anya. We're small potatoes to them. We aren't one-percenters. We're nothing as far as they're concerned."

"Seychelle." Czar turned to Savage's woman.

Savage had her on his lap. She had curled up, looking smaller than ever, eyes closed as if she was asleep. He knew she was drifting, but she could hear what was going on. She just might not care so much. He bent his head to her ear, pushed her hair aside with his nose and caught the lobe of her ear between her teeth, slowly biting down until her lashes fluttered and he felt her body shift.

"Pay attention, baby."

"I am," she lied and sat up straighter.

Savage kept his hands on her, helping to steady her as she looked around and finally focused on Czar.

"I know it took a lot of psychic energy to help Plank's people, and I certainly wouldn't ask you to do any more, but you seemed to think this was a crisis, and I have a gut feeling you're right."

She nodded. Her gaze flicked to the other members of Torpedo Ink. "I didn't get much. She planted a suggestion in both men to inform on the shipments to the Feds. I'm fairly certain she got to someone in the Demons club as well. I couldn't see who; it was a vague impression only. Whoever it was hadn't met her at the De Sade. She just felt smug to me until she suddenly was thinking of you. That came out of nowhere."

"What about her? Did you get any impression of what she looked like? Her age? Anything at all?" Czar persisted, glancing over his shoulder at Absinthe.

Savage stiffened. He wasn't having his brother question

Seychelle. Absinthe could get the truth from anyone, but it could be a very painful interrogation.

Seychelle shrugged. "I told you, not much. I got the impression she was young and originally from Russia. There must be some record of her at the De Sade. Maybe surveillance tapes Code can get?"

"We have no real timeline," Czar said. "No way of knowing when she was there."

Absinthe approached the picnic table. Savage surged to his feet and set Seychelle down, sweeping her behind him as he faced his fellow Torpedo Ink member. "I think we're done here, Czar." He didn't take his gaze from Absinthe as he made the declaration to his president. "We're all tired and need rest."

"If someone is going to assassinate me, especially someone from my own club, it might be good to know who it is," Czar pointed out.

Seychelle slipped her fingers into Savage's back pocket, connecting them. He liked when she did that as a rule, but right now, he felt threatened—or, more importantly, he felt as if she was threatened. He needed room to fight, if necessary.

"Why would you need Absinthe to question Seychelle when she's voluntarily told you about this Russian woman and the danger to you?" Savage asked. "She didn't have to say a word."

"Absinthe might be able to see more than she's remembering. No one thinks she isn't telling the truth, Savage," Czar said patiently. He ran a hand through his hair. "This night has been tough on everyone, especially Seychelle. All of us have fucked up with her. I know she's tired and needs to sleep. Do you think I don't want that for her?"

"What I think is a better use of Absinthe's time is to check everyone to see if they attended the De Sade and interacted with a Russian woman," Savage said. "I don't mind if he starts with me. I've been there enough times, and if it happened before Seychelle and I were together, then I could be programmed and not remember."

Czar sighed. "It might come to that. I'm hoping Seychelle has more details than she knows. I can't imagine what your objection is."

"You can't? After what you heard this evening? I fucked up and left her when she needed me the most. Maestro and Lana treated her like shit. They went so far as telling her she wasn't the right woman for me and she shouldn't be here. That she couldn't see to my needs and other women here could. Hell, you made her feel like an outsider as well. Our club was more than willing to use her for our purposes, no matter how difficult it was on her, but we still treated her like an outsider. I'm not willing for that to happen again."

There was a soft murmur of objections that ran through some of the club members. Maestro and Lana looked down at the ground. Destroyer and Reaper both moved closer to Savage. He couldn't tell if they intended to protect him or Czar. He didn't care which at that point. He just knew he was standing between Seychelle and anything that might harm her.

"Every word you say is the truth, Savage," Czar acknowledged quietly. The moment he did, the club members who had been objecting to Savage's assessment went silent. A few looked at Maestro and Lana with a kind of shock. "I understand you wanting to protect Seychelle. She is your first priority, and you nearly lost her tonight."

"I still could lose her."

"Okay, that's enough." Seychelle suddenly stepped around Savage to stand beside him. "I'm right here, Savage. It's not like I can't think for myself." Her gaze went from Savage to Absinthe. "What do you do when you ask questions that makes you a threat to me, Absinthe?" Deliberately, she challenged him directly. If she was supposedly a part of them somehow, then Absinthe would answer truthfully. Clearly, she didn't believe he would.

"My talent isn't the same as yours, Seychelle, although I can use my voice to persuade others, and I can hear thoughts, which can drive me insane. I touch you, wrap my hand around your wrist where I can feel your pulse. When you lie,

I can send impulses to your heart that impact your brain in very painful ways."

"I see."

Seychelle's palm slid down Savage's arm to find his hand. She curled her fingers in his. She moved her body under his shoulder, unconsciously seeking protection. He could feel the slight tremors, although he wasn't certain if she was aware of them.

"How would you know if I was lying?"

"In this case, I'm looking for details, not lies. I would ask a few questions about what your impressions of this woman were when you were talking with the two Diamondbacks."

"Let's just do it, then," Seychelle said. She looked up at Savage. "I just want this night to be over."

He hesitated. He just wanted to be alone with her, to work everything out with her. He wanted to know they were back in sync. He brought her knuckles to his lips. "You absolutely certain you want to do this, baby?"

"I don't want anything to happen to Czar. Blythe and those children don't need the trauma. Quite frankly, neither do any of you." She turned her head back to face Absinthe. "Let's do this. I hope you get something."

In the end, Absinthe didn't get anything Seychelle hadn't already told them. He confirmed there was danger to Czar. It was immediate, the threat was hostile and the woman had focused her anger and need for revenge on Czar. She wasn't connecting Czar to the Demons or the Diamondbacks in terms of the two clubs getting their wives back through Torpedo Ink. One of the Demons told her that Czar introduced them to the Diamondbacks, and she connected the dots over time when she learned he was Russian. But how?

"You're going to have to speak with each member, Seychelle," Czar said. "I'm sorry. I know you're tired."

She nodded and sank down onto the top of the picnic table, avoiding Savage's outstretched hand. He didn't like that. She'd been relying on him; now she was avoiding him. That pit of anger was coming close to overflowing.

"You may as well start with me." He stood in front of her.

She shook her head. "I'd rather not at all if I can help it, but if I have to, I'll check you last, Savage." She refused to look into his eyes.

"Babe. Anything you find with me and that club came before you."

"It will still hurt. Talking about it, knowing about it and even thinking about it isn't the same thing as sharing it, Savage," she replied very quietly, but firmly. "I'll check you last so I can get this done."

Great. She would not only see what a first-class bastard he was, she might see other things he definitely didn't want her seeing—like him taking a human being apart. He hoped she was only going to see whatever went on in that club, nothing more, because that would be bad enough.

One by one, the members of Torpedo Ink came up and had a brief conversation with Seychelle. Czar sat on the other side of the picnic table, watching the proceedings. Savage sat on the table but apart from Seychelle. Absinthe sat on the very edge, just in case she needed him. It was clear using her psychic energy to entice a hidden memory out was tiring her out. Twice she suddenly stopped and frowned once at Storm and flat-out told him not to drink so much, that it was affecting his liver.

The moment she said anything, Savage interrupted. "Seychelle, did he have interaction with the Russian woman?"

She blinked several times to bring him into focus. Steele moved between her and Storm. Master stepped up as well.

Savage caught her shoulder in a tight hold, his fingers digging deep. "Is Storm clear?"

"Yes, but his liver . . ."

"You're not taking on his liver. We'll make sure he stops drinking so much, but Steele can work with him, not you," Savage said decisively.

Since Master was right there, Seychelle checked him next. He definitely had interacted with the woman but had turned her away when she sidled up to him, wanting him to take her into one of the private rooms. Seychelle kept him talking, trying to get to his memories of the woman, what she looked like, her age. She had managed to blur them, just as she had with Tony and Leonardo. She sent him to Absinthe.

Destroyer was the second club member she frowned over. Her hand went to her throat. She cleared it twice and then coughed.

"Seychelle." Savage was off the picnic table to stand between her and Destroyer. "Look at me. Only me. Stop what you're doing right now."

She moistened her lips and blinked several times as if trying to focus on him. She was resistant to breaking off attempting to heal Destroyer's throat.

Savage framed her face with his hands. "Right here, baby. Eyes on me." He waited until she focused completely on his eyes. "Did Destroyer interact with this Russian woman?"

She nodded her head. "Several times. Again, he passed on her."

"Destroyer, you're up next with Absinthe," Savage said without looking at him. He glanced at the line. Only Maestro and Lana were waiting. Lana looked extremely uncomfortable. Guilty even. Maestro wore no expression whatsoever.

Lana stepped up. "I want to apologize for making you feel as if you weren't wanted, Seychelle. You're the best thing that's ever happened to Savage. *Ever.* You're right, I was afraid to have you come on the run because I didn't want you to see anything that might make you leave him. All I did was drive you away from him and us. I've felt edgy and moody for a while now, and I guess I took it out on you."

Seychelle studied Lana's face for a long moment, and then she nodded. "It happens. I know I look like I'm fragile, but I have unexpected, very deep wells of strength. Savage knows I can handle whatever he needs. If you don't yet have faith in me, and that's understandable, you should have faith in him. What is it about me that most puts you off?"

Lana shrugged. "I find myself wanting to protect you all the time, even from Savage. You look so innocent. Sometimes I want to scream at him that he chose wrong. That he can't pull you down into the wreck of our lives. I hate it for him, that none of us can save him from what he needs, and I hate it worse for you." Her hands shook as she pushed at the dark strands of her hair. "I want to shake you until you see sense. You don't belong with us, and yet you fit with him so perfectly. I see you two together, and you blend. It doesn't make sense, but he laughs. He's never really laughed before, not really. He's different around you, and even I can see that."

Savage was watching his woman concentrating on the notes emerging from Lana's mouth as she spoke. Her notes were strong, like the woman, a deep red mixed with a lighter red and, strangely, light purple and aqua. It took a moment before he saw the other woman's deceptive notes emerging as well. Lana had been around the Russian woman for certain.

"What you need to remember when you start feeling that way, Lana, is none of you had a choice. I do. Savage *always* gives me a choice. I choose him. I choose our life and what we do together. I say yes, or I say no. Not him. Me. He doesn't have that choice, but I do. He's always aware of it. Mine is from free will. His isn't."

"Does loving him give you a choice, Seychelle?"

Seychelle had already sent out her golden net and looped the notes that didn't belong, following them back to the source. "Of course. I told you, I'm much stronger than anyone believes, and if I don't believe Savage is as committed to us as I am, I will walk away. I refuse to have anything less than I deserve. Putting myself entirely into my relationship is scary and difficult, so I expect—even demand—that he does as well. That was a promise he made me."

Seychelle had a little frown of concentration on her face that told Savage something wasn't quite right. He glanced at Czar. Czar was aware that something was different as well, but he didn't ask questions. He just waited.

The president of Torpedo Ink had sent most everyone who had been examined to their campsite for the night, leaving only his guards, mostly because they refused to leave. Savage knew that was partly because he hadn't been examined yet and neither had Maestro. No one wanted either of them to suddenly turn on Czar.

"You didn't spend much time at the De Sade, did you?" Seychelle said, flicking a quick glance at Absinthe.

He moved closer to Lana. Lana's brows drew together. "I don't think so. I've actually lost some time, and it bothers me. I've asked Maestro about it. He said we went to the De Sade together. I remember going in. I sat at the bar. A couple of guys approached me, and I waved them off."

Savage saw the exact moment when Seychelle was able to extract the notes from Lana, but they were so faint he could barely see them.

"Maestro, will you come over here and tell us about that night?" Seychelle asked. "What you remember?"

"Sure. Lana wanted to see what all the fuss was about, and I told her I wasn't babysitting her. I left her at the bar, but I didn't feel right about it. I went back after a few minutes, and she was sitting with a dark-haired woman. I'd never seen her before. She was asking Lana questions about Czar. Not the club, but about him specifically. She actually used his given name, Viktor, not Czar. Lana was very uncomfortable and tried to change the subject. I could tell the woman had been at her for a little while, so I just stepped in between them. She instantly looked me up and down and gave me the submissive shit, pretending she was all about that and wanted to go with me to a private room."

"I vaguely recall that," Lana said, rubbing her forehead. "It's like it's really far away."

"I can tell someone who likes to switch back and forth but is really not in the least submissive. That chick wanted to go with me, but she was playing a part. I left with Lana."

"Do you remember what she looked like?" Seychelle asked.

Savage could see that she had been watching Maestro's notes carefully. His were strong, but there were no other colors than his. She shook her head. "He's clear."

"Yeah. She was Lana's height, or maybe taller by an inch, with dark brown hair. Nice-looking. Dark eyes. Nice figure, a bit on the thin side. She looked more like a model than what I prefer, but some men go for that. No lines on her face. She spoke English with an American accent, but I could hear the Russian under it."

Czar shook his head. "Doesn't ring a bell at all. Shit. I ran so many missions. Maybe I assassinated her brother or husband." He looked at Seychelle. Then at Savage. She had one left.

Savage hated that there was an audience. He wanted them gone. At least Lana. He didn't know why it was important she wasn't there if it all went sideways, but he knew this examination could be humiliating for Seychelle.

"You finished with Lana and Maestro?" he asked Absinthe.

Absinthe nodded.

Lana hesitated as she slid off the picnic table. "I feel different, Seychelle. Lighter. Not so edgy. I'm really sorry for the way I treated you. I know that's just words right now, but you'll see I mean them. Thank you for whatever it is you did for me." She gave a little wave and sauntered off into the night.

Maestro stood for a moment in front of Seychelle, and then he shook his head. "Wouldn't want Savage to have any other woman, Seychelle. Don't want you hurt. Don't want him to lose you either. I went about this all wrong, and I shouldn't have said anything when I didn't know what was going on." He put his hand on her shoulder and then slipped into the shadows.

Savage knew he didn't go very far. Putting his hands on Seychelle's thighs, Savage gently opened them so he could wedge his body between them. He needed the intimacy. "Let's just get it over, baby. If you need me to talk, I'm just going to come right out and tell you how much I love you. I hate that this night went so wrong for us. I wanted you to have one fucking night where you had fun."

"I had fun on the ride here with you," Seychelle said. "I always love riding with you. It's very sexy."

He could see their notes intertwining, silver and gold together. He didn't see any other color, pale or otherwise. Her hands covered his as his palms pressed into her thighs. He knew she was looking at the De Sade. The dungeon there. A woman tied to a St. Andrew's cross as he flogged her. She could see him when he flung the flogger to the side and stalked to the moaning woman, caught her hair in his fist and yanked her head back.

"Baby, get the fuck out of my head. She isn't there. That isn't her. You don't need to see what a dick I am."

He was cruel. Brutal even. He was worse than a dick. She was never going to look at him the same again. Savage started to step back, that ever-present rage swirling so close to the surface it was terrifying, because he feared he wouldn't be able to contain it. Seychelle caught his hands and held them tight.

"He's clear, Czar, and I'm so tired I can't keep my head up. I really, really need to sleep. Can all of you please leave us alone?"

Czar stood up. "Thanks for all your help. Sadly, we're going to have to ask for more tomorrow. We have to keep the Demon informer from going to the Feds and also try to find any women Campbell may have planted suggestions in. Savage, you have work to do with those names we got."

Savage didn't reply. He just stared down at his woman. She wasn't looking at him like she was running. She was looking at him like she belonged to him again. He wasn't sure why, not after what she'd witnessed. He waited for the others to leave.

"What is it, baby?"

"You told me the truth."

"I always tell you the truth. I want Campbell out of your

head and my ring back on your finger. How do I get what I want?"

"You just got rid of Brandon for me. As for the ring, it's in the pocket of your jeans. I need the restroom, and then we're going to bed. I promise you can do dirty, sinful things to me tomorrow if you can wait that long. I'm just too tired tonight."

SEVENTEEN

It was a shit day as far as Savage was concerned, but for one thing. His woman. The tiny RV stunk of feces, urine and blood. Death definitely had a stench. It permeated the small RV, getting into the barrier-covered walls, the soundproofing on the ceiling and same on the floor. It didn't matter how many times he showered, he couldn't scrub the smell off of him.

He went up front into the cab and shoved the slider into place, separating himself from the next asshole he had to question, giving himself a brief respite. All he wanted to do was get back to his woman. What the fuck was wrong with so many brothers willing to turn on their kind? He didn't get it. He would never get it.

Babe. You missing me?

Why would I be missing you? I have a good book, a comfortable chair and my booty doesn't hurt anymore. I'm also eating all the chips.

Damn, she made him smile. The woman had attitude. **Stay away from my chips. I can't eat sandwiches without them.**

Don't be such a baby. You can, you just don't want to.

I need the chips, woman. He sent growling emojis. He knew they would make her laugh.

Fine, I'll leave crumbs. And not the barbecue. Those are my favorite. She sent licking emojis. Just not the crumbs of the barbecue chips. I'm licking those right up. Yum.

Angel. He sent angel wings and halos to remind her she was sweet.

Fallen angel. She sent an angel with broken wings crashing to earth on his butt.

Savage glanced sideways at Maestro, who hadn't said a single word. "You okay?"

"We're not getting much. At least not what we want. Nothing about Czar and the Russian woman."

"No, but we have identified the men who were going to kill Plank, Shark, Lion, Pierce and Judge. And the one who was after Jeff Partridge, president of the Venomous club and four of his inner circle. They really were planning to wipe out several clubs here. We're still looking for the hit men with our names. Shit work though." Savage glanced down at his phone again.

"Who do you have on Seychelle?"

"Czar is with her. We have to keep him safe too. He's too smart to go wandering around. Alena and Keys are with Code nearby. I'm trying to make things look casual to her. She knows, but I don't want to ram it down her throat."

Maestro glanced at his watch. "Destroyer back there doing his thing?"

Savage nodded. "He does good work. Keeps them alive until they give us what we need to know. That's damn hard to do." He looked around the front of the RV. "I hate this fucking thing. I can't breathe in it."

"Yeah, I know what you mean," Maestro agreed. "Anyone any closer to figuring out the Demon informer angle with the Feds? It would be nice to know who the fuckin' Fed is. Or how many they have here."

"Not so far. We have eyes on them and are ready to intercept," Savage reported. His phone vibrated. He pulled it out to look at the text message from his woman. The smile faded. It wasn't from her. It was from Czar. "Fuckin' Plank sent a few of his men with a 'couple of women' for Seychelle to check out. Like she's his fucking property."

He texted Czar back. This is bullshit. Plank can't just treat her like his servant, Czar. We have to put a stop to this. Not only that, it's draining on her, but also dangerous. If someone is sick, she could get sick. Libby Drake told me she takes on the illness.

I'm well aware he's overstepping, and I told Judge that. Tried to send them packing, but his old lady, Theresa, started sobbing and your tenderhearted woman gave in instantly. She told me she'd take a look. What was I going to say then?

You overrule that shit. Damn it. Savage glared at his screen as he texted his woman. She had far too much compassion in her for everyone. You tell Theresa you can't help her until I get there. Tell her she can just take her ass and go back to the Diamondback campsite. If you're feeling sorry for her, think about what she and Tawny did to Alena.

He waited, staring at the screen. Waiting. Wanting to throw the damn thing.

"You having trouble with your woman, Savage?" Maestro asked, not bothering to hide his amusement.

"If she was standing in front of me right now, she'd be smiling that sweet smile of hers like she'd do just about anything I said, but she'd just do whatever the fuck she wanted."

"You ever think of punishing her?" Maestro asked.

"Hell yes. Considering the fact I enjoy that shit, I'd say it happens more often than not. It doesn't do a damn bit of good if she decides she wants to do something. You have no idea what she's like. She looks all innocent and sweet, and really, I suppose she is, but she doesn't obey worth shit."

Maestro grinned at him. "Nasty little problem for a man like you to have."

Savage would have been grinning right along with him, but he was genuinely worried about his woman. "Any one of those women she examines could have an underlying sickness, Maestro. I'm not there to stop her. She can't stop herself. It could be a disaster."

"Czar's there; he knows her problem. Key's there. Send a reminder if you're worried. They'll look after her. We have too much work to do here for you to have your mind on your woman."

One informant led to the next, and they uncovered one paid hit man after another. It was Savage, Destroyer and Maestro's job to get the information any way they could, and then kill the hit man and or informant while Ink, Storm and Ice tracked down and brought the next victims to them. The bodies were stacking up, and it wouldn't be long before they would have to be driven off-site, bodies set on fire and dumped into the chosen ravine.

The RV had been stolen from an old site where the rigs no longer worked. Transporter and Mechanic had fixed the engine up and then driven the rusted RV right off the back side of the hill, where it had been half-buried for nearly two years. They'd spotted the hulk and begun to work on it at night, when no one was around, knowing someday they would need it for just such a use. It still smelled like rust and dirt. Now blood, urine and feces were added to the mix.

By the end of the day, with night closing in, Savage was sick of the smell and sick of betrayal. He didn't need to bleed rage from Destroyer and Maestro or any of the others to overflow what he was already feeling, but the compulsion to do it was too strong to stop. It was shitty work and a shittier day. He didn't envy Transporter, Ink and Mechanic having to get rid of the entire rig with the bodies they'd disposed of that day. The body count was one of the highest they'd ever had in a day, and they couldn't call this war. Transporter would drive the RV, and Mechanic and Ink would each take a vehicle and run interference just in case there was trouble with the cops.

Savage was damn tired of the work. He had to shower in the tiny little cubicle there in the RV. He didn't envy Destroyer trying to shower in the little box. The man would get stuck in there. After he showered and changed, he left his clothes and shoes behind and went to the larger Torpedo Ink RV to shower again. He took his time, allowing the hot water to pour over him, hopefully getting as many of the kinks out as possible and removing the stench of torture, blood and death from his body so that when he went to Seychelle, he went as clean as possible.

He was pissed as hell at her. He'd been texting for the last three hours and she hadn't answered him once. Not one fucking time. He might strangle her. She might be upset because he'd quit texting her in the middle of the day for a block of hours. She'd texted him several times and he hadn't responded. He'd been in the middle of taking an asshole apart, one that had come to kill Alena. He wanted to know who'd sent the man, but he got nowhere.

Czar had the grill fired up, and the smell of steak, vegetables and his famous mini potatoes greeted the three of them. Destroyer and Maestro had accompanied Savage back to his campsite in order to give him a full report. Savage was anxious to see Seychelle for himself to make certain she was all right. He might be pissed as hell, but it was unlike her not to answer him. She didn't play games. Surely, Czar would have texted him if she had been ill.

He strode right past Czar and the great-smelling food that reminded him he hadn't eaten all day, and went deeper into the camp area, looking for his wayward woman. He spotted her curled up on her sleeping bag. She was on her side, knees pulled to her chest, her arm under her head. She was sound asleep. She looked smaller than usual, there under the trees.

Savage stood over her, his anger at her fading as he stared down at her face. She did remind him of an angel. There were no lines on her face, her skin smooth, those long lashes, two thick crescents, her mouth a bow. He had a ridiculous desire to lie down and curl his body protectively around hers, just to feel her close. She had a way of calming the raging demons in him, and they sure as hell were raging. He needed her desperately, but she needed rest. Whatever had gone on while he was working for the club had exhausted her.

He made his way back to Czar, and the others crowded around the grill and picnic table. Czar nodded at him. "Long day," he acknowledged. "Every time I thought she could rest, more of those women would show up and she'd have to start all over again."

Savage glanced toward the sleeping figure curled up in the dark of the trees. "She didn't have to, Czar."

"She has way too much compassion in her to turn down crying or scared women," Czar said. "You know that. I said no, but she just gave me that little smile of hers and went right to them and started talking. She's a handful. So damn sweet and does whatever the hell she wants."

Savage nodded. "She is sweet. She nods and smiles, and everyone around us thinks she's my little submissive baby, but that woman is going to please me when she wants to and then go her own way when she feels like it."

Destroyer gave a little sound in his torn throat that sounded like a growl. "Women need a firm hand, Savage."

"Preferably right on their ass," Maestro added. "Hard."

"Grateful for the advice from two men who don't know shit about women," Savage said. Czar handed Savage a plate with his steak. "It's best not to listen to them. Neither one of them knows what they're talking about."

The three men filled Czar in on what they had found out as they ate. The hit men had each been contacted via email. They were instructed to pick up their assignment and money and where to do the job. The Venomous club had three men, the president and two of his highest-ranking members, targeted to be killed. At approximately the same time, four of the highest-ranking members of the Diamondbacks were to be removed. And Torpedo Ink had the most on the list. The men who had taken the job had no idea who put out the hits or why. They had provided many of the names on the hit list, which was how Savage and the others were able to get the identities of the others so quickly.

"So we still don't know who is behind this?" Czar said. "It's a pretty damn brazen hit."

"If we separate it from what Seychelle told us about the Russian woman and the Ghosts it brings it back to Brandon," Savage said. "Look at who they wanted killed in Torpedo Ink. Reaper, Ice, Storm. Alena. Those four are enemies of Tawny. She hates them. You threw her out, Czar. If she is partners with Brandon, or thinks she is, then he wants me dead and she wants all of you dead. All those other suggestions he planted in those women are for his amusement. He wants to create chaos. In a way, he already has among the clubs."

"There could be something to that," Czar said.

Reaper nodded. "The little pissant. He needs to go, Czar."

"I agree, but I'm betting if we take this to Plank, he'll pull the plug on him and it won't fall on us. Lana managed to intercept the Demon informer to the Feds and bring him here to Seychelle. She got rid of the suggestion. That wasn't on Brandon for sure. That was definitely our Russian woman who works for the Ghosts," Czar said.

"Seychelle," Savage whispered under his breath. He pushed his empty plate to the side and got up, going to the largest tree straight beyond the firepit. He took his time before he found the perfect branch, a thin one he cut off and brought back to the table.

Most of the members had drifted off, leaving only Destroyer and Maestro drinking beer with him while he trimmed the branch into a perfect switch. Once he had that ready, he set the scene he wanted, pulling out the few tools he would need if Seychelle was up for his kind of kinky needs, then he went to her with a cup of coffee in his hands, the to-go mug with a lid that she particularly liked. "You're waking up for me, baby."

It took a couple of moments of calling to her before she blinked up at him as she sat up, pushing at her hair. "You're back." A slow smile of welcome lit her face. Her eyes.

His stomach performed that slow somersault he was used

to now. "Have dinner ready for you, Seychelle. Did you see any of my text messages?" He'd given her a few instructions just in case she was up for a night of dirty, sinful lessons.

Her blue gaze clung to his. "I must have fallen asleep. I'm sorry, babe. I should have stayed awake just in case you needed me earlier." She picked up her phone where it was lying on the sleeping bag beside her.

"It's no big deal, angel. Czar told me you worked on those women all day, even though I told you not to do it without me." He didn't bother to sound stern. It wouldn't make a difference. She'd already done it.

Her lashes fluttered, and a small smile curved her mouth, that mouth that drove him crazy if he thought about it too much. He hadn't yet taught her to suck his cock, but that was supposed to be one of those sinful, dirty lessons he had in mind for their camping trip. Now he was probably going to take that off the table.

The moment she turned on her phone it began to ding, over and over. All the text messages he'd sent her. She stared down at them, a flush spreading over her beautiful skin. Her gaze slid from him to the lingering members of Torpedo Ink. Two were still at the table, finishing their beers. He knew they would be gone by the time he walked her back from the restroom. He'd made it clear he needed to be alone with his woman.

"I'll walk you to the ladies' room. Grab whatever you need for the night." He was giving her a choice. She didn't want to play, she didn't have to. He would be in bad shape until they got home, which would make life rough for both of them, maybe even the other members of Torpedo Ink, but that was just too damn bad. He wasn't going to push any-thing on her, not after what happened the night before.

She stuffed items into a small bag and then sipped at the coffee as they walked the short distance to the restrooms. Music blared and again, as the night before, laughter and conversations were loud. He didn't try to talk, he just stayed close to her. She would know soon enough that he had done what he needed to do for the club. He'd tell her while she ate, just not the details. He had to; she'd likely catch them anyway when he had his hands and mouth and cock all over and in her.

She came out of the restroom dressed in one of her favorite pairs of denims, very old, the kind that buttoned up rather than zipped, and a tank, with just a cardigan over it. She was still resisting wearing the club colors he'd provided for her. She would be wearing them the next day, she just didn't know it. At least she was wearing his fucking ring on her finger.

They had to walk through the outer circle of the Torpedo Ink campground made up of the Trinity chapter. There was a lot of activity. They knew how to party. Seychelle got her first taste of an authentic Torpedo Ink party, with couples not paying any attention to their surroundings. She tried not to stare at the naked bodies, the women dancing around the firelight, or the men drinking whiskey out of a bottle, stroking themselves in anticipation while they watched the dancing.

Savage kept her walking straight through to their campsite. He was happy to see that his brothers had taken the hint and left. "You hungry, baby?" He pulled a fresh, cold beer from the cooler and offered her one.

She shook her head. "I ate earlier, before I fell asleep. Water is fine for me."

"You insisted on helping those women without me being around. Czar told me a couple of them had a few illnesses. You were lucky no one was really sick. We talked about that, and when I texted you, you just didn't bother to answer me."

She shrugged, not looking in the least bit remorseful, but he knew she wouldn't. He went to his favorite spot to sit on the top of the picnic table. She wedged herself between his thighs and reached up to stroke his jaw. "You're having a difficult time, aren't you, Savage? Was it bad today? I'm sorry I fell asleep."

Bog. Every time he thought it was impossible to love her
any more, she overwhelmed him. Swamped him. She saw
him. Stripped him naked. "Yeah, babe, it was bad. Shitty
work. I don't know who wants to kill so many people, but I
suspect Brandon is behind it. I just couldn't get the confirmation, and I tried. I suspect Tawny and Brandon are con-
spiring together, but they had to go to someone else to get
the money to fund that many hits."

She moistened her lips. "You had to interrogate them?"
She swallowed hard and lifted her lashes so her blue eyes
met his. Compassion. Sadness. A little bit of fear. "It
was bad."

"Any time I have to question people and they don't want
to give me the answers I need, it gets ugly, baby. I don't want
you to ever see how ugly."

Her fingers stroked his jaw. "I'm sorry, Savage. I'm especially sorry I wasn't awake when you needed me. I could
have at least answered your text. I know that helps you a
little. I'm here for you now."

His heart jumped. His cock jerked. She was offering herself to him. Her body. Her gaze didn't waver from his, not
even when he pushed her sweater from her shoulders and
helped her take it from her arms. The cool night air showed
him she wasn't wearing a bra. Her nipples turned to two
tight pebbles, pressing hard into the thin, pale pink tank. He
stepped off the table so he was close, so he could put his
arms around her. Hold her. Support her. Let her lean on him
while she fully made her decision—hopefully in his favor.

"You sure you're up for this, baby?" Even as he asked her,
giving her the choice, Savage's long fingers caressed her
breast and then found her nipple, tugging and rolling. She
leaned into him, thrusting her breasts forward for his attention. He pinched. Hard. She gasped. He pushed the tank up,
letting the dancing flames from the fire show him her skin.
He loved her skin so much. He ran his palm over that soft,
perfect canvas. Unmarred. Flawless. He could decorate it so
beautifully.

His hand slipped to her face, cupped one side, his thumb sliding gently over that beloved mouth. Her lips. That tender expression of such love only she ever gave him. Only Seychelle ever felt for him. He kissed her. Gently. Trying to show her he loved her. Telling her she was his world, pouring that truth down her throat and into her body to give her the courage she would need to face the monster raging in him if she consented. When he lifted his head, he stared down into her eyes, letting her see the blue flames there, the dark, ugly flames that burned with need.

"Yes," she said simply. "I came here for you, Savage, and you need me."

"I'm not at my worst, but I do need you," he admitted. "I've thought a lot about what we could do here without breaking our rules but still bleed off some of my needs." He cupped the weight of her breasts in his palms, thumbs strumming her hard nipples, watching her shiver in response, watching her eyes darken to a deep blue of pure desire.

"I told you I would be willing to bend the rules if we needed to," she whispered.

"I brought your jewelry, baby, the kind you hate to love." He whispered it into her ear as he went back to playing with her nipples.

Her gaze jumped to his, and he found himself smiling. She loved nipple play, and she loved clamps. She didn't like the clover clamps he sometimes used on her. Well, she did and she didn't. That was one of those things she still couldn't quite fathom, how it could hurt so good. She swallowed back a protest and leaned closer to him, as if for reassurance. He gave it to her, turning her around, one arm sliding around her ribs to lock her back to his chest. Her breasts jutted out, with the firelight playing over them; he continued the assault on her nipples, pulling and stretching, teasing them into tight buds.

"You like this, Seychelle? You're already slick and hot for me, aren't you?" He whispered the query into her ear as he tugged roughly.

She made a soft sound deep in her throat and then looked over her shoulder at him. "Yes, you know I like it."

He waited, staring down into her eyes. He could see desire. Lust. He saw trepidation. Reluctance for what was coming. There was love. Soft. Tender. His.

She moistened her lips. "I'm always ready for you when you touch me, Savage."

"And these really are your favorite clamps, aren't they, baby?"

She hesitated.

"Your body doesn't lie, Seychelle. You're so slick you can barely keep from rubbing your thighs together, and I haven't even put them on you yet."

"I know, but . . ."

Already, the sadist in him was rising like the tide, that rush of domination, of power. He enjoyed the confusion on her face, the mixture of lust, desire to please him and trepidation. "Turn around for me."

She took a deep breath and did so, turning to face him. He pulled her tank over her head and tossed it onto the picnic table before lowering his mouth to suckle her right breast. He kneaded her soft flesh as he sucked hard, using his tongue and teeth to elongate her nipple and ready her for the clamps. He took his time, watching her face as he brought the little clamp with pronounced bumps on the rubber surface up where she could see it.

He loved watching her expression. "Look at me, Seychelle," he commanded. He wanted her looking into his eyes. She was tense. Any time he brought out the clover clamps, she was tense. He wanted her full attention on him at all times, not on the fact that they were outdoors and there were others around them, in the distance maybe, and they were guarded, but that didn't mean she wasn't aware of others close by.

Her gaze jumped to his. There was pleading there. Resignation. She knew he wasn't going to reconsider. There was also need. A dark, growing need in her he could see. Her breathing had already gone ragged.

"You have somethin' to say?"

"I'm just nervous because there are people around us."

"Can you see anyone here? No one is here, baby. I'm clampin' your nipples because right now I'm in a fuckin' foul mood and I need you to get me out of it. If you don't, we're going to be having a long session and you're not going to be able to get up or go anywhere for a week or so." He bent his head and kissed her. "You won't be able to ride on the Harley home and we'll be stuck in this fuckin' place forever. Either that or I'm going to pick a fight with someone and kill them with my bare hands and go to prison for the rest of my life. I won't look good in prison clothes, babe."

He told her the truth. The rage was there once more, building and building until he thought he'd go insane with it, even though he tried to make a joke out of it. "I want you wearing these while I stripe you. I'm going to fuck you, baby. Hard. Ride you hard. Smack your ass. I won't take your ass here, but I'm gonna play. This one isn't for you, this one is to keep the demon under control. You up for that shit? Because I need you up for it. If you're not, say so now, so we can stop and I can try to get myself under control until we get home."

He needed her to be. God, he hated himself, but she had to do this for him. He couldn't be alone with her, not when he was so close to being out of control. His brothers would stop him if he lost his mind. She needed to be safe, and he needed her to put the monster back in the cage. He waited for her to nod. For her to give her consent. He needed that too. Needed to know Seychelle was his partner and with him every step of the way. She had to consent to suffer for him. To give him her pain. To give him her tears. He was that big of a fucking monster, and there was no way to stop it unless he put a bullet in his head.

Her blue gaze moved over him. "If I say I can't do it, what are we going to do?"

His heart sank. "We stop, baby. We stop and I get myself under control. We'll pick up at home."

If it was possible for her blue gaze to soften more, it did. "I love you, Savage. I'm up for this." Her voice was low, a mere thread of sound, barely there, but it was there.

Triumph swept through him. He didn't wait. Never once had he taken his gaze from hers, refusing to allow her to look away. He controlled her, mesmerized her, completely dominated her with his gaze. It always made clamping her so much more intense. Pinching her nipple hard once more, he stretched it and then attached the clover clamp. He was deliberately slow, taking his time. Her "jewelry" was really three solid beads, each a little larger than the next. He had been careful, making certain they weren't too heavy, but every time they moved, that clamp pinched tighter and sent fire flashing through her.

Her breath hissed out, and she bit her lip, but she didn't cry out as the clamp settled and bit into her. He flicked the little chain of balls, sending them swinging. Her eyes filled. Those liquid tears, so beautiful. One spilled over, and he leaned into her and licked it from her face. Tasted what he needed. What she gave to him. Her gift.

He took her other breast in his mouth, taking his time, gentle, tender even. Unexpectedly biting down so that she gasped and instinctively pulled back, only to have his teeth settle around her nipple. Pulling. Pinching hard. He let go, watching her face the entire time as he clamped that throbbing nipple. It was there. That look he needed. That expression.

"Would you do anything for me, Seychelle?" He stroked caresses down the back of her head, feeling the silk of her hair. She wore it long because he'd asked her to. She hadn't worn a bra because he'd asked her not to. He knew her pussy was bare because he'd insisted she let him shave it. He wanted her bare so she would feel every delicious thing he did to her and he could see the marks stark on her flesh.

Instantly, she looked leery. "Almost. I have limits."

He knew her limits, and he was grateful she had them.

The clamp had pinched hard enough to bring more tears, and he licked at each one, grateful for them, sipping on them

as if they were the finest wine. To him, they were. He needed
them. He needed to cause them and ease them. He was that
fucking sick. He flicked the balls, both strands, and watched
her face as they swung.

"What's that feel like, baby?"

"Pain. Fire." Her body shuddered. "Good. Bad. I don't
know."

He smiled and flicked the beads again. Her entire body
shuddered again.

"Maybe we need to see how it makes you feel. Let's ask
your little pussy." His hand dropped to the buttons of her
jeans. He opened them and then slid the denim off her hips,
down her legs to her ankles. He waited for her to step out of
them. She hadn't worn panties because he told her not to in
the text he'd sent. His hand slipped between her legs. Heat
poured off her. His palm found slick honey.

"Your pussy says it's good."

Keeping one hand tight over her slit, his thumb flicking her
clit, he flicked the chain of tiny spheres again in time to his
thumb, his gaze on her face. Her eyes. She couldn't look away.
Couldn't close her eyes. Another shudder went through her. Her
breath hissed out again. A low moan escaped her throat. Hot
liquid spilled like tears into his palm. He gave her a wicked
smile and brought his hand up for her to see the evidence.

"Good for certain, baby." He licked at the spice on his
palm, loving her taste. He loved everything about her. Every
single thing.

He attached a fairly long chain that went from one nipple
to the other. "My leash. I love to be connected to you. Do
you feel our connection, baby? Do you feel how close I am
to you right now?"

She didn't know it, but when he was at his absolute worst,
when the demons rode him so hard and he needed to do this
to her, to see that she would stick with him, give him everything he needed to get him through, that was when he truly
felt closest to her. He felt his love for her overwhelming him.

She nodded her head. "Yes."

Her voice, so soft. He loved that voice of hers. Acceptance. She didn't loathe him the way he sometimes could loathe himself. That wasn't now. Now, when she was giving himself permission to be himself, euphoria was beginning to sweep through him.

Savage tugged until she stepped toward him. He sank down on the table and indicated for her to climb onto the bench and then onto the table beside him. "Want you up here, Seychelle. Kneel up right next to me."

Seychelle obeyed, facing him. The moonlight spilled over her, and she looked beautiful, with her breasts clamped and the chain hanging low, long enough to touch her bare mound. He couldn't help brushing that pale space with the pads of his fingers, wanting someday to see his name there permanently.

"I'm going to do some things that will make you wild and probably afraid, but you'll come hard, I promise. I'll make certain to take care of you. Are you still with me? Can you do this?" Always, always, he had to check with her, know it was her choice. Hear her confirm it. Know she was all right.

"I love you, Savage. If this is what you really need, then I can do it. I want to do it."

"I need it, or I wouldn't ask. You know that."

Her face relaxed into that tender, sweet love that made him want to melt at her feet. Made him wish he had his whip with him and that she would give him permission to use it any damn place he wanted to use it. Made him almost wish he weren't so fucked up.

"Lay across my lap."

She swallowed hard, but she did as he said, groaning as the little weighted balls tugged on her nipples and fire flared through her body. That long, fine chain slithered down as well, pulling on her breasts, adding to the weight. He rubbed her bare bottom and then delivered several very hard slaps, leaving dark red handprints on both cheeks. He pushed his fingers into her slick entrance, collecting the thick liquid.

"Naughty girl. You like those clamps far too much. I

don't think you get to protest again. Or is it the combination of the clamps and the hard spanking?"

But there was so much more he needed. Her body was pristine. A canvas. The rage was too deep. The darkness consuming him. He was drowning, and she was his only lifeline. Did she know that? He was just warming up. He needed so much more to bleed off the rage to get through the fucking night and rest of tomorrow so he could make it home. He needed the sanctity of their home, where he had no restrictions. Where he could just fucking breathe.

He took his time opening the small jar of oil Preacher had prepared for him. "This is a little surprise, baby. You're going to love it."

He dipped two fingers in the jar and began to paint her clit, circling and then painting until the little hood and the hard bud were coated. He went back, dipping his fingers and then applying it to her bare lips and sliding them inside her entrance, curling them deep, over and over, pushing more and more of the oil inside her until he was certain he'd gotten enough. His fingers returned, and this time he began sliding the oil between her cheeks. He could see the oil glistening from the dancing flames in the firepit. He added more and more and then pressed into that forbidden star. She moaned and writhed, but he slammed his palm hard on her cheeks until she settled. He pushed his fingers deeper, opening her, and then added more of the oil.

"That's going to make you feel so good in a few minutes, Seychelle. I told you I'd think of special things we could do together. You're going to need my cock like you've never needed it before."

He could see the oil was already beginning to do its job. It had hints of ginger in it. He hadn't wanted to start her off with ginger right away, but he'd asked Preacher to create something that would set her body on fire for him. Something that would heat up with every movement of her body. He spent a few more minutes spanking her, enjoying the way she writhed and cried, panting and pleading with him.

Savage let up and indicated for her to crawl off the table, moving with her, controlling her actions with the chain leading to the clamps. Every movement sent fire through her ass and over her clit. Her nipples were on fire. By now the oil and the spanking had her desperate for his cock.

With Seychelle kneeling at his feet, he found his beer on the table and deliberately took a long, slow drink. "You want my cock, baby?"

"Yes." She nodded.

"How bad?"

"Need. I need it."

"There's a switch over there on the other side of that tree. You can get it and ask me to use it on you. You ask nice and I'll do it, and then you can have my cock." He folded his arms across his chest, the action drawing the chain up, forcing her breasts up as well.

She cried out, her breath catching as the clover clamps bit down viciously. "Savage . . ."

The soft quiver in her voice was an aphrodisiac. Was everything he needed. The liquid glittering like diamonds on her lashes were all his. He jerked his chin toward the spot where he'd left the switch, hoping like hell she'd remember the two little scenarios she'd told him that had turned her on when she'd watched porn. He had re-created them for her, putting his own spin on them.

Her eyes were on his. He could see the blue darkening even more with lust. With need. Yeah, she remembered. Her body was already burning for his. He hadn't done the things he needed, not yet, but hot blood rushed through his veins at the sight of her kneeling, her round breasts covered in the marks of his hands and teeth, her nipples clamped with those little weights swinging merrily if she dared to move or he tugged on the chain. Her skin was flushed, lungs desperate for air as she panted raggedly, fighting the burning hunger between her legs. He'd known she'd be sensitive to the oil.

She didn't stand, she simply nodded, her tongue touching

her lower lip so that it glistened temptingly, and then turned and began to crawl toward the larger tree that was behind them. It was at the very edge of reach of the firepit, where the light from the flames could reach, but he'd set a low gas-fed lantern in the branches.

Savage walked with her, using the chain like reins, tugging every few steps so that her breasts swayed and she gasped softly as the clamps bit down. The weights pulled her breasts and tugged on her nipples, increasing the flames licking at her body.

"Think about those clamps coming off, baby," he counseled wickedly. "All that fire rushing through you, consuming you. What a burn. There it is." He indicated the switch on the ground. He'd swept the ground earlier with a branch of leaves to get rid of the rocks, so when she crawled, she wouldn't get hurt, but still, the idea of her willingly suffering for him added to the excitement.

A fresh flood of tears on her upturned face rewarded his reminder. She reached down and picked up the slender, flexible switch he'd made and handed it to him. He tugged until she was forced to stand. That made her clench her little red ass, and she made another little cry that sent heat sizzling through his veins like a drug.

"You dreamt of this, didn't you, baby? Right out here in the open? Someone could walk right up on us, couldn't they? You wanted this. You have to tell me what you want, baby."

The switch wasn't a whip or a flogger, but it would leave the marks he needed, and it would hurt—but it wouldn't damage her, not like any of the tools he had at home. He'd still have to be careful. He'd need control. He didn't want this to be over until the dark pool of rage had dissipated enough and he knew Seychelle and everyone else around him were safe.

EIGHTEEN

Seychelle shook her head, but Savage could see how bright her eyes were, the pupils dilated. She wanted this. Anticipated. But the trepidation was there, and it was thrilling. She kept looking at the thin branch he'd shaved so carefully while he'd been sitting at the picnic table, talking with Maestro and Destroyer, and drinking his beer. He'd been anticipating, just like she was now.

"Are you lying to me, baby? Because that wouldn't be a good idea. Not with the way I'm feeling." He stepped close, using the chain to force her back against the tree trunk. It wasn't exactly smooth. "What do you want?" His heart was beating right through his cock.

"You. This."

That was all he needed to hear. "Put your arms back around the tree, Seychelle, like you're hugging it."

She swallowed hard, her eyes on his, but she complied without hesitation, wrapping her arms around the tree in a backward hug. He walked around behind the tree, pulled the ties from his pocket where he'd stashed them and yanked her wrists together. He'd eyed the trunk earlier to make certain she could circle it with her arms, and she just barely made it. The bark would be pressing uncomfortably into her back. He tied her wrists so she couldn't move and then walked with deliberate slowness back around to stand in front of her.

The position he'd put her in forced her generous breasts outward, jutting them right at him, the little balls still swinging from her body. "Spread your legs. I want your feet planted beyond your shoulders." He walked back to the table with that same deliberate slow stride, took his beer and drank, watching her struggle to get her feet in position without moving her upper torso.

She was beautiful. Tied to that tree, she was gorgeous, waiting for him. Waiting for his switch. Or whip. Or any damn thing he chose to do to her. The rush was on him now, the monster fighting for supremacy. He put his beer down and walked back to her, watching her gaze dart around her as voices rose and fell, sounding close.

"Savage . . ."

He didn't let her finish. He knew no one was approaching their campsite. The voices came from those camping close. He wanted her to hear them, just like in the film she'd watched. He unhooked the chain and slipped it in his pocket. He smiled at her. "We can't keep those clamps on, as much as I want to. They have to come off, baby. They've been on too long already."

Instantly, she broke out in a sweat and shook her head. His smile turned very wicked as he slid three fingers into her slick heat and began a slow pumping while his thumb strummed at her clit. Every line in his face was stamped with a sinful, sensual cruelty as he reached for the clamp on her left breast. He took it off fast and watched her face as the blood suddenly rushed back into her nipple, causing an excruciating, almost agonizing pain. His fingers pumped faster, and his thumb and forefinger suddenly pinched her burning clit.

She came with a wild choked cry, the orgasm crashing through her in waves, even as tears poured down her face and he licked and kissed them away. When the last rolling wave was gone, he held out his fingers to her, and smiled as she sucked them clean.

"There's still one more clamp, baby," he reminded her. His gaze never left her face. God. That face. So beautifully expressive, just as much a canvas as her body. So his. So much beauty. Such a gift. She was wild with need, but just as fearful of the pain. She wanted both. Hated that she did. He needed that confusion. Craved it.

He dropped the chain so that it hung from her nipple, the other clamp and three small weights pulling as well. She gasped and cried out, helpless to do anything to stop the pain with her arms wrapped around the tree. Savage leaned in close and pressed a kiss to the corner of her left eye and then took her tears.

"What did I tell you about making a sound, Seychelle? We have our rules, don't we?" He kept his voice low, but added a menacing quality as he once again slipped his fingers into her hot little pussy. It was already slick with anticipation. He circled her clit. This time, he wasn't going to give her the end result she wanted. He needed so much more. He was just getting started.

Savage reached out, staring straight into her eyes, and pulled hard, yanking the clamp away from her nipple. Seychelle nearly cried out, but caught herself as the blood rushed back into her nipple. The ropes binding her to the tree kept her up as her knees sagged. Her hips rode his fingers frantically, but he pulled them away, depriving her of her pending orgasm just before it roared through her. He leaned forward and took her breast into the heat of his mouth, soothing away the pain.

"Savage." The ache in her voice was real. The pain. The need. "Please."

"I'm going to decorate your body, that little pussy and ass, and then I'll give you my cock the way you need it, Seychelle."

She was so delicious. She didn't fight him or protest. She

straightened her knees, wincing a little as her back hit the bark, thrusting her breasts forward for him. He picked up the switch. She would see this coming. Each stroke he put into it. He knew the places that would really injure her, and he was always cognizant of how hard he struck her. But the beast was screaming for pain. For action. For retribution.

He slashed a stripe across the front of her thighs. Her mouth opened in a silent scream. The oils in her pussy and ass had to be building a fiery desire when she clenched in preparation for his strikes. He was faster, delivering several more up her legs to her mound, that pretty little bare mound that belonged to him and was so sensitive. He was good. He was an artist. He could write his name if he wanted, but he had another goal in mind.

He stepped up to her, his fingers trailing up her thigh to find her heat. The oil had spilled out of her along with her spicy honey. "You're so hot for me. You like this, don't you? You're just waiting for my cock." *Bog*, he loved to hear her say it for him.

He let her ride his fingers frantically, her moans growing louder, and then abruptly he stepped back and began to tap her needy little pussy with the switch while he sucked on his fingers, watching her expression grow more and more desperate. He increased the power behind the swing of the switch, all the while staring into her eyes. He knew exactly where his target was, and he hit it every single time. He watched as pain and pleasure rushed through her. She tried to resist, coming to her toes, but she didn't move her legs, didn't try to pull them together, and she didn't stop him by giving him her safe word. Then she was actually moving her body into the switch, meeting the stroke as he increased the power just a little more.

Seychelle cried out, a loud, sobbing cry of shock, as her body exploded with a powerful orgasm. Immediately, he gave her two more swift, hard taps, and then he slashed his way up her body to her breasts. He put more power into the next few stripes. To those beautiful rounded curves. Under them. Over them. The sides. One straight across those in-flamed nipples for him. For the monster in him. For his hungry, dirty cock that waited so impatiently for its prize.

Her eyes went wide in shock, and her mouth opened, but no sound emerged. Tears poured down her face, but her body was still orgasming, wave after wave. Savage stepped close again, giving her his fingers, rubbing her clit with his thumb where the oil, the switch and the thundering blood were making her nearly convulse with one powerful orgasm after another.

The master. He was that. He had learned almost before he was a teen and perfected the art by the time he was twenty. His hands moved up and down her body, stroking those dark streaks, and then he stepped back and walked around the tree to untie her hands.

"We're not finished, baby. Turn around and put your arms around the tree again." He waited for her to comply. She was shaky, and he wrapped an arm around her waist and slid the switch between her legs as he guided her around so she would face the trunk this time. "Hug the tree, baby. Close. Put your upper body tight against it and push your ass out toward me. Just like you saw in that porn flick. I'm going to give you a spanking, Seychelle, and then you'll get my cock, just like I promised, unless you want to stop. Do you want to use your safe word? Are you finished?"

She was riding the switch. Pushing her perfect cheeks back at him. Sobbing for him. Begging him, but so softly he could barely hear her.

"Seychelle?" He pulled his hand and the switch away. "Answer me, baby. I need to know if you want this."

"Yes." She hissed it at him. "I need you to give me your cock."

Savage knew she was giving him what he needed. She was his partner. She gave him permission every fucking time to let his sadistic monster rule. He pulled the switch back, the rush of power on him. That feeling of domination. He was riding high.

He could flay the flesh off a man with one stroke, and he was careful not to do more than leave a nice long red lash across her thigh, just above her knees, that first perfect opening of his artistry on her backside. His heart jerked hard in his chest. It was gorgeous. He laid three more going up toward her ass.

He knew the oil in her ass would be at its hottest and she would clench as he laid the stripes across those perfect cheeks. He spent time there, decorating her cheeks, watching her quiver, watching her body react to what he was doing to her. The endorphins released caused goose bumps to rise and sweat to glisten on her skin. Every time the switch licked flames across her flesh, she clenched beautifully, and the oil licked flames internally, sending them straight to her fiery little pussy.

He stopped to use his fingers on her, to stroke her nearly to orgasm, just stopping when she was close. So close. Her clit was swollen, screaming at her. Desperate for him now.

Her tears excited him. Her pain put absolute steel in his cock. Those stripes across her ass and going up her back and down her thighs made him so fucking hard he wanted to rip his jeans down and fuck that slick little pussy right then, but his monster was howling with joy, urging him on. He swung harder, watching the dark streaks rise on her cheeks with satisfaction.

Seychelle hissed. Pressed her forehead against the tree trunk. "Yellow. Savage. Yellow."

Shit. What the fuck was wrong with him? She should never have to give him a warning. Not unless he was too far gone, and he wasn't out of control, was he? He flung the switch far away from him and reached for her, his hands at her hips.

"Do you want to stop? I want to fuck you, baby, but we can stop, and I'll carry you to the bedroll and put the lotion on you," he whispered against the small of her back. A temptation. Yet it was also a plea. He fucking needed to bury his cock in her like the brutal animal he was. Like the sadistic monster from hell they'd created and he couldn't shed.

"No, don't stop. Give me your cock." There was an urgent plea in her voice.

"Baby, you know when I'm like this, I'm going to be violent. You sure you're okay with that?" One hand was already unzipping his jeans, freeing his brutal, vicious erection. The scars were stretched and painful. They needed the lubrication of her body, that special oil Preacher had made for them.

"I want you any way I can get you. Just hurry, please." She pushed back against him.

Savage leaned into her because he couldn't stop himself, his fingers sliding down her body possessively, from her shoulders to her ass. She hissed and clenched and then cried out softly. He slapped her left cheek hard and then her right.

"No sound, Seychelle. You know that."

He repeated the motion over and over, using the pads of his fingers on her back and then his nails gently on her ass— watching her body's reaction, letting her pain feed that place inside him that needed to see his woman fight for him. He reached between her legs and found her slick with need, hot with fire that was all for him. She tried riding his fingers, but he flicked her clit and pulled away, leaving her wanting, leaving her desperate.

He rubbed her cheeks again with one hand as he stroked himself, moving behind her to settle the broad head of his cock right at her slick entrance. She felt like an inferno beckoning to him, trying to drag him deep. He caught her hips and yanked hard as he drove forward, slamming into that tight tunnel. He threw back his head, wanting to roar into the night. She was fucking paradise every single time, taking him far away from his own head. He loved this. Fucking loved this. The monster roaring. This feeling of euphoria. Of Seychelle and Savage coming together in a wild fury of sheer vicious, mind-blowing sex.

He stared, enthralled at the mesmerizing welts on her

body. At times he couldn't resist slamming his hand against her striped cheek or running his fingernails over the curve of one to feel her shudder. Her body bathed his scarred cock in hot, spicy liquid even as she hissed a pretend protest. She pushed back frantically into him when he hammered into her as brutally as possible.

He refused to let this end. He took her up so many times. So many, holding her on the brink, then stopping her abruptly by pressing hard on her clit. "Not yet, baby. Not yet. You're so out of control, you'd take me with you, and I don't want this over."

Savage bit the command out even as he continued to yank Seychelle back into him while he slammed his body into hers. The action smashed her against the trunk of the tree, and another low cry escaped her as he drove into her over and over. She tried to pull her torso away from the tree, even as she pushed her hips back onto him.

Her tits were taking a beating from the tree bark. He didn't like that. It wasn't his intention. He could put stripes on her, but he wasn't bruising her body with the fucking tree. His hands went to her breasts, filling his palms, pulling her back away from the tree trunk, squeezing hard with every ferocious pump. Her breath came in ragged gasps as he mashed and kneaded her breasts, holding her to him as he rode her body hard. All the while, he kept his hands between her breasts and the bark of the tree.

Her body grew hotter. Scorching. Like the lava pools in a volcano. His girth swelled impossibly, forcing the soft tissue to accommodate his size as he pounded into her. Deep. Deeper. He wanted to stay buried in her forever. Powerful waves broke over her, sweeping through with gale-force intensity. That silken tunnel, already so fucking tight, clamped down like a vise, squeezing, strangling his cock. He threw back his head and roared to the night. She cried out, the sound beautiful to him. Her pussy was greedy, milking his cock hungrily, so that it felt as if a thousand tongues were lapping at him, fists squeezing to drag every drop from him.

His head spun as euphoria settled over him, and for a time he couldn't think or move, barely able to breathe or stand. All he could do was feel that bliss, making him feel he wasn't really on this planet but somewhere else entirely. He came back to himself slower than he ever had out in the open. He could only hope someone had been watching his back, because he sure as hell didn't know what was going on around him.

Savage could barely stand up, and his woman was collapsing, would have gone straight to the ground had it not been for the ties, her breath coming in ragged sobs as her legs gave out. He tightened his hold on her waist, refusing to allow her knees or bottom to touch the ground. Quickly, he untied her, and then, managing to get his cock back in his jeans with one hand and zip his pants, he took her weight.

"Shh, baby, it's going to be all right. I've got you." He repeated the mantra over and over, burying his face against her neck. He had to find the strength to get them both to the sleeping bags. He hadn't thought the tree was that damn far when he'd set the scene.

She didn't answer him, her body still almost a dead weight, but he could tell she made an effort to stay upright and hold herself away from him. He didn't like that. She'd done it before. When they had intense sex like this, she needed him afterward just as much as before and during. She needed care from him. She needed to know they were a couple, and she was loved.

"Baby, put your arms around me and let me take care of you."

She shook her head, trying to stay where she was, but he reached down and managed to get an arm under her knees and lift her, cradling her against his chest. Savage felt the strength returning to his body, and he straightened, taking her with him. She turned her tearstained expression away from his gaze as he tried to assess her condition. She buried her face against his chest so he couldn't see jack, but he could feel how wet her face was.

He was still fully clothed where she was completely naked. He made his way back to the sleeping bags, soothing her gently, talking to her in Russian, scattering kisses on top of her head. She didn't look at him. That was a bad sign, but she'd done that before. He was just going to have to teach her that aftercare was every bit as important as what they did together during sex.

Savage sank down onto the sleeping bag, Seychelle on his lap, cuddling her close to him. He felt her movement, as she tried to squirm off. "Stay still, baby. I have to get this lotion on you. Once I get it on your front, especially your breasts, you can lay on the sleeping bag so I can get your other side. It helps with any bruising or swelling. It also has a numbing agent in it."

He'd been damn careful with the switch until that last strike. He'd laid that one on her ass just a little too heavy. It was going to leave a bruise for sure. Every other stripe would fade within twenty-four hours. He'd been that careful. It was difficult to tell in the dark. He had to light the gas lantern he had waiting next to the sleeping bags.

Her body was shuddering continually, tremors running through her until he thought she might shake apart. She covered her face with her hands and rocked her body back and forth. "Hurry, Savage. Just get the lotion." Her voice was muffled. Laced with pain.

That jerked his head up. He had been holding her on his lap with one arm and fumbling in the dark for the lotion with the other, but now he narrowed his eyes and dragged the lantern to him.

"Babe. This shouldn't be hurting any worse than . . ." He trailed off. He'd been consumed by rage all day. He'd been collecting the anger from his brothers and sisters and storing it up for weeks. Cursing under his breath, he managed to get the lantern lit and shone it on her body. His mouth went dry. Sweat broke out on his body.

"Fuck me, Seychelle," he whispered between clenched teeth. This wasn't supposed to happen. Not here. Not now. Not when neither of them was prepared. Not with a fucking switch. She wasn't trained for this. He hadn't brought her in gently. Lovingly. What the fuck was wrong with him that he'd been so out of control he hadn't known? This was why he needed his brothers around him. He shouldn't have been alone with her when the monster was so close. Fuck. Fuck. Fuck.

He caught up the lotion and poured it over the slashes to her front. So many of them. Many more than he'd thought he'd put on her. He tore a strip of cloth from his shirt and soaked it with lotion to lay over her breasts. The entire time he whispered to her that it was going to be all right. That he'd take care of her. That the lotion would numb the pain. He had something in his pack that would help. He just had to get this on her first.

It wasn't going to be all right. He knew that. He could barely breathe. Barely think. His heart was racing, and his mind was all over the place. There was a roaring in his ears. Blood thundering. No one could ever love a fucking monster. Not really. He'd lied to himself. Let her in. He'd let himself believe. Let his guard down. He wanted her so much. And then he'd done this. He'd fucking done this to her.

He wasn't going to put his screwup on Seychelle and ask her why she didn't stop him. She'd given him a yellow. This wasn't on her. This was on him. He'd known he was on the edge. He still was. This wasn't as bad as he could get. Not by a long shot. The idea was to ease her into his life, not crash her into it. Not hurt her when he'd promised her he wouldn't, with the others around them. He'd broken about every fucking promise he'd ever made to her. She'd made it clear she was damn sick of his broken promises. He'd thought he'd come up with something special for her, and instead, his true identity had rushed forth and taken over, and now she was lost to him.

"I'm going to wrap you, Seychelle, and give you painkillers, get you to sleep and then put you in the truck and head for home tonight."

She shook her head and pressed her face against his

chest. "You have to work tomorrow." It came out muffled between sobs, but she got it out.

"Fuck that, baby. Reaper or Keys can take my place. I'm taking you home. They can bring my bike. I've done enough for the club this run. Both of us have." He kept pouring on the lotion and smoothing it over the stripes until he thought he could safely lay her down. "Careful, baby. I need to get the other side. Don't try to move around. Let me do this for you."

He smoothed her hair back and kissed her face. "I swear, baby, I didn't mean to break my promise to you. I'll get you out of here before anyone sees you."

"I know you didn't." There was conviction in her voice.

Why she would believe him, he had no idea. He just counted himself lucky that she did, but he knew it wouldn't matter in the long run. The lotion was beginning to do its job. She would remember later, and she would leave him. His angel. She took away the demons of his past just by being in his bed. Her laughter cleared out the ghosts, drove them away when they were too close.

Savage soaked strips of his shirt in the lotion and covered the worst of the stripes on her backside with them and then covered her with his sleeping bag. He found two heavy-duty painkillers in the first aid kit and gave them to her, even though she resisted taking them. It didn't take him long to break camp, group texting Czar, Reaper, Destroyer and Maestro that he was leaving and taking one of the trucks. He added that he wanted them to bring his bike safely home.

Czar texted first. We haven't gotten to the bottom of the problem.

Another brother will have to do it. Broke another promise to my old lady. Taking her home. She didn't ask. I need to take her home. That should be all he should have to say—and it was.

Immediately, because they were his brothers, they offered to help. Destroyer brought the truck as close to the campsite as possible. Reaper packed Savage's gear in the truck while Savage placed Seychelle carefully in the sleeping bag. She kept her eyes closed, but he could tell she was awake when he put her in the seat and buckled the seat belt.

"Watch Alena," he warned his brothers.

"We're packing up as well," Czar said. "We did as much as we could for Plank and the others. We'll see if the Diamondbacks still try to pin anything on Alena. If they do, I might take Plank out myself after all we've done for him."

Savage understood. He nodded and slid behind the wheel. "Meet you back home. Take care of my bike for me."

"Transporter and Mechanic will keep it safe," Reaper assured him.

Savage set out on the road, putting on soft music in the hopes to lull Seychelle to sleep. The road was nowhere near as smooth as he would have liked, but the truck was in perfect shape and had a full tank of gas. He could make it home before morning easily without pushing it too hard. Still, with few people on the road, he made good time. The truck was a rocket if need be. His gut knotted more every time he glanced toward his woman.

She hadn't said a single word of recrimination. Not one word. Her body, in spite of the lotion that should have numbed her and the pain pills, still shuddered occasionally. She had her fist pressed tight against her mouth. Her hair had spilled over her face, but he could see her cheeks were wet from her tears. She tried to turn her head away from him, but he refused to let her. He dropped one hand onto the top of her head, preventing movement, and slowed the truck.

His own eyes burned. Shit. For a moment, his vision blurred. That was all he fucking needed. To kill them both because he couldn't see. He slowed the truck even more. He wasn't holding it together. Where was his famous control? This wasn't going to work. He thought he had it all with her, but it wasn't going to work because he wasn't doing this shit to her. He was taking her home, cleaning her up and then he'd take her back to Sea Haven. To her cottage. She loved that little house. He knew she was leaving him anyway. He'd had her in his life for months, and he wasn't going back to living without her. He just couldn't do that.

There was a gun in his boot. Another one in the glove compartment. Another hidden in the compartment between the seats. He had a spare in a holster under his arm. Once he had her safe, he didn't need his bike to exit, driving it over a cliff. He just needed one of those guns. He fucking knew this was going to happen sooner or later. He'd known it all along. How could she really love him? It wasn't possible.

Seychelle groaned as she shifted her weight in the sleeping bag, struggling to sit up.

"What the hell are you doing? Stop moving around."

Deliberately, she looked at him, tear-wet face, spiky eyelashes dripping water, eyes swollen, her gorgeous face red and puffy from crying. Hell, she was still crying. Still silent, just like he ordered when they had sex. Her defiant little chin lifted and, looking him right in the eye, she released the safety belt. When she did, the sleeping bag slithered down her body and pooled around her waist.

He was forced to look back to the road to see where the fuck he was going before they wrecked. Fortunately, the road was straight. "Put your damn seat belt on, Seychelle."

She didn't answer him, and he glanced at her again. Her tits were jutting out, the welts from the thin branch showing very clearly over the curves. The thin band of his shirt was still plastered to her nipples, which meant at least the lotion was sticking there. But the sight of those dark stripes over her generous curves put so much steel in his fucking cock he had to adjust his jeans as he drove. He hated himself for that reaction.

He clenched his teeth, doing his best not to swear at her. He really wanted to swear at himself. He'd done this to her. She was sitting in the truck with a monster, and she knew it.

Except she was no longer sitting. She was up on her knees, her tits against the backrest. She pressed so hard as she leaned over, she flinched. His fucking cock noticed and jerked.

"Seychelle." Savage poured a warning into his voice. Damn her, she just couldn't sit still. What the hell was she doing? Didn't she know every move she made was pure temptation to a man like him when her body was decorated like that?

She totally ignored him, just the way she did whenever she decided to do what she wanted. She turned completely on the seat, rising up again on her knees, heedless of the sleeping bag sliding down while she reached into the back seat to snag the bag closest to her. It was dark on the road, with only one or two cars coming their way. The headlights acted like a spotlight, because, as she bent over, her ass was pushed out, and those headlights landed precisely on the stripes crisscrossing the cheeks of her bottom. The stripes were thin, dark red, and angry-looking. They were sexy as hell. Gorgeous.

"Seychelle, I'm not playing around. Get back in that seat, right now." He put a growl in his voice. Total command.

She hung over the seat, unzipping the bag and dragging out one of his shirts, ignoring his orders as if she didn't hear them. The temptation to spank her ass was overwhelming.

"If you don't turn around right now, I'm going to smack your ass, and it's going to hurt like hell." His cock hurt like hell. What difference did it make if he went that far? He'd already lost her.

She didn't even look at him or act like he'd spoken to her. He waited, his heart accelerating, his mouth dry, the blood pounding through his cock. Before he could stop himself, adrenaline poured through his body, and he slammed his palm on her perfect round left cheek and then her right, over the long, thick welt that was darker than the others. She jumped and whipped around, her hand coming up like she might cover her bottom, but she didn't.

She had his tee in her hand. "That really hurt, Savage."

She gave him her long, spiky lashes. That pouty lower lip he liked to bite. *Bog*, he needed to pull over and kiss the hell out of her, tell her he needed her, and she could never leave him. She took away his past. Drove away his demons. Gave him laughter and taught him what fun was. She was his world.

"Punishments are supposed to hurt. Turn around and put your fucking seat belt on or I'm going to pull this truck over and you're going to be hurting a lot worse than you do now."

Now his cock was so swollen with need he wanted to tell her to lie across the console and put her mouth on him. Fuck him. He really was the devil. Her face was still wet with tears, and they had been driving for miles. It didn't matter to the monster. If he didn't have to keep the truck on the road, he would have made his demands. She pulled the tee gingerly over her head. He had to keep casting little glances at her as he maneuvered several curves in the road before he was finally on a straight stretch.

Seychelle struggled to get her arms carefully into the tee and pull the material over her breasts. She made a single sound of muffled pain, turning her face away from him toward the window. Her hands were shaking when she placed them on her knees, which were still inside the sleeping bag.

"What do you think you're doing?" he asked again, this time forcing a gentleness into his voice.

"I want to sit up when we talk. I don't think you're going to take me seriously if I'm laying down." She clenched her teeth and dashed at the tears running down her face.

"You're supposed to be sleeping, not talking. Babe, I put that lotion on you for a reason. You've taken half of it off you. How do you expect it to work?"

"I expect you to listen to me." She lifted her chin at him. *Bog*, he loved that little chin lift. "I always listen to you." He had to clear his own eyes. The fucking road kept blurring.

"Evidently, you don't, Savage. We talk, I think we're on the same page and then you pull this bullshit."

Seychelle didn't swear. He swore. He thought she was the most beautiful thing in the world. "You knew what I was, Seychelle. I never lied to you," he said in a low voice.

"Sometimes I want to shake you." She pressed her fingers to her trembling lips. "We're supposed to be partners, you asshole. *Partners*. You don't get to negate what I do for you. You don't reduce it to nothing. You took on the rage for your brothers, and I took on the pain for you. That was the pact we made. That's what we both did. You don't get to sit in this truck and think about taking your life and leaving me alone because you think you screwed up. That's not how it works. You make me so angry sometimes, Savage. Why don't you take on *my* anger?"

Her blue eyes flashed fire at him. It took a few minutes for her statement to actually penetrate when he was expecting something altogether different.

Shit. Shit. That look on her face. Those eyes of hers. They had softened into that unusual teal color. She took his breath. Robbed him of his ability to think with his brain. He had to be realistic. *She* had to be realistic. No one, *no one* could love a monster, least of all an angel.

He couldn't fucking drive when she was looking at him like that. He did pull to the side of the road. His hands were shaking. She couldn't look at him like that. She couldn't. Rage was close, welling up like a volcano. He left the engine running, and he gripped the steering wheel with both hands hard because he didn't trust himself.

"Do you think that's the worst it gets?" He spat the truth at her. Snarled it. She couldn't look at him like that. She had no idea what was close to being loose in the truck with her.

"No, I don't. I believe it will get much worse than that." Seychelle spoke very calmly and swiped at the tears on her face with the pads of her fingers.

She looked so fucking young. So innocent. Her face was soft. Adoring. Her eyes so damn blue and looking at him with . . .

"For fuck's sake, Seychelle," he exploded. He reached across the console, turning fully toward her. "Stop looking at me like that."

"Like what? How am I looking at you, Savage?" She challenged.

He knew it was deliberate by that defiant little chin lift.

Her eyes just got bluer. Went to pure teal. Underwater. Completely immersed with those tears, but still her gaze clung to him, refusing to look away. She defied his command completely, staring at him with that look of utter and unconditional love. There was no such thing.

She was going to leave him. She would. It wasn't possible that she really felt that way about him. She couldn't love him. He was ugly to his core. He didn't have a soul anymore. They'd ripped it out of him when he was a child, and no matter what he did to those fuckers, how many he took out to save other children, he couldn't redeem himself and get his soul back.

He would forever have this cycle of rage and the need to see his woman suffer for him. Prove to him over and over that she was willing to give to him what he gave to those he loved. Pain. He took their anger and rage, and it became his pain. He gave that to Seychelle. That cycle would never stop. He *needed* to feel the whip in his hand to gain back control. He needed to see those welts and red stripes on her body to settle the terrible chaos in his mind. To take away the demons ruling his world and restore order. To make him man enough to be with a woman he loved. He needed *her*. Seychelle. And he was driving her away because he knew the longer she stayed and gave him that solace, the more he would need her. Depend on her. Believe in her. He already believed.

"Damn you. Fuck you, Seychelle. Stop looking at me like that. I fucking mean it. I'll put you out of the truck right on the side of the road dressed in nothing but my T-shirt."

She shifted her weight slightly, easing off her sore left cheek to give herself a reprieve. He could tell her it wasn't going to help. Her ass was a mess, and she needed to be off it. He let his gaze travel over her body, a slow, leering, possessive inspection, down to the hem of his tee, where her hips showed the dark welts. She shifted again, easing up on her sore ass.

Deliberately, he gave her a shark's smirk. "Hurts, doesn't

it, baby? Even with the painkillers I gave you. You move around and keep your weight on it and it will only get worse. You know what that does for me?" He dropped his hand to the bulge in his jeans and slowly opened the zipper, giving his aching cock some fucking relief from the tight restriction. "Makes me hard as a rock knowing I put those hot welts on my woman and she's going to wear them for a long time." He rubbed his palm over his cock, watching her face.

She was watching him just like she had that first time in the hospital, with just a little hint of amusement. "Damn you to hell, Seychelle. Don't you dare laugh. I will throw you out of this truck. Stop looking at me like that."

She sighed and wiped at the tears on her face again. This time she pressed a hand to her stomach. "I can't stop looking at you this way. I'll never stop, so you're going to have to get used to it. You're having a panic attack, just like I did. I can love whoever I want to, Savage, and I chose you. I will always choose you."

"You were going to leave me last night."

"Because you wouldn't listen to me, not because I didn't love you. You chose the club. You refused to be committed to *us*. I'm loyal, Savage. One hundred percent. You promised me the same. You're giving me that now and giving me the emotional support I need. I'm giving that back to you. That's called a relationship." She pressed her hand tighter against her stomach. "Will you please roll down the window? I need some air."

He immediately hit the button to roll her window down, letting the cold night air into the truck. She was still shivering. He zipped his jeans up slowly. Carefully. Now he just wanted to hold her. Take care of her. He didn't like her color. It was way off.

"I made you a promise that we wouldn't do anything like that with the others around, and I fucking broke that promise to you."

"Your intention was to give me one of my little porn flicks, and we were away from everyone."

"Yeah, and I got out of control. I didn't even know I was out of control. And you didn't fucking stop me." He tried not to put accusation in his voice, but he knew it was there.

"Savage, you don't even realize what you did, do you? *I* was the one in control the entire time, not you. When I indicated through body language, deliberately, I might add, that the tree was hurting my nipples, you immediately cushioned them with your palms. The backs of your hands are all scraped up from keeping me from hitting the bark when you were fucking me. When I said yellow, you didn't slow down, you stopped. I said yellow because I knew you were at the edge of your control and that when we were home and you were going to have to really let your demons go, I needed to know I could stop what was happening. I needed to know I could control the situation."

Shit, she had known all along that he was losing his mind when he was swinging that switch and decorating her sweet body. His woman. Not too much got by her. She had her fingers covering her mouth now. Brows together in a frown.

"You fucking tested me."

"Do I look stupid to you? Of course I did. That was the closest you were ever going to get to being the real thing without being there. I had to know I could take it and that you would respond if I said stop. What I didn't realize was that even when you're close to being out of control, you still protect me. You do look out for me."

Savage found himself speechless. Seychelle. His angel. She was driving his demons away. "Do you really believe you can love me just the way I am?"

He wished his voice didn't sound so fucking choked up, like some pussy about to cry. He wasn't a man who gave in to emotions like this. He took care of her after shit went down between them. She deserved the care after what he'd dished out to her, not the other way around.

Seychelle didn't answer him for a long time. He reached for her hand and pressed her fingers into his thigh, needing the connection.

"I love you more with every breath I take, Savage. Just like you are. I've never asked you to change. Just grow. I want you to see me the same way I see you. I thought tonight, for the first time, you did. You try to avoid emotions. I'm very emotional. I need to hear those reassurances. I guess you do as well."

Did he? Hell yes, he did. He felt for a long time that Seychelle was just out of his reach. He was always going to think that, because who would ever believe a woman like her could love a man like him? It didn't make sense. He tried to twist it around in his mind and make it fit, but it didn't. Sometimes in the middle of the night, he woke up and just stared at her, trying to comprehend how she was in his life, in his bed, how she could possibly look at him, let alone have genuine feelings for him.

She knew everything about him now. What he was. What he did. His many flaws. He had shown her too soon, without getting her body ready, what kind of sick fuck she was tying herself to, and he'd done it while breaking a promise to her. No matter how much he loved her, no matter how many good things he did for her, there would always be this—his cock hard as fucking steel to see the stripes he put on her body. There was no getting around that. No running from it. No changing it.

Did he believe her that she loved him? That she would stay? He knew she was his angel. She believed she loved him. But how long could a woman face his kind of monster and love him through it? Fuck it. He was going to believe the fairy tale because he had to. He needed her desperately just to breathe.

"All right, baby. Tell me what you want right now."

She caught the handle to the door of the truck, shoving, and pressed a little desperately. "I think the pain pill made me sick, Savage, just like alcohol. I'm going to throw up. I can't get out of the sleeping bag. You're going to have to forget all about sex and help me."

Then his woman was puking her guts out, just as she had

when she'd had a couple of drinks. He was out of the truck and around the hood to pull her out of the cab and help her so she wasn't trapped in the bag. He got her to the side of the road, away from any prying eyes. Eventually, he texted Steele and then Preacher. Preacher texted Hannah Drake Harrington in the hopes of having something to help by the time Savage got Seychelle back to their home.

NINETEEN

"We've got company, baby," Savage said. "A whole slew of company. I'm going to fire up the grill. Looks like they'll be staying for dinner, since they invited themselves right at the dinner hour."

Doris Fendris pushed her way right past Savage and marched out onto the large octagon-shaped deck that was a little more secluded than the front deck. The solid redwood deck with its firepit and carved railing overlooked the ocean, jutting out closer to the ravine and bluffs. Thankfully, there were several chairs, as behind Doris came Inez; Eden Ravard; Marie Darden, another close friend; and even more women.

"Don't worry, Savage, we brought drinks," Doris called out as she bent to kiss Seychelle on the cheek. "Don't get up, dear. Hannah told us you were sick. Something about an allergic reaction to a pain pill. That's so terrible."

"She can't drink worth shit either, Doris," Savage announced. "She's allergic to alcohol as well, so don't offer her a drink, even if she begs. She thinks she can drink one of those ridiculous frou-frou drinks you're always making." He winked at Seychelle, brushed the top of her head with a kiss and gave Doris his stone face.

Doris sputtered, looking outraged. "Frou-frou drinks?" she echoed.

"Is that true, Seychelle?" Eden asked. She laid a hand on Seychelle's wrist. "How awful for you to be allergic to alcohol."

"We don't know for *certain* that I'm allergic to alcohol," Seychelle said. "I've only tried it a couple of times. Both times I was horribly sick. Maybe I just haven't built up a tolerance."

Her phone began to play "Wrong Side of Heaven" by Five Finger Death Punch. She pulled it out of her pocket and glanced down. **You looking to get in trouble at your own party? You are not drinking tonight. Bog, you make me crazy sometimes.**

Seychelle did her best to smother the laughter and sent him a series of laughing emojis interspersed with cocktail glasses.

"I don't make frou-frou drinks, Savage," Doris declared indignantly, following Savage across the deck to the barbecue, where he was pulling off the cover and opening the lid.

"Doris. They're pink. You make pink, girly drinks and you know it. Just own that shit." Savage ran a large wire brush over the grill a few times.

Seychelle's phone vibrated this time because she had the good sense not to let it blare at her every few seconds. There were hand-spanking-the-bare-butt emojis, half a dozen of them running across her screen. She glanced up at him to see him diligently working on the grill. How did he do that?

"Where do you want the side dishes, Savage?" Rebecca Jetspun asked.

"And the plates," Ava Chutney added. The two women had followed Doris and the others onto the deck and were asking Savage as he made his way back into the kitchen.

Seychelle swiveled around in her chair. The slider was

open to the house. Six women were now on her deck. There were eight chairs out. A sideboard had been placed outside already, and Savage was back, carrying out a platter of steak and chicken that he'd clearly marinated ahead of time.

She stared down at her phone and finally sent him a text. **You planned this.**

She couldn't help the way her heart did that little melty thing it did whenever she realized Savage did something completely out of character for him. The women hadn't just shown up. Savage had invited them.

Sometimes, like now, he made her want to cry. For the last two days, packages had arrived from the Floating Hat. Hannah had delivered all sorts of lotions and creams as well as bath products in person the first two days they'd been home, and a variety of organic drinks and powders she had come up with to try to help Seychelle feel better.

Seychelle knew that Savage had consulted with Hannah and Preacher in an effort to ensure she got the best of care. He insisted Steele see her every day. Hannah had sent Sabelia that very morning with various teas, jellies and fresh scones.

Didn't plan it. Doris did. Said one or two of your friends should drop by for dinner. Not a fucking army of crazy women.

She laughed as she watched Inez and Marie put stacks of plates and cups out on the sideboard and return to the kitchen as if they'd been there a hundred times. Anat Gamal and Harriet Meadows followed them out with more food.

You just happened to have enough steak and chicken marinating for eight guests? That's usual for you? Seychelle challenged Savage as she said hello to the newcomers.

Never know when Torpedo Ink is going to drop in. Have to have food on standby.

She stared down at her phone, smiling. He made her happy with his blatant lies. He wanted her close to the women of Torpedo Ink, but he knew she wasn't quite there yet. These women were her go-to posse. She loved them.

She loved to be around them. These women made her happy, and Savage knew it. The Red Hat Society. There were others. He'd probably invited them as well, but they couldn't make it.

I love you even if you are a terrible liar.

"Inez," Savage called out.

"Right here, Savage."

"My fiancée thinks I'm not telling her the truth when I say I didn't plan this event. You, Doris and Anat planned it, didn't you?" He sounded pious.

Inez laughed. "You know better than to try to trap a wily fox like me, Savage. As a matter of record, we did plan the actual party, but only after you called us and asked us to do it."

He groaned and slapped his forehead with his palm. "Making your steak well done for that, Inez. You could have left that last part off."

The ladies burst into laughter along with Seychelle.

"We thought maybe it was her birthday. Or your birthday," Doris said.

"Not her birthday. Don't even know when my fucking birthday is. I don't celebrate it."

A collective gasp went up. "Savage," Rebecca said, her voice, as always, gentle. "You have to celebrate your birthday. Why wouldn't you?"

He pointed to Seychelle. "Look at her. She's a baby. If I get any older, people will say I'm a cradle robber, which I am, but I refuse to let it get any worse."

Again, there was a round of laughter. Seychelle stared down at her phone for a long moment and then sent him several kissing emojis interspersed with old-man-with-a-long-white-beard emojis. She was rewarded when his gaze lifted from the delicious-smelling food on the grill to her and he gave her his little grin, the one that could make her toes curl.

"How many idiot vegetarians are there in this crowd, because tonight, I've got the real deal. I've got mushrooms and

corn on the grill, some squash and zucchini for you. Toma-
toes. Green peppers. Anat made a Greek salad you're going
to love, baby, and Harriet made a Caesar salad with no an-
chovies just in case you don't eat the little fuckers."

"Savage, really? Language," Inez scolded.

"She needs to eat. She never eats enough. I was just teasing her about eating steak. She's a vegetarian, and you gotta
respect that. Rebecca took care of the potato salad, Seychelle. Ava contributed avocado pasta. Eden wanted to
make certain you had enough protein, so she insisted you
have a bean soup. She claims she's famous for it. Doris
brought her garlic sticks. I tried them and have to say they're
especially good."

"She can't possibly eat all that food, Savage," Inez interrupted, laughing.

"Don't let Inez fool you, baby." Savage's voice went a
little softer. It was clear he felt great affection for Inez. "She
brought you her famous spinach lasagna. Marie, not to be
outdone by any of the other Red Hat ladies, decided to show
off her talents by bringing a roasted cauliflower pasta. Has
all kinds of fun stuff in it you'll like. And if that's not
enough, they all brought some kind of dessert for you to try
as well."

Seychelle looked around her at all the women now lounging in the comfortable deck chairs, one of Doris's frou-frou
drinks in their hand, enjoying the night with her. "It all
sounds delicious. I'm so glad everyone came to visit."

Are you leaving? After you grill, are you leaving me alone
with everyone? She texted him, suddenly worried that he had
somewhere he was going.

No, babe, I'm staying close. Just wanted you to have some
fun with your friends. I'm just making sure you know you're
surrounded by people who love you and you have somewhere
to go if you need to. People to talk to if you need to work
things out.

Oh God. She knew what he was telling her. If she needed
to talk about her relationship with Savage to someone out-

side of Torpedo Ink, meaning their sexual relationship, he
was giving her his permission. He was telling her he wanted
her to be comfortable if she needed advice. Or if she wanted
out. Or just needed someone else to lean on. She didn't. She
knew what she was doing. She had her eyes open. There
were no rose-colored glasses. But it was nice to know she
had her Red Hat ladies as her posse should she need them,
because she knew they were formidable.

**Thank you, honey. I've got things worked out just fine, but
this is the most perfect gift you could have ever given me.**

Savage turned from where he was grilling the steaks and
chicken and looked at the woman he loved. Right there in
front of all those women, he gave her everything she deserved. He let her see he loved her. There was no saying it
because he just couldn't, not without being alone with her,
but he could give her this, an open look, stark and raw and
real. Because he meant it. He didn't understand how she
could love him, but he was choosing to believe she really
did. Regardless, he knew his love for her was as real as it
could get.

The evening was full of fun and laughter. He went inside
and left them to it after he saw to it that Seychelle had a
plateful of food and all the ladies had their steaks or chicken
grilled just the way they preferred them.

Seychelle blew Savage a kiss and proceeded to try to eat
everything on her plate, the food was that delicious. Each
dish was amazing. It was quiet for about all of five minutes,
and then the conversation started up again. The women
talked about everything from knitting to quilting and gossip
Inez had heard in the store.

"Did you hear about the murder near Caspar?" Doris
asked. "Everyone's talking about it. The woman lived in Sea
Haven for a while. I think she worked at one of the hotels as
a waitress. You remember, don't you, Marie? She was a
pretty thing, but hard features. Her name was Tawny
Farmer."

Seychelle stilled, a forkful of apricot scone halfway to

her mouth. She put it back on her plate and reached for her phone with shaking hands. She just needed to feel Savage close to her. Tawny was dead, and she'd been left practically on the club's doorstep.

Marie nodded. "I remember her. She actually grew up just outside of Fort Bragg. Always wanted to leave, she said, but kept coming back, even after her mother was long gone."

"She ran with the wrong crowd," Inez said. "There was no stopping her." She shook her head. "There was no talking to that girl."

"Still," Marie said. "She didn't deserve to be murdered and left on the highway like garbage. It was terrible what they did to her. Beaten and strangled."

Doris nodded. "It was grisly. Beaten almost beyond recognition and then strangled."

Seychelle could barely breathe. Her lungs burned. Grateful for the cover of semidarkness, she could only sit very still while her mind tried to process what the women were saying. Someone had killed Tawny and left her close to Torpedo Ink. Had Pierce implicated Alena? Did Savage know and he just hadn't told her?

Did you know that Tawny was murdered and found near Caspar?

"So close to Sea Haven. Practically on our doorstep," Anat said. "There aren't that many miles between Sea Haven and Caspar but so many places to hide a body." She gave a little shiver. "Still, they dumped her right on the highway, where they must have killed her."

Just getting the news now from Czar. He sent out a mass text.

Marie and Doris said she was beaten and strangled. That lets out Alena. The cops would never buy that she could beat and strangle her.

Best not to talk about this on phones, baby.

She hadn't thought about that. She had so much to learn. She wasn't happy that Tawny was dead, but then she hadn't asked very many questions about the woman. She knew that

Tawny had hated Torpedo Ink, that she had some grudge against them all.

"Thankfully, there was a witness. At least, it sounded like the cops did have a lead of some kind," Anat said. "Hopefully, they'll solve the murder very fast."

Inez gave a sniff. "Ha. Don't believe everything you hear, Anat. Witnesses crawl out of the woodwork saying they saw all sorts of things, when they didn't really see anything."

"Do they really?" Rebecca asked. "I would think when it comes to murder, people would be afraid to talk."

Seychelle noticed the women had no trouble eating their dessert, or downing their drinks and getting up to pour themselves more from the pitchers Doris had put out.

"Some are," Inez conceded, "but others want their fifteen minutes of fame any way they can get it."

"We should solve her murder," Eden said. "We could do it. We're all smart. We just need to get the facts and then sit around and figure it out like we do everything else."

Seychelle was instantly alarmed, especially because, instead of the women disagreeing, they were all nodding, as if they thought Eden had had a fantastic idea.

OMG. The Red Hat ladies are going to try to solve the murder.

The talk instantly began to swirl around how they would come up with the clues. Reading reports and writing down every detail, no matter how small, from every source. Several of them knew reporters.

"Inez, you have an in with Jonas and Jackson," Doris pointed out, referring to the sheriff and his deputy. "You could casually bring up the murder and see if they say anything."

Inez sighed, not denying it. "It's true, I do. I'll do my best, but they're both notorious for playing everything close to their chest. Sometimes it's absolutely maddening how closed-mouth they are when I need information."

In spite of everything, Seychelle found herself trying not to laugh at the pure exasperation in Inez's tone and the murmurs of sympathy going around the deck.

Baby, stop worrying so much. Laughing emojis followed. Several of them. Followed by red and purple hats.

Perversely, Seychelle didn't think it was all that funny that the women were locked in on finding a murderer. Especially Eden. She didn't want Eden to go anywhere near the investigation. Savage thought it was funny, but every single one of the women was intelligent. They might get a lot closer than the cops—or the club—thought they could.

The evening wore on with the ladies discussing how they might get clues, some of the suggestions so absurd that Seychelle couldn't help sharing them with Savage.

Now they plan to get Sabelia and Hannah involved, using some spell to temporarily loosen Jackson's tongue so he'll spill everything to Inez.

That had her laughing. The women were laughing. Savage actually came to the slider and stood looking at them all, shaking his head. He had a grin on his face.

They are drunk off their asses. Best idea yet. Want to be there for that.

How are they all going to get home? There isn't a sober one in the bunch. Truthfully, Seychelle was a teensy bit worried about that. None of these women should be driving.

Savage came out onto the deck. His hand drifted up the back of her neck under her hair, fingers finding her scalp in a gentle massage. He tilted her head back so she was looking up at him. "I've got this. Already called Transporter. He's bringing the van. We'll get them home safely. You don't think I'd let anything happen to Sea Haven's finest treasures, do you?" He bent down to kiss her.

◦—

Lunch was late afternoon the following day. Seychelle was looking much better. She hadn't once complained about the marks on her body. It was the effects of the pain pills and how sick she'd gotten from them that worried him the most. She'd been weak afterward and so pale it had scared him.

He'd never seen anyone so violently ill. She'd thrown up

until there was nothing more, and then the retching continued as if her body had more to dispel but just couldn't. She eventually needed fluids, and Steele had given them to her. All over the pain pills.

Savage hadn't cared if Hannah saw marks on Seychelle's body; he just wanted her better. She hadn't, but it wouldn't have mattered to him. Only that she was better. Now, he watched over her very carefully. He wanted her eating, drinking and resting, the way Steele had said she should. He was very mindful of the advice Libby Drake had given him, to take care of his woman if he wanted her to stay alive.

Seychelle kept telling him she was doing so much better and he didn't have to hover, but he just ignored her and followed Steele's regimen to the letter. Sitting across from her off the little deck where he'd held the party for her with the Red Hat ladies, the alarm on his phone went off.

Savage glanced up from the alarm to his woman. He pushed the remote on his phone to allow the gates to swing open.

"Seychelle, the cops are here. No matter what happens, you don't say a word to them. I've texted Absinthe, and he's on his way. This is a club matter. We don't talk to cops. They might threaten us, but we keep our mouths shut."

Seychelle nodded. "Czar was very clear on the rules."

"If things go south and I'm arrested, or you are, or we both are, and you're offered a deal of some kind, there are no deals. Do you understand? Not to save me. Trust Absinthe to do his job." Savage issued the command as they walked together toward the living room.

"Why would either of us be arrested, Savage?"

"I honestly have no idea, baby, but it could happen. Pierce was going to manufacture evidence against Alena. He could have just as easily manufactured evidence against me—or you. Although that seems rather ludicrous. Just stay quiet as much as possible and let them talk. We want to stall, appear cooperative, and let Absinthe get here." He looked her over quickly as the doorbell chimed. "You good with this? Can you handle this?"

Seychelle lifted her chin at him, her blue gaze steady. "I'm with you."

He went to the front door, taking his time, Seychelle one step behind, her fingers in his back pocket. Those fingers were as steady as her eyes had been. Savage nodded to the two men standing on his front porch. "Gentlemen. To what do we owe this pleasure?"

"Savage." Jonas Harrington, the local sheriff, and Jackson Deveau, the sheriff's deputy, greeted him. Jonas's gaze shifted to Seychelle. He smiled at her. "Seychelle. Nice to see you. It's been a while."

"It has. How's everything going?"

"Good. We need to talk to Savage about a matter that's come up."

Savage raised an eyebrow. "You need to speak to *me*?" He sighed and glanced back at Seychelle as if to say he'd told her so. "Since I haven't done a damn thing lately, I can't imagine why, but you may as well come in." He stepped back and allowed the two men into his home.

Jonas took in the high ceilings and walls of glass with the floor-to-ceiling stone fireplace. "Nice place, Savage."

Savage waved the two men toward the sofas. "Thanks. It suits us." He threaded his fingers through Seychelle's and took the sofa opposite Jonas. "May as well sit instead of slinking around, Jackson. You're not going to find any contraband."

Jackson lifted an eyebrow, remaining silent, but he stopped moving around the room and looking through the glass at the views from every direction. He came back to drop into one of the chairs at an angle where he could easily see their faces and cover the door at the same time. Jackson was known for not taking any chances.

"It might be best if we talk to you alone, Savage," Jonas suggested. He did look uneasy, as if whatever he needed to speak with Savage about, he might not want Seychelle to hear.

"That isn't necessary. My woman can stay. I don't have secrets from her."

Jonas sighed and shook his head. He looked at Seychelle apologetically. "I'm just going to get right to it, then, Savage. I have to read you your rights before we go any further." He proceeded to do so. There was a small silence after he did. Jonas asked the standard question. "Did you understand your rights, and do you wish to have an attorney present during questioning?"

"What's this about?" Seychelle asked before Savage could answer. "Jonas? Are you arresting Savage for something? What do you think he's done?"

Savage remained silent. He brought her knuckles to the warmth of his mouth, his mind quickly running through the possibilities. Had the bodies been found in the RV they'd used to interrogate the hit men? If so, had they left any evidence behind that any member of Torpedo Ink had been involved? Had anyone recognized the burned-out RV or the incinerated bodies? They'd burned them down to ash before the RV had gone over a steep ravine. They'd chosen that specific ravine ahead of time because it was difficult to see from any direction and the likelihood of discovery for a few years would be extremely low.

Thankfully, he heard the roar of pipes, two bikes coming fast. He sat back on the sofa. "I believe that would be Absinthe now. We can just wait for him, as I have no idea where the hell you're going with this."

Absinthe and Czar entered without knocking. They sauntered in, nodding to the two men. Absinthe had a briefcase with him. He immediately sat down facing Jonas. "What can we do for you, Sheriff?"

"I've read Savage his rights," Jonas explained. "Are you willing to answer questions, Savage?"

"As long as Absinthe is agreeable."

"How well did you know Tawny Farmer?" Jonas asked. He purposely avoided Seychelle's gaze, uncomfortable with her in the room.

Savage's thumb slid across the back of Seychelle's hand very gently. "Tawny was a patch chaser, hung around the club for a while. I fucked her mouth a couple of times, but we didn't exactly hang out or talk. I'm not the kind of man who had a lot of conversation with women I used that way, as a rule. So I knew her, but not very well."

"Were you seeing her recently?"

"Seeing her? Seeing her how?" Savage sounded genuinely puzzled. He looked at Absinthe as if for guidance. "I don't know what you mean, Jonas. Seeing her how? You'll have to be more specific. And recently as in how recently?"

"Were you having sex with her recently?" Jonas asked bluntly.

"Hell no. I'm engaged. I'm with Seychelle."

"You were on a run recently. Did you have sex with her then? *Sex* is covering oral as well as penetrating her."

Savage was starting to get pissed. "Did you not hear what I said? I *never* penetrated her. I fucked her mouth a hell of a long time ago. Certainly not on the run. I had no interest in having sex with her. Or having her blow me, if that's your next fucking question. I'm in love with my fiancée and don't want any other fucking woman to touch me."

"Savage," Absinthe said quietly. "Jonas is just doing his job."

"Seychelle was with me on the run," Savage bit out between clenched teeth. "She was with me Saturday night when we fucked liked rabbits. She was with me when we drove home in the truck Sunday morning, leaving the campground around three A.M. because she was so damn sick, she couldn't stop puking. And she's been with me this entire time, right here in this house, ever since."

"You drove home in the truck Sunday at three o'clock in the morning because she was sick?" Jonas echoed. "Why was she sick?"

"I don't know, Jonas, why do people get sick?" Savage snapped.

"I can't drink alcohol or take most kinds of pain relievers; I'm allergic," Seychelle supplied. "I was pretty sick."

Jonas flicked his gaze toward Jackson, and Savage wanted

to tear his head off his shoulders. He knew Jonas was confirming that Seychelle told the truth. The club would have done the same thing, asking Absinthe, but it still angered him that Jonas didn't believe Seychelle. Jackson was Jonas's lie detector, just as Absinthe was Torpedo Ink's.

"How did you get your bike home?" Jonas asked.

"Mechanic or Transporter drove it home." Savage turned to Seychelle just to give himself a little breathing room. "Which reminds me, babe, I still haven't picked up my bike. I'll have to get on that."

"Your statement is you drove home Sunday at three o'clock in the morning in the truck with Seychelle and you were here in this house all day Sunday."

"That's correct."

Jonas sighed. "Girlfriends and fiancées don't make the best alibis."

"Oh my God, he thinks you were the one to murder that woman Tawny Farmer," Seychelle said. "Doris and Inez told me about the murder when they came over for dinner last night. Jonas, he really was with me."

Jonas glanced at Jackson, who nodded almost imperceptibly. The sheriff still shook his head. "She isn't going to be a credible witness, Absinthe. You know that."

"When did this murder actually take place?" Absinthe asked.

"She was killed on Sunday," Jonas answered.

"Seychelle isn't my only witness, Jonas," Savage said. "I have one I doubt you'll question. Go ask your wife. She was here talking to me in person."

"Hannah? Why would Hannah be here?"

"I told you, Seychelle was very sick. Hannah came to help. She was here for quite a while both Sunday and Monday. Sent Sabelia here Tuesday."

"Why would you think Savage had anything to do with Tawny Farmer's murder?" Absinthe asked.

"Call-in witness said they saw him arguing with her on the side of the rode. She'd been on his bike and they stopped, and he got physical with her. That was the last they saw. Described Savage perfectly and his bike. Described the exact place we found the body."

"Tracks of a bike?" Czar asked. "Just out of curiosity."

"Could be why we're sitting here instead of in an office somewhere. Car tracks on the side of the road."

"You think she was killed somewhere else?" Czar guessed shrewdly. "And dumped close to Caspar in order to implicate Savage?"

"You know I can't answer that," Jonas said. "But you got enemies, Savage, and I'd watch your back." He stood up. "The word is, Tawny was a government informant. But then word had it she ran with the Diamondbacks. She supposedly ran with the Venomous club. If she was playing the clubs, and informing on them both, she wasn't going to live a very long life, and her handler had to know that." He sighed again. "I hope you're feeling better, Seychelle."

Savage waited until their vehicle had driven off before he was up and pacing across the floor. The rage in the room was alive and growing with every step. Czar was right there with him. Even Absinthe wasn't far behind in his anger.

"Those fuckers," Czar all but snarled. "Pierce didn't throw the blame on Alena. He put it on you, Savage. After all we did for Plank, that little fucker still went ahead with his plan. We showed him loyalty, worked our asses off and he didn't call it off. I should have let those hit men slip past us and cut his throat."

"Unbelievable," Absinthe said. "We had so many damn bodies stacked up. We gave him his answers. Made certain he knew he was safe and his crew was safe. Seychelle made certain the women were, at great cost to herself. And he pulls this shit. He has that punk enforcer who can't keep his dick in his pants kill Tawny and blame Savage. We can't let him get away with this shit, Czar."

Savage was seething. "There's a possibility that fucking Pierce did this without Plank's consent. He knows we're going to come after him. He hurt Alena, and he's going to pay for it. He can pretend to try to save her all he wants to, but he was banging Tawny and every other bitch he could when she wasn't around. He disrespected her by passing on that video to Plank and sharing it with his brothers. He didn't even try to protect her. Their relationship from the beginning was all about him. This setup stinks of him."

"Did you hear what he said?" Czar asked. "Tawny was informing on the clubs to the Feds. I don't think there was a mysterious Russian woman behind her informing. I think she did that all on her own. She liked to play her games. The Feds were there on the weekend, looking to talk to the members of the clubs that were willing to sell their clubs out. Of course, the members had no idea what they were really doing. They were under the influence of the Russian woman. Tawny was playing her own game."

"As if we don't have enough trouble with the Ghosts after us," Absinthe said.

"The Russian woman is definitely connected to the Ghosts," Savage affirmed, looking to Seychelle for confirmation. She had drawn up her knees and wrapped her arms around them and was resting her chin on top, her eyes following his every move. He was aware, instantly, that he had been doing what he always did, automatically draining off the anger from the other two men, just like an eager PAC-MAN, gobbling it up, storing it like a dragon in his secret vault. He cursed under his breath. There was no condemnation in her eyes, only that quiet acceptance she often got, as if she knew the one night they'd shared was nothing compared to what he would need after this.

"Tawny was not connected to the Ghosts or to the Russian woman. She was running her own game with the clubs and the Feds," Czar said.

"And Brandon," Seychelle murmured softly.

Savage's head went up alertly. "What did you say, baby?"

Czar and Absinthe turned toward her.

She looked uncomfortable, rubbing her chin back and forth on top of her knees. Her eyes met Savage's. "Tawny was very involved with Brandon. If she was pitting the Venomous club against the Diamondbacks for him, and I'm fairly certain she was, but she was also informing on both clubs to the Feds, then I doubt that Brandon knew that. If he found out, he would be really angry with her."

"Go on," Savage encouraged.

She hesitated again, no doubt feeling the level of anger the three men had toward Pierce. "It's just that Brandon had a very intricate revenge plan. He was in it for the long haul. It wasn't about involving law enforcement. He wanted to be a part of a club. His ultimate goal would be to take over a club, rise to the top. He uses women for his purposes. It would amuse him to see the clubs torn apart by these women gossiping and whispering conspiracy theories to their men. He wanted the Venomous club to eat away at the Diamondbacks until they started a war."

"The hit men, what about them?"

"The women were his, a fun little idea to stir the pot and see if he could pull it off. Can you imagine, on a run, if the women in a club started off giving their men blow jobs and ended up murdering them? This run was his ultimate revenge, where it all was supposed to come together. He'd arranged it all. The women were his perfect diversion. They give blow jobs and kill, and while everyone is looking at them, the real hit men go after the presidents of the clubs and their closest men. That's checkmate for Brandon. He didn't care about Torpedo Ink, other than Savage. Tawny did. Every person named was someone she had a grudge against. He was nowhere near the run, so he couldn't in any way be implicated."

Czar leaned against the back of the sofa, regarding Seychelle with his silvery, piercing eyes. "You fucked it up for him, Seychelle. You quietly stopped those women by removing the suggestion Brandon planted."

She nodded. "Even the president of the Venomous club brought his women to me Saturday and asked me to check them. I think Plank talked to him, or the women talked to each other. In any case, Torpedo Ink stopped his hit men. Brandon had to be furious that he put out all that money and nothing came of it. Not one single thing."

"Why didn't I think of all this?" Czar asked.

"Because all of you despise Pierce and you want to blame him. I think you're just looking for an excuse to go after him," Seychelle said.

"Honey, that was a rhetorical question," Czar said. "And we already have our excuse, although you're right. We went off half-cocked. I should have thought it all the way through."

Seychelle rubbed her chin along her knees again, and this time she bit at the end of her sleeve, one of her nervous habits. Savage moved close to her, leaning his hip against the sofa.

"Do you think Brandon was acting alone?" Absinthe asked.

Again, Seychelle hesitated and looked up at Savage as if for guidance. He sent her a small, encouraging nod. She moistened her lips and shrugged. "I wouldn't know."

Absinthe's head jerked up, and his eyes met Savage's, a dark frown on his face. Savage pulled out his phone and texted one-handed.

Not a good idea to lie with Absinthe in the room, baby. Tell the fuckin' truth.

At once, color heightened her high cheekbones as she read his text message. She didn't look at him or the other two men. Her fingers gripped her legs until her knuckles turned white.

"Seychelle." Savage crouched down in front of her. His voice was very gentle. "You had a lot to say here that was valuable. What don't you want to say? Do you think we aren't going to listen?"

Her small white teeth sank into her lower lip, and she raised her eyes to his. There were tears in her eyes. "I think you will listen, Savage. I think all of you are going to listen to me, and maybe that isn't such a good thing. I could be wrong."

"But you aren't wrong, are you, baby?" Savage coaxed the truth out of her. He used the pad of his thumb to erase the tears escaping down her cheek. "Tell us. Brandon isn't quite as smart as we all give him credit for, is he? He didn't think his revenge plan up. Someone helped him. Who was it? Not Tawny. Who was the real brains behind Brandon's carefully thought-out revenge on his half brothers?"

"Brandon is a half brother. They share the same father, don't they, Seychelle?" Czar said. "That's why they have the same eyes. Lion, Shark and Brandon all have those eyes."

"Eden and Brandon's mother are sisters," Seychelle whispered. "Their father, Reggie, was with Brandon's mother, Nina, first. He got Nina pregnant when she was just out of high school. Eden said it was a terrible scandal. Her sister left the baby with Reggie and skipped town. Nina wanted to be an actress. The last thing she said she wanted was a child. Eden was younger by quite a few years, but she felt responsible and did what she could to watch the baby when she wasn't in school so Reggie could work. They ended up falling in love and getting married. When Brandon was five, Nina came back and demanded they give Brandon to her. She would leave on and off, just take off in the middle of the night, and Reggie would have to go get Brandon, but Nina poisoned him against them. She drank a lot at that time."

"So Nina is the mastermind behind Brandon's revenge on his half brothers," Czar said.

Seychelle nodded slowly. "I spent all day Saturday undoing Brandon's suggestions on I don't know how many women. I began to hear her voice. It was subtle at first, but then I could hear her quite clearly. I know it will break Eden's heart if she ever finds out. These past few years, they've grown closer. She thought because Nina had quit drinking, she recognized how important family was and wanted their relationship as much as Eden did. She talked like she did and had begun to do a few things with Eden."

"What else do you know or suspect, Seychelle?" Savage pushed.

She looked up at him and then back down at her hands. "I think Nina knew Tawny's family. Her mother at least. Eden said Nina drank a lot. Tawny's mother drank a lot. If Tawny knew Brandon and Nina, she would most likely go to them whenever she needed anything. She'd do whatever Nina or Brandon asked of her."

"Where did they get the money to pay to have all those people they wanted killed?" Absinthe asked.

"That's something I really don't know. Nina could have a sugar daddy, for all I know. She may have saved money. Brandon works, and he controls women. We saw it with Sahara. He may have gotten women to sign over bank accounts, who knows? I just know that before you decide someone is guilty, you need to look at this from every angle."

"She's right," Czar said.

"And if Brandon is the one who called in the tip to the cops that Savage was the one who had an argument with Tawny on the side of the road, we have to stay away from him," Absinthe advised. "Let's back off and see what Plank has to say about all this. If the other clubs don't handle him, we can always arrange an accident later."

Savage didn't like later when now would do, but he could live with it.

TWENTY

Savage and Seychelle spent yet another entire day lounging in the house. Savage didn't want Seychelle to do much of anything but heal. An entire week had gone by since the run, and there wasn't a mark left on her body but that one faint stripe across her bottom—and it was faint. While the stripes were fresh, he'd used the time to make love to her as often as possible. He hadn't had to get rough. He could be playful or loving; he could take his time, treat her the way she deserved. He wanted her to have everything good he could possibly give her, because she was going to have as bad as it could get very soon. She would need this to hold on to in order to get her through.

After he fed her dinner, she wanted to go to her cottage in Sea Haven. They hadn't been there since they'd returned, and she wanted to spend the night there. He found he did as well. He liked that bed of hers and the way they were able to talk so openly together. There was just something about the intimacy of the way they could lie together and play their question game that he loved. She did too. It never felt like prying when they were in her bed.

Savage thought it was because the room was small and

held an intimate warmth. She made him feel cherished and accepted when she put her hands on him, massaging his scalp and neck with unexpectedly strong fingers. She always surprised him with her thoughtful answers to his admittedly provoking questions. Yeah, he loved that room. It was their room. He'd fallen in love with her in that room.

"You just want to go to the Floating Hat for tea in the morning," he accused, because he wasn't going to sound like he was all choked up thinking of that room and lying on the bed with her, falling hard for her.

Seychelle laughed. "That could be true. Actually, before we left, I stashed some tea there from the Floating Hat. I wouldn't mind going for breakfast if you'd like though. The scones are so good, aren't they?"

Joy radiated through him. She did that to him. That laugh of hers. The way her smile lit her face, changed the color of her eyes to that particular shade of blue that got him in the gut every time. "They are, baby, but just sittin' across from you anywhere does it for me."

Her smile got even brighter. Turned mischievous. "I've been saving up questions, Savage. I think this time, I'm going to have you on your toes."

He drove one-handed, reaching for her hand, capturing it and pressing her palm tightly against his upper thigh. "You always have me on my toes, angel. Love our little cottage. Lookin' forward to your questions."

She gave him a pretend frown. "That never bodes well for me. You come up with the *worst* questions."

He threw back his head and laughed, bringing her fingertips to his mouth. "You love my questions."

"I do not. They're always about sex. Or something equally difficult for me to answer."

"You never have trouble answering. You just don't always want to tell me your fantasies. I don't mind telling you mine."

"Yes, we're going to make new rules about those questions," she declared.

He laughed again. Real, genuine laughter. "I don't think so. We get to find out so much about one another. Don't be such a little coward, baby."

She laughed at him. "You wish I was a coward. I somehow manage to best your ridiculous questions. When I do, you retaliate and start getting all twisted."

"Babe. Seriously?" He put the truck in park in front of the cottage and turned off the engine. "I am twisted. You already know that."

Her eyes went soft as she took off her seat belt, leaned into him and cupped the side of his jaw with her palm. Her thumb brushed along his bristles. "I love you, Savin Savage Pajari. I always will. That twisted part of you is what matches the twisted in me."

He shook his head and leaned in even closer to steal a brief kiss, his heart reacting with that strange squeezing like a vise that always felt like maybe he was having a heart attack. "There's not one fucking thing twisted in you, Seychelle. Not one."

"You know there is, and I'm happy there is. I fought it before, because I thought it meant there was something wrong with me. I realized it didn't mean that at all. It meant I like our sex a little different than other people like theirs. That's okay. I'm not as wild as you are, but that's okay too. We don't have to go there every time. You're satisfied with some of the time, and I can give that to you because I love you that much."

"That's your takeaway from what happened when I lost control on the run?" Now his stomach knotted up. "Because that wasn't losing control. Baby." He could feel himself start to sweat. "When it happens, I don't want to lose you because you think it's going to be like that."

"That's not what I think. I'm telling you what I learned about me, not you." Her voice was very gentle. Those blue eyes never wavered but held his gaze steady. "I know you don't think I could really love you as you are, Savage. You had that drilled into you, and somewhere, as a child, you began to believe it." Both hands went to frame his face. She knelt up on the seat of the truck. "I would walk through hell to find you if you were lost. I would walk through hell with you. You don't have to believe me now. Actions have always spoken louder than words. You listened to me when I told you I needed emotional support. I realized you need the same thing. I'll be giving you that every day the way you give it to me."

He caught her by the nape of the neck and dragged her to him. Kissing Seychelle was being caught in the catastrophic eruption of a volcano. They both detonated, an explosion of fireworks. That red-hot lava moving through his veins in a rush of heat and fire and adrenaline was as addicting as her laughter and sweetness. Kissing Seychelle was drowning in love.

When they came up for air, he pressed his forehead against hers. "I fucking love you so much, Seychelle. If you keep saying things like that to me, you're going to turn me into a pussy, and I'm the one the club counts on to scare the crap out of people. It's best not to give me that when we're around other people."

She leaned into him, and he felt the velvet flame of her tongue along his bottom lip. "Like the Red Hat ladies?"

He groaned. "*Especially* the Red Hat ladies. Those women are a menace."

Seychelle's laughter was more like a giggle, and he shook his head. His phone rang, the tune tipping him off that it was Czar calling. "Gotta take this, babe. You go on into the house and I'll be right behind you."

Still laughing, Seychelle slipped out of the truck. He did too, and rounded the hood, so he could lean against the passenger door to watch his woman saunter up the cobblestone walkway to the cottage door. Today she was in leggings and a long shirt that covered the curve of her ass, but there was no stopping that feminine sway she had. She had her hair down. It fell in wild waves down her back, that honeyed, gold-and-platinum hair that was like silk to the touch. The wind caught at her hair and playfully ruffled all that silk, making him wish he had his fingers buried deep in it. He still couldn't believe she was his.

She stopped just inside the door and stood there as if she were frozen. She didn't turn to look at him, but she didn't move forward or close the door. She just stood there, her entire body stiff. Something was wrong, and he ended the call abruptly, not even warning Czar, just sprinting along the walkway, pulling his weapon, his heart in his throat, pounding out of control.

He came up behind his woman, looking over her shoulder, and took in the sight of her destroyed home. Everything was smashed. Everything that could be gotten to. Pictures on the wall had been torn off. Drawers had been pulled out, items dumped onto the floor and the drawers broken until they were nothing but splinters. The table and chairs had been destroyed with what could only have been a sledgehammer. Every kitchen pot and pan had been drilled through, so they had holes in them. Dishes were shattered and in pieces on the floor.

This was done out of pure hatred. The walls practically breathed hatred. It was impossible not to feel it. Savage wanted to shelter her in his arms, drag her out of there, but she was already moving to the bedroom, picking her way through the rubble, glassware crunching beneath her boots.

"Baby, wait. Let me." He tried to caution her. He knew what she was looking for. He knew the moment she saw it. Her parents' remains—their ashes. The beautiful, handblown entwined-roses sculpture smashed on the floor by some contemptible, disgusting human being.

Seychelle crouched down beside the shattered glass, her fingers pressed tightly over her mouth as she slowly looked up at him. The sorrow on her face tore his heart out.

"Don't move, angel. We're going to collect all those pieces of glass. Every last one of them." The sculpture had been shattered against the dresser, and fortunately, there hadn't been any other glass for the intruder to break there in that particular space. Savage found a bag to put the pieces in and began gathering each one off the floor.

Seychelle helped him, but her movements were jerky. More automatic than as if she knew what she was doing. "This can't be glued back together. It has to be in a million pieces, Savage. Some of them are so small I can't even tell which rose they went to."

"Just keep picking up the pieces, baby," he said gently.

"They could have taken every single thing in this house and I wouldn't have cared if they just left me this." She pushed her hands through her hair. "I should have taken it over to your house. I almost did. It has better security. Why was I so resistant? I just should have moved all the way in."

"This is our house, Seychelle," he corrected. "We have both houses. This isn't either of our faults. Who knew a crazy person would do this? Do you have a small handheld vacuum?"

"In the garage, hanging up. If they didn't smash that too."

"Go get it for me," Savage said. He took out his phone and texted Casimir as he watched Seychelle pick her way carefully back through the mess toward the front door.

Casimir was married to Lissa, who was a famous glass-blower. He had no idea if she could do anything at all with what was left of the glass that had the ashes of Seychelle's parents embedded in it, but he couldn't think of any other solution. He took several pictures of the shattered glass and sent them to Casimir's phone to show Lissa.

While he waited for Casimir to confer with his wife, he went into the bathroom to see what damage had been done there. Like every other room, this one had been destroyed as well—the mirrors, the toilet, even the bathtub and shower had been cracked.

Savage pulled up the security cameras. At the back door was a clear shot of Shari using a crowbar to pry open the door. She systematically used a sledgehammer and drill to destroy every room. She came as soon as they had left for the run and returned Saturday and Sunday. She was lucky no one had thought to check on Seychelle's home. He didn't want Seychelle to see the feed, although he sent copies to the other Torpedo Ink members. He didn't want her to call the cops either. Torpedo Ink would handle this on their own.

He proceeded to take as many pictures of the kitchen as he could before Seychelle returned with a small vacuum. He cleaned the basket thoroughly, making certain there wasn't a speck of dirt in it before he used the vacuum to get the last little pieces of glass up from the floor. He put them in with the larger ones in the bag to take to Lissa.

"Did they destroy the garage too?"

"No, it was fine. I don't think they even went into it. But I looked in the closets and drawers, Savage. All my clothes are cut up. Everything."

"We can replace clothes, Seychelle," he said gently and took more pictures of the rooms, showing the state in which Shari had left Seychelle's home. Finally, when he was certain he had enough photos, he picked up the bag containing the remains of Seychelle's parents' ashes and urged her toward the door.

"Come on, angel, let's go. You don't need to be here. I'll get cleaners to come in and take care of this."

"I should do something, Savage." She looked up at him again, but she wasn't really seeing him.

He swept his arm around her and walked her to the truck. "There isn't anything for you to do, Seychelle. We have what's most important to you. The boys are here, and they'll seal everything up tight."

"I don't think that's really necessary. There isn't much left for anyone to destroy."

He opened the door to the truck. "Get in, baby. You're in shock. I think we need some of Hannah's special tea."

"I just want to go home and lay down."

"One stop, then, I promise." He shut the door and walked around the bed of the truck, where Reaper and Maestro waited.

"Where the fuck is that bitch?" Reaper demanded in a

low voice. "You can't go near her, Savage. I'll take care of it."

"This one's mine," Maestro declared. "You have Anya to worry about."

Savage glanced down at his phone. "Code said she checked out of her hotel."

The sound of motorcycles had them turning their heads. Czar and Keys stopped beside them. Czar raised an eyebrow when he saw Reaper and Maestro huddled next to Savage.

"We do this the way we've always done things. It's a job. We do the job," Czar said. "Code is already getting us information. No one is going off half-cocked. You understand? We'll bring this to the table."

As much as Savage didn't want him to be, Czar was right. This was a relatively easy job. They couldn't come at it from an emotional standpoint. This had to be impersonal, like every other job they did. That was what had kept them from ever getting caught. They were meticulous about getting information and carrying out an assignment. They let time go by.

"We're all pissed at ourselves and for a damn good reason. We didn't treat Seychelle right on that fucking run," Czar said. "None of us were thinking straight then, but we'd better be now. She's one of ours, and she's taking a lot of hits all at once. Anything we can do, Savage, let us know."

"Her cottage is a fucking mess. Thought maybe we can get a couple of dumpsters. Get the word out that the brothers are doing a remodel so if any of her lady friends see the mess they won't be wondering what happened. The entire place needs to be cleaned out. You'll have to shovel that shit out of there. Shari did a hell of a job on the place. Anything of Seychelle's that can be salvaged, do, but I don't think there's much. I'm heading over to Casimir and Lissa's. Sent Lissa a picture of a sculpture Seychelle had that held her parents' ashes. It was smashed. We gathered the pieces. Lissa is going to see if she can do anything with it."

Czar swore under his breath. "She smashed the sculpture with her parents' ashes?"

Savage nodded and glanced into the back window of the truck. Seychelle wasn't looking back at him, and she hadn't texted him. Her head was on the backrest, and she stared straight ahead. He fucking hated that.

"We'll start on it, as soon as we can get organized," Maestro promised.

"She looks so damn lost, Czar," Savage said.

"I'm sorry, Savage. I know this has been a nightmare for her." He studied Savage's face. His eyes. "With more to come. You want someone with you?"

Savage understood what Czar was referring to. His president knew Savage was close to the end of his cycle. This was going to tip him over the edge. The last thing his woman needed was his monster coming at her on top of everything else and him losing all control. "I do. She doesn't. She says she can handle it if it's just the two of us. Not if someone is a witness."

"I get that," Czar said. "Can you handle it?"

"Yes. We're strong together. But then it scares the shit out of me. If I make a mistake, just one, I know I couldn't live with it. She says it won't happen. She believes in me that much."

"Do you believe in you?" Czar asked.

Savage was silent for a long time, weighing his answer. "I believe in the two of us. I love her more than I ever knew it was possible to love someone. If she says *stop*, I will hear her and stop."

Czar nodded. "There's your answer. Plank wants an informal meet, was hoping to drop by the bar tomorrow night. Given what's going on here, you can skip this one if your woman needs you home with her."

Savage didn't want to skip it. "We'll see how things go. If it's informal, she may want a night out. She likes singing with the band. I'll let her know what's going on and ask her what she wants to do." He was firm about that. There was no reason not to let Seychelle know Plank would show up with a few other Diamondbacks. She would know it was to talk.

Czar nodded. "Get out of here. The brothers will fix the door and lock it up tight until we can get the rebuilding underway."

"Thanks."

Savage slid behind the wheel of the truck, once more grateful that he hadn't yet retrieved his Harley. He'd asked Mechanic to go through it for him since it was already at the shop and make certain it was in perfect running condition. Once he was on the highway and moving in the direction of the large farm Czar and Blythe shared with several others, including Casimir and Lissa, he reached over and took Seychelle's hand.

"I'm sorry about the cottage, baby." He kissed her fingertips. "The boys promised they'll fix it up as good as new. I know you love your house. I do too, as it turns out. We talk better there. I have a good memory for the exact position you like the bed so the moon can come through the window perfectly. I swear I'll have it ready for you fast."

She turned her head to look at him, her blue eyes moving over his face. He couldn't look at her when he was driving on the road, not when it was right along the oceanfront, but he felt that intense scrutiny. Her fingers curled in his.

"I know you will, Savage." Her voice was soft. Loving. "Thank you for being with me. It was really nice that some of the brothers showed up."

"They're all going to help, Seychelle. They'll get your house put back together, although I'm going to practice saying *our* house. We do need to get married."

She gave him a faint smile. "Why? Are you pregnant? You really should tell me these things, Savage."

"Very funny, angel. No, I just would like to get it done." He made the turn onto the farm property, driving through the open gates.

He didn't want to tell her he wanted her married to him before the rage overflowed and the sadistic monster got loose. He knew he would never believe she loved him again. His insecurities would get the better of him. How could they not when he let go of his control? He gripped the steering wheel tighter with one hand while carefully holding her gently with the other.

"Get it done?" she repeated softly.

There was the tiniest thread of amusement in her voice, although she still sounded desolate overall. He was grateful he could interject even just that little bit of humor into her.

"As in get married? That's how you view our getting married? Getting it done? That's a very interesting way to put it. And it isn't the first time you've said it like that. You aren't exactly a white-dress-and-veil-in-the-church-with-a-thousand-witnesses-watching kind of guy, are you?"

The house was on top of a small hill surrounded by tall, beautiful redwood trees, the trees a good forty or fifty feet from the house, a perfect spot for defense. The clearing in between was planted with low-lying shrubs, ground cover and colorful flowers, so no one was going to sneak up on the occupants easily. Beautiful metal structures turned with the wind, adorning the yard closer to the house. The sculptures created movement, flowing with breathtaking colors in the moonlight, giving visitors the idea that this was the home of an artist. Savage looked with different eyes. He believed each of those sculptures hid something much more lethal. He noted all the cameras and motion detectors that were in plain sight and knew it was the ones no one could see that visitors—or enemies—should worry about.

Two stories, the house appeared to be built like something out of a storybook, with its wraparound porch and many gables. He drove up the long drive leading to Casimir's home. As they approached the house, they could see the beautiful art sculptures closer. Because it was night, the lights on the spinning blades spun dazzling colors into shapes and patterns that were sideways rather than upward.

"You knew I wasn't a hearts-and-flowers kind of guy, baby," Savage reminded her, parking the truck. He passed the pad of his thumb over the ring on her finger as he took

in their surroundings, judging how safe it was to allow his
lady out of the truck.

Because Casimir wasn't one of the original eighteen Torpedo Ink members, he tended to dismiss the lethal side of
the man—and his woman. Now, seeing their setup, he realized that was a big mistake. Casimir was a fully patched
member of Torpedo Ink. A brother. But he wasn't one of the
original eighteen charter members, and Savage didn't know
him all that well yet. He was Czar's birth brother, and he'd
attended one of the four schools in Russia. None of the
schools had been easy. Casimir had trained as an assassin,
and he'd served their country. With Lissa, Casimir had been
the one to free all of them by killing Sorbacov and his son.
Every single one of them owed Casimir and Lissa a debt that
could never be repaid.

"Actually, honey, that's exactly what you are. You are a
hearts-and-flowers kind of guy, very romantic at heart. I
count on that."

She could slay him with just that look she gave him and
a few soft words. He kissed her fingers, her knuckles and
that sacred ring, making up his mind. Casimir was a brother.
He was Torpedo Ink and Czar's birth brother. It was time
Savage learned to trust him. "Come on, babe."

She looked around her. "Where are we? It's late. We can't
just visit people this late at night, Savage."

"I texted them we were coming to see them." He slid out
of the truck before she could protest and went around to
open her door.

Savage kept Seychelle tight under the protection of his
shoulder. He had never been big on asking favors of others,
yet it seemed he was learning he could do so for Seychelle.
He only hoped Casimir's woman could come through for
him. He knew the chances were slim. Fucking Shari had
shattered the roses. There were some larger pieces, but most
were small, and a few pieces were powder. Still, Lissa was
a talented glassblower.

Savage didn't even know the proper protocol for asking for something like this—a favor. A huge favor. That didn't matter. Only getting his woman what she needed mattered. He'd texted that they were coming along with the pictures of the original sculpture and what was left of it. Lissa had said she thought she might be able to do something. It wouldn't be exactly like the original, but she could preserve the ashes in a sculpture. Casimir had texted immediately back that they would be expecting them.

Savage glanced at his watch as they went up the stairs onto the porch. He hadn't paid attention to the lateness of the hour. He probably should have.

"You okay, baby?"

"I don't know why we're here, Savage," Seychelle whispered, looking up at him. She looked vulnerable.

He leaned down and gently kissed her because he couldn't bear that look on her face. His thumb slid over her lips as if he could erase it. "Baby, we're going to fix this. I know you're upset, but we'll make it right. Trust me on this." He had no idea if Lissa was really that much of a miracle worker, but he wanted her to be. This one was too important.

He knocked on the door, shifting his body slightly to put Seychelle away from the opening, where he could protect her even better. Casimir opened the door immediately. The porch light had been blazing, as had the lights along the path leading up the walkway through the artwork in the front yard.

"Savage. Good to see you, brother," Casimir greeted. "You both all right?" His piercing eyes, so like his brothers', swept over both of them with concern.

Savage noted he was armed. He'd stated it was an emergency in his text, but he would have expected a fellow Torpedo Ink member to be armed at home anyway.

"Yes, we're fine. You've met Seychelle. We've had an incident, and I was hoping Lissa could help us. It's important, or I wouldn't ask." He hadn't needed to add that. It was a given. This was probably shocking both Casimir and Lissa that he had come to them.

He didn't see Lissa, but she was nothing like Seychelle other than she was small. She might look fragile, but she wasn't. She was backing up her man, somewhere in the shadows. She had been trained as an assassin, just as they had been, and she was lethal as hell. She suddenly appeared in the foyer, smiling a welcome as Casimir closed the door behind them. To her left was an imposing, muscular black dog, looking both powerful and intelligent. Savage was well aware the dog was a Black Russian Terrier. Czar and Blythe had one as well. Those very intelligent eyes had targeted him the moment Casimir had allowed them into the house, and hadn't taken his gaze off him since. Clearly, he knew who the true threat would be.

Both Casimir and Lissa gave the dog a hand signal, and it relaxed and trotted to a dog bed that was placed between two very comfortable chairs.

"I have to apologize, Lissa," Savage said immediately. "I didn't think about the time, and I should have. We made a run over to the cottage in Sea Haven, intending to stay there for the night, and when we got there, we found the house vandalized. And by that, I mean whoever had done it had completely wrecked it. Everything. All of her belongings. Cut up her clothing, drilled her kitchen pots and pans, smashed even the walls, shower, bathtub and toilet."

Savage pulled Seychelle even closer to him, her side to his front, wishing he could turn back the clock and be there in her house when Shari had come.

"How terrible, Seychelle." Lissa indicated the cozy chairs in the living room. "I saw the damage in the photographs you sent, Savage. "I'm so sorry, Seychelle. It must have been a terrible shock to you. Please come in and sit down."

Savage was a little uneasy. He didn't visit people, and he didn't go sit in their snug little rooms, where they had the advantage in a firefight. He noted the exits and every item he could use as a weapon in the room. He was armed, and his body was a weapon. Still, his woman was with him. He took the love seat and pulled Seychelle down beside him, one arm around her, the other still holding the large but fragile package.

"I've made some tea, unless you think it's too late for that." Lissa indicated a red-and-black inlaid tray. On it sat a black teapot decorated with a fiery red dragon and two matching mugs. It was clear she knew Savage because the other two mugs held coffee.

"Tea is perfect, thank you, Lissa," Seychelle managed. "The tea set is lovely and very unique. I've never seen anything quite like it."

"I actually made it myself," Lissa confessed. "I went through an experimental phase, making pottery. I've been considering giving lessons to Lucia and Lexi. Lexi suggested it. Lucia is Airiana's oldest girl. Maxim and Airiana rescued Lucia and her brother, Benito, and sisters from one of those horrible ships where they kill the victims after using them. We've all been trying to find ways to make Lucia feel at home here, but also to give her things she loves to do. She's an incredible chef already. She has an affinity for the dogs and helps Gavriil train them. She keeps up with her schoolwork and is always there for the children and Airiana, but we wanted to give her something else, something that's just hers. She told Lexi once that she always had wanted to take a pottery class, but when she looked them up at the arts studio in Sea Haven, they were just too expensive."

Savage frowned. "Maxim is loaded."

Lissa shrugged. "Lucia already feels he's taken on so much. She refuses to be a financial burden to him any more than she already is. I actually think it would be fun to have her here, and it gives me a chance to spend a little time with Lexi. I haven't worked with pottery like this in quite a while, so I've begun to fool around with it. Casimir is helping me."

Savage raised an eyebrow.

Casimir grinned at him. "You ever see the movie *Ghost*? If not, you need to."

Seychelle laughed softly. It wasn't much of a laugh, but it was enough of one that he decided they'd have to find the movie and watch it together. "Must have missed that one. We'll have to watch it, babe."

Seychelle nodded. "It was really good."

"The boys look over the cottage?" Casimir asked as he took the seat across from Savage.

"Yes, they're doing so now. I'll take Seychelle back to the house, and we'll stay there while the cottage is being fixed up. Be interesting to see if the bastard tries to break in there."

"It might have been just a random break-in," Seychelle said, a hopeful note in her voice. "It wasn't that long ago that there was a group of robbers breaking into the homes of the elderly. I'm sure my cottage looked deserted. Or it could have been mistaken for a vacation home." She took a sip of tea, her eyes meeting Savage's over the rim of the mug.

Savage kept his expression purposefully blank. He held out his hand for the mug. "This is really beautiful, Lissa." It was. The dragon was far more detailed than he'd thought possible with pottery. Lissa's hair was nearly as fiery red as the dragon. The scales were touched with gold to add accents. The lip of the mug was thinner, and the handle was part of the tail.

Lissa looked pleased. "Thank you. I made it on a whim."

Seychelle accepted the mug back and regarded all three of the others with her intelligent blue eyes. Savage wanted to groan.

"Casimir, you don't believe for one moment that it was a random robbery, do you?"

"Probably not," Casimir answered. "The destruction was far too much for it to be anything but personal. I'd like to tell you different, but that would be doing you a disservice."

Seychelle nodded and took another sip of tea. "I thought that too. I just hoped I was wrong. Savage doesn't lie to me, and I didn't ask him because I didn't want to put him in a position of having to deliver more bad news to me." She leaned into Savage, tipping her head back to give him another wan smile.

He slid his arm along the back of the love seat, finding the nape of her neck beneath the thick layer of silky waves so he could ease some of the tension out of her. "You don't have to think about it anymore, baby. Let the brothers fix up the cottage. We'll get first-class security on it. I should have been all over that already."

"Don't, Savage. You know I never even locked my doors until you came along."

Lissa gave a little gasp. "With your voice when you sing? With your looks? Surely, you had to realize men could get obsessed with you."

"Well. No, actually, I didn't," Seychelle admitted. "I never thought of myself like that. When I sing, I get caught up in what I'm doing. I love it. I can feel the energy of the crowd. When the band is good, like it is with Torpedo Ink, that just adds to the magic of the feeling. I can see the musical notes floating in the air like these beautiful gold shimmering fireflies. Sometimes, when people are feeling down, I can weave a net and bring their emotions up, make them feel happy. That makes me happy." Enthusiasm poured into her voice.

"Are you going to sing with the band tomorrow night?" Casimir asked. "I know they're playing."

"Tomorrow night?" She looked at Savage.

"I haven't had a chance to tell you," he said, keeping his voice casual. "Plank asked for a meet, and Czar is going to indulge him at the bar tomorrow night. The band is playing. Of course they want you to sing, but it isn't something you have to do if you don't want to. Czar isn't asking for a command performance. It's only if you want to sing."

"Are you going to the meeting?"

Savage shrugged, watching her face.

She smiled at him. "Of course I'm going to sing. You have to be at the meeting, and I'll need you there to make sure the room is clear for me to sing."

"Clear?" Lissa asked.

"Sometimes, when people are really ill," Seychelle volunteered, "I can't help myself, I take on their illness. It can be . . . challenging."

"Life-threatening." Savage all but growled it.

"Let's go back to singing," Seychelle said. "And forget the other. What were you saying about that, Lissa?"

"You have a real gift," Savage said. "I'm in awe of your talent." He was.

Lissa nodded in agreement. "I was there the other night. Believe me, I know you do. That's why it's so important to always have security in your home and around you when you go out. I was terrified of dogs until we got Baron. Gavriil talked me into taking one of the puppies his pair had, and he's come every day to help me train him. Lucia babysits him and helps out to reinforce Baron's training. I have to admit, I love him and don't know what I'd do without him."

"Is he fully grown?" Seychelle asked.

"Yes, he's grown now; they get their full growth at two years. He's a big boy," Lissa answered.

Casimir put his arm around his wife. "Lucia has a special affinity with dogs, and Lissa uses every excuse to have her come over and help out with the dog or the cooking or learning something new."

Lissa laughed and shrugged, not bothering to deny it. "It's true. I like the girl. A lot. I can't help myself. I don't like that she takes the world on her shoulders. She lost her little sister on that ship, and she looks after her siblings as if she's their mother. Now I feel as if she's taken on Airiana as well. I don't want her to turn out like me." She gave a little chin lift to her husband.

He caught her chin in his hand easily and brushed a kiss over her lips. "If she turns out like you, she will be brilliant and wonderful, a miracle for her partner."

Lissa smiled at him, the smile lighting her face. "Is that how you see me? A miracle?"

"That's exactly how I see you."

Lissa swallowed and shook her head, blinking rapidly. "You always say things that make me want to cry." She

turned back to Savage and Seychelle. "I think I can do
something with what is left of the sculpture, Seychelle, but
it won't be the same. It will have your parents' ashes in it,
but they'll be mingled together rather than apart in two separate roses. There is no way for me to figure out which
pieces of glass have who embedded in them."

Seychelle took a deep breath and tightened her fingers
around Savage's hand. "I think Casimir is right, Lissa. You
are a miracle. Thank you for even trying to save the sculpture any way you can. It doesn't have to be roses, or flowers
for that matter, just anything with my parents' ashes in it.
This means a lot to me."

Seychelle sat with her back to the headboard, wearing nothing but a nearly transparent crop top that clung to her generous breasts. She wasn't wearing panties, because, really,
what was the use? Savage lay with his arm around her hips
and his head on her belly while she massaged his scalp. It
was his favorite place. He found peace right there. Utter con-
tentment.

He'd tried to re-create that same feeling of peace for
Seychelle that she had in her little cottage, but the bed was
enormous. The sea was closer, the waves louder as they
crashed against the bluff and sea stacks. Still, she was getting so she seemed to find peace there as well.

"Are we going to ask questions tonight, baby?" he asked,
keeping his voice gentle. He didn't care one way or the
other. He didn't mind lying there with her, listening to the
ocean and drifting off with the scent of her in his lungs.

"Not tonight, Savage. But I do have a few questions." She
looked up at him with her sea-blue eyes. "Do you know who
destroyed my home, Savage? Does the entire club know?
Has the destruction of my home become a Torpedo Ink
thing that we can't talk about?"

He nuzzled her bare belly with his chin, all the while
meeting her eyes. "Baby, I've given this a lot of thought.

How we should be. What kind of relationship we need to have. I have to protect you. You have to have certain things in order for me to meet your emotional needs. When we had a meeting with Blythe and Czar, Blythe said something that really resonated with me."

Her fingers continued to massage his scalp. "What was that?"

"She said she only asked questions when she really wanted to know the answer and knew she could handle it. She also said if she got the answer, she wouldn't judge. I'm asking you to let this one go. If you ask, anytime you ask me, I'm going to give you the absolute truth, just like Czar does Blythe, and hold you to the no-judging rule. But, baby, I'm asking you, for me, to let this one go, if you can." He held her gaze steady. "I know you love that house. I know those things destroyed were personal and yours. You have every right to know who did that to you, but I'm asking you to let this one pass."

"Because Torpedo Ink is going to handle it."

"Yes."

She was quiet a moment, but she didn't flinch. "And when they handle something, it tends to be in a permanent way."

"Not going to lie to you, baby." He nodded.

Her teeth bit down on her lower lip, and then, very slowly, the tension eased out of her. "I guess it is a Torpedo Ink problem. I'm going to just go to sleep and dream about really wonderful things, such as singing with the band tomorrow night. That sounds like such fun."

"Even knowing Plank and his crew are coming?" *Bog*, he was so in love with her. He pressed kisses to her hip bones and then lower still to that freshly shaved mound with the little airstrip of tiny curls. He nuzzled them with his nose. She squirmed and he inhaled her scent, that fragrance that was all Seychelle.

"What are you doing?" There was a hint of laughter in her voice, but also that note that told him she was already growing slick with need.

"Making sure you're relaxed and ready to sleep," he murmured, kissing his way down to her bare lips. His shoulders were wide, keeping her thighs spread for him. And yeah, all that delicious honey and wild strawberry was right there waiting for him.

He took his time, making a thorough job of it. Savoring her. Savoring her taste. His time with her. Bringing her pleasure. There was no other thought in his mind but giving her as much pleasure, as much love, as possible, showing her with his hands and mouth just how much he worshipped her.

He wrung multiple orgasms out of her, leaving her limp and exhausted but happy, no longer capable of thinking. He wrapped his arms around her, holding her close as she fell asleep. The soft sound of her cries of pleasure replayed in his mind, along with the sound of the waves crashing against the bluffs, allowing him to drift off with her.

TWENTY-ONE

"What do you mean the ladies have a birthday surprise for me?" Savage said. He looked out the clubhouse window warily. Sure enough, the parking lot had three cars in it filled with women and their absurd red-and-purple hats. "This is fucking not happening. I don't have birthdays. I have no idea when my birthday is, so how would the ladies know?" He glared at Seychelle.

Seychelle put her hands up in the air in surrender, shrugging to show him she wasn't involved in any way. He could tell by the look on her face that she was as shocked as he was. She wasn't behind whatever was going on, which didn't make him any happier. In the clubhouse there were tables set up with food, and a large cake was in the middle of one table. Paper plates and napkins were sitting there beside the cake. Some of the older women in the parking lot were carrying trays of cookies. That didn't look too bad. He could live with that. The majority of them gathered outside, while Inez and Doris brought the trays of cookies in.

Inez beamed at him. "Happy birthday, Savage. Come outside and see your birthday present. We really had such a good time coming up with the perfect present for you."

"But it's not . . ."

Seychelle kicked him hard and then elbowed him in the ribs. Reaper grinned at him. Keys and Master sauntered right out the door. Storm lingered by the cake, but Mechanic and Ink caught him by the shoulders and marched him outside.

Destroyer jerked his chin toward the parking lot. "Mama Anat is out there, birthday boy. You're not disappointing her."

This was going to be bad. Savage was certain of it. Just about every old lady he'd helped at one time or another was out in the parking lot. Some of the older men were there. Most of his club was there. Cell phones were out to capture the moment when he opened his present.

"I'm hoping for a dog, Seychelle," he whispered into her neck. "Otherwise, we're heading out of the country. They've cooked up something really bad, I can feel it." He held out his hand. She took it and he closed his fingers tightly around hers for courage. "A dog like Casimir has. We could use one of those."

"Why do you think what they got you would be bad? They love you. They wouldn't do anything bad to you," Seychelle assured him.

"They won't *think* it's bad. They never think anything they do is bad, but trust me, baby, I need my reputation to stay intact."

"I didn't know you wanted one of those huge dogs. What are we going to do with a dog like that, Savage?" Now she glanced nervously out the window. "Do you think that's what they got you? Did you mention you wanted one to them?"

He instantly wrapped his arm around her. "If they got us a dog, we'd get someone to help us train it." He'd be so relieved if they got him a dog. He didn't think he'd be that lucky.

He'd spent the morning worrying about Seychelle, taking care of his whips and other tools, knowing he was far too close to the end of his cycle, and the meeting with Plank tonight at the bar was bound to push him over the edge. He'd made plans. He was going to have everything ready at home, but he was going to go to the fight club first, try to burn off as much rage as possible before he went to Seychelle.

Mechanic texted him in the early afternoon and told him to come to the clubhouse, that there was a quick meeting before they would see the Diamondbacks, but to bring Seychelle as Alena had put together some new concoction she wanted them all to taste. Instead, it turned out, it was a big celebration of his "birthday" that wasn't his birthday. He looked around the yard, his arms around Seychelle, holding on to her as if she was his safety net, which she was.

The entire Torpedo Ink club was there, which didn't surprise him when there was food and cake involved. "Let's just get this over with," he whispered into Seychelle's ear.

He didn't like the way his brothers were grinning at him. Really grinning at him. That gave him a bad feeling. The little old ladies were beaming. That gave him a worse feeling. The brothers parted for him, allowing him to see his Harley. It was parked innocently enough just a little apart from the other bikes. It was clean and shiny. He loved that bike. He looked from Transporter to Mechanic. They'd had his most treasured possession in their garage these last few days, fine-tuning it. It was a road rocket already.

"Why the hell is everyone grinning like idiots, Seychelle?" His fingers bit into her hips. He gave the two men a look that told them he would fuckin' pull them limb from limb if one little thing had happened to his bike.

The older women had crowded around it, all looking enormously pleased with themselves. Too pleased. He was beginning to sweat. His bike was set up exactly how he wanted it. Perfection. Something was really off here.

"I'm not sure." Now she sounded wary. Her hand came down over his. She really didn't know, he got that much, and she was becoming worried and reminding him that these women were important to both of them. "Man up, honey. Just face it. We'll deal with whatever they've done after."

"I might have to kill someone," he whispered, his lips against her ear.

"So long as it isn't one of the Red Hat ladies," she whispered back.

Just the fact that Seychelle was agreeable to him killing someone boded ill for his birthday present. He manned up, stood up straight, stepped out from behind his woman, took her hand and walked into the middle of the Red Hat Society women. They fluttered around him instantly, laughing and giggling nervously like schoolgirls. That did something sweet to his insides, so he promised himself no matter how bad this was, he was going to be okay with it.

Doris Fendris stood in front of the left side of his Night Rod Special. It was painted all matte black with dull gunmetal-gray trim and blacked-out chrome. The only artistic touch was the image of a dripping gray skull and . . . Doris moved out of the way. And . . . His heart nearly stopped beating, then began to pound hard, accelerating madly. There was an addition to his bike that hadn't been there before.

To hide his expression, Savage crouched low to study the new design. His mouth went dry. No one touched a man's bike. That was a sacred rule. He had the right to beat the crap out of a man for touching his bike. Or pull out his gun and shoot him. But this—this deserved slow torture before death. Seychelle crowded close to him, her heat at his back, no doubt to remind him of the ladies all around so he wouldn't erupt like a volcano.

He continued to stare at the new decoration welded onto his bike. It was a little broad-brimmed hat made of gems—real ones, bright red with a purple band, glittering every time the sun hit. There were feathers made of purple, green and blue gems coming up from the band. As hats went, it was quite charming and delicate. The entire thing was actually quite small, and there wasn't a single doubt in his mind that Ice had made it for the women. It looked like his work. He was certain the women weren't happy it was so small, but on his bike with its black coloring, the red stood out vividly, and the blues, purples and greens stood out like a sore thumb.

He took a deep breath and reached for Seychelle's hand as he stood up. "It's beautiful," he managed, looking around at all the eager faces.

Inez and Doris nodded. "You're an honorary member, Savage, of the Red Hat Society. Both chapters, Sea Haven and Caspar. We thought it was going to be too small, but it looks perfect on your bike, doesn't it?" Doris said, pride in her voice.

Mama Anat nodded as did all the other women. Savage found the anger that anyone had dared to touch his bike fading. He looked at the hat again. The brothers had welded it in the least conspicuous place possible. Maybe he could live with it just for a little while to make the ladies happy. They were beaming. Glowing. *Bog.* He'd never seen them all so happy. He transferred his arm to circle around Seychelle's shoulders.

"Never thought I'd wear a hat covered in gems on my bike."

At least his brothers hadn't welded it onto the top of the skull. They had to have thought of it and laughed their damned heads off. He sent Mechanic and Transporter a look over his shoulder. He wanted them to worry about a visit from him in the middle of the night. Both their smirks faded, and they looked a little uncomfortable. There was no use giving Ice that look. All he would do was laugh. It wasn't like he was expendable, and he knew it. He had Soleil.

"Don't know what to say, this is pretty huge. No one's ever done anything like this for me before." He tightened his hold on Seychelle, unexpectedly feeling a lump in his throat.

It wasn't really about that silly red hat, it was the intent behind it. These women had taken him in just the way he was. All of them. They'd just accepted him. Not just for Seychelle. For himself. He had no idea why. He was rough and, for the most part, stayed out of sight if he could help it, but they didn't seem to mind his foul mouth or his coarse ways.

The ladies beamed even brighter.

"Shall we go inside and eat that delicious-looking cake Alena made?" Rebecca asked. "We wanted to have the party at her restaurant, but you would have known something was up immediately."

"After cake and ice cream, we can take your bike home for you," Mechanic offered.

Savage lifted an eyebrow. "I'm fairly certain you have the ability, Mechanic," he said. "But whether or not you can be trusted is another story altogether. I think I'll swap trucks with you and drive her home myself."

Mechanic turned away, but not before Savage caught his grin. He wasn't nearly as sorry as he should have been. It was a sacrilege to touch a man's bike. Let him worry about Savage showing up in the middle of the night. That was always a possibility. He flicked a glance at Transporter as he moved past him into the clubhouse, letting him know he held him just as accountable.

That little red hat just might grow on him. If it didn't, he'd leave it for a couple of days and then take it off his bike and keep it where the ladies could see it at the cottage. He'd just have to find the perfect spot for it.

"You're amazing," Seychelle whispered. "You made them very happy. Thank you for being so gracious about the hat. It couldn't have been easy."

He thought about letting that go, but it wasn't right. "Maybe not at first. Never wanted anyone touching my bike. Never had anything that belonged to me until I got the bike. And that bike is part of me. It represents so many things to me. No one ever lays a hand on it, other than Mechanic or Transporter, and that's because they're turning it into a rocket."

"I hardly think you need to make it faster, honey." Seychelle cuddled into him as they made their way around the room, greeting each of the women.

One by one they hugged him, pressing kisses onto his cheek. He never thought that would happen either. He kept his hand on Seychelle, not allowing her to abandon him. He wasn't altogether certain he would be able to handle all the attention. Around them, his brothers and Alena and Lana grinned like idiots. Seychelle was his anchor, allowing him to be gracious when he was on unfamiliar ground.

"The point," he whispered, in between the hugs, "is that maybe I don't mind quite as much as I thought I did. I'm thinking about it."

The door opened, and Jackson Deveau sauntered in, carrying several brightly wrapped packages. His gaze swept the room, missing nothing, settling for a moment on Savage, a hint of satisfaction showing just for a moment. He wasn't in uniform, but there was no doubt he was armed.

"Hannah heard it was Savage's birthday, and she sent a few things for him," Jackson said. "Jonas had a meeting, or he would have delivered the package himself. Instead, I offered." He eyed the baskets of chicken Alena had put out on the table along with all the other food.

"You can put that right here, Jackson," Inez said helpfully, leading the way to the gift table.

Savage watched Jackson trail along behind her, carrying the brightly wrapped packages from Hannah. The deputy's features were always the same: totally unreadable, except for that one moment when his eyes had met Savage's. He kept looking at the chicken, not at Savage, but suspicion crept into Savage's mind and took hold. Where had the women gotten the idea to make him an honorary member of the Red Hat Society? Jackson Deveau, that was where. That underhanded bastard of a sheriff's deputy, that was who had planted the seed and poured water and fertilizer on it until it grew. Savage knew absolutely that he was right. And he was there to gloat. To see how Savage was taking his little prank. He knew how sacred a man's bike was. Jackson's father had ridden with a club.

"Take a breath, honey," Seychelle advised. She hooked

her arm around his neck and went up on her toes to brush kisses over his mouth. "Think about all the packages your brothers have on that table. Most likely, they gave you really preposterous sex toys just to freak me out."

She was more than likely right about that. "Jackson Deveau is behind this. He just threw down the gauntlet. It is *on*." He whispered it into her mouth. "He has no idea who he's fucking with. I'm going to get the club to help me with the next prank. We can get very creative." He licked the curve of her lower lip and then tugged at it with his teeth.

"In the meantime, show him you're such a good sport," she advised. "You *love* what the ladies gave you. That will get to him more than anything. Act like you don't have a clue he had anything at all to do with it."

"If he wasn't married to Hannah's youngest sister, I'd ask her to fill his entire house with toads," he muttered under his breath.

Seychelle burst into laughter, her arms going around his neck, head tilted back, looking up at him with pure joy. Pure love. What the hell did anything matter when he had her? He laughed with her and spun her around, taking her with him to the food table. He would have opened some of the gifts if no one but Torpedo Ink had been there, but he wasn't going to embarrass Seychelle in front of her friends—or the cop. Although, looking at the older women, he had a sneaking suspicion some of them might have enjoyed whatever Torpedo Ink had given to them in those packages sitting so innocently on the table.

The bar seemed overflowing with bikers, not just Diamondbacks but members of the Venomous, Twisted Steel and Headed for Hell clubs. They'd brought their women with them and they weren't causing any trouble, but the underlying mood, at times, was tense. Savage just plain didn't need that shit, not with his woman onstage. It was supposed to be a relatively easygoing evening. Fun, even. He didn't want her to think the club was using her to calm everyone the fuck down. He wanted her to know the club was looking out for her. Taking her in. Enfolding her into their family.

He was in a fucking foul mood, and it was getting worse by the moment. He made his way around the crowd, trying to stay to the shadows as much as possible by hugging the edges of the walls as Seychelle sang an upbeat song that had most of the crowd going. He edged close to the stage, keeping his eyes not on his woman but on the occupants of the bar. Reaper, Storm, Destroyer and Ink stayed in the shadows, along with Savage. Preacher was behind the bar with Anya and Sabelia serving drinks. Sabelia was a little tentative, but she was catching on fast. Heidi, Betina and Delia moved around the tables, taking orders.

Scarlet, Lissa, Lana and Alena sat at a table with Soleil and Zyah, close to the stage. Savage was particularly happy to have the women together so close to Seychelle. The band, Master, Keys, Player and Maestro, were with her, but having the women looking as if they were just out enjoying the evening, knowing if anything went wrong, Scarlet, Lissa, Lana and Alena would have the other wives safe and under cover immediately.

Casimir and Gavriil stayed close to the door, acting as bouncers. Absinthe was on the security screens with Code. They had the bar covered, but Savage knew, with the amount of bikers from different clubs inside, one little match could set off a shit storm of trouble in an instance.

Bannister sat at the bar, close to the stage. He wasn't a member of Torpedo Ink, but he was always ready to back their play. Anya was extremely protective of him. Delia and he had grown very close in the last few weeks. He lived in one of the two apartments above the bar. Delia lived in the other one.

The band was giving one of their best performances, at least Savage thought so. Few of the customers could stay in their seats for long. Most were already paying more attention to the music than trying to converse with one another.

He let himself look at his woman for just a moment, take in her beauty as she sang, her rhythm as she moved in time to the beat of the song making her seem like she was part of the music. Seychelle glowed when she sang. Her skin. Her hair. Her eyes. She had a siren's voice—at least for him. Her voice was compelling, filled with emotion and transferring that emotion to anyone who could hear her.

The band kept the songs upbeat, so that those in the room were continually on their feet, in a good mood, rather than surly or wanting to pick fights. Savage could feel Seychelle's subtle influence in that energy. He could see the golden notes climbing the walls to the ceiling, forming a net to enfold her audience in good vibrations that rocked the bar and kept everyone laughing and upbeat.

Savage loved seeing her power, but he didn't love that he had promised her a good time and she'd gotten something different. He saw her gaze shift to someone in the crowd and then to Alena and then to him, clearly warning him. She never missed a beat, her singing smooth and easy, rocking the throng. He followed the direction of her gaze and saw Pierce making his way through the door. His gaze had already found Alena, moved on to ferret out every potential threat to his president and then come back to Alena.

Plank is here with eight more of his men. Pierce, Lion, Shark and Judge are with him, along with four others, Gavriil reported. **You figure with those already here, the Diamondbacks have a large presence in the bar.**

They want trouble after this Tawny thing, they can find it right here, Reaper responded. **Trying to shove that shit on us.**

He meant on Savage. Savage could feel the rising tension. The anger. It wasn't just his own. Plank had a lot to answer for. If he arranged for Tawny's death and tried to pin it on Savage, or Torpedo Ink, there was no saving him. Their club had saved his life as well as the lives of his top men. Brandon and his mother, Nina, may have put the hits out on them, but Torpedo Ink had shut them down whether Plank wanted to admit it or not. If he had repaid them by murdering Tawny and then attempting to pin her death on their club, he was definitely a dead man.

Pierce walked up to a large table and stood there waiting. It was occupied by members of the Venomous club. There was a tense moment while the members continued to sit stubbornly. Savage and Reaper moved out of the shadows to stand beside Pierce, although Savage would much rather gut Pierce than show any solidarity toward him. The moment the Venomous club members stood and retreated, one knocking over a chair, Heidi was there to clear the table.

Savage turned and disappeared, leaving his older brother to right the chair before he moved into the shadows as well. Neither greeted Pierce, or even acknowledged him. As far as they were concerned, he was a dead man. He'd hurt their sister. It didn't matter that he kept coming around, acting like he wanted to make amends. Pierce had shared a video that he'd insisted she make for him alone with his president, who shared it with other members of his chapter. That was so disrespectful in the eyes of Torpedo Ink that no matter what Pierce did, none of them would be able to forgive that shit.

Already Savage could feel Alena's pain. An ache for what she'd lost. Or for the fact that she'd trusted someone, and he'd betrayed that trust. He wasn't the only one to feel her pain. All of the members were woven together, and they could all feel it, whether Alena tried to hide it or not. Alena was soft inside. She had learned, over the years, to hide that softness from others, but she was much more vulnerable than any of the rest of them. Essentially, she was their baby sister, and Pierce had torn her apart.

The anger was there, smoldering in each member, kept under control because they dared not feed that explosive mixture of dynamite in the bar, but it was there all the same. Savage absorbed as much as he could, allowing the rage to pool in that reservoir so the others could function unimpaired.

Heidi took the orders at the table, smiling and flirting just a little, laughing with the Diamondbacks easily. She was the consummate professional, a real asset to the club. She was extremely loyal to them, never gossiped about them or anything she may have inadvertently overheard, but when she picked up information, she passed it on to one of the club members or Anya immediately.

She moved easily through the crowd, so experienced she was barely touched by any of the many bikers crowding around the bar unless she wanted to be touched. "Preacher, table seven orders," she called out and leaned in close to Bannister. Bannister was always on the same bar stool, the one nearest the band, and Anya covered that section. By calling out to Preacher, that meant she had a note or information of some kind to pass down the line.

"I'm free," Anya made a point of saying. She smiled and began filling the drink orders even as she slid the note off the bar. Preacher stepped behind Sabelia, one hand on her shoulder as if checking her work.

Sabelia glared at him. "I've got this. I'm slow, but I'm getting the hang of it. No one's complained yet."

"Don't want you poisoning the customers, *malen'kiy ved'ma*. Just making sure."

Anya deftly slid the note in Preacher's pocket as he turned away.

Sabelia narrowed her eyes. "Did you call me a witch?"

Preacher moved away from her with an easy roll of his shoulders. "Some might use that word for *witch*. I personally prefer it for *hellcat*."

"Lovely. Just lovely. You're going to find out what a hellcat I can be," Sabelia muttered under her breath, but she kept working.

Anya burst out laughing. "Preacher is a pain in the ass. Don't let him get to you. You're doing great, which is why he's all up in your business. You were supposed to fall on your face and need his help so he could be all superior."

"That's enough of that bullshit," Preacher called out.

Sabelia and Anya exchanged a smirk that included Heidi. *See?* Anya mouthed.

Savage leaned over the other end of the bar, calling out for a beer. Preacher shoved a cold one to him, along with a napkin. He took it and disappeared back into the shadows, moving toward the hall. He walked to the very end, where Czar and Steele had come in the back way.

"Heidi sent a note, Czar," Savage greeted. "Too many clubs out there. And that fucking Pierce walked in like he owned the place."

Czar glanced at his watch. "Have ten minutes before the meeting. Plank must like the band to come this early."

"I hope that's his reason," Savage said, but he didn't believe it. Pierce was too cocky. He was back in Plank's good graces, and that didn't necessarily bode well for Torpedo Ink.

Czar glanced down at the note and scowled. Savage felt the burst of black anger the president of their club hastily got under control. Savage did what he always did—bled most of that rage off. Czar was going to have to face Plank and look as if he was in complete command of his emotions at all times.

"They came early so they could listen to the band and Pierce could have another shot at talking to Alena. Heidi overheard them talking. Plank and Judge told him to take his chance while he could, before things had a chance of heating up."

Savage swore under his breath. He needed to get back out there. He knew he was too late. He felt the shift in the other members' emotions immediately. Seychelle's voice changed subtly, pouring a calming vibe into the notes as she sang. Pierce had clearly insisted on Alena dancing with him, pulling her into his arms in spite of the song being on the faster side.

Could use a little help, here. One of you come and dance with me, Alena sent to the brothers. He's all over me.

Was there desperation in her voice? Was she falling for Pierce's shit?

Tell him to go to hell, Ice demanded. I'm your fucking brother. I can't go rescue you.

Tell him to get his fucking hands off you. He's dancing with you, Destroyer snapped. He doesn't need to be grabbing your ass. He's just showing off to his friends that he can.

I've moved his hands several times. Unless you want me to break them and start a war, get your ass over here and help out, Destroyer. You're the only one he doesn't know, and he thinks we're together. Alena sounded pissed. And you owe me big-time.

Don't dance. And where do you get the idea I owe you?

You kissed me when I was a kid and then won that damn contest and left me in that hellhole.

There was a moment of silence while all the members of Torpedo Ink digested that information. The band continued to play. Seychelle sang. Pierce pulled Alena closer to him, his hands roaming her body while she shoved at his chest, glaring daggers. No one was quite certain who she was glaring daggers at.

Are you shitting me? You were nine years old, and I kissed the top of your head. A brotherly kiss, by the way, to try to convey that not every man was an asshole.

I don't care if it was on the top of my head. I made it into something else in my mind. I needed it to be, so it was.

You're saying I owe you because you had a childish fantasy over a kiss that didn't actually take place in the way you made it out to be in your head?

Savage could see how that was totally fucked up, and Alena wasn't going to back down. Once she got something in her head, she was so stubborn, nothing could move her. Destroyer didn't have a prayer in hell of winning this one, even if she was totally illogical. Destroyer was fairly new and had no idea how truly stubborn she could be.

Bet your ass you do. Now get over here and act mad and jealous. I'm sure you can manage that.

You are one totally fucked-up woman. And you're going to owe me, Alena. Meals for weeks. Months. I detest dancing.

You like scaring the shit out of Diamondbacks. So don't pretend you're all put upon.

Of course Alena would find a way to make it seem like she was doing Destroyer a huge favor by making him dance with her. If it wasn't so fucked up, Savage would have laughed. Alena thought Destroyer had kissed her when she was nine? Really kissed her? Didn't she know Czar and Ice would have conspired to kill him? Hell, everyone would have killed him. There wouldn't have been a contest for him to win because he would have been dead.

Destroyer moved out of the shadows, and when he came out of them, he came out looking like a berserker. He didn't look at Pierce, as if he was a loathsome insect, so far beneath his notice. He towered over the Diamondback. His shoulders appeared nearly twice as wide, his chest nearly twice as thick, yet there wasn't an ounce of fat on him. He caught Alena's arm and pulled her to him.

"Woman, what the fuck do you think you're doing? You want to dance, you dance with your old man. You've been independent way too long, and that's the only reason you're getting away with this shit."

Reaper, Storm and Savage moved out of the shadows to insert themselves between Pierce and the couple as Destroyer whirled Alena away from them, his larger frame nearly engulfing her smaller one. Her slender arms went around his neck, and she leaned into him as if in total surrender, and then the crowd of dancers cut them off completely.

"Who is that guy?" Pierce demanded. "Where the hell did he come from?"

Savage raised an eyebrow. "He's Torpedo Ink. You threw Alena away, Pierce. Did you think she wasn't going to get snapped up?" He turned his back on the man before he gave in to the need to sink his fist into his mouth. He was skating on the very edge of his control. Even Seychelle's sweet, calming notes, as golden as they were, couldn't settle the burning in him any longer.

He shook his head and glanced down at his watch, a kind of despair settling over him. He would have to head to San Francisco to the fight club. He had no other choice. He needed to work off some of the rage before he went to his woman, and he had to do it after the meeting tonight. He couldn't wait.

Reaper led Plank, Judge, Pierce, Shark and Lion into the meeting room. Savage followed them and closed the door. Absinthe, Keys and Maestro were already inside with Czar and Steele. They had argued with Czar and Steele about allowing both men in the meeting with the Diamondbacks. If everything went south, they didn't want the president and vice president in jeopardy, but Czar and Steele had been adamant that they both be present. They wanted to see Plank's face. Hear his voice.

"When you come into this meeting room with us," Absinthe said, "you want to tell us the truth."

The Diamondbacks looked at him with a small frown. It was Plank who answered. "We requested the meeting. That's what we're here for."

"Do you have any recording devices on you?" Absinthe asked.

"No," Plank answered for all of them.

Absinthe nodded and indicated for everyone to take seats around the table. Savage and Reaper draped themselves against the doors, where they usually blended with the shadows. Maestro and Keys seated themselves on either side of Czar and Steele.

Plank didn't waste time. "I know you have to believe that we had something to do with Tawny Farmer's body being dropped near your clubhouse. We didn't. I came here knowing I could put us in jeopardy with you by you recording this conversation, but we owe you. We didn't set you up. We could have set up a member of your club, but we chose not to. We burned all evidence we had that would have pointed in that direction. Tawny was slated to be . . . ended, but she was gone when we went to get her. We would have just disposed of her body where no one would have found her, but someone else got there ahead of us."

Savage flicked a quick look toward Absinthe, as did Czar. Absinthe was seated the closest to Plank. His nod was nearly imperceptible.

"You don't believe any member of your chapter killed and dumped her without your consent?" Absinthe asked.

Pierce started to speak, but Plank lifted a hand, and he went silent.

Plank shook his head. "Absolutely not. I questioned everyone. I brought them together and questioned them all. Pierce was very upset. He knew I would take a close look at him. He had the most to lose if Tawny was killed and dumped in your territory. He wanted to get back with Alena. No way did any of my men do this."

"Alena has moved on. She has an old man in our club," Czar said. He leaned back in his chair. "I have some information, but it is unconfirmed." He raised his gaze to first Lion, and then Shark. "I believe both of you are targeted and will continue to be targeted, as will your chapter as well as your brothers' chapter eventually. We believe this is a vendetta specifically against you. It was meant to internally turn the chapter against itself. The money is being traced right now, but we have a suspicion we know where it will lead back to."

Lion and Shark shared a look. Plank and Judge waited in silence for them to speak. When neither was forthcoming, Plank snarled at them. "You know something, now would be a good time to tell us what you know."

"That's the problem, Plank," Lion said. "We don't actually know anything." He tapped the table and then looked directly at Czar. "Are you referring to our half brother? Do you suspect him in this? Because we considered it, but he really isn't that talented or smart."

"Not if he was acting on his own," Czar agreed. "The

Diamondbacks turned him down. He has a big ego. A really big ego. He uses women. He wanted to show you he could take you down and take down the club that dared to refuse him entry."

"He might want that, Czar," Shark agreed, "but he doesn't have the kind of smarts to set it all in motion. That kind of long-range planning. And the hits? I can see him thinking up the women and blow jobs, but the hits on the presidents of the clubs? Planning to throw the clubs into chaos? He wouldn't think about that."

"*He* wouldn't," Czar agreed and fell silent. Waiting.

The clock ticked. Plank stirred but then didn't speak, realizing Czar was giving Shark and Lion the opportunity to put it all together. To figure it out.

Lion swore under his breath and then turned to his brother. "Aunt Nina. She orchestrated this. She's cunning enough to do something like this, and she hates Mom. I've seen her looking at Mom sometimes with this look on her face." He stood up suddenly, shoving back his chair so hard it nearly fell over, but his brother caught it. "I should have done something about her years ago. I was always afraid she'd do something to Mom. Hurt her."

"I thought maybe she'd changed over the last few years," Shark said.

"That's what she wanted everyone to believe so she could help Brandon carry out his revenge plan," Lion said. He shoved a hand through his hair. "Aunt Nina knew Tawny's mother. They were drinking buddies." He looked at Czar. "How soon can your man get the information on the money trail?"

Czar looked at Steele. Steele texted Code. They waited a few minutes. Steele glanced down at his phone. "Code will provide you with the information when you leave. Not text."

"Good enough," Lion said. He looked at Pierce. "We'll take care of the problem from here."

Pierce nodded in agreement.

Plank stood up. "Appreciate your help as always, Czar."

"Always good to see you, Plank," Czar responded.

Absinthe opened the door and led them down the hallway back into the bar. They sat down at the table and drank another beer, listening to the music until Heidi came to the table and leaned over Lion's shoulder, all flirty. In her hand, she had several folded papers, which she tucked into Lion's jacket.

Immediately, the Diamondbacks stood. They threw several wads of big bills on the table and left. The other members of their crew in the bar followed them out. Heidi gathered the enormous tip and grinned at the other two waitresses and the bartenders as she made her way through the crowd to hand over the tip to Preacher.

He whistled softly. "Nice, babe."

"It's this top. It's always lucky."

Sabelia coughed behind her hand and continued to serve drinks as fast as she could while Anya laughed and the band played.

TWENTY-TWO

~≈≈~

Savage tossed the keys onto the nearest end table instead of hanging them up. This wasn't going to be easy. Seychelle moved ahead of him toward the bedroom, not bothering with lights. At the sound of the keys dropping, she stopped and turned back to face him. The floor-to-ceiling windows allowed so much light in despite the night, he could see the sudden apprehension on her face.

"Savage?" She took a step toward him.

He held up his hand to stop her. It was best she didn't come near him. Not now. Not when his demons were riding him so hard.

"Babe." He kept his voice casual. "Was thinkin' it was time to take a trip with a couple of the brothers to San Francisco."

Seychelle's head turned toward his, her blue eyes opening wide. Already she was shaking her head. He ignored her first response and kept on.

"I know my cycle, Seychelle. I need to hit the fight club. I'll take Maestro and Keys with me. They'll look out for me. When I've worked a little energy off, I'll come on home."

She stopped in the middle of the living room, regarding

him with her large, all-too-seeing eyes. She gave another shake of her head. "We talked about this."

"Yeah, babe, we did." He didn't want to look at her, so he moved to the large glass window and stared at the crashing waves. He was like that inside. Roiling. Fighting. Complete chaos. "I explained to you very carefully how I went to the clubs and took a few fights. I'll text the brothers and start out this evening." It was already two in the morning. He was feeling like a maniac. Too close to the edge of madness.

"We do this together. If you need to go to a fight club, that means it's time."

The sadistic monster in him roared for release. He wanted nothing more than to take her out in the moonlight and tie her where he could use his whip. His entire being craved that release. Needed it. He tasted that need in his mouth.

He forced himself to speak when his body rebelled. Everything in him rebelled against it. He didn't want to save her this time—and a part of him feared that. His voice came out a dark rasp. "It will be safer for you if I go to the club first, Seychelle."

"It's safer for you, and much more enjoyable, if you stay right here with me, Savage." She tilted her chin, but her eyes met his steadily. "I'll need instructions."

He could see the trepidation. That little hint of fear. A flare of excitement rushed through him. She awakened the beast like no one else ever could. He was roaring now. Hungry. Greedy. Eager to devour her.

Savage stared at her for a long moment, the fight in him all too real. "I can't lose you, Seychelle. I can't. This goes wrong and I lose you or I hurt you, it's over, baby. There's no coming back from that. It's just safer to go to San Francisco . . ."

She closed the distance between them, reaching up to curl her palm around the nape of his neck. "Savage, I love you. *All* of you. We knew this was coming. This is your time to be this part of you, to let it out. I'm here for you. I told you I would be, and I will. I'm nervous, but we both expected that. And you need that." She pressed her lips to his.

He felt that soft brush of her mouth right through his body. An offer. Her love. The tip of her tongue ran along the seam of his mouth, and he opened to her. There was no holding back against the overwhelming tide of need. He wrapped his arms around her and dragged her against him, fitting her body to his, locking her there while he kissed her.

Lust rushed through his veins like a dark predator, mixing with love to create a fireball hot and wild. A turbulent storm that already bordered on pushing the limits of his control. He lifted his head, gripping her arms, ready to thrust her away from him. Seychelle clung to him.

"Savage. I'm sure. Absolutely certain. You need to let this part of you have free rein without fear. Let yourself have complete freedom. This is your time. You only get to allow this once in a while. This is my time to give it to you. Let me. Have faith that I'll bring us both home safely. I'm giving you permission to be you so there will never be a need to be ashamed by anything you do here. This is my decision. My choice."

He stared down into her blue eyes, his darkest cravings warring with his deepest fears of losing her. Her eyes were clear. Held love and acceptance. He had to believe in her. He slid the pad of his thumb across her delicate chin.

"Follow me." He walked ahead of her to the grotto, turning on the taps himself, reaching for the special jar of purple-and-blue bath salts that looked so innocent. Preacher had devilishly come up with the formula. He poured a generous amount into the water so that it sparkled invitingly. "You can touch yourself all you want, but you're not to get yourself off. Do you understand me? That's a hard rule, Seychelle."

"Of course."

So innocent. She should know him by now. Maybe she did. He framed her face with his hands and took her mouth gently. As gently as he could when he was already slipping into that sadistic beast wanting to take what was his and claim every inch of her his way. Make her prove to him she meant every single word she said. That she loved him. She either did or she didn't. He would put those vows to the test tonight. She would suffer for him. Give him her tears. Offer up her body. See him for what he was, see his worst cravings and the dark satisfaction he got when his whip decorated her pristine skin.

He made his way to the shower and took his time in the hot water, washing himself thoroughly before pulling on a loose pair of soft drawstring pants. He opened the top drawer containing his collection of coiled whips. He kept them oiled, kept them in perfect condition in anticipation of this night. Each was a work of art, made specifically with purpose.

He touched his bullwhip, an easy favorite, but too easy. There was the Devil Harpy. He was drawn to that one, black and red, starting out with a twelve-plait single tail and ending up with evil tails of fire, three of them, as intense as the wielder of the whip wanted them to be. The overlay and falls were all in one piece, and it had a heavy fully flexible handle. It was a unique whip and one he enjoyed using.

The other he considered also started out as a twelve-plaited single tail but ended in five very, very thin, long fingers of stingy plaits. Between the last two choices of whips, he could produce a multitude of unique patterns on Seychelle's skin. He pulled all three whips from the drawer and walked outside to set them up on a table across from the posts where he was going to tie her.

His music was ready. The crash of the waves was a perfect match for the blood rushing through his veins. His heart pounded as he checked the rings set deep into the posts. He wanted to make certain the cuffs were at the right height. Nothing could impede his movement—or that of his whips.

By now, the salts he'd poured so generously in the water would be acting on her body, working their way inside, and she'd be rather desperate for his mouth. His fingers. His cock. He smiled to himself. She would be so needy—a good thing. She would need that.

He heard her and turned. She was on the deck, wearing nothing but small beads of water on her skin. Her hair was down, flowing around her body, until a capricious wind gusted and sent it flying. She was trembling, perhaps from the cold, perhaps from fear, but she stood her ground.

Savage went to her, curling his palm around the nape of her neck and looking into her eyes. "I love you more than anything, Seychelle." He was all too aware his voice was strained. Rough. He knew he looked different even. He hoped she could see past the monster in him to the man who loved her. Even the monster loved her. He pressed his forehead against hers. "We can stop this right here. I can head to San Francisco and you'll be a hell of a lot safer. I'm going to tell you, straight up, I don't want that. But I do want you safe. I don't know if I can stay in control."

Her hands came up to frame his face, her eyes meeting his. "I'm telling you, straight up, Savage, you don't need to stay in control. This is my gift to you. Kiss me now and then tell me what to do."

"You're absolutely certain?" He wanted her to be. He needed her to be. Those eyes didn't so much as flinch. He took her mouth and let flames consume them both.

The moment he broke that kiss, he let himself believe. He took her at her word. Her body undulated, and her hand slid down toward her mound with a soft little cry. He caught her wrist and tugged, taking her straight through the yard to the poles, where he stretched her arm out and bound her wrist with a cuff.

"Didn't I say not to get yourself off?"

She squirmed, trying to rub her thighs together. "I really want you, Savage. Before we start, could you just use your mouth? Or your fingers?"

He stretched her other arm out and cuffed that wrist to the pole. "You have to learn patience, baby. You never have patience." He poured amusement into his voice.

Savage checked the bindings on Seychelle's wrists. She was trembling almost uncontrollably, feeding that dark lust that welled up like a volcano inside of him. The cool night air played over her body, adding to the illusion of fingers touching her in the dim light. He went silent, knowing the sound of his voice grounded her. He didn't want to give her that, not yet, when it wasn't needed. Later, she would need his voice; she would need much more from him.

He hooked her bare foot and shoved it wide and then bent to secure her ankle to the post with a cuff. As he rose, he ran his fingers up the inside of her thigh, over her bare pussy lips, feeling the slick heat, smiling when she shuddered with need, and then down her other side, trailing that sweet honey in a little intriguing smear along her thigh. He shoved her left leg wide and secured that ankle as well.

He circled her again, tugging on the ankle bindings that kept her legs spread apart, exposing every inch of her naked body to him. The bath salts had done their job. He could see the slickness forming on her tight little opening. That was all his. Not hers. This night wasn't about her at all.

He swept her hair into a knot on top of her head and then wrapped it into a silken scarf that was tied to the crossbeam above her, so she didn't have a lot of room to move. He needed her hair out of the way, so he had access to both the front and back of her—all that satin skin. As he moved around her, he deliberately ran his hands down her soft skin—skin that belonged to him.

"You're so fucking beautiful, Seychelle. I knew you'd look like this with the moonlight shining on you."

The music pounded through him the way his heart beat. He had put on his favorite band, Five Finger Death Punch. He identified with so many of their lyrics. The beat crashed through his blood, straight to his cock, finding the same thundering roar as the waves smashing against the rocks.

His woman was beautiful in her fear of the unknown. He stood behind her and pressed his body against hers, his palms cupping her tits. She had good-sized breasts. More than a handful, high, round and firm, her nipples standing out, already hard pebbles, telling him that she might be scared, but she was very aroused. Her waist was small, her hips flared. He loved her ass, and he pushed his erection tight against her generous cheeks.

"You're ready for this, baby. So ready. You're dripping for my cock, and we haven't even gotten started." He whispered the truth in her ear like a sin. His teeth closed on her delicate lobe and bit down hard enough to sting, making her gasp. She tried to move her head, to rest it on his shoulder, but her hair tied into the scarf above her made that impossible. He licked at the sting.

"Remember how it felt? That fire? So good, Seychelle. You loved it. Your body was made for mine. This is going to be so much more intense. That only means when I let you have my cock, it will be like nothing you've ever experienced."

He stepped in front of her again, this time picking up his coiled bullwhip. He showed it to her, watching her eyes widen with both trepidation and anticipation. Deliberately, he caught her left nipple, that beautiful nipple he had clamped before to prepare her for this moment. He pinched hard, as if she wore clover clamps. She gasped, and the demon in him roared with approval, thundered for more. His cock pulsed for more. His mouth clamped down on her right tit, sucking hard, drawing it into his mouth while the fist holding his bullwhip brought the handle between her legs.

She was needy. The moment he touched her clit with the braided leather, she reacted helplessly, her hips pushing against it, a moan escaping. He bit down on her nipple, using his teeth mercilessly, allowing her to ride against the whip handle while his fingers and teeth tugged and pulled her nipples harshly.

Tears formed in her eyes, liquid gold as far as he was concerned. He let up the pressure and used his tongue to ease the sting. "It hurts so good, doesn't it, baby?" He kissed his way down her belly, sliding the whip handle back and forth over the insides of her thighs.

"Please, Savage." She whispered the entreaty.

He licked at the honey spilling along her bare lips. Her entire body jerked. She was ready. More than ready. He straightened and backed away. "You do please me, Seychelle. What is the rule? Tell me." He poured steel into his voice, keeping his tone low, a velvet demand.

She swallowed hard. "No screaming unless I'm having an orgasm. I can cry silently, but my tears belong to you."

He nodded. "What do you say if you need me to slow down and give you a moment?"

"Yellow."

"And to stop?"

"Red."

"If you say *red*, we end everything. You're in control here. Remember that, baby. You're done, you say that. Promise me."

She nodded.

"I need to hear the words."

"I promise."

"This isn't like the flogger I used on you before. This is going to be intense. Each whip is going to be harsher. Much more extreme. You have to surrender completely to the sensations. Give yourself to it. Let the fire take you."

She nodded, but her blue gaze had dropped to the coiled bullwhip. Her tongue touched her lips. Moistened them. He stepped forward again, not wanting to take a chance of losing her, his palm cupping the side of her face for one moment, his eyes looking into hers.

"You ready?" She had to be ready. She was ready. She was dripping. Her breathing was ragged. Her pupils were so dilated, and endorphins were already kicking in. Her gaze kept returning to the whip, curious, needy, a kind of craving mixed with fear. She tried to nod, but her hair was tied too tight.

Savage let her go and trailed his fingers down the side of her neck. Gently. Trying to give her courage, looking into her eyes. Trying to tell her without words that he would watch out for her. Look after her. Make it good for her, no matter what he said. He saw acceptance of the demons in him. Of his terrible cravings. Of his needs. Of whatever he had to do this night.

He walked a few feet from her and shook out the whip. The moment he did, he felt the pounding beat of the music moving through his body. The well of rage boiled and seethed like a giant lava pool, spewing volcanic heat through his system, taking him over. He let it. Feeling alive. Letting the power, the domination, rule him. Take control.

He turned, the single tail snaking out. The crack of the leather was loud in the night, the sound beautiful. So fucking beautiful. He didn't touch her yet, just cracked the whip in the night, feeling the leather as an extension of his arm, his body, again. That was the way it always was. It was part of him. His brain moved it automatically, almost without thought, in the way his brain told his arms or legs to move.

He walked around her, using that same slow pace, knowing she couldn't hear him, couldn't turn her head. She could only wait for the sound of the whip, the first streak of fire as it fell across her flesh. He chose an easy overhead flick to warm her up. Although it didn't have the same savage sound of the original cracking of his whip, in the night, it was loud enough to be ominous. The thin braid of leather hit her back in a precise line. She gasped, choked back a cry of shock. That single soft stroke of the whip lit her on fire far more than any of the harder blows he'd given her with the flogger. He used those flicks fast to cover her back, buttocks and thighs, bringing the blood to the surface and getting her used to the shock of the single tail striking her.

Each time that he added a little more of a flick to increase the fire, he stepped into her and gave her his fingers, or his mouth, making certain her body reacted with need. With craving. He took his time with her, enjoying the night, the crash of the waves, the heat of his blood, the way she looked tied in the moonlight, her body on display, so open to his every whim, to that lash. More and more, he could view her as he wanted. That perfect skin, visualizing the patterns he would put onto it, that he would create.

Savage coiled the whip, and, running the pads of his fingers down her back, he moved around her to stand in front of her. He had marked her skin, but barely, and there was satisfaction in knowing she was eager for more. Almost desperate for more. He stepped close, using the handle of the whip to push her chin up so he could capture her mouth with his. At the same time, he slid his fingers into her slick pussy.

Seychelle had been intrigued with the whip and what she'd seen him do with it. She'd enjoyed the flogger. So far, her body had responded positively to her warm-up. He wanted her feeling mindless. Desperate for release.

Once more he stepped back, flicking her belly gently, bringing the blood to the surface, letting her nerve endings feel the glow, using a fancier figure eight so she was mesmerized by the action of the bullwhip, the sound of it moving to the beat of the music. She loved music, and it all worked together.

He continued gently a few more times—her breasts, her belly, that sweet little mound, the tops of her thighs and then the insides of her legs. A preview. She had no idea what was coming, but he did, and the thought of it flooded him with a savage kind of rush. He took his time, carefully lulling her into a false sense of security, watching her body grow needier as the streaks of fire danced over her skin and every nerve ending flared into life.

He coiled the whip, tossed it onto the small table and picked up the second, shorter one. His heart accelerated. His cock jerked in anticipation as he stepped close to her, one hand sliding down her belly to find her needy clit, his thumb and fingers moving in time to the wild beat of the music, in time to the hot blood rushing through his veins like jagged lightning.

"That was just a warm-up, baby. This is the start. Are you ready for more?" His fingers continued to circle her clit, flicking the hard little bud and then curling into her slick entrance, stroking deep until she was riding him helplessly, moaning continuously. "Do you want more?" He whispered the temptation. "Do you need it?"

His tongue licked at her tit, the idea of using the whip putting his cock into a frenzy of need. He wanted her mouth on him. She'd never once gone there. He'd never demanded that of her.

"Yes," she managed.

"That's not good enough, Seychelle."

"Please, more, Savage," she choked out, her hips trying to press down onto his fingers.

"That's my girl." He took his hand away, bringing his fingers to her mouth. "Lick me clean." His voice roughened with demand, a rasp of steel.

She did exactly what he ordered, her eyes on his. He watched, his blood roaring through his veins. Pounding. Fuck, she was beautiful. Perfect. Made for him.

Very slowly, he brought the new whip into her sight, shaking it out so she could see it, and watched the dilation of her eyes. He didn't blame her for the fear that rolled off her in waves. The whip had a bit of an evil appearance, with the three red long tips that looked like long, wicked Harpy talons coming off those thin, black braided falls. They were evil and wicked in the right hands, and he was a master of pain. He was the Whip Master. This particular whip was shorter in length, only thirty-nine inches. The handle was flexible, giving him so much control.

He dangled the black-and-red whip in front of her and then slid the falls over the curves of her breasts, lower until those red talons met her mound. He was grateful that he'd shaved her and there was nothing marring his vision of the thin red and black braids against her bare skin. He enjoyed the contrast between the stark colors of the whip and her pristine skin. He hadn't left any real marks with the bullwhip, but he would with this one, and the idea of it was exciting.

Savage was capable of delivering wicked blows. He'd trained for years. He knew exactly what he was doing. Few could wield crops, floggers or any other type of pain-giving weapon as he could. He knew exactly how to deliver the most pain possible when he needed—or when he wanted—to do it. He was breathing hard, and his cock was filling with scorching-hot blood, a demon rising, fighting for control. Now he could feel his heart beating right through his cock.

Seychelle took a deep breath as Savage stepped back. Where before there was little expression, now those lines in his tough features were carved deep, a mixture both sensual and cruel. He studied her body as if she was his toy, his possession. This was the sadist wholly engaged, fully functioning, a cruel, sensual being intent on his own pleasure. He was fascinating and, she had to admit, hot as hell. She was in such a heightened state of sexual arousal, her body desperate for his, all she could think about was getting his cock in her.

Seychelle couldn't take her eyes off him. The whip seemed an extension of him. He was all flowing muscle, scars and burns, arrogance and dominant power, but it was more than that, so much more. The moment he stepped back, everything about him changed. She was seeing a side of him she'd never seen before. This was the part of him he called the sadistic monster, the one he'd been afraid for her to meet. This one truly enjoyed inflicting pain on his woman. There was no conflict on his face. He wasn't afraid now. He wanted her to meet him—or he didn't care.

He snapped his wrist without warning, and the black tail snaked out fast, those three red talons seeking a target, striking the top curves over her breasts, but two of them, the very tips hitting her nipples. For a moment, Seychelle felt nothing at all, and then the shocking burn was like being branded with a live flame held to her skin so that it traveled deep beneath.

She clamped her lips together tightly, but tears instantly formed in her eyes, blurring her vision. Her entire body shuddered. Her knees turned to jelly. She couldn't do this. Nothing had ever hurt like this. Nothing. At the same time, a wave of fire burst through her core until her sex clenched and blood pounded in a dark, demonic response in her feminine channel.

The evil whip struck along the side of the curve of her right breast, two of those wicked talons once again striking her nipple. She came up on her toes, shaking her head, her breath exploding out of her lungs. Her nipples peaked. She felt them. It was sick how her body reacted, the way the flames spread like a wildfire straight to her sex. Her nipples and breasts were so sensitive to a mix of pain and pleasure, but this was too extreme.

Beads of sweat broke out on her forehead. Seychelle couldn't catch her breath. Just watching him through the tears pouring down her face, seeing him, that expression of sensual cruelty, of total concentration, of pure sexual lust, added to the arousing need coiling so tightly, like a terrible fist deep inside her. At the same time, those terrible red talons were evil claws, just waiting to slash into her skin.

Savage stepped into her, the flexible handle of the whip finding her slick heat unerringly while his fingers traced the bright red welts over her right breast and then to the side. "You have to stay very, very still, Seychelle, for these next two lashes. You'll do that for me, won't you, baby?"

He lapped at her inflamed nipple with his tongue, soothing the terrible pain, then sucking it into the heat of his mouth. At the same time, he pushed the thick braid of leather into her and rubbed the abrasive knot over her clit. She nearly cried out, but at the last moment was able to clamp her lips together, even though the tears continued to flow.

He pulled back from her breast. "You'll stay very still, won't you? This is very precise work, and I don't want it to look sloppy on your gorgeous tits. You loved the way it looked on the mannequin, so I chose the pattern just for you."

He sounded like he was giving her such a gift. She wished he hadn't stopped. The night air was even colder. The music sounded more ferocious, as did the pounding waves. Savage's eyes had gone so arctic blue, so ice-cold and remote, but filled with a lust that bordered on animalistic.

The whip he held up gleamed in the moonlight with liquid from her, and his smile was cruel as he licked the leather, those eyes watching her as he stepped back. He was clearly waiting for her answer. She forced herself to nod, giving him what he wanted, when he had the evidence that she was so needy. There was no hiding it from him.

He struck fast, just a flick of his wrist, two flicks, and those three talons struck once, then again. The first strike laid lines under her right breast, with the tips so painful on her generous flesh, one striking precisely on her wet, inflamed nipple. The second strike somehow landed on the *inside*, between her breasts, those tips striking the sensitive mound, completing the cup of the bralette, and one of those tips hit her nipple again. The sting was so painful she would have gone to her knees if she wasn't tied.

She opened her mouth to call *yellow*, but he had coiled the whip and sauntered around behind her. When he did, he trailed his fingers along the nape of her neck.

"You are doing so well, angel. I didn't think you could really do this for me." He caught her head, tilting it, pulling on her scalp where her hair was tied, licking at her tears. "You're so beautiful like this, taking my real lashes. My patterns. They'll last a long while on your body. Every time I see them, I'll be so fucking hard. I didn't need to go to the underground club. I just needed you." He trailed his hand down her back to her bottom. "Just this body you're giving to me."

Seychelle did her best not to tense up when she couldn't see him. She thought it was bad when she saw the whip coming at her, but with Savage standing behind her, she feared it was going to be far worse because she didn't know what he was doing. When the lashes fell on her, from the neck down, forming the sides and back of the top, the streaks felt as if he touched her with a living flame and burned each one deep. He came around to her front and finished, that violent red and black whip snapping and flicking to draw the cup on her left breast, the talons every bit as wicked and sharp as a predator's claws.

Seychelle could barely see Savage through the tears in her eyes, but it was impossible to take her eyes from him. He was a man possessed, the pounding music and crashing sea reflected in the sheer poetry of his fluid movements. The lines in his face were carved deep with sensual cruelty. He was dazzling, mesmerizing, even as he wielded the whip, making it whirl and dance to the beat and rhythm of the song playing.

Abruptly, he stopped, and she found herself trying to breathe through the pain, through the horrifying awareness of her need of him. He tossed the whip carelessly onto the table but then picked up more items. A small sob escaped as he turned back to her. He stood beside the table for a moment, lifting a water bottle to his mouth while he studied her as if she were one of the mannequins he'd practiced on.

"Looks gorgeous, baby. Your tits were made for the whip."

A little shudder went through her body, but it didn't stop her sex from clenching at his words, or the way his gaze slid over her so possessively. He put the water down and sauntered over to her.

"Need you to take a little more for me, angel," he whispered. "I brought a couple of things to make it easier for you. Can you do that for me, Seychelle?"

She was so tired. The pain of that horrid whip had been excruciating, but her body was so desperate. How much longer could he go before he would have to take her? She could see the huge bulge at the front of his thin pants. She'd never seen his cock straining so much.

She moistened her lips and forced herself to really look at his face, at his eyes, to see beyond the cruelty of the sadist to the man who had taken on the rage of his fellow brethren for the last couple of months. She wanted to make certain they drained most of that away, if not all of it, so that reservoir was as empty as they could get it.

He wasn't nearly done. She could see the rage still burn-

ing hot and wild beyond the brutality of this part of Savage
that had been set free.

"I can do it." The consent came out in a whisper. Her
voice wouldn't go above that. The knot of tears in her throat
blocked sound.

His fist in her hair tilted her head back farther, and he
kissed her. It wasn't a gentle or loving kiss. It was possessive. Hard. He took his time removing the tears from her
face before he dropped to a crouch between her spread
thighs. Her heart jumped, accelerated. She felt his hot
breath.

"Brothers gave me a few intriguing toys for my birthday.
Knew you'd love them, so I laid them out to use. This little
button was programmable. Preacher made certain I had
enough oil that would heat up and make you feel good. I also
had Mechanic program it to the beat of my music."

He fit the button over her clit and secured it and then
moved behind her. "I used that oil on this little toy as well.
It's also programmable. Pulses like crazy to the music, massages and pounds to the beat. You're into music, baby, so I
know you're going to love this."

Without warning, he poured oil between her cheeks and
pressed something that felt far too big into the forbidden star
there. She gasped, resisting. His hand came down hard on
her left cheek. The pressure never let up, steady and very
strong, sliding the toy in deep until it was seated. He'd used
plugs before, but nothing that long or wide.

Savage walked back around to stand in front of her. "You
have to stay very still. I'm going to form the bottom half of
your outfit." Seychelle looked dazed. Confused. On the
brink of calling everything off, but not certain she would—
or could—make herself do it.

Smirking, Savage pushed the thin material from his
hips. Her gaze immediately jumped to his straining cock.
He fisted the wide girth casually, knowing she was desperate, watching her strain toward him without realizing she

was doing so. He caught up the third whip as he passed by the table and walked back to her, taking his time.

Standing close, he curled his fingers into her sweet, slick pussy, so hot now and greedy with need, she didn't know if she was sobbing for his cock or from the pain of those wicked red talons on the whip. He licked up her neck and over her cheek, tasting her tears, reveling in each one of them. These were for him. All his. She gave them to him freely.

"Savage, please." She pushed into his fingers, rocking her hips in desperation.

"We aren't finished, baby. You have to ask me for more." He trailed the handle of the whip over the curves of her breasts, those beautiful lines rising in red welts that showed his precise pattern, the one that looked as if he'd created a bralette on her body. "You want my cock, you earn it."

He kissed his way down her tear-wet face to her chin, to her neck, his teeth nipping. Stinging. All the while his fist pumped his cock, his rough hand scraping along the scars. It felt so fucking good. His mouth wandered lower, kissing his way down her throat, to her collarbone and then the top of those sweet curves where the first of his beautiful bright red welts formed her bralette. His lips and tongue teased over the raised surface, the lines that formed a cage around her right breast. Those lines spread out from her erect nipple much like a spider's web.

He didn't know a single person who could rival his work. This was sheer beauty. He kissed his way to her nipple and flicked it with his tongue. She shivered, a groan escaping. She thrust her breast into the hot cavern of his mouth while her eyes devoured his fist wrapped around the scarred ridges of his brutally erect cock.

He sucked her nipple into his mouth, the nipple he'd slashed each time with those wicked red talons when he'd formed that beautiful bralette with his whip.

She nodded. "I said I'd do it."

"Not the same thing as wanting it, babe. You have to say

you want the fire. Tell me you want the fire, Seychelle. You want to burn with me in it."

She swallowed hard, but he knew he was going to win. He saw capitulation in her eyes first, and it was all he could do not to howl at the moon in triumph.

"Yes, Savage, I want the fire."

He grinned at her, letting her see his cruelty. The rush. The euphoria when he held such power over her. "You can't move, Seychelle. Stay perfectly still or you'll mess up the lines."

He stepped back immediately and pointed to his player, turning up the volume, as Five Finger Death Punch's *Jekyll and Hyde* burst out into the night. As the music swelled, pouring what he was into his veins, he saw the same beat take hold of the little button at her clit and the merciless plug in her ass. She would need the pleasurable sensations to counter the new whip he was using to form the cute little decorative shorts he would cover her ass and thighs with, and that gorgeous mound of hers.

He shook out the whip. It was a single tail leading into five thin braided fingers, long ones. Each finger ended in a single knotted tiny decorative rose. He'd braided the whip himself. The handle was flexible, just as the other whip had been, giving him plenty of control and movement. The first strike had a satisfying crack as he snapped it using a well-practiced flick of his wrist. The tail was fast, a blur, as it whipped out those five long, wicked fingers seeking their target unerringly.

He saw them hit perfectly just below her hips, all five laying those stripes that ended in the gorgeous roses pitting into her delicate skin. The fingers stung like a mother, and she reacted with a stifled cry, her body flushing, endorphins bringing a fine sheen of sweat and goose bumps to the surface. A fresh flood of tears trickled down her face.

The power settled into him, drove him higher. The music took him, thundered through his veins, pounded through his blood as he rained lash after lash down, over and across, creating the perfect pair of shorts to go with the bralette. The welts were a darker red, and there were more of them, the lines curling around her thighs and hips. This whip was a step above the last one, and he put a little more punch into it.

Savage moved around her continually, the whip never stopping, although he had to remind her not to move. Her body shuddered. Her breathing was ragged. She struggled not to move her hips when the wicked stimulation at her clit pounded to the beat of the music. All the while, the plug in her ass pulsed and massaged in counter rhythm. She needed those pleasurable sensations desperately to counter the terrible pain of those stinging fingers.

He found himself putting more and more strength into that flick of his wrist, just a little harder, watching her closely, seeing how much she could—and would—take for him. The high was getting higher. The rush stronger. His cock was close to exploding.

She had such a perfect ass, and he made certain that those curves had perfect lines all the way around, the welts raised and dark, especially on her sit spot. He studied his handiwork, his heart nearly exploding with the high.

"Yeah, baby," he said softly, as he moved around once again to her front. "Let me see you cry for me. Give me your tears. Those are mine. All for me. That's you loving me."

Power and control wrapped him in euphoria and arousal beyond anything he'd known. Dominance and a primal feeling of sheer ownership, as if she belonged to him and he could do whatever he wished with her, settled over him. He needed this. He wanted it and he needed it. The craving was so strong, and she was his to do with whatever he willed.

He sent the whip snapping through the air, those beautiful, wicked roses with the tiny thorns hit in a beautiful fall, one after another, like a flowing waterfall this time, right on her mound. He didn't wait, bringing it back and snapping it out again and again. Five times in a row.

The world seemed to stand still. Stop. Or maybe time did.

Seychelle thought that whip was agony, but she'd been determined to bear it until she was certain Savage had purged the deep well of rage in him. But this . . . This was beyond any pain she had ever thought possible. She truly thought he was ripping her body open with the whip, and if she could look down—which she couldn't because he'd tied her hair and trapped her—she'd see blood running like a river. But she could see him.

Savage looked insane with sensual power. He was definitely out of control. So high, she would have thought him on drugs. For the first time, a shadow of a doubt passed through her mind that she might not be able to stop him. She was entirely alone with him, and he was definitely out of control. All of that flashed through her mind with the first fall of those evil roses on her mound. She opened her mouth to scream, to put a stop to the whip, but no sound emerged, the pain was too excruciating. He struck so fast he'd managed to lash her several more times before she was able to find her voice.

"Red." The first was a whisper. Her eyes were on him. Watching. Willing him to hear her. To listen. "Savage. Red." Her eyes burned, she'd cried so much. This had to be enough for him. It was all she had to give, but more than that, she knew she had to stop him before he went any further. The next step, he might do something he would regret.

The hand holding the whip froze so that the tail and the wicked fingers fell close to his side. His eyes moved moodily over her body. At first, she didn't think he really heard her. His eyes were so dilated, the pupils looked almost blown, but he coiled the whip and then tossed it aside, coming to her, stepping close.

She couldn't stop her hips from moving, or the tears from flowing. She was sobbing uncontrollably. Chanting his name. A plea. She needed him.

He pulled the button from her clit. "You want my cock, baby, or do you need to go inside?" His hands were up, releasing the scarf tying her hair.

She wanted his cock desperately. She wasn't certain she could live without it. That was always the way it was, but she didn't know why. The tears wouldn't stop. Savage leaned down and released her ankles from the cuffs and then her wrists before swinging her up to cradle her in his arms.

She shook her head, burying her face against his chest. "I need your cock. I do. Please."

"I know, baby. Not like that, not in the cuffs. Somewhere a little more comfortable for you. You took a lot for me. You're still going to be taking it because you know I'll be rough."

Seychelle didn't care. She needed his roughness. She needed his cock. She needed him. Still, being in his arms hurt like hell. He kept leaning his head down and nuzzling her breasts with his chin. The bristles rasped over those dark, sensitive welts, sending stinging darts that became streaks of fire straight through her skin, setting her squirming to try to stop the sensation from traveling through her body straight to her sex.

Savage hadn't removed the plug, and as he nudged open the sliding glass door leading to the master bedroom, another song began to play, and the plug pulsed and moved to the pounding beat. The music filled the room, already lit with candles and the scents he loved. Red wax fell like tears through the black honeycombs on the tall pyramid stands where the large candles sat.

He took her to the bed and laid her on her back, a shocking move when he usually liked to take her from behind after one of his heavier sessions. Even so, he positioned her with her legs wide, draped over the sides of the bed. He didn't wait, just stepped to the end of the bed and slammed his cock into her. She was slick and hot and so in need, but still his girth was big enough that with his scarred ridges, it felt as if he were splitting her in two. Still, fire streaked through her and she nearly shattered.

His hands gripped her hips, and he yanked her body into his. "You are so fucking tight every damn time, Seychelle." He wasn't looking at her, only at the dark welts on her body.

"Look at your tits, baby. Look at how beautiful that pattern looks on you."

He kept surging into her, nearly lifting her off the bed with every stroke so that he drove the breath from her lungs. The pain was almost unbearable, but there was so much pleasure streaking through her, consuming her. It mixed together until she couldn't tell one from the other and she didn't care. She only needed him filling her, stretching her to the breaking point.

He took her up so high, that terrible tension coiling tight, and then he leaned over her, his mouth on her nipple, teeth clamping down, tugging with the other hand, fingers biting into the roses while his thumb thumped her clit hard. She exploded into impossible cataclysmic waves, so powerful she screamed and screamed, trying to hold on to him for an anchor, but he was riding her hard. Then he flipped her body over, uncaring of the welts, as she came, belly down on the material.

He dragged her legs over the edge, yanked out the plug, kicking her legs wide apart, and once more began to surge into her like a madman. Every wild hammering drive into her sent her body skidding across the bed, so the material rubbed over the whip marks. It was her mound, with those terrible roses, that added to the coiling heat that wouldn't let up in her body. It was as if she had caught fire with him and they were burning together, a firestorm out of control. It went on and on, with Savage smacking those whip marks, or raking them, but that only seemed to drive her higher. Then they were both shattering, exploding, coming apart together in a way she didn't think they'd ever be able to come back from.

She floated for a long time, barely aware of Savage taking care of her, washing her carefully, applying the numbing lotion, whispering to her, soothing her, turning her gently to do the same to her front. She drifted off, only to have Savage wake her so many times she lost count. Most of the time, she couldn't move, but her body exploded every single time. He always did the same thing afterward. Holding her close, rubbing the lotion gently on her. Whispering to her, rocking her tenderly, sometimes showering or bathing her. Telling her to sleep. Then waking her again to repeat the savage fucking.

During the day he wanted her to wear a see-through shirt and nothing else. He cooked for her, waited on her, took care of her, but out of the blue, he would set her on a counter, shove her over a couch or a chair, take her on the floor, up against a wall. Outside on the porch. It didn't matter. He was insatiable. The moment he looked at her with those patterns on her skin, he was as hard as a rock and all over her. It hurt and yet, she had to admit, he always made certain her orgasms—and they were always multiple—were explosive and amazing.

He was rough and demanding. Attentive and even loving outside of the sex. The sex was just that: sex. It wasn't loving, and it didn't feel loving to her. But she did begin to feel in control. She did begin to understand his cycle. She could look in the mirror and admire his ability to put the patterns on her skin and never once break her skin. There wasn't one single spot where he'd struck so hard that she'd bled. It might have felt that way, but she hadn't.

As the days passed, he began to ease up, and she caught more and more glimpses of Savage. Her Savage. She began to make an effort to converse with him. Just a little. Tease him. Make him laugh. She asked to see his whips. She really was interested in the way he'd braided the leather. She wanted to see the floggers and understand why some he considered "toys" and some were too intense and even dangerous in the wrong hands. She asked lots of questions and tried to get as much information as possible.

By the second week, Savage had come back to her. He still loved to see the fading welts on her body, but when he rubbed his hands over them, he wasn't trying to hurt her. She could tell the difference. She didn't want him to feel shame, not when she had insisted they were partners and she *felt* like his partner. She reiterated that he had stopped the moment she had given him the word.

They laughed hysterically together when she tried her hand at just cracking one of the whips, but it was fun practicing, with Savage showing her how. She knew it gave him a sense of companionship. She wanted him to know she was with him 100 percent. All in. Committed. She did her best to show him.

TWENTY-THREE

"Babe. Want to talk to you about something important before you head out." Savage watched his woman as she stepped out onto the front porch. He was always fascinated by the way she moved. She was wholly feminine, her hips swaying in the dark lavender yoga pants she wore to minimize the discomfort of those remaining stripes on her rounded bottom.

She arched her left eyebrow, calling attention to the small scar that bisected that eyebrow, the one she'd gotten saving his life. The moment he noticed it, he was hot all over, just as he was thinking about the way she took his whip for him. She looked so damn innocent and young, with her thick, wild hair falling in waves around her face and down her back. He loved it the most when she just let it be instead of trying to tame it.

"Sit down with me, baby." He indicated a low-slung Adirondack chair made from redwood slats. No cushions. There was a small table made of the same redwood. His chair was across from hers so he could look at her face, see every expression. Ordinarily, he would have talked things out with her right after they had wild sex, but not when he was so out of control. He had to work it completely out of his system first.

Seychelle sank gingerly into the chair, keeping her legs a little apart. She wore soft gray boots to match the sweet little dark lavender sweater with the thick gray lines zigzagging through it. The sweater didn't cling to her generous tits like most of her clothes. She was wearing a bra, but it was one that was lacy around her breasts, so that the mesh caged the weight but didn't press against her nipples.

"I don't want to make you late for your meeting, Savage." She looked a little worried, brushing back a strand of hair that was persistent in falling across her face.

"There are things that need to be said." He was decisive. "I have plenty of time." There was no way he could be away from her without clearing things up. He leaned toward her, his eyes meeting hers. "I'm not saying there's a hope in hell of this happening, but I gotta know, Seychelle, if you want out."

Her brows drew together. "Out of what, honey?"

She wasn't playing him. There was honest puzzlement in her voice. On her face. She spread her hands out in front of her.

"Us. Me and you. Do you want out?" He could feel the familiar panic rising. His chest hurt. His heart beat too fast. Sweat was beading on his forehead. She couldn't love him because he was a fucking sadistic monster.

Her blue eyes drifted over his face with that same expression she'd been giving him consistently. No holding back. Stark, raw love. She didn't try to contain it. Or hide it from him. She just gave it to him, whether he deserved it or not. All of him. Every bit of him. A slow smile made her look even more angelic.

"You're not getting rid of me that easily, Savage. Just because I make you pick up wet towels and throw them in the laundry basket isn't a good enough excuse to try to shove me out."

He pushed his palm hard against his chest. "You think it's the wet towels?"

She shrugged casually. "Probably not. You caught me studying the patterns on your mannequins and you know my evil plan, don't you?"

It was his turn to raise an eyebrow, because she had been in the courtyard with the mannequins. She'd been there for some time, studying them, tilting her head from side to side, walking around them and looking from every angle.

"You weren't just admiring my skills?"

"I was, actually, but I was also going to match the whips with the patterns. That way, I could kind of build up to the harder ones. I thought the one you did on me was beautiful, but it hurt like hell. When I say *hurt like hell*, I really mean that. Those whips were the very devil."

"I was careful with you," he pointed out. "Didn't break your skin."

"You didn't. I was impressed," she admitted. "But I still thought we'd talk about working up to the harder patterns." Matter-of-fact. Easy. As if they were discussing the weather. Interested, even.

She sat there calmly across from him, her body still bearing the welts from their last session, and she was talking about preparing for his next cycle. He turned his head away from her to stare at the pounding waves. He didn't dare keep looking at her. She was going to make him believe she loved him just the way he was and that maybe, just maybe, she'd keep on loving him year after year when he couldn't stop being the monster.

"That's a good idea, Seychelle," he agreed, when he could finally get words out. He still sounded gruffer than he wanted.

"I tried to work out from looking at them which ones were more intense, but I really have no way of knowing. I thought maybe next week you could show me the whips again and explain which ones do what and which are used to create the artwork on each of the mannequins. I find all of it beautiful. Your accuracy . . . astounds me."

She sounded like she meant it, almost admiring. Okay.

Not only admiring, but respectful. He couldn't help himself, he had to look at her even if she saw too much on his face. Because if she was looking at him with that same uncondi- tional, stark love he'd seen earlier, he was going to break down. He fucking knew it. Like some damn pussy with no discipline. She was turning him inside out.

His eyes met hers and then took in the expression on her face. There it was. Open. No reservations whatsoever. Just like the first time he'd met her. Seychelle was genuine. She took him with every single one of his flaws. He was so bro- ken and damaged. No good or decent woman should have anything to do with him, but she loved him in spite of every- thing. *All* of him. She accepted him. He had no idea how. Or why. But he wasn't questioning it.

"Honey." She whispered the endearment softly.

"I think it would be a good idea to wait a couple of weeks before we explore which patterns we decide to use next. We have plenty of time now. I'm speculating, but it could be as long as three months before I get that bad again. You really came through for us, Seychelle."

She smiled at him, that angelic smile she seemed to re- serve just for him. "You told me what to do, over and over, ahead of time. I just listened to you. I'm good at listening, especially under duress. And I'm good at reading the man I love. I just had to make certain you had gotten to a place where you were good." Her smile widened. "You didn't warn me about the week following the main event. It would have been nice to know about the week of staying naked and the wild, unbelievable sex ahead of time."

His gaze moved over her body. "Hard to stay away from you when I finally, after all these years, have my patterns on the only woman who means everything to me."

"Are we good now?" she asked.

"Yeah, babe, we're better than good." Savage stood up and went to her. "Don't know how I got so lucky, but I'm grateful to the powers that be that put me in front of that truck that day. Just glad you're mine."

She wrapped her arms around his neck. "I feel the same way. So lucky to have you. I'll be in Sea Haven, Savage. I know you have your meeting at the clubhouse, but I have to see Eden. Tony called and asked me to . . ."

Savage stiffened, his hands biting down on her shoulders as he held her at arm's length so he could look down into her face. "*Tony?* As in the fucking Diamondback *Shark* Tony? He called you?"

"Tony Ravard called me. Eden's son. That's who called me, Savage."

"You didn't think maybe this warranted sharing with me right away?" Sometimes his woman was enough to make his head want to explode. One minute he was feeling loving, and the next he wanted to turn her over his knee, and not in a good way.

"I was going to share, but you were on the phone with Czar, and then before I could say anything, you told me we had to talk. I assumed what you had to say was way more important than what Tony had said to me."

He resisted shaking her. "Any time a Diamondback talks to you—and why would he have your cell number?" He was getting her a new number. "That man is becoming a problem."

"Savage, don't go off the deep end. He isn't a problem. He has my number because his mother has it. He's worried about her, and he asked if I'd call her and set up something with her and a couple of the other women. She's so upset over losing Nina and Brandon in that car accident. Since you were going to your meeting, I agreed—and before you flip out, I didn't tell him you had a meeting."

"He going to be at this thing you set up?"

She had the fucking nerve to roll her eyes at him. If she wasn't so damn cute, he'd yank her over his knee right then. He still might do it, but he'd run late, and he didn't want to do that.

"Of course not. He's just worried about her."

She leaned in and brushed his mouth with hers. He felt that touch right through his heart.

"We'll be going to the Floating Hat. I tried to choose the women who would ease her suffering. Torpedo Ink can't be there because of the meeting, or I would have asked Lana, but Blythe is wonderful in situations like this. I was very happy that you didn't have anything to do with their car accident, Savage, even knowing Brandon and his mother deserved everything they had coming to them."

She kissed him again. This time a little longer. With a little more fire. His heart turned over, and he was happy he didn't have anything to do with Brandon's death either. He wouldn't have minded slicing that asshole into pieces, but he had to admit, it was nice to be able to be with his woman with hands clear of blood.

Savage wrapped his palm around the nape of her neck. "Player told me Hannah makes up special baskets, like the ones she did for you when you were so ill from the painkillers, but for other things. I'll put in a call and see if she can put together a few things for Eden that maybe will help ease her grief."

She cupped the sides of his face. "I love you, Savin Pajari."

"Enough to add another ring onto this finger?" He pulled her left hand to his chest, his fingers rubbing over the engagement ring there.

"You do like to take advantage."

"Have to while you have that soft look in your eyes, babe. Gotta go. Glitch is gonna be lookin' after you."

"Do you think that's really necessary? He gets so bored."

He didn't answer her, just put the tip of her ring finger in his mouth and bit down. She yelped and pulled her hand away. "You're so oral. Go away. It's time you rode your bike. I've been worried you'd forget how and you'd fall over or something equally lame and I'd have to pretend I didn't know you."

He yanked her completely out of the chair and smacked her hard on her already tender bottom. She was laughing too much to care. He was as well. He waited until she was in her ridiculous little car and out of the garage, heading down the

drive toward Sea Haven, with Glitch following her, before
he swung his leg over the Harley and got on the road, taking
his time.

The day felt perfect to him. His woman had stuck with
him through the worst of who he was. She had gone into it
with her eyes wide open, no rose-colored glasses. She hadn't
exactly enjoyed it, and she'd ridden it out as long as she
could in order to drain off that well of rage in him before
calling him back. *And she'd done it.*

No one else had been there. He had considered asking
Reaper to stay in the shadows just in case, but he'd given his
word to her. He had to believe in the two of them the way
she did. They were a partnership. She was strong. She said
she could do it, and she would, no matter how much he ma-
nipulated her or her body. She'd been on fire, and he'd
been . . . gone. Out of control. She'd called him back.

A new kind of euphoria settled over him. Different. He
recognized love. It ran deeper than that red reservoir of rage.
He would always be a sexual sadist. That wouldn't go away,
but she wasn't making him apologize for it. The well inside
him would fill with anger from the past and future, from his
memories and those of his brothers and sisters, but he could
handle it better now. There would be balance.

He parked his Harley among the long row of bikes in
front of the Torpedo Ink clubhouse and stepped to the curb
as he took out his phone. Seychelle wouldn't have quite
made it to the Floating Hat yet.

**Forgot to tell you. Glitch can read lips. He's going to sit in
that shop facing you and let me know every single thing
you say.**

He smirked as he sent the most outrageous thing he could
think of to her. Glitch would lose his mind if he told him he
had to do that.

**You wouldn't dare. There has to be a law against that kind
of invasion of privacy.**

**I already told you, I don't believe in privacy between us. No
locked doors or locked lips.**

It was all he could do not to hold his stomach laughing. If he looked toward Sea Haven, he was certain he would see smoke coming out in two long, black columns.

There were a few moments of silence. He couldn't help grinning as he walked into the clubhouse. His phone vibrated.

Well, then. I suppose it's war and poor Glitch is caught in the middle. Sabelia has promised classes to some of us and he's going to hear all about retaliatory . . . There were toad emojis and snails and all kinds of other little creatures. Next came a series of remote control emojis and on/off buttons and emojis of men.

Savage was pretty darn certain he knew what that threat meant. Between his laughter, he managed to send her bare butts and paddling emojis. Then he added text. **You're not supposed to be texting and driving.**

I could be parked. You don't know. Glitch got caught at the stoplight. So slow, that one. Lots of laughing emojis. **He can't possibly be telling you where I am.**

"You're in a good mood," Czar greeted.

Savage looked up from his phone. "Seychelle is a riot when she's texting. She drives like a bat out of hell. If I wasn't holding a grudge against that bastard Deveau, I'd ask him to lie in wait for her and give her a ticket for speeding." He smirked at the thought.

"No, you wouldn't."

Savage followed Czar into the meeting room. "No, and I'm betting my little angel could just smile and get out of any ticket she deserved anyway. Seychelle said Blythe was meeting her at the Floating Hat to have tea or something like that with Eden and a couple of her friends."

The other members of Torpedo Ink were drifting in, taking up their regular places around the large oval table.

"Yeah, Blythe told me Seychelle said Eden was taking her sister's death pretty hard," Czar acknowledged as he took his place at the head of the table.

The rectangular room was large, with a bank of windows

that looked out over the wide expanse of meadow leading to the bluff overlooking the crashing waves. The view was priceless and gave them the illusion of freedom. They were Torpedo Ink and took nothing for granted, least of all freedom and safety—every window was bulletproof.

The long wall opposite the windows was painted with a mural of their colors, a tribute to those who had fallen and a reminder that together they could be indestructible. To the left of the colors was a row of names painted in beautiful calligraphy. The flowering shrubs surrounding the names were covered in webs that shimmered in the morning light, forever iridescent, caught with the mist from the sea in those fine filaments, forever weeping tears for the fallen. Brothers and sisters they failed to bring home.

Four armories were secreted in that room, and four ways to escape. They left little to chance. They had practiced using every one of their escape routes under every possible circumstance they could come up with or Code's computer could simulate. The common room held even more, as did their barracks and the kitchen. Each of their chosen homes had safe rooms and passages to escape should they need it. They had go-bags with passports and money stashed. Czar had several children. Steele had a son. Plans had been worked out to get them all out as fast as possible, the entire club working fast to move them to safety. The children would be their first priority.

"Savage?" Reaper called his name. Got his attention. "Czar said Eden was taking it pretty hard that her sister died in a car crash."

"And Brandon, her nephew," Savage added. "She was afraid of him, but she didn't wish him dead. Eden isn't like that. She and Nina, her sister, hadn't gotten along for years. Nina drank a lot, and she'd turned Brandon against Eden and Reggie, her husband. Nina had gotten sober and acted as if she was making amends. She visited Eden, did her hair, seemed closer. It was the first time in years Eden had hope that they were going to have a good relationship. Family means something to her."

"That sister of hers was a piece of work," Code said. "She did have a far-reaching plan to put Brandon in a position of power in the Diamondback club. She was furious with Brandon and Tawny for fucking it up by insisting on putting out hits on us. We were of no consequence. That was all Tawny's doing, from the emails flying back and forth between the three of them. Brandon wanted Savage dead, and Nina was fine with getting him out of the way, but all the others were too much money. She didn't want to go to her source for more."

"Who was her source?" Czar asked.

"I traced the money back to a man by the name of Walker Thompson," Code said. "It took a while for me to find any connection between Thompson and a business corporation, but he's part owner of a group of casinos in Nevada and Louisiana. They run the casinos on the river and on the beachfront along the Mississippi. He's the younger Thompson. His father, Mathew Thompson, is also a part owner, but he generally runs the Nevada side and from what I understand is very serious about his casinos and keeps them clean."

"What do you know about the son, Code?" Czar asked. "How did he get involved with Nina? And why would he give her that kind of money? Why would he bankroll the destruction of two chapters of two clubs?"

"I found a thread in one of his emails that leads me to believe he's a member of the Ghosts, one of the founding members. I think they want an in with the Diamondbacks and couldn't get it when we took back Plank's wife. They want to get their hands on the counterfeit money and drugs as well. At least what they consider their share of the money. Taking out the main leaders, Thompson thinks he can set up his own leaders. He was going to put Brandon in a position of power. That was part of the deal," Code said.

Savage made a sound of derision in the back of his throat.

"Nina and Brandon didn't understand the clubs very well. Brandon wouldn't have survived five minutes. He would have been challenged and probably killed."

"He would have tried using his voice," Alena said.

"His voice didn't work on everyone," Savage pointed out.

"It's a moot point now," Steele said. "Brandon's dead. The plan went to hell once again. Before, we weren't really on the Ghost's radar. I suspect we might be now."

"Maybe, but they don't know we wiped out the hit teams," Keys said. "No one knows for certain we did it. We didn't let Plank know where we were."

"Doesn't matter," Czar said. "Ghosts are going to hear about us sooner or later. We have to prepare for that. We need to take a close look at all of Thompson's friends. Go back to his childhood. This feels like someone or one or two others that he has very close ties with. They hashed their plan out together and they're keeping it close to their chest. They somehow found the Russian assassins and hired them to do their dirty work. How? How did they find them?"

"The casinos," Mechanic said. "The Russians were looking for work. Hungry for it. If we weren't settling down, we'd be looking for anything with an edge. They might have tried bouncer work in a bar, but going to the casinos and trying something like that on, yeah, I can see them doing that. Even if Thompson Senior turned them down or hired them for shit work, Junior was watching, and he pounced. He gave them the work they were best at."

Czar nodded. "That would make sense. Nina was most likely in his casino and she screwed up. Owed him money. That's how she came in contact with Junior. Had to be. Can you put her anywhere he might have been, Code?"

"Nina liked New Orleans," Code said. "And he makes that his home base. She wasn't the best at gambling, but she liked it when she was drunk. There are a few, not many, and very terse on his side, exchanges between them in the form of emails. Nothing incriminating. The plan is all laid out in the exchanges between her and Brandon. Nina let Junior know she had an in into the bigger MCs. In exchange for making her debts go away and a few other things, she could get him just about anything he wanted from a couple of the chapters."

"Nina was playing a dangerous game with men like Junior and two clubs like the Diamondbacks and the Venomous," Keys said. "She couldn't have been that naïve. Even Tawny should have known better."

"Tawny didn't know about Junior. She thought the Feds were going to protect her," Savage pointed out. "All three of them were stupid. Brandon, Nina and Tawny."

"At least we have a line on Junior now," Czar said. "Are we any closer to the Russian woman?"

Code shook his head. "She's dropped off the face of the planet. No one seems to know anything about her. I tapped into the cameras at the club—they were wiped clean. The most we know is that she has some psychic ability and she doesn't like you. She wasn't looking for you to start with, but then she accidentally ran across you. It seems to be a personal matter."

"We have to tighten security around Blythe and the kids," Czar said with a small sigh. "And the Russian running the pedophile ring? Where do we stand with him? Any closer to his identity? We're on his radar as well."

Code shook his head. "He's buried deep. I'm looking. My best bet is to keep following the assassins the Ghosts use. The Russian runs them. He's the mastermind behind them. Sooner or later, one of them is going to screw up, and I'll catch him."

Everyone believed him. Code was that good.

"You keep hitting them where it hurts the most, their bank accounts," Czar decreed, "but make certain it can't be traced back to us."

More than once, Code had hit the assassins' bank accounts and drained them. Now that he knew Junior was part of the Ghosts, he was going to get creative with everything the man was a part of, as long as it involved his personal finances.

"I'm always careful, Czar," Code assured him. "I never take chances."

Czar nodded. "I'd rather wait months than put you or the club in jeopardy. We use patience. We always have."

"We getting any hits on the online auctions for kids?" Transporter asked. "Seems to me, if they are putting it together that Czar is in any way involved in taking down their ring, it's a good way to bait him."

Maestro nodded. "I was thinking the same thing."

"What does that mean?" Alena asked. "We don't go after any children Code finds?"

"It doesn't mean that," Destroyer countered, watching Czar's face.

"No, Czar agreed. "We aren't going to let anyone stop us. Taking back kids and taking down the trafficking rings is our mission. When we decide we've hunted enough, we'll stop. These are children no one else can recover. If we can let law enforcement get them, we give that to them; otherwise, we don't leave them out there suffering on their own. Not because we're scared of someone in the shadows."

Savage had to agree with that. They'd spent their entire childhood with the boogeyman lying in wait in the shadows.

"We just have to be doubly cautious," Steele said. "In a way, this is a good thing. We don't want to get complacent. We're building a good life here. Settling. Until we decide to stop this, we still have to stay sharp. Knowing we're hunted too is going to keep us sharp."

Savage agreed with that assessment as well. "Has it been that quiet, Code?"

Code shook his head. "It's never quiet, Savage. I'm monitoring a few murmurs right now. One is of a place holding pregnant girls. That just popped up on my radar. No information yet. I have no idea if it even really exists. So many times these rumors are just phantoms. Twice some asshole looked as if he was putting a little girl up for auction, but he pulled out at the last moment. There's an auction coming up in a couple of weeks as well, but so far, the merchandise isn't listed. Only the notice went out."

"Isn't that alarming? Why wouldn't they advertise?" Player asked.

Code shrugged. "Depending on who it is, they send the notice and try to avoid law enforcement by not listing product."

Savage hated that Code had to continually see the things they'd all escaped. He'd never thought about it and the toll Code's job of constant hunting for pedophiles online could take on him.

"Code." Deliberately, he waited until the man looked up and met his eyes. "Don't tell you near enough how much you're appreciated for what you do for all of us."

The others immediately nodded. "Yeah, brother. The best."

Savage rubbed his thumb along the edge of his phone. Never, not in a million years, would he have thought to thank a brother for the service he performed for all of them. He could see it meant something to Code.

Wanted to say you matter to me, angel. Hope things are good there. Reaching out to her brought emotion under control.

Love you so much, Savage. The basket they delivered to the table from you was amazing and so thoughtful. Eden cried. She's doing all right though.

Basket was from us.

Savage doesn't like anyone knowing he's an—and there was a series of angel emojis.

Damn, the woman made him laugh. He looked up and met Czar's eyes. Shit. Blythe, no doubt, had texted him about the fucking basket. He shook his head, grinning, and looked back down at his phone and the taunting emojis. That woman.

"This fireman," Storm said. "The one Darby was dating. What do we have on him?"

"Asher Larkin," Czar announced. "Has a two-year-old son, Caleb. Reggie, the man Eden was married to, has a sister, Lydia. Asher is her son. He's an only child. He has sole custody of Caleb. He's a hard worker, and he seems to really like Darby. She broke it off with him after he mentioned to Shark that we had dinner reservations at Crow 287. He came to me like a man and said when Tony asked him if he would let him take Eden out that night, that he didn't know it was anything more than just that. He hadn't realized why Darby broke things off with him until Tony said it was a possibility that it was because of their relationship and the reservations."

"You believe him?" Reaper asked.

Czar nodded. "I didn't want to. I can tell when a man is lying. He's a straight shooter. And Darby's been miserable. Asher doesn't have anything to do with the Diamondbacks."

"It's still dangerous," Reaper pointed out.

"Darby knows that. She knows what she can and can't say around him. I'm letting her make up her mind."

"Shit, Czar," Storm said in disgust. "It would be a whole hell of a lot easier to kill the bastard. Now we've got to watch our girl like a hawk."

"You were getting lazy," Alena pointed out. "Gives you something to do."

Storm glared at her when they all laughed.

"Where are we with Shari Albright?" Savage asked. "I'm not forgetting that she completely demolished Seychelle's cottage and ruined her parents' sculpture."

"While you were holed up in your little love nest with your woman, Savage, Shari went back to San Francisco and hit the clubs hard. She was well known in the party crowd. Liked to do a lot of drugs and party at the edgier clubs. She was with a group of her friends, and right in front of them, Saturday night, she was hitting it hard: mixture of alcohol and drugs, dancing, sex with not-so-nice men, went out on the balcony with her girls and she went over the side. She was laughing too, they said. No one thought she did it on purpose. She was fooling around, doing a striptease on the railing, and then she went over."

Savage stared at them all. Finally, he shook his head. "No

way. The balcony, in front of everyone? We haven't pulled that one off in years. No cameras? Someone had to have had their cell phone out filming her fooling around like that. Everyone has cell phones now."

Mechanic grinned at him. "I'm hell on wheels with those cameras now. I practice all the time. No one got a shot of Lana with those women. Even if they did, she was wearing a really cute face that no one would ever recognize. Our resident artist is really getting good."

"Soleil?" Savage guessed. Ice had married a woman who was an amazing artist.

"She's mind-blowing with facial masks. She makes them so real. The material is like human skin. Even when you're wearing it, the mask doesn't bother you at all. The makeup is superb," Lana said. "Soleil is a huge asset. She doesn't have a clue what I'm using it for, but if she did, it wouldn't matter. She's so loyal to Ice, she'd never say a word."

"Thanks, Lana," Savage said. "And Seychelle's cottage? I'll start helping now that I'm halfway decent to be around."

A round of laughter eased the tension in the room.

"The house is completely cleared and gutted. We're starting on the walls," Master reported. "Keys and Player are working on the bathrooms. Maestro and I are concentrating on the kitchen. Once we have those rooms done, we'll tackle the easier ones. The others join us when they're off work."

"Thanks, everyone, we both appreciate it so much."

～

"Got something for you," Savage said. He was lying naked in his favorite spot, his arms around Seychelle's hips, his head on her belly, while she sat, back to the headboard.

Seychelle's fingers massaged his scalp, the way she did most nights when they lay together like this. Happy. Lazy. Drifting.

The sex had been amazing. It always was with Seychelle. The marks of his whip were fading, the patterns mostly gone until only a few lines continued to show on her skin. He'd

kissed them a hundred times. Kissed her more. Worshipped
her body in every way he knew how. Worshipped her even
more. She'd given him life. Joy of living. Laughter. Those
older women who'd thought it was okay to put a hat made of
gems on his Harley. Made him think it was damn funny that
a fucking cop would pull a prank on him and think he could
get away with it. Never mind he'd started it in the first place.
Seychelle had given him fun.

"I don't need anything more, Savage," Seychelle murmured softly. "I've got everything. I mean it. You're everything. This house. What we have."

Savage rolled over, sat up and reached under the bed.
There were two packages. Both were of significant size, and
both were heavy. He sat facing her and put the first brightly
wrapped gift in front of her.

"Open it, baby."

The wrapping was purple, blue and white tissue paper.
She looked at him. "This is signature wrapping from Judith
Henderson's store. She makes gorgeous kaleidoscopes."

As guesses went, it could have been a good one. He
wouldn't mind having a kaleidoscope in the house. A big
one. He watched her expression as she carefully took the
tissue away and uncovered the delicate sculpture. Savage
didn't realize he was holding his breath.

Seychelle's eyes widened. Her facial expression, if possible, got even softer. She lifted her lashes and looked
straight at him, the love there so easy to read. She never held
anything back from him.

"Lissa finished the sculpture. It's so beautiful."

It was. He thought it was even more impressive than the
first one. The roses were entwined, the petals a dark red
and the stems dark green. It was thicker and much sturdier
than the first sculpture but gave the appearance of being
delicate. The scattered ashes and former glass embedded in
the piece lent it texture and brightness. He thought Lissa was
a miracle worker. It wasn't anything like the first one, but it
was beautiful.

"She hoped you'd like it. I didn't want you to be disappointed that it wasn't like the first one. She couldn't make it the same."

Her fingers trembled a little as she followed the path of the stems. The base was sturdy and could sit easily on a stand if she wanted to light it the way she had the first piece. "I didn't need it to be the same, Savage. I just needed it back. Thank you. I would never have thought to bring the smashed pieces to her. I love you so much. I really do."

He took the sculpture from her and handed her the second package. The sculpture he set on the long, wide railing that ran the length of the room. He had thought a lot about where to place it to keep it safe and yet still have the piece prominent for her to see whenever she walked into the master bedroom.

He turned at her gasp. She stared at the second piece of artwork he'd asked Lissa to make for his woman. It was the most beautiful piece of blown glass he'd ever seen, but then he was biased. A single black rose with dozens of thorns twined tightly around a beautiful red rose with no thorns on its stem. When they were apart all those weeks, he had come to her at night, leaving behind a black rose with thorns and a red rose without. Again, the sculpture was sturdy, the bottom able to stand on its own or be fitted onto a base so it could have light under it. His angel. Him.

"Savage." She breathed his name.

Yeah. She liked it. "Had to get you something that was me, baby."

She smiled. Just smiled. But when she did that, he could see he had everything.

RESOURCES

Advocates for Youth

1325 G Street NW, Suite 980
Washington, D.C. 20005
1-202-419-3420
advocatesforyouth.org

Against Child Abuse Hong Kong

Wai Yuen House
107-108 G/F
Chuk Yuen North Estate
Wong Tai Sin, Kowloon
Phone: 2351 6060
Hotline: 2755 1122
aca.org.hk

American Academy of Child & Adolescent Psychiatry

3615 Wisconsin Avenue NW
Washington, D.C. 20016-3007
1-202-966-7300
aacap.org

American Academy of Pediatrics

345 Park Boulevard
Itasca, IL 60143
1-800-433-9016
aap.org

American Counseling Association

6101 Stevenson Avenue Suite 600
Alexandria, VA 22304-3300
1-800-347-6647
counseling.org

American Psychological Association

750 First Street NE
Washington, D.C. 20002-4242
1-202-336-5500
Toll-free: 1-800-374-2721
apa.org

Bikers Against Child Abuse (BACA)

bacaworld.org

Casa Alianza

Moctezuma #68 Col. Guerero
Alcaldía Cuauhtémoc CDMX. CP. 06300
Mexico
casa-alianzamexico.org

Center for Healthier Children, Families & Communities

10960 Wilshire Boulevard, Suite 960
Los Angeles, CA 90024-3913
1-310-794-0967
healthychild.ucla.edu

Child Exploitation and Obscenity Section

Criminal Division
U.S. Department of Justice
1-202-514-5780
usdoj.gov/criminal/ceos

The ChildTrauma Academy

5161 San Felipe, Suite 320
Houston, TX 77056
Toll-free: 1-866-943-9779
childtrauma.org

Child Welfare Information Gateway

330 C Street SW
Washington, D.C. 20201
Toll-free: 1-800-394-3366
childwelfare.gov

Child Welfare League of America

727 15th Street NW, Suite 1200
Washington, D.C. 20005
1-202-688-4200
cwla.org

Dunkelziffer e.V.

Albert-Einstein-Ring 15
22761 Hamburg
Phone: 040 42107000
dunkelziffer.de

PAT International

Phaya Thai Road Ratchathewi
kok 10400 Thailand
e.org

ECPAT-USA

EPCAT-USA
86 Wyckoff Avenue, #609
Brooklyn, NY 11237
1-718-935-9192
ecpatusa.org

European Children's Network (EURONET)

europeanchildrensnetwork.org

Frauenberatung Sexuelle Gewalt

Phone: 044 291 46 46
frauenberatung.ch

Institute on Violence, Abuse and Trauma at Alliant International University

10065 Old Grove Road, Suite 101
San Diego, CA 92131
1-858-527-1860
ivatcenters.org

International List of Sexual & Domestic Violence Agencies

hotpeachpages.ne

Justice for Children

justiceforchildren.org

KidsPeace

5300 KidsPeace Drive
Orefield, PA 18069
1-800-25-PEACE
kidspeace.org

MaleSurvivor

350 Central Park West, Suite 1H
New York, NY 10025
1-800-738-4181
malesurvivor.org

Mental Health America

500 Montgomery Street, Suite 820
Alexandria, VA 22314
1-703-684-7722
Toll-free: 1-800-969-6642
nmha.org

National Association for Prevention of Child Abuse and Neglect

9/162 Goulburn Street
Surry Hills NSW 2010
Phone: 02 8073 3300
napcan.org.au

National Association of School Psychologists

4340 East West Highway, Suite 402
Bethesda, MD 20814
1-301-657-0270
Toll-free: 1-866-331-NASP
nasponline.org

National Center for Children in Poverty

475 Riverside Drive, Suite 1400
New York, NY 10115
nccp.org

National Children's Alliance

516 C Street NE
Washington, D.C. 20002
1-202-548-0090
nca-online.org

National Data Archive on Child Abuse and Neglect

Surge 1—FLDC
Cornell University
Ithaca, NY 14853
1-607-255-7799
ndacan.cornell.edu

National Domestic Violence Hotline (Canada)

All provinces; bilingual (English & French)
Toll-free: 1-800-363-9010

National Indian Child Welfare Association

5100 S. Macadam Avenue, Suite 300
Portland, OR 97239
1-503-222-4044
nicwa.org

National Organization of Battered Women's Shelters (Sweden)

Roks, Hornsgatan 66
118 21 Stockholm, Sweden
Phone: 08-422 99 30
roks.se

Provincial Association of Transition Houses and Services of Saskatchewan (PATHS)

abusehelplines.org

Rape, Abuse, and Incest National Network (RAINN)

1-800-656-HOPE

Reporting Crimes Against Children

Federal Bureau of Investigation
fbi.gov/report-threats-and-crime

Scottish Women's Aid

132 Rose Street, 2nd floor
Edinburgh EH2 3JD
United Kingdom
Phone: 0131 475 2372
24-hour help line: 0800 027 1234
womensaid.scot

S.E.S.A.M.E. (Stop Educator Sexual Abuse Misconduct & Exploitation)

10863 Florence Hills Street
Las Vegas, NV 89141
1-702-371-1290
sesamenet.org

Silent Edge

108 Terrace Drive
Syracuse, NY 13219
silent-edge.org

The United Nations Convention on the Rights of the Child

unicef.org/crc

U.S. Department of Justice

Project Safe Childhood
810 Seventh Street NW
Washington, D.C. 20531
AskDOJ@usdoj.gov
justice.gov/psc/index.html

U.S. ICE (Immigration and Customs Enforcement) Cyber Crimes Center, Child Exploitation Investigations Unit

1-866-DHS-2-ICE
ice.gov/features/cyber

Women Against Violence Europe (WAVE)

Bacherplatz 10/6
1050 Vienna
Austria
Phone: 01-5482720
wave-network.org

Women's Aid Federation of England

PO Box 3245
Bristol BS2 2EH, England
womensaid.org.uk

KEEP READING FOR AN EXCERPT FROM
THE NEXT THRILLING NOVEL IN
THE GHOSTWALKER SERIES BY CHRISTINE FEEHAN

PHANTOM GAME

AVAILABLE MARCH 2022 FROM PIATKUS

The mountains rose up, climbing higher and higher, towering all around, the peaks reaching for the clouds. All along the mountainsides and in the valleys between, red cedar, whitebark pine and spruce trees vied for space. This was true forest, two million acres of actual wilderness, most of it left to the animals that were native to the area. Grizzlies, black bears, mountain lions, moose, timber wolves, mountain goats, elk, bighorn sheep and mule deer all made the vast forest home, along with a range of smaller animals.

Jonas "Smoke" Harper, Dr. Kyle Forbes and Jeff Hollister, three of the genetically and psychically enhanced members of GhostWalker Team One, continued along the nearly nonexistent game trail they'd been traveling for the past three hours.

"You still getting that bad feeling in your gut, Jonas?" Jeff asked.

Jonas scanned the dense forest with narrowed eyes, maintaining his purposefully relaxed gait while keeping his hand close to his weapon. "Yep."

Kyle sighed. "You sure it isn't just a stitch in your side?"

"Yep."

CHRISTINE FEEHAN

"You did notice that the higher we climb, the more bear scat we're coming across," Jeff said.

"Yep."

"Just thought I'd point that out." A small grin lit Jeff's face.

"I'm not sure he actually knows how to talk, Jeff," Kyle said. "Ryland did warn us. Said if we volunteered to come with him, we'd hear nothing but grunts for days."

"Wait." Smile fading, Jeff halted abruptly and glared at his companions. "You volunteered? Ryland *ordered* me to come with you two. Said I had to protect your asses."

Jonas and Kyle stopped as well, and Jonas took the opportunity to study Jeff without appearing to do so. It had been a couple of years since Jeff had recovered from a stroke that would have put any normal soldier out of commission for good. Jeff had fought his way back.

Jeff, like men in the government's GhostWalker program, wasn't anyone's definition of a normal soldier anymore. They were, instead, the products of a military experiment that hadn't quite gone off as expected. They had gone into the program volunteering for psychic enhancement with the expectation of being of more use to their country, but along with removing filters in their brains, Dr. Peter Whitney had also performed experimental gene coding on them. That part, they had *not* signed up for.

Worse, the first of Whitney's gene coding experiments had been illegally performed on young orphan girls, with disastrous results. Those initial failures hadn't stopped Whitney though. Instead, he'd forged ahead with similar gene modifications on the soldiers, believing that grown men could better handle the pressures of the enhancements than the female children had. Team One had lost several of the men in their unit and Jeff had suffered a brain bleed and stroke. He was fully recovered, but the entire team tended to watch over him, Jonas especially.

The survivors of Whitney's experiments were all admittedly stronger, and they now possessed some very incredible abilities, but those benefits had come at a steep price. They were all continuing to learn just how steep that price could be. Lily Whitney-Miller, Peter Whitney's adopted daughter, now married to their team leader, Captain Ryland Miller, had given them all exercises to do to strengthen the barricades in their minds. That allowed the ones who had been wide open to be able to be in public without an "anchor"—one who drew emotion and psychic overload from them—at least for short periods of time.

Jeff looked good to Jonas, but still, he glanced at Kyle just to make certain. Kyle would be better at making an assessment. If the doc thought Jeff needed a break, he'd find an excuse to take one. Jeff never shirked the physical therapy designed to strengthen the weaker side of his body or the mental exercises to strengthen the barriers in his brain. He stayed in therapy the brain surgeon recommended to ensure the psychic talents he used didn't bring on another bleed. He was one of the hardest-working GhostWalkers Jonas knew—and that was saying a lot.

Their unit, GhostWalker Team One, was tight. They looked out for one another. They trusted few others, and those they brought in, they did so slowly and carefully. Years ago, their team had been set up for murder, separated and held in cages, essentially waiting to die. Ryland had planned their escape and Lily had hid them at her estate until they could get to the bottom of the conspiracy against them. In the end, they had managed to come out on top, thanks in no small part to their dedication to training hard and working together. They still ran missions, but they trusted and depended only on one another.

Now, there were three other GhostWalker teams. Whitney had used each team to perfect his technique so that each subsequent unit was able to handle their enhancements much better than the team before them. But he'd also added more and more genetic coding, turning the soldiers into much more than they ever expected—or wanted—to be.

There was a special place in hell reserved for sociopathic

monsters like Peter Whitney—or if there wasn't, there ought to be. Jonas wouldn't mind bringing a little—or maybe a *lot*—of that hell to Whitney in the here and now, especially as more and more of his most diabolical experiments, all on orphaned girls, came to light. Unfortunately, as evil as he was, Whitney had a solid network of connections among America's most powerful, including high-ranking government officials, billionaire defense contractors and bankers, as well as his own private army of expendable super-soldiers, all of them would-be GhostWalkers who hadn't made the official cut. Between his connections and his army, Whitney was virtually untouchable.

Jonas sighed as his gaze swept the surrounding forest. He used every enhanced sense he had, both animal and human. They were being watched. He had been aware of it for the last few miles but hadn't been able to identify exactly where the threat was coming from—or whom. Or rather, from what. He was certain their observers were not human.

"You feel it?" Kyle asked him quietly, turning toward him.

"Yep."

Jeff heaved an exaggerated sigh. "You ever think a word now and again might be helpful?"

"Not certain what it is yet."

Jeff shoved a hand through his perpetually sun-bleached hair. "It? Not a who. An it?" When Jonas didn't answer, Jeff rolled his eyes. "Why did I agree to keep the two of you alive? You're both a pain in the ass." He began walking again, doggedly putting one foot in front of the other. "Do we even know where we're going?"

"Nope." Jonas hid his grin. Annoying Jeff was one of his favorite pastimes, and when the tension was beginning to stretch out, like now, a little humor went a long way. In spite of his amusement, he stayed on full alert, looking for the sentries watching them.

He was fully aware Ryland hadn't sent Jeff. Jeff had come with him, like Kyle, because they were his friends and they hadn't wanted him to check out his strange feeling alone.

It had been that simple. Friendship. The feeling, at first, had been a vague calling to him. For the last mile, along with that compulsion he felt, he now felt uneasy as if there was a threat, but he couldn't place where it was coming from.

Night was falling. In the forest, especially this deep in the interior, it was always a good thing to establish a camp before sunset. Too many wild animals hunted after dark. He could connect with them and, if he was lucky, keep them away, but it was silly to take chances. The trees were thick, the brush heavy. The trail they were on was very narrow. Tree frogs were abundant, staring at them with round eyes as they passed. In the vegetation at their feet was the constant rustle of leaves as rodents rushed to get undercover.

"We should find a place to camp for the night. Build a fire."

"I tried to send word back to the others," Kyle said. "But I'm not getting through. Could be the density of the canopy, but I should be able to . . . " He trailed off.

"I'm not surprised." Jonas wasn't. There was something at work here. He'd gotten that feeling in his gut and wanted to check things out.

Jonas had told Ryland he had a strange pulling toward this side of the mountain for some time and wanted to take time off to explore. They'd just recently come off a dicey hostage rescue. They'd managed to pull off the rescue without a single casualty even though things had gone sideways twice, and they all had some downtime coming. Jonas wanted—no, *needed*—to explore the miles of wilderness around the fortress they had carved out for themselves close to Team Two.

"Have you noticed that we're losing visibility, Jonas?" Kyle asked. "The mist is getting thick."

Jonas could see the fog moving through the trees at times. At first it stayed low to the ground, gently rolling like ocean waves on a cloudless day. Then a few fingers of mist crept through the trees toward them, in an eerie display, looking like giant hands pulling an equally giant blanket through the forest until it was impossible to see through the gray vapor. Jonas glanced down at the trail they were following, but the swirling mist had thickened so much that he couldn't see even his own boots—a strange phenomenon.

There was another component to the fog he found fascinating. A warning, or dread, that acted on their bodies. He could hear both Kyle's and Jeff's hearts accelerating. His own pulse rate had tried to increase and he had instantly forced his heart under control. All three GhostWalkers slowed considerably, eventually halting altogether.

Jonas waited in silence for his eyes to adjust to the fog rolling off the ground and rising in dark tides nearly to his waist. Given time, he could see through just about anything. He was often called Smoke because he moved through and could disappear into places no one else could. He saw through things no one else could see through. It was only a matter of time before his vision would adjust to the strange mist hiding the trail.

"Looks as if the fog is dissipating in that direction," Kyle said, indicating their right with his chin.

Jeff nodded. "And our little game trail leads in that direction too, Jonas. If we're going to find a place to camp before nightfall, we should double-time it out of this mist."

Jonas didn't move, studying the forest and rocks in front of him. The path had wound through the trees and rocks earlier. He had a good memory. More than a good memory. His mind mapped things out for him in grid patterns. The game trail hadn't veered to the right. It had continued upward, straight ahead, winding around tree trunks and large rocks, but it hadn't really swung left or right.

"Give me a minute."

Keeping completely still, Jonas swept his gaze up and down the fog-shrouded forest floor in a grid pattern, paying special attention to the area where the game trail should have been. At first there was a strange shimmer, very reminiscent of a mirage in the desert. But Jonas persevered until the shimmer dissipated and what lay beneath it became clear.

"The actual trail is straight ahead. It's being hidden from us."

"That's not good," Kyle observed. "And we're being watched to make certain we go where we're directed?"

"Yep." Jonas took the first step onto the very narrow game trail to see if it would trigger an attack of some kind.

"This is some kind of crazy-ass magnetic earth thing happening, like in the Bermuda Triangle," Jeff muttered. "We're going to get misdirected all over the place, aren't we?"

"Yep."

#1 *NEW YORK TIMES* BESTSELLING AUTHOR

CHRISTINE FEEHAN

"The queen of paranormal romance...
I love everything she does."
—J. R. Ward

PIATKUS

Do you love fiction with a supernatural twist?

Want the chance to hear news about your favourite
authors (and the chance to win free books)?

Christine Feehan
J.R. Ward
Sherrilyn Kenyon
Charlaine Harris
Jayne Ann Krentz and Jayne Castle
P.C. Cast
Maria Lewis
Darynda Jones
Hayley Edwards
Kristen Callihan
Keri Arthur
Amanda Bouchet
Jacquelyn Frank
Larissa Ione

Then visit the *With Love* website and
sign up to our romance newsletter:
www.yourswithlove.co.uk

And follow us on Facebook for book giveaways,
exclusive romance news and more:
www.facebook.com/yourswithlovex

PIATKUS